T0274352

SO
WITCHES
WE
BECAME

BY JILL BAGUCHINSKY

Spookygirl: Paranormal Investigator

Mammoth

So Witches We Became

SO
WITCHES
WE
BECAME

JILL BAGUCHINSKY

LITTLE, BROWN AND COMPANY

New York Boston

Copyright © 2024 by Jill Baguchinsky

Cover art copyright © 2024 by Marco Mazzoni. Cover design by Jenny Kimura.
Cover copyright © 2024 by Hachette Book Group, Inc.
Interior design by Michelle Gengaro-Kokmen.

Little, Brown and Company
Hachette Book Group
1290 Avenue of the Americas, New York, NY 10104
Visit us at LBYR.com

First Edition: July 2024

Little, Brown and Company is a division of Hachette Book Group, Inc.
The Little, Brown name and logo are registered trademarks of Hachette Book Group, Inc.

The publisher is not responsible for websites (or their content)
that are not owned by the publisher.

Branches © Inna Sinano/Shutterstock.com
Cat © Sloth Astronaut/Shutterstock.com

Little, Brown and Company books may be purchased in bulk for business, educational, or promotional use. For information, please contact your local bookseller or the Hachette Book Group Special Markets Department at special.markets@hbgusa.com.

Library of Congress Cataloging-in-Publication Data
Names: Baguchinsky, Jill, author.
Title: So witches we became / Jill Baguchinsky.
Description: First edition. | New York : Little, Brown and Company, 2024. |
Audience: Ages 14 & up | Summary: When a curse traps a group of friends on a barrier island, they must harness the shared power of their traumatic secrets or risk being devoured.
Identifiers: LCCN 2023022692 | ISBN 9780316568807 (hardcover) |
ISBN 9780316568821 (ebook)
Subjects: CYAC: Friendship—Fiction. | Blessing and cursing—Fiction. |
Secrets—Fiction. | LGBTQ+ people—Fiction. | Horror fiction. |
LCGFT: Horror fiction. | Novels.
Classification: LCC PZ7.B14215 So 2024 | DDC [Fic]—dc23
LC record available at https://lccn.loc.gov/2023022692

ISBNs: 978-0-316-56880-7 (hardcover), 978-0-316-56882-1 (ebook)

Printed in Indiana, USA

LSC-C

Printing 1, 2024

For my mother, Jeri Baguchinsky,
who once stabbed a creep in the hand
with her charm bracelet
and still says it was no big deal.

And in memory of my father, John Baguchinsky,
who kept our island safe from hurricanes
as long as he lived.

For content warnings, Jill invites you to visit her website at
jillbaguchinsky.com/swwb-content/.

Then

Twelve Years Ago

T he girl can't move. Her eyes snap open but her limbs are stiff as stone.

The night-light her father thought would help creates as many shadows in the dark bedroom as it chases away. Those shadows shiver as lightning glints between the slats on the window blinds, chased by a low crash of thunder. The enormous Maglite flashlight, another desperate gift from her father, lies useless under the pillow, inches and miles away at the same time. She can't turn on a flashlight if she can't move to grab it.

Her gaze shifts panic-quick to the closet door. It's closed, thank goodness. Sometimes she forgets to shut it before bed, but tonight she remembered.

But tonight, the thing isn't in the closet.

Instead, it lurks in the far corner of the room, a shadow that doesn't quite make sense. It unfolds, limb after spindly limb, soft-edged and indistinct. Watching it is like watching smoke wisp from an extinguished candle—there's no substance, only movement. What begins as smooth and fluid turns jerky and jittering, a creeping creature that shivers like static on an old television, and all the girl can do is stare. She almost can't even see it when she looks head-on; its outline is clearer if she peeks from the corner of her eye. That's changing, though—last night it was a little easier to see than the night before, and tonight it's darker still, and more solid.

It's growing stronger.

She wants to open her mouth, wants to scream for her mother, but her mother isn't here. And besides, what if the shadow unspools itself while her mouth gapes open? What if it reaches a thread-thin arm inside her, right down her throat? The thought makes a gag rise, sticking like gristle on the back of her tongue.

The shadow stares without eyes, its head tilting to the left. Its only facial feature is a gaping maw of a mouth, always open. When it moves toward her, it neither walks nor floats. It almost seems to pulse from place to place, vibrating like a sound wave. It drags one arm—a jagged tendril where a hand should be—against the wall, loud and hard enough to leave a scrape, but the girl knows that when she checks tomorrow, the drywall will be unmarked.

She hears the shadow breathing. It takes in air through that unhinged mouth, stealing the oxygen from the room.

She shoves against the paralysis, fighting invisible bindings like a fish tangled tight in a net. Fear fuels her struggle, and as the thing stretches, as its thread-thin arm drifts closer, closer, almost touching her cheek, she wrenches her jaw open. And for just a shimmer of a second, she forgets.

"MOM!"

Victorious and petrified, she clamps her mouth shut against the reaching tendril. But the shadow is already gone.

For tonight, at least.

Thunder growls once more outside the window as the paralysis fades and the girl sits up in a tangle of bedsheets. She screamed for her mother, but it's her father who will scurry in and fuss. "Nellie, again?" he'll say, his exasperation clear even as he gathers her in his arms. "How many times do we have to do this? It was just a dream! Did you use the flashlight?"

"I couldn't."

"Honey . . . you have to *try*." He doesn't understand. He thought the big, heavy Maglite would make her feel safer. *Just turn it on and the shadow will disappear.* As if anything could be that easy. As if she could ever move enough to do so in the shadow's presence.

Tomorrow there will be another conversation with the therapist the girl has been seeing for her recurrent night terrors. She'll be asked to draw more pictures of the shadow, to describe it, to practice visualizations and reframings and meditations meant to diffuse its terrible hold. The therapist will repeat to her father that the sleep paralysis, the hallucinations, the panic attacks, all of it is just a manifestation of Nellie's anxiety over her parents' recent separation and her mother's abrupt departure. She'll even try to blame some of it on the late-spring storms that have begun coasting through at night as Florida's rainy season settles in.

Nellie will insist, once again, that she's not afraid of storms or thunder or lightning. She'll speak up, but no one will listen.

3

The shadow is just a phase, the therapist will say. It's Nellie's brain working things out, and someday soon it will fade away into nothing. She keeps saying that, keeps making the same prediction, but it never seems to come true.

And tomorrow night, Nellie knows, the shadow will be back.

Chapter One

Is that a ukulele?" Harry asks.

I glance at the uke case in my left hand. "Yeah."

He carries a few of my other bags down the driveway for me. "Cool. I know you're in chorus—"

"Used to be," I remind him, trying to keep my words from forming sharp points. Chorus is a delicate topic for me.

"Okay, used to be—but I didn't know you played an instrument, too." He hefts my suitcase into the hatchback of his green SUV, tucking it next to his and Harper's luggage, and a thick lock of slightly sweaty chestnut hair falls over his forehead. He shakes his head to keep it out of his eyes. "Going to give us a little concert this week?"

"What? I wasn't...I mean, maybe. I don't..." I stumble over my refusal, regretting that I didn't stow the case in a tote or a duffel bag to keep it from drawing attention. "No," I manage finally.

Harry tilts a brow. There's a question on his tongue, so close to escaping that I can almost hear it already, and my thoughts spin, searching for a believable excuse, wondering why I didn't think to come up with one before. But after a pause he lets it go and nods toward his SUV. "Is that everything? Ready?"

"Yeah." I get in back and stash the case by my feet while he folds his lanky form into the driver's seat. I've known Harry for years, for as long as his younger sister, Harper, and I have been friends, and he's always been just a little too tall for his own good, like he's never quite grown into himself.

If we—Harper, Dia, and I—have to have a chaperone this week, though, Harry should be a bearable one. He's only a year older than us, and he used to tattle on Harper and me for all kinds of things—doing messy art projects in Harper's carpeted bedroom, racing our bikes through Winter Park's congested downtown, giving my Barbies edgy haircuts and experimental surgery—but he got a lot more tolerable three years ago, after we caught him sneaking vodka from his stepfather's liquor cabinet. We struck a compromise: Harry laid off his tattling, at least somewhat, and we kept our own mouths shut in return. It's not like either of us cares if he drinks—Harper sneaks booze all the time—but having something to hold over his head made things easier for us.

Plus, years of taking care of his sister while their then-single mother worked multiple jobs had forced him to learn how to cook once they tired of peanut butter and boxed macaroni and cheese. I can whip up some decent meals, too, but I can't begin to match what he's taught himself from YouTube tutorials. A week with Harry looking out for us means a week of his cooking, and I'm definitely looking forward to that. Harper told me he's already planned several menus, which is just...*so* Harry.

"Seat belt?" he asks, watching me in the rearview mirror. *There's* the chaperone. I nod, holding back a snort-laugh. I didn't even get a lecture from my father about behaving myself while I'm away. He knows we won't have many opportunities for trouble with Harry around.

Harry checks his blind spots twice before backing out of my driveway. "We'll get Dia first, then swing by the office for Harper."

"Did she really get roped into working this morning?"

"You know how Charlie is," he says, referencing their step-father. "There's always time for just a little more work."

Harper and Harry's mother was practically a hippie back before she met Charlie, and I've never understood how the two of them clicked—how does a laid-back single mom end up with an uptight, type A entrepreneur? Charlie shoved his way into their family and took it over, and now Harper gets to be the weekend receptionist at Charles Warner Incorporated whether she wants to or not.

We pick up Dia on the way. She's on her front porch, waving from beneath a floppy hat, her spring tan glowing against her white eyelet sundress. Dia likes to brag that, because she's Cuban, she never burns. By the end of our trip she'll be gloriously bronze while I'll turn neon pink despite my SPF slathering. Her embroidery tote sits next to her suitcase; I'm not surprised that she's taking her favorite hobby along for the week.

"Nell!" She envelops me in a hug, then gives Harry the same treatment, turning his cheeks pink. She's had a crush on him since the day they met. I wish she'd chill, especially since Harry just broke up with his boyfriend two weeks ago. That's not the issue—Harry's bi, so theoretically, he and Dia could work—but I don't want her throwing herself at him all week and ending up in rebound territory.

In the SUV, she tosses her hat back with the luggage and runs her hands over her auburn ponytail.

"No hat hair," I reassure her softly, and she grins.

"How's school going?" she asks Harry on the way to Charles Warner Inc. "I keep hoping I'll see you around campus on Thursdays." She never misses a chance to remind Harry that, thanks to her dual-enrollment status, she's technically a University of Central Florida student, just like him.

"Fine. Stats is kicking my ass."

She leans forward. "Maybe I could help you study sometime."

"Um..." Harry's ears turn as pink as his cheeks.

"Wasn't your spring break last month?" I ask, jumping to his rescue. "Are you off this week?"

He shakes his head. "My World War I presentation for European History is on Monday, and I've got a stats exam on Thursday, so I'll need to drive back for those. The three of you are going to have to behave yourselves while I'm gone."

"Okay, *Dad*." I chuckle.

He catches my eye in the rearview again. "You aren't the one I'm worried about, Nell."

"I could go with you to campus on Thursday," Dia presses.

"We're here!" Harry says a little too loudly, pulling into a spot at the business complex that houses Charlie's main office. "I'll run in and get Harper."

"No need." I point to the building's glass door as Harper strides out, her expression less than happy.

"You're late," she says, jumping in up front next to Harry.

"You were scheduled until noon. It's 12:05."

"That was five minutes too many with Charlie." She twists

around and plasters on a smile, and it's dazzling even though I know her well enough to tell that it's fake. Harper is like a living photo filter, the kind that gives the illusion of poreless skin and long, sooty eyelashes—only the lashes that frame her enormous brown eyes are 100 percent real, and her lips are a rosy flushed pink with no need for gloss, and her deep brown hair is somehow always perfect, with shiny tendrils framing her face even when she twists it into a clip for work. "Hey, babes! Can you believe that dickwad made me work all morning?"

Harper is no fan of her stepfather, and neither am I, but I can't bring myself to complain about the person paying for this extravagant trip. Or for Harry's car, or the family's house, which is a hell of an upgrade from where Harry and Harper grew up. "At least you escaped," I say as Harry gets back on the road, pointing us toward I-4.

Harper hums in agreement, settling back in her seat, then wiggling to pull out her phone when it chimes with an incoming message.

"Gavin?" Dia guesses as Harper's manicured nails dance over her screen, typing a reply.

"Of course." Harper laughs a little. "I'm not sure the poor boy's going to survive the week without me."

Gavin.

Back in February, when Harper first proposed the spring break trip, I had one question. "Will Gavin be there?" We were eating lunch on Winter Park West High's senior patio. Maybe I imagined it, but I thought I saw her fingers clench her water bottle just a little tighter when I said his name.

"Mom and Charlie would kill me," she responded after a beat.

9

"And you know Harry would rat me out. So what do you think? You, me, Dia. Nice house. Private island. Our own beach."

"And Harry."

"We'll ignore him."

"Dia won't."

Harper laughed. "I thought she was going to explode when I mentioned he'd be there. I kept expecting little hearts to start spinning around her head like in a cartoon."

"You already asked her?"

"Yeah, last night. I knew she'd be at UCF today."

I tried not to let it bother me that my two closest friends had been planning this trip without me.

"So you're coming, right? Mom already convinced Charlie to pay for the whole week as a graduation present."

"Just us and Harry," I said. "No Gavin."

"Jesus Christ, Nell." Harper's expression hardened. "Look, I know you hate my boyfriend for whatever reason, but—"

"I don't hate him," I lied. "And yes, of course I'll go." How could I not? In the fall, Harper, Dia, and I would all head in different directions. I couldn't even fathom that yet. If we didn't do this now, when would we? Besides, Harper and I needed some quality best friend time, especially after the past year, when our bond had grown increasingly brittle.

I wanted to make her promise about Gavin, but I held back.

Now, as we head northeast away from Winter Park, I picture a week spent lounging on the beach. Reading on the porch while the breeze off the Atlantic teases through my hair. Exploring the hidden corners of St. Felicitas with my two best friends.

A week hours away from Gavin.

Chapter Two

Charlie might be a pain in Harper's ass, but his money pays for a hell of a lot. Like a week on a private barrier island just off the Atlantic coast. An entire *island*.

We drive through downtown St. Felicitas, which is all palm trees and tourist-packed sidewalks and Spanish-inspired architecture with curved archways and colorful tiled roofs. "We should spend some time in town while we're here," Harry says. "There's so much history."

"Oh God," Harper mutters.

He ignores her. "We can tour the old fort. Or the lighthouse. It's supposed to be haunted. That should be right up Nell's alley."

A year ago, when I was still writing horror, it would've been. Still, I speak my agreement, trying to sound enthusiastic. "That could be fun!"

"Ooh, look at all the bars," Harper says as we pass places with names like Dolly's Tavern and the Crow's Nest Lounge.

"Nope." Harry turns right, heading out onto the A1A. "And by the way, Harper, don't be surprised when you can't find that whiskey you hid in your beach bag. I put it back in the liquor cabinet."

Harper turns toward him, fire sparking in her narrowed eyes. "You went through my stuff?"

"The bottle was leaking. I could smell it. It got on your towel."

"You couldn't just let us bring one stupid bottle." Harper flops back against the seat and crosses her arms. "And now I'll have a smelly whiskey towel all week. Great."

"The rental has a laundry room," I say, "and I brought some detergent."

Dia giggles. "Of course you did."

"You probably brought an entire convenience store." Harper grins over her shoulder at me.

The mood in the SUV lightens at my expense. "Yeah, yeah. Wait until you need a bandage. Or some ibuprofen. Or you lose a button. Or, you know, your towel stinks like whiskey. Then we'll see who's laughing."

"It's smart to be prepared," Harry says.

"What about tampons?" Harper crows to make her brother uncomfortable. It works. His ears go red again.

I roll my eyes. "Of course."

Harry jerks his thumb toward his sister. "Got any big enough to plug up this one's mouth?"

Dia pats my hand. "We really do appreciate how you think ahead," she says, but her eyes still glitter with constrained laughter.

We skirt south along the coast for a few miles, passing vacation homes with towels drying on porch railings and rented bicycles leaning against front steps. Finally the GPS directs us left toward a gate, beyond which a small, flat bridge passes over a narrow inlet. Harry rolls down his window and enters a code on a keypad, and the gate swings open. We pull through and cross the bridge, passing a carved wooden sign: STRAIGHT SHOT.

"How heteronormative," I say, and Harry snorts.

It's a fitting name, though, for this sliver of island, a straight north-to-south shot of perhaps two miles of sand with an unpaved road and plenty of pines, palm trees, and beach grass. I could probably walk from west to east—from the bay on one side of the island to the Atlantic on the other—in under ten minutes. I'm surprised it hasn't been built up like other Florida islands. I'm even more surprised that it hasn't been swept away by a hurricane. I've never understood why people build on barrier islands—they literally are barriers, patches of elevated sand built by the ebb and flow of the tide to shield the mainland from the brunt of ocean-borne weather.

Not that we need to worry about that this week. Hurricane season won't start until June.

The bridge is on the south end of Straight Shot, and the vacation house sits about a quarter mile from the island's northernmost tip. It's two stories tall, freshly painted, with a wide porch that stretches all the way around and a detached garage. There are generous growths of pine trees to either side of the house, a matched set of forest-patch bookends probably left in place to anchor the sand during storms.

"This is amazing," Dia breathes, staring out the window of the SUV. "And it's all for us. Harper, your stepdad is so great."

Harper looks down, concentrating on her phone like she didn't hear Dia, or like she's pretending she didn't.

The weather is already almost summer warm, but the breeze off the ocean cools us as we lug our things up the front steps. On the porch, a large metal planter overflows with various herbs, each identified by a handmade marker stabbed into the rich soil. "These will be great to cook with," Harry says almost reverently, pausing to inspect the plants. They're lush and thriving; when he plucks a mint leaf and rubs it between his fingers, I can smell it from yards away. The scent of mint always turns my stomach a little, so I breathe through my mouth until it fades.

The interior of the house is bright and beachy—whitewashed shiplap walls with just the right amount of trendy distressing, an enormous blue-and-white-striped sectional couch and decorative driftwood in the living room, gauzy drapes over the windows. Tiny succulents in miniature terra-cotta pots and planters line the sills of the east-facing windows. An index card leans against one planter, with *Please don't water!* written in neat script beside a smiley face. The handwriting matches that on the herb markers outside.

A hand-painted sign over the wide kitchen doorway reads THE ISLAND OF NO STORMS. I doubt the veracity of that claim—this is Florida, after all—but the sentiment is nice.

Dia and I claim rooms on the second floor. I try not to make too much of a show of my uke case, tucking it beside my bed instead of leaving it out in the open with the rest of my luggage. I'm still unpacking when I hear Harper yelling downstairs.

"Harry, that's not fair! You don't just get to claim the master."

I go downstairs and see Harry in the doorway of another bedroom, his arms crossed. "Mom and Charlie said it was fine. A trade-off for babysitting all week."

"A trade-off for keeping us from having any fun, you mean. We should at least flip a coin or something."

"Nope. Mine."

Harper's voice goes shrill. "Let me have it or I'm telling Mom about the vodka!"

"Then I'll tell her about the whiskey!"

I step between them, faking a bright laugh to help de-escalate. "Okay, you two. Enough." It's like I'm six years old again, listening to them bicker over a toy, so I do what I learned to do back then when Harper gets like this. I take her by the arm and lead her away. "Come on, let's take a look out back."

Harper glares from Harry to me, but she lets herself be led.

The backyard is huge, with a gradual slope down toward the bay. A raised deck with a sparkling blue pool and a built-in grill hugs the rear of the house. Beyond that, chairs nestle around a firepit, and the manicured lawn gives way to beach grass and thick clumps of sea oats farther down. A path cuts through the beach grass, leading to a long dock that stretches over the marshy shallows out into the bay. The dock ends at a covered platform on high stilts. The bay itself sits wide and deep beyond the shore, with sunlight glinting bright and sharp off lapping waves.

As I knew she would, Harper has already forgotten the argument. "We should get Harry to rent us a boat this week," she says, taking off across the backyard. Dia joins us outside, and we follow Harper beyond the lawn and along the sandy path. Harper sets off down the narrow dock, its wooden boards bleached pale by sun and salt. The platform at the end sits at least six feet above the bay, even now when the tide is high. A ramp leads down to a floating lower platform for boats and Sea-Doos and swimmers. I see other

15

docks across the bay, several with people fishing or lounging. The sharp grumble of a motorboat engine revs to life not too far off.

Harper scampers down the ramp and sits on the edge of the floating platform, slipping off her sandals and dangling her feet in the water. "Gavin would love this," she says. "He'd already have a fishing rod out."

"Is the water warm?" I call down, ignoring the mention of her boyfriend.

"Could be warmer, but I'd jump in." She touches the hem of her T-shirt like she's thinking about yanking it over her head and splashing into the bay in her shorts and bra.

That's when I hear the music. It floats out over the water from the direction of the island, like a half-forgotten dream—a delicate tinkling, dancing sound. It might be a melody, but trying to make it out is like deciphering a murmur from another room, so familiar but so faint. "Do you two hear that? What is it?"

"Hear what?" Dia says.

Harper cocks her head back toward the house. "It sounds like a music box."

Dia listens and perks up. "I think that's an ice-cream truck! One of those old ones that plays music." She turns, staring back down the dock.

I pause. "How did an ice-cream truck get on the island?" The sound definitely carries from the direction of the house, not from across the bay.

"Who knows? Maybe Harry didn't close the gate right. Let's see if we can catch it!" Harper steps back into her shoes, races up the ramp, and takes off down the narrow dock, running more confidently in her sandals than I can in sneakers. Dia follows at a jog, yelling something about Creamsicles, while I lag behind, uneasy for reasons I can't define. I can still hear the tinkling music—it gets louder as we get closer to land—but I can't place the song. It tickles the edges of my brain with notes that are oddly toneless, a familiar tune played in a creeping minor key.

A memory flutters, something about strawberry ice cream, pink and sweet with chunks of red fruit. I slow to a walk. It's a hot afternoon, and we're on vacation, and ice cream should be perfect right now, but the thought of it makes my stomach churn and I can't figure out why.

Harper reaches the shore. She sprints across the yard and disappears around the side of the house.

The music stops.

Dia pauses on the sandy path, waiting for me. By the time I reach her, Harper reappears in the yard.

"Did you catch it?" Dia asks. "Did you tell it to wait for us?"

"There's no truck," Harper says, her voice flat with bewilderment.

"But I can hear it," Dia says.

I shake my head. "The music stopped a few seconds ago." I'm almost shivery, despite the warmth of the day. The memory of strawberry ghosts on the tip of my tongue like something I misplaced.

Harper's brow furrows, casting a shadow over her eyes. "It sounded close, right? It couldn't have disappeared that fast. I would've seen it driving away." The three of us stare at one another, and I see some of my uncertainty mirrored in their faces. Then Harper pivots and runs into the house.

We follow her to the master bedroom, where Harry is

unpacking. He looks up, wincing as if he's expecting Round Two in the Battle of the Master Bedroom to commence.

"Did you hear it?" Harper asks.

"What?"

"The ice-cream truck. There was an ice-cream truck outside." She peers out the bedroom's front-facing window.

"Outside where? Outside the house?" Harry heads to the front door. He steps onto the porch and surveys the dirt road, working his jaw.

Harper follows. "Yeah. Out here."

"There couldn't have been any trucks. We're the only ones on the island."

"Yeah, well, maybe you forgot to close the gate."

"It's automatic."

"Maybe it didn't lock." Harper crosses her arms.

"You saw a truck," Harry confirms. "Out here. There was a truck."

"An ice-cream truck," Harper says, frustration sharpening each word.

"We didn't see it," I clarify. "We heard it. We heard the music."

Harry's shoulders fall slightly as he relaxes. "You *heard* it." He looks at us like there's ten years between us and him instead of only one. "It must have come from across the bay."

"Maybe." I was sure of the direction before, but now doubt creeps in like fog before a humid dawn. Plus, the memory of that music still makes me queasy, and I'm eager for this debate to end. "Yeah, that's probably it. Let's just drop it, okay?"

Harper frowns and ignores my request. "It wasn't across the bay, Harry. It was right out here. It had to be. I can't believe you couldn't hear it. We heard it from the dock!"

"It carried across the water," Harry says. "That can do funny things to sound. It distorted the direction. That's all."

"Sure," Harper says, annoyed. "Or else you forgot to lock the gate and you don't want to admit it."

"I told you it's automatic!"

Harper points south. "Prove it. Let's go check."

Harry sighs in exasperation. "Fine. Come on." He locks up the house and drives us back down the dirt road. We cross the little bridge and park, and he gets out and shakes the gate, demonstrating that it's locked tight. Then we drive back, past the house, to the end of the road, where a giant banyan tree claims the northernmost tip of Straight Shot. There's no other way on or off the island, except by water.

"Whatever you heard came from across the bay," Harry says again, turning carefully on the narrow road. "I promise."

"Maybe the guy with the ice-cream truck has the code to the gate," Harper says.

"The owner of a multimillion-dollar island isn't going to give some rando his gate code," Harry says. "If you three want ice cream so much, we can find a grocery store. We need to get stuff for dinner anyway."

All I want is for us to drop the subject so my stomach can settle. Besides, it's not about the ice cream. It's about the music, that familiar sour tune, and a locked gate, and an ice-cream truck being where it shouldn't be, but how do I explain that to oh-so-logical Harry when I can't even explain it to myself? So we head into town, and Dia finds a box of the Creamsicles she was craving in the frozen foods aisle of Publix. When we get back to Straight Shot, she puts them in the freezer and doesn't touch them again.

19

Then

TWELVE YEARS AGO

Tonight the shadow crouches near the bookshelf. It's darker again, and easier to see, and stronger. The girl can hear it breathing over the growl of thunder in the distance.

And of course—of course—she can't move.

"When that happens," her therapist had said, "remember that it's just your mind playing tricks. The shadow can't hurt you." Together they practiced techniques to help the paralysis pass: repeating phrases like *I am safe* in her mind, over and over. Picturing herself in a happy place—the park, the beach, a quiet meadow. "And keep trying to wiggle your fingers and toes. That can help snap you out of it."

I am safe.

The shadow unspools from its corner, all ink and sinew, its oddly cocked head stretching toward the ceiling, its wide mouth hanging open.

The girl tries to wiggle her toes. They remain still under the blanket.

She imagines the meadow her therapist described: flowers swaying in a warm breeze, puffball clouds drifting overhead. But the wind picks up and the clouds turn black, an imaginary storm just as vivid and crashing as the one brewing outside the bedroom window.

I am safe.

It's hard to believe when she's bolted in place, frozen and stuck like a mouse on a glue trap while the shadow begins to reach. It inhales, a choking rasp building to a thin squeal that's like a knife scraping a china plate.

I am safe.

But she isn't safe. She knows that. The shadow will loom until she manages to open her mouth and scream. That always makes it go away…

…but what happens one night when it doesn't? What happens then?

The stormy meadow leaves her mind, preempted by the idea of her father hearing her scream and running in like always, ready to soothe and invalidate her fear. She imagines the thing's thread-thin arms reaching toward him instead—her father, who is all she has left. Her mother should be here to protect her, but her mother is gone, off chasing a life that doesn't include a little girl named Nellie.

The thought kindles a wisp of wrenching anger amid the fright. Her mother left and the shadow arrived, and she can't let it get her father.

No. She needs to find a way to handle this herself. Nellie needs to unfreeze.

Just as her therapist instructed, she pictures a safe place. Not the meadow—it's still storming there—but somewhere else, a spot toward which her mind hurtles instinctively: her kindergarten teacher's cheerful classroom with its alphabet cutouts parading over the whiteboard and its shelves of books, the bright spines stacked and aligned and tumbled together.

Nellie likes school. She feels safe in that cheerful classroom.

The shadow slithers closer.

Nellie thinks back to earlier that day, when she ended up coloring with the new girl in class. The new girl hid behind her straight brown hair and sang to herself as she filled the outline of a cartoon puppy with strokes of crayon, coloring far more neatly than Nellie could.

"What are you singing?" Nellie asked. The song was quiet, playful, with a whimsical tune.

It was an old song, the new girl said. A favorite of her mother's.

"I like it. Will you teach it to me?"

The new girl smiled shyly and taught Nellie the lyrics. Nellie sang it to herself all afternoon, making sure she remembered every last word. It was pretty, all singsong and cozy, with lyrics that slipped up and back like the scales they sang during Music Time on Tuesdays and Thursdays.

Those lyrics. Those words.

The memory dissolves a little of the tension locking Nellie in place. Only a little, but it's something, and as the shadow slithers closer, Nellie works her jaw until her mouth opens just enough. Instead of screaming, she sings to the shadow. She can't manage much more than a whisper, and as her mind tries to blank with fear, she clutches at the first lyric she can recall.

"I like to dream it's otherwise, pretend the world is fine."

She lets the tune tumble and flit like the new girl did, each note playing with the one before it.

"I know you'll soon be on your way, but here in the shadows you're mine."

The shadow reaches toward her.

Hesitates.

Drops its thread-thin arm.

It's working.

Nellie digs more lyrics from her memory. She sings them out of order, but the shadow doesn't seem to care. It creeps to the bed, settling on the far corner, wrapping itself around the bedpost. It goes still. It listens.

When Nellie tries again to wiggle her toes, the blanket moves. Her muscles relax as the paralysis lets her go. Beyond the window blinds, the thunderstorm fades toward the horizon without passing through.

She sings the entire song twice more, puzzling the words into proper order. When she's done, the shadow dissolves.

It isn't gone. She can tell, although she isn't sure how. It will be back. But now she knows a secret. The new girl in class gave her a great and somber gift; this realization fills Nellie with affection, and she decides right then and there that she and the new girl will be friends. Best friends, in fact.

And now she can sleep without fear.

Chapter Three

That night I close my door and dig my old Maglite out of my suitcase, the one Dad got me because of the shadow. He thought I could just shine it at the thing and all would be well. Shadows can't survive in the light, he said.

I never dared to try, even after I broke through the paralysis.

The Maglite is still useful, though. It's come in handy during plenty of Florida thunderstorm power flickers, and it's always with me when I travel. Heavy and metal and more than a foot long, it's as much a weapon as a flashlight. It's unwieldy but prudent, another example of my status as the group's mom friend—because really, you never know. I slip it under my pillow, where I always keep it.

Then I sit on the bed with my uke case, hoping the walls in this house aren't thin.

Holding my ukulele close against my chest, I strum softly and sing along, my voice barely more than a whisper. This is my nightly ritual, a habit I picked up for several years as a child. Not too long ago it became necessary again.

When I was little, soon after my mother took off, I started having night terrors. They were awful. I was too young to understand how sleep paralysis worked, and despite what my therapist told me, I was sure the hallucination haunting my bedroom each night was real. I thought there was a monster in my room, a living shadow that wanted to devour me, or break me, or crawl inside me, hiding in my throat, my head, my nightmares. But once I learned I could break its spell by singing...

I don't wake up paralyzed anymore, but a year ago the dreams began again—that shadow, that thing, darker than ever and back to lurking in the night like it belonged there. So I rescued my uke from the top shelf of my closet, and I revisited my old ritual. I sing the same song each night, an old standard—"Here in the Shadows," with its winsome melody and playful, plaintive lyrics. Harper taught me the song back in kindergarten, on the day we first met. I've never told her how desperately important it became to me. I don't know how to explain the significance of such a seemingly simple gift. She was just singing a familiar song to stave off the loneliness that came with being the new kid. It was something her mother sometimes sang while sweeping the floor or folding laundry; it felt cozy and safe, like home.

It felt like that to me, too, as soon as I heard it, so I borrowed it.

As long as I keep up with this ritual, the shadow keeps a polite distance. Most nights I don't dream of it at all.

As long as I sing.

Chapter Four

We're all having coffee when the truck pulls up out front. It's a battered red pickup, not a phantom ice-cream truck, but it shouldn't be here either way. We watch near the huge kitchen window as it parks next to Harry's SUV.

Frowning, Harry heads out to the porch as a young woman in carpenter jeans gets out of the truck, her dark skin shaded by the brim of a straw cowboy hat.

Dia bristles at the sight of the newcomer. "I should go help Harry," she says, heading out the door. Harper and I follow.

The girl in the cowboy hat is apologizing. "I'll be out of your hair soon. Dad meant to get out here on Friday, but he got tied up at another property all day. He asked me to come out and make sure the roof repair's holding before any storms roll in." She notices us and smiles.

Her smile knocks the air from my lungs for a second. In a good way.

"This is Tristan," Harry says. "Her dad owns the island."

"Tris is fine." Tris gives us a quick nod before lowering the truck's tailgate and opening a toolbox. She selects a few items and secures them to her jeans, placing them in pockets or hanging them from loops.

"Need help?" Harry asks.

"Nope. Just have to grab the ladder from the garage." She walks off.

Dia glares after her.

"Chill," I whisper.

"Did you see her smiling at Harry?" Dia mutters.

I watch Tris open the detached garage and take down an extension ladder from its hooks on the wall, hefting it without a struggle. "She smiled at all of us." The memory of that smile glows neon bright in my brain.

Tris positions the ladder against the house, giving it a shake to make sure it's set sturdily. Harry steps toward her, the compulsion to help still evident in his furrowed brow, but she leaves the ground before he can reiterate his offer.

She climbs up to the roof, confidently planting her work boots onto the shingles. I watch without breathing as she kneels, running her hands over what I assume is a recent patch. I don't know what she's looking for, but she seems pleased.

"Looks good!" she announces when she's back on the ground. "Give us a call if you notice any damp spots on the ceiling upstairs when it rains, but I think it'll be fine. Mind if I check a few other things while I'm here?"

"Go ahead," Harry says. "Give me a holler if you need help."

The smile she gives him this time doesn't quite meet her eyes. "I'll be sure to do that."

He heads back inside with Dia and Harper. I linger, watching Tris dig through her toolbox.

"Sorry about him," I say once Harry is out of earshot. "He's just really...helpful."

"I noticed." She laughs a little. "It's fine. I just get that a lot, you know?"

I search for more to say. "I'm guessing you don't need a lot of help with this kind of thing."

"Not usually." She drags a telescoping rod with a blade on one end from the truck bed. Then she glances at me. "You mind giving me a hand?"

"I thought..."

One corner of her mouth quirks upward, forming a dimple in her left cheek, and suddenly I'm out of breath again. Hell yes, I want to give her a hand, even though I know full well she doesn't *need* the help. I nod and follow her to one of the tall palm trees in front of the house, where she lengthens the rod and saws away at a drooping frond. When it falls, she has me drag it to the truck. It's larger and heavier than it looked on the tree.

"There are work gloves in my toolbox if you want them," she says, but I'm not concerned about my hands or nails. We take down a few more fronds, her sawing and me dragging. It's satisfying work. It's also quiet work, and I'm grateful for the lack of awkward small talk.

After a few minutes Harper reappears on the porch. "Nell? You good to head to the beach soon?"

"Sure," I say, hauling a frond into the truck.

"Okay." Harper glances from me to Tris before going back inside.

Once the palms are trimmed to Tris's satisfaction, she glances at the stand of pines to the left of the house. "There are a couple of dead branches I should take down before they land on the garage." She trades the telescoping blade for a saw, which she has me hold while she leans the ladder against the tree. Then she climbs up to a large branch with drooping brown needles, and she saws through it, cutting close to the trunk. When I go to drag the branch to the truck, she signals for me to wait.

"We'll leave the branches by the side of the house for now," she says after taking down a few more. "They're big enough to chop up for the firepit, but firepits are pretty low on my list of priorities right now." She shoves her hat back and wipes her brow, staring at the pile of branches. "I always feel a little bad."

"About what? Trimming the trees?"

"They feel like…friends, I guess? I don't like to go around sawing off my friends' arms."

"I would hope not." I laugh. The sound comes out a little higher than I meant, thin and nervous.

She grins. "Sorry. I didn't mean for that to sound as macabre as it did. Besides, trimming is good for trees. It's part of taking care of them, as long as it's done right."

"How do you know which branches to take?"

She frowns like she's not sure how to answer. "Instinct, I suppose. It's almost like the trees tell me." Then she shakes her head, sheepish. "It's stupid, I know."

"It's not." I could never consider what she's telling me stupid, not when she's sharing it with such sincerity. "Are the succulents in the living room yours?"

Her eyes brighten. "Yes! I propagated them myself. Aren't they cute?" She hesitates. "You're not watering them, are you?"

"I wouldn't dare. I've never been able to keep a plant alive for more than a month."

"Good. They're fussy. It's too easy to drown them. The herbs on the porch, on the other hand, are thirsty little freaks." She glances around like she's trying to think of other things to take care of while she's here. "How's the dock looking? Any wasps' nests out on the platform?"

"I haven't seen any."

"Let's check anyway. They're sneaky bastards." She hands me a can of bug spray and picks up a drill. "I can get the new hammock hooks up while we're out there."

"There are hammocks?"

She nods toward the garage. "In there. Bikes and stuff, too. Dad's been meaning to add a kayak."

No wasps lurk around the covered platform. "Just in case," she says, stashing the spray behind a roof brace so it'll be handy. Then she has me hold the hooks while she drills holes in the pilings.

She definitely doesn't actually need help.

When the hooks are anchored and secure, she sits on the edge of the platform. "Out of all of Dad's places, this one's my favorite."

I sit nearby. "Does he own a lot of properties?"

"He's up to almost a dozen. They're not all this snazzy, though. This is his newest. We just finished renovating the house earlier this year."

"And you help with that kind of thing? Renovations, upkeep?"

She nods, leaning back against a piling and turning to face me. "When I'm not in school. I'm a freshman at Flagler up in St. Augustine, and I help Dad on the weekends. I grew up doing this stuff with him and my grandma." She takes off the cowboy hat and holds it in her lap, keeping her fingers loosely wrapped around the brim to protect it from the breeze off the bay. Her dark hair is pulled back, secured with an elastic band at the nape of her neck.

That same bay breeze is pulling at my own hair, riling it up into something more unruly than usual. I smooth my hands over my dark blond waves, catching them in a loose ponytail. "That sounds like a lot of property to keep up with."

"It is. Dad had a business partner who helped out for a while, but he likes to be as hands-on as possible. Especially with this place. It's his favorite, too." She tilts her head a little. "You know, I thought he said a couple rented the island this week, not a bunch of spring breakers."

"That was Harper and Harry's mom and stepdad."

"Ah. Where are they?"

I swallow, wondering if us being here without them is a violation of the rental agreement.

She grins. "Hey, don't worry about it. Just don't wreck the place, okay?"

I relax. "Wrecking isn't an option with Harry around, I promise."

"That's the impression I got of him." She laughs. "Hey, so I didn't catch your name earlier."

"Nell," I say, trying in vain to keep from blushing.

"It's nice to meet you, Nell. Thanks for the help today." She leans toward me, offering her hand to shake. Her grip is strong, as confident as her footfalls on the roof.

"Nice to meet you, too, Tris."

"Where are you from?"

"Winter Park."

31

"Interesting. Do you go to UCF?"

I shake my head. "I start at Eckerd in the fall."

"That's all the way down in St. Pete, isn't it? Over on the Gulf Coast?"

I nod.

"Flagler's pretty great. I think you'd like it. Just saying."

I feel my face flush a little again. Flagler does suddenly sound appealing.

"Why Eckerd?" she asks.

"They have a really good creative writing program." I set my heart on Eckerd well over a year ago, back when I still wrote. Now I second-guess the choice every day, but I've already confirmed my attendance and accepted a scholarship and applied for loans and submitted deposits, and I feel like I'm past the point of hitting the brakes.

"You're a writer?"

"Sort of. It's...awkward?" I give her a humorless grin and hope she picks up on the fact that I don't want to talk about it.

I think she does, but then she says, "You probably need to get back to your friends, huh? Head to the beach?" She stands up and brushes her hands together, and the abruptness of it makes me suspect I screwed up somehow.

I stand, too. "Yeah, I probably should."

"Got your phone?"

Surprised, I pull it out of my pocket.

"Cool. Let me give you my number, in case anything breaks while you're here. Or, you know, if you just need me to look at something."

Okay, so maybe I didn't screw up. My cheeks flush again as I save her number in my phone, and then I text her so she has mine.

She puts on her hat and leads the way back down the narrow dock. "Hey, weird question," I say behind her. "Who has the gate code?"

"Just y'all and us," she says over her shoulder. "We change it every time we rent the place."

"So you wouldn't give it to, say, a delivery guy or something, right?"

"Of course not." She turns to face me. "Why?"

"We thought we heard a truck out front yesterday, but when we went to look, nothing was there."

"Nah, can't happen. If y'all order pizza or something, you'll have to meet the delivery person at the gate. Don't give them the code."

"That's what we figured." I remember that distant, echoing music, and I shiver, and I tell myself to stop dwelling.

Back at the house, Tris starts her pickup. "Remember, if anything breaks, you've got my number."

"Got it." I pat my phone through the pocket of my cutoffs.

"And if nothing breaks and you just need an excuse…" The dimple in her left cheek reappears. "Go ahead and break something, Nell."

She drives off before I can come up with a response. I watch the pickup grow smaller as it heads south; I don't notice Harper coming to stand beside me until she says, "So. Beach?" Dia and Harry are nearby, too. All three of them are staring at me.

"Sure. Yeah. Just let me go grab my stuff." I run into the house to gather my beach tote and a towel.

I can't help glancing around for things that might be worth breaking.

Chapter Five

"So?" Harper hands me back the bottle of sunscreen and rubs what's left on her hands over her face.

"So?" I echo, raising my brows at her before offering the bottle to Harry, who eagerly accepts. Of course I'm the only one on this trip who remembered sunscreen. I've already applied a thick glaze of it over my own burn-happy skin; despite that, I can feel the sun licking at my vulnerable arms and shoulders. I'll have to shrug my cover-up back on before too long.

"That girl," Harper clarifies.

"Tris?" I shrug. "She just needed to take care of a few things on the island."

Harper's smile is sly. "What was she taking care of all the way out on the dock?"

"She put up some hooks so we can hang a hammock." The flush returns to my face. I turn toward the sun, a convenient scapegoat, and notice a dark ink-slash of a storm lurking along the horizon, far away.

"And you were out there with her."

Dia sits up on her towel and glances at Harper over the frames of her sunglasses. "Leave her be, Harper."

"I'm just saying, it's not every day we see our Nell flirting."

I sigh. "I wasn't flirting."

"If you say so. It sure as hell looked like *she* was."

I hate it when Harper gets like this. "Were you watching?"

"We saw you two walking back up the dock," Harper says, grinning like a Cheshire cat.

"She *was* really smiling at you," Dia adds. So much for her having my back and getting Harper to lay off.

At least Harry stays out of it, busily glopping on sunscreen.

"Um, need some help?" Dia asks hesitantly when he struggles to reach between his shoulder blades.

Harry swallows. "No, I don't...I mean..."

"It's fine," she says quickly. "You've got it handled."

He pauses. "Actually, I...wouldn't mind a little help."

Dia scoots over and kneels behind him, moving slowly and deliberately, like she's worried she might scare him off. She tosses me a quick grin and goes to work with the sunscreen as Harry loosens his shoulders and settles into her touch.

"So do you like her?" Harper asks.

Harry whips his head around to glare at his sister, his expression panicked.

Harper rolls her eyes. "*Nell.* Do you like Tris?"

"I don't even know her." I stiffen my spine and try not to bristle.

My love life—or lack thereof—is a regular topic of conversation for Harper, who always insists I need to *put myself out there* more. "We talked for like ten minutes."

"That's not what I asked."

"I mean…" Usually I try to shut her down when she goes in this direction, but for once she's not entirely off base, and that somehow annoys me even more. It hurts that she nudges like this; it makes me feel like I'm doing everything wrong. Like *I'm* somehow wrong. "Maybe?"

"Is our late bloomer finally blooming?" Harper asks with cooing enthusiasm.

"You act like I've never dated anyone." I turn my attention to the Atlantic and watch as sunlight glints off the deep blue waves, turning the ocean into a faceted sapphire. Despite the brightness of the day, a distant ghost of thunder echoes from the darkening horizon.

"You saw a movie with Noah and met that Audrey girl for coffee a few times. Meanwhile, you have more options than any of us." She looks at Harry. "Well, almost any of us."

"That doesn't mean I find most of those options appealing." I know she just wants to encourage me, to push me out of my nest and into the dating pool, but most of the time I think I'd rather stay single than date someone for the sake of dating. Besides, if you made a Venn diagram of people I'd like to date and people who are interested in dating me—a quiet, sturdy introvert with hyper-vigilant control issues and weird ukulele fixations—the two circles would barely intersect, if they intersected at all. I'm an acquired taste, and I'm okay with that. I like my softness, the way my hips sway when I walk, the deep curves of my strong thighs, but not everybody does. That's their loss. Besides... "I don't know if Tris even likes girls."

"Did she give you her number?"

"Well, yeah."

"She likes girls," Harper confirms, her tone a little too smug. "She likes *you*."

"It was in case we need any repairs this week!"

"She likes you," Harper repeats, standing and turning away. "I'm going swimming before that storm gets here." She grins over her shoulder at me, then runs down to the water in her pink bikini. I wouldn't mind a swim, but I don't want to risk this conversation continuing, so I lie back and close my eyes and stare into red nothingness, letting the salted breeze soothe my baking skin. I hear footsteps crunch through the soft sand as Dia moves her towel next to Harry, and the two of them talk quietly, their words carried away on the light wind. When I peek a few minutes later, they're sitting close together, and Harry's giving her his best ducked-head, shy-boy smile.

Maybe Dia will get what she wants this week after all.

The ink-slash storm clouds fade without coming near, and the heat combined with the growl and sigh of the Atlantic waves lulls me into a stupor. I doze until my phone vibrates. I fish it out of my tote and find a message from Tris. In case you were curious, I checked. Flagler doesn't have a writing program, but they do have a creative writing minor. Just saying.

Too bad, I answer. I was all set to transfer. Is this flirting? Whatever it is, it's easier than being face to face. What's your major?

International studies. Minoring in prelaw.

Wow. So... you're going to be, what? A diplomat-lawyer? I ask. Who fixes houses on the weekend?

Haha, more like an international studies prof who fixes houses on the weekend, probably. Speaking of fixing stuff, did anything else break yet?

I smile. No, but we can hope.

She sends a GIF of a cartoon character crossing its fingers.

When I spot Harper heading to shore, I pull on my cover-up and step into my sandals. "I'm going back to the house for a drink. Anyone need anything?" Harry and Dia both request water, and I promise to bring bottles for everyone.

The path from the beach cuts through rolling dunes and up a short flight of rough wooden steps; the walk takes only a few minutes. Back at the house, I fill a small cooler with ice and water bottles.

My phone vibrates in the pocket of my cover-up. So what kind of stuff do you write?

My heart dips downward. Horror, mostly.

Really? Horror's my favorite!

When I don't answer after several minutes, she tries again. I'd love to read something of yours sometime. Are you working on anything now?

I press my lips together. When I tell people I'm not writing, they always ask why. That's not something I want to explain.

But I'm flattered that she's interested. And I do have plenty of older stories saved on my laptop. She doesn't need to know if it's been two weeks or two years since I wrote a certain piece. I could email you something.

Awesome! She sends her address.

I should get back to the beach, but instead I run upstairs for my laptop. I'm not about to ignore the delicious little surge of ... of *something* flickering in my chest. It won't take long to decide on a story and send it.

I haven't even opened my writing folder in almost a year. I tried a few times early on, pulling up a draft or a blank document and sitting, fingers poised over keys, waiting for the words to flow like they used to. It never worked. My breathing would grow shallow, and my heart would hammer in my throat, and my head would float with woozy vertigo.

But this isn't writing. This is just opening a file or two, and old stories are like old friends. I sit at the kitchen table, skimming file after file, debating what to send. The one about the blue-faced woman who haunts a seashore cottage, her skeletal hands forever clawing at her throat? Or wait, maybe the zombie outbreak story, or the serial killer hiding in an amusement park fun house, or the one about the orphanage and the unquiet bones? I wonder what kind of horror Tris prefers. Spooky atmospheres? Straight-up gore? Horror-comedy? I used to write it all. I could send more than one.

But what if she was just being polite when she asked? Bitter doubt nips at the edges of my brain. I add a *no worries if you're too busy to read* line to my email to give her an out, and I slip back into indecision.

When the front door opens, I jump.

Harper comes in first, followed by Harry and Dia and a rush of sun-warmed air.

"Drinks!" I stand up so sharply that I nearly knock over my chair. "I'm sorry. I got distracted." I hold out the cooler as if the three of them can't just go right to the fridge.

"Don't worry about it." Dia takes a water. "We had to come back anyway. That storm's rolling in after all."

I check the time and realize I've been poking around in my story files for over an hour.

Harper peeks at my laptop screen and sees the open email draft. "TrisCanFixIt at Gmail?"

"She wanted to read one of my stories." I shut the laptop without sending anything.

Harper elbows Dia. "Oh my God, it's getting serious."

Harry frowns at her. "Jesus, Harper. Cut it out."

Harper rolls her eyes. "Come on, Nell knows I'm just teasing her. Right, Nell?"

"Sure. Yeah." My face burning, I take the laptop back to my room and shut the door, and I sit on the bed and stare at the email draft. Maybe I shouldn't bother.

I remember Harper's tone when she called me a late bloomer.

Before I can lose what's left of my nerve, I attach the unquiet bones story and send the message.

Great. Now if I just never check my email again, everything will be fine.

To distract myself, I get up and study the small bookshelf next to the window. It holds only a handful of books, mostly dog-eared beach reads that I assume were left behind by previous renters. The only hardback has a plain red cover with *Guest Book* embossed in looping gold font.

I open it to the first lined, cream-colored page. It's blank. "Well, yeah," I mumble to myself. "How's anyone going to know to sign it if you keep it up here instead of down in the living room or the kitchen?" Then I notice a ragged bit of paper near the spine, and I realize I'm not looking at the first page at all. There was another, but most of it has been torn out; all that remains is a thin, blank strip at the bottom. Whatever memories were recorded in this book, they're just…

Gone.

That unsettled feeling creeps through me again, damp and clammy like fingers reaching through fog. It's the same feeling I had when I heard the ice-cream truck. Something's not quite right. Someone wanted so badly to hide a secret, a terrible memory, that they tore a page from this book.

Or else someone wrote something gross and Tris or her father ripped it out to avoid offending other guests. That's the more likely explanation. I shake my head and shove the unsettled feeling away.

Someone knocks. "Nell?" Dia's voice.

I put the book back. I'll try to remember to take it downstairs later. Maybe we can write in it this week, give it a fresh start. "You can come in."

She does. "Want to talk?"

I shrug as thunder growls in the distance. The light outside the window softens, muted by approaching clouds.

"I'm sorry Harper's being annoying."

"It's fine. She's just...being Harper." But she wasn't always *this* version of Harper.

Dia sits beside me and leans, letting her shoulder brush mine. "I just hate seeing you two like this. I don't know what's up with her lately."

"It's not just lately."

She nods. "I haven't known her as long as you have, but I get that she wasn't always like this."

Another shrug. It's not like I haven't analyzed the crumbling edges of my friendship with Harper a thousand times. "People change. We used to be a lot more alike than we are now." Best friends in elementary school. Matching misfits and zine publishers in middle school, at least at first.

Then Harper grew perfect curves, and I just sort of grew everywhere. She fascinated boys simply by existing, while I just existed. Her mom married Charlie, and suddenly she could afford trendy clothes and makeup and other things she'd never expressed much interest in before.

Things got even worse after Gavin moved to Winter Park. Harper kept changing, and it felt like she began to resent me for not following along. For not keeping up. "She thinks she's being helpful," I say. "She thinks she and I want the same things, and if she just pushes and pressures and teases until I get brave enough to go after them..."

"But you don't want those things."

I stare at the closed laptop, at the way its brushed steel case stands out against the blue comforter. "It doesn't matter. In a few months I'll be in St. Pete, and she'll be all the way up in Connecticut."

"I still can't believe she wants to go so far away."

I don't answer. We both know why Harper chose the school she did. It's where Gavin is going.

"Why does she single you out?" Dia asks. "She doesn't give me a hard time for being single."

"You've had boyfriends. You're not refusing to justify her chosen way of life the way I somehow am. Besides," I say, smiling a little, "if she bullies you into finding a guy, she knows which one you'll go for."

She grins and chews her lip. "I think that might actually happen."

"Don't come on too strong." I chuckle. "Harry's a total cinnamon roll. You don't want to scare him off."

"We actually had a really nice talk after Harper went back for another swim," Dia says. "He's still a little down about Randy, but he says it wasn't going well for a while, so he wasn't exactly surprised when they broke up. And then we just... talked. About all kinds of stuff. We've never done that before. For once I didn't feel like I was just another of his little sister's friends."

I think again about talking her down, warning her about rebounds, but I can't be the mom friend all the time. "Good," I say instead. "He's a really decent guy. I want both of you to be happy."

"I hope Harper feels that way, too. If it happens."

"How Harper feels doesn't have to matter," I say as raindrops begin to patter the window. Words I never thought I'd say about my best friend. I swallow that thought down, vowing not to let it mar the entire trip. There's too much to look forward to this week.

Then

TEN YEARS AGO

For a time, the shadow visits Nellie every night—all through kindergarten, then through first grade, and on into second. It slips and slithers into the bedroom, eager for her offering. It sways along with the soft lilting of her voice as she sings, and later with the gentle strumming of the ukulele. It's her mother's old uke, unearthed from the back of the hall closet where it had been abandoned after her parents' separation; the hum of its strings reminds Nellie of being younger and snuggling close while her mother played before bedtime. Nellie finds chord charts and instructional videos online and teaches herself to play. The first song she learns by heart is "Here in the Shadows," the song Harper taught her on the day they met. It seems to be the shadow's favorite.

She sings and she strums, and in an odd way, she starts looking forward to her nightly concerts. She likes having an audience of one. She even learns to like the shiver that creeps down her spine each time she sees the shadow. It almost seems to grow alongside her, becoming darker, larger, more distinct as the months and years go by, but also more familiar. It's still frightening, but now that she and it have reached this understanding—become friends, even, in a way—that fear is strangely delicious. As long as she sings, she is safe with her shadow.

That's a new discovery—the idea that fear can be fun, as long as she stays in control of it. The concept fascinates her, and she searches for other ways to spur those feather tickles of harmless fright. She lists the scariest things she can think of—monsters from old movies, lonely ghosts in endless hallways, witches huddled in forest huts—and she lets them whirl wild in her imagination. These nightmares are delightful, not like the ones in the real world—people you love leaving you, people you trust hurting you—and she dives into that escape like a desert wanderer into an oasis.

Every day she tells herself the scariest stories she can manage. The more she delights in spooking herself, the less she sees of her shadow. Gradually it fades away, as shadows always do. When she no longer needs her singing ritual, and she finds herself with a little extra time before bed...

Nellie begins to write those stories down. She doesn't want to forget a single one.

They're mostly just for her, although she does share them with her best friend from time to time. It feels like a fair trade; after all, Harper shared the shadow's favorite song, even though she has no idea what an important gift that was. Nellie reads stories out loud to Harper while the two of them sit on Nellie's bed or huddle in a blanket fort in the living room. Sometimes Nellie pulls the curtains shut and reads by the glow of her Maglite, pausing now and then to smile ghoulishly with the flashlight under her chin while Harper chews her nails in gleeful anticipation.

They incorporate some of Nellie's stories into the games they play at recess, pretending to search for the witch of the wood or recasting a jungle gym as a haunted estate. After one lecture too many about frightening or upsetting their classmates, Nellie and Harper resolve to keep most of their games between just the two of them. They don't need other players, not when they have each other.

Chapter Six

SUNDAY, APRIL 19

I don't check my email for the rest of the day. I even disable my account's auto-updates on my phone so I won't get any notifications. As long as I don't check, it's like Tris both has and hasn't responded. She both has and hasn't liked the story about the unquiet bones.

Schrödinger's inbox.

The rain moves through quickly, returning the heat and leaving the air heavy and thick with humidity. We've had enough of the sun, so Harry suggests we drive back into St. Felicitas for the afternoon. I almost stay behind to avoid Harper, but Dia convinces me to go. We park downtown and walk, poking through souvenir shops and gathering silly, touristy ideas for places to visit and things to do later in the week—the old Spanish fort, a pirate museum, an after-dark ghost tour on a trolley.

Harper spots a used bookstore and pokes her brother's shoulder. "Maybe you can find something for your collection in there."

"What collection?" Dia asks.

Harry's face flushes. "It's nothing."

"When he visits a new place, he always has to get a history book about the area," Harper says.

"It's silly." Harry dips his head and tries to keep going down the sidewalk.

"I don't think it's silly." Dia grabs his arm and pulls. Harry's face goes so red that I'm afraid he might pass out, but he smiles at Dia and relents, letting her tug him into the store. We follow, drawn in mostly by the chilled sigh of the place's air-conditioning. It doesn't take him long to find a suitable book, and we continue on.

Back on Straight Shot, Harry grills pork chops for dinner, using his recipe of secret spices, along with fresh rosemary and cilantro from the porch. He wraps ears of corn in foil, roasting them on the grill as well, while I melt cheese on garlic bread and Dia tosses a salad.

I avoid Harper's eyes as she sets the table. We haven't spoken much since she carried on about Tris earlier. But I can't hold on to my bruised feelings too long in the face of Harry's amazing cooking. We all stuff ourselves silly, and the high of a good meal softens the jagged edge of my frustration.

After dinner, we head out back with big glasses of iced tea, and although the evening is a little too warm and muggy to bother with the firepit, Harry gets it going anyway. The last whisper of daylight fades, leaving the sky a starry indigo with a vanishing strip of deep pink hanging low over the bay. Lights flicker on and glow yellow in the windows of the houses across the water. Frogs and crickets call from the patches of piney woods that bookend the house, and an osprey wails softly overhead, on its way to roost for the night.

Dia brings out her latest embroidery project, its fabric pulled taut in a wooden hoop. She's meticulous about her hobby; her stitches look like they were done by machine rather than by hand. She always has a piece going, and Harper and I have both gotten finished hoops from her as birthday presents. Mine was a quote by Stephen King about writing. Tonight she sits near Harry and stitches by firelight. She's working on a new piece, one she's been secretive about since she began it, and I wonder if it's meant to be a gift for him.

She puts her work aside, though, when I reveal one of the surprises I have for this week: a bag of marshmallows and a handful of skewers, along with graham crackers and chocolate bars. The smoky air turns sweet as we magically find room in our stomachs despite the dinner we just shared, and soon we've demolished my supplies and we're licking the last hints of melted chocolate and charred marshmallow from our fingers.

The s'mores melt away what's left of the tension between Harper and me, at least for now, and before long we're all laughing at the memories that come up in the flickering shadows. I keep an eye on those shadows, but none of them are anyone I know.

"We're the only ones on this whole island," Harper says. "It's creepy, but in a good way, you know?" The firepit pops, sending a shimmer of embers into the air as the burning wood resettles.

"It's like that time my parents took the three of us camping." Dia snickers. "Remember?"

"We were all sitting around the campfire," Harper tells Harry, "and Nell told the scariest story. Wasn't it the one about the blue-faced lady, Nell?"

My stomach twists a little, but I smile and shrug. It's odd to remember that there was a time in my life when I shared my stories so freely. "Could've been."

Dia's grin widens, the firelight painting it as a leer. "Then that branch fell nearby at just the right moment, and my mom freaked out. She was sure we were all about to get murdered by a vengeful ghost. And we never went camping again."

"Got a story for us?" Harry asks me.

"I haven't come up with a new story in a long time."

"Then tell us an old one," Dia presses. "I never get tired of them."

"Please, Nell?" Harper gives me a small smile. "That was such a fun night. I miss your stories."

"I don't remember any of them well enough."

"You could just read one off your laptop," Harper says.

And just like that, I'm out of excuses. I don't want to go upstairs for my laptop, but . . . "I can get to one on my phone. Okay."

Dia claps her hands and Harper grins.

Opening my email app forces an inbox update that tightens my chest. There's no reply from Tris. Ignoring the letdown, I go to the sent folder and open the attachment from my email to her, and I read out loud about the orphanage and the unquiet bones. The story mingles with the fire's crackle and the songs of the island's crickets, and the effect is almost creepy enough to give me the kind of delicious shiver I used to savor.

As she listens, Dia wraps herself into a ball, drawing up her knees like she's cold. When Harry notices, he shrugs off the plaid button-down he's been wearing over a concert T-shirt and passes it to her. She smiles at him and drapes it over her shoulders.

After my story, Harry fetches his new book. It includes a

chapter on occult legends about St. Felicitas and outlines which locations in the city are thought to be haunted. This isn't Harry's usual area of interest, but the theme fits the evening, and he reads out loud about the ghosts rumored to creep through the Fulton Cemetery at night, and the women who escaped a seventeenth-century witch hunt by fleeing to a nearby island and vanishing, and the long-dead soldier sometimes spotted at twilight in the old fort. Mysterious lights flicker after dark in the Grand Felicitas Inn, and the ghosts of drowned children giggle through the city's old lighthouse. The legends Harry shares make me wish I still enjoyed scary stories; I could find so much inspiration here, especially now, as the darkness presses in and the slowly dying embers in the firepit coax the shadows closer, closer.

Later, after we've all parted ways for the night, I sit cross-legged in bed and tune my uke. I'm just about to strum the first chord when my phone vibrates on my nightstand.

A message from Tris. Holy shit, you are GOOD! That story's going to give me nightmares.

At least when I'm alone in my room I can blush without getting teased by Harper. Thank you! And I hope not. About the nightmares.

Nah, it's cool. I like nightmares. I don't usually sleep well. If I'm having nightmares, at least that means I'm sleeping.

I bite my lip. I mean, if that's the way you feel, I could send another nightmare your way.

Please do! she responds, and I'm already sliding out of bed to grab my laptop. Reading to my friends around the fire made me realize that I've missed scaring others instead of just myself. I've missed it terribly.

51

Then

Nellie, can I show you something?" One day during fifth-grade lunch, Harper pulls her sketchbook from her backpack. "You know the story you let me read last week?"

"The one about the swamp hag?" Nellie asks. She and Harper no longer play pretend games based on her stories, but she still offers to share them with Harper, and Harper always eagerly accepts. Nellie is especially proud of her latest, a tale of the monstrous hag who haunts an old bayou, damned to wander for all eternity as punishment for neglecting her children and letting them drown in the swamp's stagnant waters.

Harper nods, flipping through the sketchbook until she finds an inked drawing of a half-rotted old woman rising from a fetid swamp. What's left of the woman's hair hangs in slimy tendrils around her face. She reaches out with one gnarled, grasping hand like she might escape the page and come to life right there in the cafeteria.

Nellie gasps. "That's my swamp hag! You're such a good artist."

"Your story inspired me." Harper grins. "It scared me so bad I couldn't sleep, so I stayed up and drew this."

Fascinated, Nellie brushes a finger over the remnants of the hag's hair. The drawing creeps her out. In a good way.

"I could do more if you want," Harper says.

"That would be amazing," Nellie says. "But...why?"

"Well, I kind of had this idea...."

Nellie raises a brow.

"Remember how Ms. Miller had us make those zines last month?"

"Yeah, of course." Their language arts teacher had explained that a long time ago, back before the internet was a thing, people used to share their work in little homemade magazines. She had each student staple together booklets of poetry, artwork, stories, random thoughts—whatever they wanted. Some people still created zines, she'd said, although blogs and Tumblr and other sites had made them all but obsolete.

"What if we started a horror one?" Harper asks. "Your stories and my illustrations. A collab."

"That..." Nellie pauses. She was ready to turn down the idea, to keep her stories mostly to herself, but then she looks again at the drawing. It's satisfying to know she inspired that. Someone read her story and ran with it; the resulting feeling is intoxicating, a strange mix of possession and pride, and she wants more. She wants other people to read her stories and share the harmless horrors in her head.

She could just put the stories online somewhere. That would

be the easy way. But the idea of putting together a zine—sharing tangible copies, holding her work in her hands—charms her.

Finally, she nods, the giddy excitement of a new project effervescing in her head. "I love that idea!"

Harper grins. "When should we start?"

"Come over after school today and we'll figure it out. Or maybe we can go to your apartment?"

"Harry will be there. He'll bug us."

"I don't care. We can deal with Harry." Nellie loves Harper's tiny apartment. It's bright and threadbare, full of Harper's mother's secondhand treasures, and it always smells faintly of cinnamon-vanilla incense that makes Nellie think of cookies and hugs. She loves slipping into the place's only tiny bathroom and seeing Harper's mother's toiletries and cosmetics scattered across the counter; sometimes she sniffs bottles of moisturizer or body spray and tries to remember if her own mother ever smelled like any of them. Even though Harper's mother is nearly always at work, or occasionally out with her boyfriend, the apartment always feels like her. Like a home.

Plus, while Harry might be annoying, lately he's been teaching himself to cook. He may need taste testers for whatever he'll be experimenting with this afternoon, and his dishes tend to be yummier than the peanut butter sandwich Nellie's father slapped together for her lunch before leaving for work that morning.

Harper nods. "Okay, fine." She's about to continue when a boy from their class walks past their table and gives the strap of her new training bra a stinging snap before hurrying off. "Ouch!" She glares after him and reaches back to gingerly rub her shoulder blade. "What the heck?"

"Boys," Nellie says, also glaring in solidarity. Something dark and angry licks to life inside her.

"Why are they like that?"

Nellie shrugs, trying to let the anger settle. "My dad says if a boy teases you, it's because he likes you." She finds that idea ridiculous—why would liking someone make you want to hurt them? But anytime she's complained to her father about a boy mocking her or pulling her hair or touching her, his response has always been the same—a knowing smirk and a he-must-like-you comment. She no longer bothers to tell him about most of it.

Harper gives the retreating boy a final derisive glance. "Gross." She turns back to Nellie, smiling a little too brightly, looking for distraction. It's like she folds up the moment with the boy and the bra strap and locks it away somewhere dark and deep, where she won't have to think about it. "Okay, but now we have to figure out something really, really important."

Eager to make her friend happy, Nellie mirrors her sudden enthusiasm. "What?"

"We have to name the zine."

The girls brainstorm through the rest of lunch, until Nellie comes up with an idea that grabs them both. "What about *Here in the Shadows?*"

"Like the song? Oh, that's so creepy! That could work!"

Her old friend the shadow would be pleased, Nellie thinks. Not that she ever sees it anymore, but it always loved that song.

Chapter Seven

MONDAY, APRIL 20

I wake up stoplight red. So much for the sunscreen I used the day before. I slather myself in aloe vera gel, leaving the tube on the bathroom counter in case anyone else is similarly afflicted, and pull on a soft jersey dress that won't irritate my sore skin. By the time I get downstairs, Harry has left for Orlando and Harper is out on a morning jog down the unpaved road.

"Ouch." Dia looks at my Day-Glo complexion and hands me some coffee.

"Caffeine," I coo lovingly into the mug.

"Didn't you sleep well?"

"I was up late." I sent Tris three more stories last night. She read them right away, texting her reactions in real time.

She makes me wish I could still write.

"Up late? Me too." Dia smiles slyly over the rim of her cup. "You know how Harry had to stay outside for a bit to put out the fire?"

"You joined him?"

"He loaned me his shirt, remember? I had to give it back."

I give her a short, amused chuckle. "Yeah, I'm sure that's why you went back out. So what happened?"

"We talked some more, and . . . I'm sure he was flirting. Or trying to." Her smile widens, causing her nose to wrinkle.

I know I decided not to get involved, but the urge to protect her heart—and Harry's, too—is rising, and I can't wrangle it back down. "Dia, I don't know whether to cheer for you or tell you to be careful."

"Cheer, Nell. Definitely cheer."

"He and Randy only just broke up."

"I know. I do." The words come out quickly, and she punctuates them with a solid nod. "I don't want to be his rebound."

"Good."

"I just feel like time is running out, you know? Soon I'll be up in Tallahassee and he'll still be in Orlando."

"That's not for another four months." As soon as I say it, I wish I could take it back. The words feel thick and foolish on my tongue. Four months is nothing.

Four months until everything changes.

Harper opens the front door, and Dia tosses me a pointed look. I give her a quick nod—no more talk about Harry and rebounds, not while his sister is around.

"Ouch, Nell." Harper eyes my arms. "You weren't even outside that long." She has some extra pink across her cheeks and the bridge of her nose, and maybe a few more freckles than yesterday, but that's it. At least the sunscreen worked for someone.

"Some things never change," I say. The cliché rings false after the discussion Dia and I just had. "Remember that time your mom took us to the beach and I ended up in the ER?"

"Oh my God, yes." Harper gets some coffee and sits down with us. "Sixth grade, right? Mom forgot the sunscreen and we stayed all day. You couldn't stop shaking after. First I was scared you were going to die. Then you were okay and I was scared your dad would be mad at my mom, and we wouldn't be allowed to be friends anymore."

Back then, the idea of losing Harper's friendship was like standing at the edge of a canyon, staring straight down until I was dizzy.

That day happened a year or two before Dia moved to Winter Park, but she's heard the story before. "I'm so glad I never burn," she says.

"Sure, rub it in." I finish my coffee and rinse the mug.

"What should we do today?" Harper asks. "I'm thinking another beach morning, since it's not like we can get Harry to take us anywhere. He won't be back until late this afternoon."

"I'm in," Dia says, but I opt to stay behind. I can't imagine baking in the sun all morning when I'm already extra crispy.

After they leave, I get my uke and head out to the bay. The sun is merciless on the narrow dock, but once I reach the covered platform, the breeze cools my burns. The tide is low, the air so briny that I can almost feel the salt settling on my skin.

I didn't sing last night, for the first time in a year. I fell asleep with my phone in my hand. Tris kept messaging me while she read my stories, and I couldn't pull myself away from her reactions long enough to grab my uke, and then I opened my eyes to the morning. When I saw the uke case on the floor, I froze, just for a moment. But if the shadow had come by, looking for its song, perhaps it had decided to let me sleep instead, at least for one night. I didn't play, didn't give in to that compulsion . . . and this morning everything was still okay.

The realization made me want to play my uke—not for the shadow, but for me. Not hidden away in my room at night, but here, where the morning light flashes off the gentle waves of the bay and the wind combs invisible fingers through my hair.

I love playing. I love singing along. Why not let it be something gorgeous and joyful and full of light?

I strum the strings and start to sing, letting the breeze steal each word from my lips. There are a few people visible across the bay, on docks and in yards, but they're far away and I'm as good as alone. I lose myself in song after song. I close my eyes and play until my calloused fingers start to go numb, and it's all just for me, and it's glorious.

"Hey, Nell."

I yelp and lose my grip on the uke. My hand darts out to catch it, my fingers nearly grazing its narrow neck, but I miss. It cracks against the edge of the dock, hollow against solid, wood against wood, and then it topples out of view. "Damn it!" My throat tightens when I hear the tiny slap of a splash as my uke hits the water. I scramble to my feet and spin around, nearly snarling, hackles up. "Gavin?!"

"In the flesh." He leans against a piling, arms crossed, and grins at me. "Sorry. Didn't mean to scare you."

"What the hell are you doing here?"

Then

The first issue of *Here in the Shadows* contains Nellie's swamp hag story, with Harper's art on the cover and additional illustrations throughout. They create thirty copies, printing the pages on Nellie's father's laser printer and then folding and stapling each volume by hand. Harper uses a highlighter to turn each printed hag a sickly green.

They hand out copies at school the next day. Demand is high. They run out before lunch. Nellie's stomach flips at the thought of sharing her work with so many people, but the reactions she hears are overwhelmingly positive, stoking her confidence. The second graders who feared her and Harper's playground games have grown into fifth graders who are eager to prove how brave they are.

That evening, Harper shows up at Nellie's door, upset. "I told Mom about the zine and her boyfriend overheard. He said we were stupid to give it away. He said we should charge."

"He's the one who's stupid." Nellie isn't a fan of Harper's mother's boyfriend, Charlie. Nor is she a fan of being called stupid; she bristles alongside Harper, tensing in time with the echo of thunder on the horizon. There had been a time when she and Harper had plotted possible ways to set up Harper's mother with Nellie's father, so that the girls could be sisters as well as best friends. Now Charlie is in the way, and Harper and Nellie are eager for him to move on and let the two of them get back to their plan.

However, what if Stupid Charlie has a point? "Then again," Nellie says, "if we sell copies, we can use the money to buy better paper. Maybe we can even get the covers printed at Staples. They could be in color!"

"Color?" Harper brightens.

"Yes!" Nellie grabs Harper's arm and tugs. "Come on. We can start planning the next issue." They collaborate for hours, writing and drawing and chatting wildly. Outside, the thunder fades without any rain falling. Florida storms can be fickle.

Nellie and Harper print and compile fifty copies of the next issue and charge a dollar apiece, and they sell out by lunch.

During sixth period the principal summons them to his office and informs them that they cannot sell zines on school property, especially not ones full of gruesome stories and horrific drawings. He's too late; demand is skyrocketing among the girls' classmates.

They can be discreet, they decide later, but they're not stopping.

They print a hundred copies of the third issue—this one with a color cover—and sneakily sell them all.

Chapter Eight

I didn't know you still sang," Gavin says, ignoring my question. The breeze musses his ash-brown hair and teases the untucked hem of his blue polo. "We miss you in chorus."

"Why. Are. You. Here?" I try again, spacing the words out like I'm talking to a toddler. I want to glance over my shoulder and look for my uke—I'll have to retrieve it before the current takes it too far down the bay—but I don't dare take my eyes off Gavin. I hear another splash from below, like a fish cresting and going back under, and a gentle bubbling.

"Harper invited us over for the day."

"Us?"

"Me and Christopher." Gavin jerks a thumb over his shoulder. In my peripheral vision, I see his best friend and fellow swim team member standing at the end of the long dock, a turquoise baseball cap pulled low over his blond crew cut. He waves.

I don't wave back.

"Harper shouldn't have done that. It's against the rules." I force my tone into something resembling calmness and consider my options. The adrenaline in my veins screams for me to slip past Gavin and hurry down the dock. I don't want Christopher to head toward the platform before I can escape. I don't want to be trapped between them.

But I also need my uke.

"The rules?" Gavin steps in front of me. He grins, subtle crinkles appearing near the corners of his green eyes. I smell mint on his breath, and the scent twists my stomach. "Chill out, Nell. It's spring break."

I keep my face carefully expressionless. I can't—won't—let him know how freaked out I am. *He startled you*, I tell myself. *That's all.* At least he can't hear the pulse slamming in my ears or feel the prickle of the tiny hairs rising on the back of my neck. "You made me drop my uke."

He chuckles, holding my gaze. "I didn't make you do anything. All I did was say hello."

"Whatever." I force my eyes away from him and look down toward the bay. "Now I have to…" My voice trails off. Below us, shadow-dulled waves lap gently at barnacled pilings. My uke should be right there, but nothing's floating under the platform.

"What?" Gavin peeks down beside me.

I straighten and skitter down the ramp to the floating dock. If the uke were nearby, I would certainly be able to spot it from here. "It's gone. What the hell?"

"Guess it sank." On the platform, Gavin shrugs, his eyebrows raised in a look of oh-well nonchalance.

Tight frustration ticks to life in my chest, forcing a little of my panic to the side. "A ukulele would float," I say as I climb back up the walkway toward the platform, shoulders squared. My uke is hollow and made of lightweight wood; it's more air than solid instrument. It might sink eventually, after growing waterlogged over the course of hours or days, but there's no way it could disappear in seconds—but then I remember that second little splash and the bubbles that followed, and I picture my uke filling with water and sinking.

Sinking... or maybe being dragged. But what would do that?

"Damn it, Gavin, I—"

"Jesus, Nell. Calm down." He tosses me an easy smile that's slightly bemused but also thoroughly unconcerned. "If it's such a big deal, I'll buy you another."

A big deal. I want to spit at him that the uke was my mother's. He can't replace its scratched finish or the way parts of its fretboard are worn shiny from her grip and mine. But my eyes start to burn, and I refuse to let my anger turn to tears in front of him. Instead, I duck around him and head down the dock. At first I'm not sure Christopher is going to step aside and let me pass, but I narrow my eyes at him as I approach, and he finally moves over, grinning and tipping his head downward so that the bill of his cap shadows his eyes.

"Nell, wait!" Gavin is still behind me. I do *not* want him following me anymore. "Where's Harper?"

"The beach. That way. Can't miss it." I point east, then head for the house, wanting nothing more than to get inside and lock the door behind me.

"Maybe we'll come in and wait," Gavin says.

My throat constricts. I don't want to be inside with the two of them. "I'm actually about to head out for a walk," I lie. "I'm just getting a water first."

"Mind grabbing us some?" Gavin asks, putting a hand out to keep the door from closing.

I hate this. I *hate* this. He stands in the open doorway while I scoot inside. My stomach twists when I spot my empty uke case on the kitchen table; I tuck it on top of the fridge like that's where it belongs, and I grab a few bottles of water. After distributing them, I again point toward the beach. "Harper's right down there. Dia, too."

"Dia's here?" Christopher says. "Nice. Come on, Gav." The two of them finally head toward the path that leads down to the beach.

I send a silent apology Dia's way. Christopher has been smitten with her for years, and she's never returned his infatuation. But I need them to get away from me so my heart can stop pounding.

I watch them from the porch, waiting for them to disappear from view. Of course I'm not actually going on a walk. All I can think about is slipping back inside. Closing the door. Locking it tight.

But then Gavin glances over his shoulder, his steps slowing. I need to keep up with my lie. If I don't vanish, he might come back.

I consider returning to the bay to look for my uke, but I can't risk being cornered again. It's gone, and of course I can get another one, but it won't be *my* uke, and how am I going to appease my shadow in the meantime? I'll figure it out, but for now, I need to disappear. Frustrated nearly to the point of bursting, I head toward the thicket of pine trees that bookends the house on its right side. I'm not dressed for a walk in a miniature forest, but there aren't many places to disappear on such a small island, so I'll have to make it work.

I pick my path through a carpet of pine needles, dodging the sharp reach of an occasional saw palmetto. Sand works its way between my feet and the soles of my sandals, scratching at my toes. While I walk, I take out my phone and message Harper. Really? You invited Gavin. You gave him the gate code. REALLY?

It's just for the day, she replies after a minute.

HARPER.

Look, he wasn't going to stop bugging me until I let him come over!

Harry's going to be so pissed. You KNOW he'll tell your parents.

Do NOT call Charlie my parent, Harper shoots back immediately. He is NOT my dad.

Whatever. He and your mom will make us all come home early. Right now I'd be thrilled by that outcome.

They'll leave before Harry gets back. So unless you tell him . . .

I'm so focused on my phone that I almost bump into the bus. By the time I glance up, I'm nearly on top of what's left of its hood.

"What the hell?" For a moment I forget about bitching out Harper.

It's a school bus. Or it used to be. There's still some faded yellow paint peeking out from around the devouring rust and creeping moss. The windshield is smashed, the remains of a large branch dangling from the jagged hole in the glass. The tires are gone.

The bus isn't that far from the road or the house, but none of us noticed it before now. The vegetation here is effective camouflage—trees have grown up around the vehicle, crowding it, imprisoning it. Vines wind and knot around the axles like the chains of anchors. It looks like it's been here for years. If someone tried to remove it, I suspect it might crumble.

And there's that feeling again—that crawling, unsettled

discomfort, like the tickle of a spider up my spine. The bus, the ice-cream truck, the damaged guest book. Something's not right.

And yet…I need a place to hide. Just for a little while. No one would know to look for me here.

What's left of the folding door is half closed, but a shove sends it creaking open and wobbling on protesting hinges. I climb the stairs, alert for broken glass and the scuttle of large insects. The interior stinks of mildew, but I expected worse. At least the busted windows allow for some airflow.

The seats near the front are ruined, the vinyl torn and chewed, the stuffing bulging and dotted with mold. The rear of the bus is in slightly better shape, with intact seats and a scattering of old Solo cups on the floor, the red plastic faded and cracked from the heat. I nearly head all the way back, but that crawling tickle of dread spikes and I freeze. *Too far.* I choose a seat a few rows forward that doesn't look in danger of giving way or being full of roaches, and I perch gingerly on its edge.

It's not lovely in here, but it's bearable. I just need a few minutes to regroup.

My phone displays three more messages from Harper, all either begging or ordering me not to tell Harry what she's done. Jesus, Nell, it's really not a big deal. The text comes from Harper, but I hear Gavin's voice read it in my head.

It *is* a big deal to me, and I can't tell her why. There's no explanation that won't backfire on me. At least it's not like Gavin and Christopher can stay for too long. They'll have to leave before Harry gets back. I just have to grit my teeth and bite my tongue until then.

I close my conversation with Harper and message Tris instead, as a distraction. So what's with the bus?

I assume she's in class and won't answer right away, but she responds in seconds. What bus?

The old school bus in the trees by the house.

The hell? On the island? There's no bus there.

Then what am I sitting in right now? I try to follow up with a photo of the bus's interior, but it won't go through.

Are you messing with me? What's the punch line?

If I were messing with you, I'd come up with something more plausible than a broken-down bus, I promise.

There's a bus. In the woods. On Straight Shot.

Yes. I swear it. I keep trying to send a pic but it won't work.

Class lets out at 11:30. I'll be by after to check it out.

I know she's only coming to investigate my bizarre claim, but I feel a little better knowing that Tris will be here soon.

And I didn't even have to break anything.

Chapter Nine

I wait in the bus until Tris messages me that she's close. Then I make my way back to the dirt road to wait for her, keeping an eye out for Gavin. Relief loosens my rib cage when I spot the red truck kicking up dust to the south. She parks near Gavin's BMW, giving it a brief frown as she gets out.

Her cowboy hat is gone today, and her hair is loose and thick and natural, parted in the middle. She wears jeans, boots, and a faded T-shirt advertising a band I'm pretty sure my dad used to listen to in the '90s. "Okay, show me the bus." She still sounds doubtful, but she smiles when our eyes meet.

"This way." I lead her back into the trees, trying to take the same path as before, when I was texting Harper instead of paying attention. I'm going the right way, I swear I am, but the bus doesn't appear. "It was kind of hidden," I say, confused.

"It's a school bus." Tris pushes a branch out of the way. "How hidden could it be?"

I shake my head. "It was right around here, I swear. Look, I still have the pic I tried to send you." I scroll through my photo feed, but the picture isn't there. It's not in my deleted folder, either. Suddenly a little desperate to anchor myself in reality, I press my palm against the trunk of a nearby tree, focusing on the rough prickle of bark against my skin. "I don't get it. I feel like I'm losing my mind."

"Hey, it's okay. We'll keep looking." She sounds uncertain.

I'm about to keep walking when I hear voices echo up from near the house. The others are back from the beach. I don't realize I'm trembling until Tris puts a hand on my arm and asks if I'm okay. "I'm fine," I say. "It's just this sunburn. It's giving me a weird chill or something."

"Let's go back to the house."

"No." My shoulder blades clench.

"Nell? What's up?"

I sigh. "One of my friends invited her boyfriend over. He and I don't get along, so I'm kind of avoiding everyone right now. That's why I was wandering around out here to begin with."

"Need somewhere to disappear for a while?" she asks. When I nod, she gestures for me to follow her north through the trees.

Aside from the brief drive with Harry our first day here, I haven't been to Straight Shot's northern tip. Beyond the reach of the dirt road, a huge banyan overlooks the spot where the bay meets the ocean. I remember how Tris talked about the pines and the palms, and the succulents that line the living room window, and I'm not surprised that her solution to my bad day is a tree. She leads me into the shade beneath its canopy, and we pick our way among knobby roots and outstretched vines that remind me of shadowy, thread-thin arms reaching between treetop and ground.

Banyans are stranglers, Tris explains. This tree grew by twisting and twining and throttling another, until that host rotted away within. "She's hollow but thriving," Tris says, touching the trunk. She hoists herself onto a thick branch that curves about four feet off the ground, creating a natural cradle large enough for two. She pats the bark, inviting me to join her.

"I'm not sure I can get up there," I say. I've never been much of a climber.

She reaches out a hand. "I'll help."

I hesitate, shyness and doubt burrowing into my thoughts. I'm sure she could help lift someone smaller, like Dia or Harper, but...

Tris raises a brow at me and wiggles her fingers.

My hand clasps hers. Her palm is warm, and then she pulls, boosting while I haul myself up. It's not easy or elegant, especially in a sundress and sandals, but I plant myself on the branch without too much of a struggle. "You're strong," I say, and she laughs and flexes a bicep. Then she tilts her head, a signal for me to turn and look.

The banyan's canopy blocks part of the view, but what's visible is gorgeous. This far north, the island is so narrow that I can see ocean to the right and bay to the left, with the inlet where they meet directly in front of us. We're surrounded by waves—whitecapped on one side, gentle on the other—and sheltered by the tree.

"Like it?" she asks.

"It's perfect." I watch a pelican splash into the shallows of the Atlantic, its dive eager and lacking in grace.

"It's my favorite part of the island." We're sitting close enough together for me to feel the slight brush of her arm against mine. "Dad keeps talking about cutting this tree down. Can you believe that?"

"Why would he want to?" The thought of it feels criminal.

"He thinks we should put a gazebo up here. Take advantage of the view without the banyan blocking it."

"Don't let him!"

She chuckles. "I don't plan on it. Besides, the tree is part of what anchors this section of the island. All these roots help keep the whole place together. I don't know how it's thrived for so long with all the salt in the groundwater, but it obviously belongs here." She gives the branch an affectionate pat.

I stare out over the water. "I think I'll stay out here for the rest of the week."

"Because of the boyfriend? If your friend is letting him stay overnight, I can claim that's against the terms of the rental agreement and get Dad to come out and make him leave."

My laugh is soft and humorless. "Not overnight. He has to disappear before Harry gets back."

"So how come you don't like... what's his name?"

"Gavin. We just don't get along." I force myself to breathe normally and focus on the solidity of the branch beneath me. "He made me drop..." I bite back the words, both because remembering the loss of my uke constricts my throat with regret, and because I don't want to admit to Tris that I had it in the first place. What if that leads to questions about my singing and playing? Sharing my stories with her was a big enough step; I'm not ready to share my ritual as well. "A book," I finish, although the lie makes a tiny ache bloom in my chest. I don't like lying to this girl. "If you dropped something off the platform out back, where would it probably end up? Would it wash up in the shallows?"

Tris's brow furrows. "If it's something that floats," she says, "the current would probably carry it down the bay for a while, until it gets caught up in the vegetation somewhere. I think your book's probably a goner, though."

"Yeah, I guess so." I close my eyes, letting the hushed roll of the waves and the cries of distant shorebirds lull me, and I try to accept that my uke is long gone. Maybe someday I'd appreciate the wistful romanticism in the image of a ukulele drifting off into gentle oblivion, buoyed on the backs of sun-dappled waves.

Sure, maybe, if it had actually been floating. The memory of watching the water and seeing nothing itches like the welt of a mosquito bite. There's something uncanny about it, something not quite right that I can't quite crack.

"When's Harry supposed to be back?"

I shove my mourning for my uke aside. "Not until later. Six, maybe."

"Want me to hang around until then?"

I open my eyes and look at her. "Don't you have to get back to campus?"

"Nah. Already skipped out on my last class of the day."

"I'm sure you have things to do." It sounds like I'm blowing her off, encouraging her to leave. That's the last thing I want. But I also don't want her to feel obligated to stay. Harry won't be back for hours.

She grows serious, her brows tilting downward as she studies me. "Want the truth?"

"I'm not sure. Do I?"

"The way you talk about this guy is giving me creeper vibes. I don't know why you don't like him, and I don't know what he's done, but I feel like maybe I should hang out until he's gone."

73

"I'm that transparent, huh?"

She shrugs. "If you want the company, I'll stay."

The vise that's been tightening around my chest since Gavin surprised me loosens. "I want the company."

"Then company you shall have." She gives me an easy, almost languid smile, bringing our conversation back to casual. "Hey, guess what?"

"What?"

"I had a nightmare last night. About the woman with the blue face."

"Oh God, I'm sorry."

"Don't be. What did I tell you about me and nightmares?"

I frown. "At least you got some sleep?"

She grins. "Exactly."

Then

Hey, can I ask you something?" Harper says while she and Nellie ignore their eighth-grade algebra homework in favor of stapling the spines of the latest issue of *Here in the Shadows* on Nellie's bedroom floor. They've released an issue a month without fail for the past three years, selling them in school and online in Nellie's Etsy shop. Ever since Harper's mother married Stupid Charlie last year, dashing the girls' hope for official sisterhood, all zine production has shifted to Nellie's house. Nellie misses how the early issues always smelled a little like cinnamon-vanilla, but it's not like Harper's mother burns incense anymore anyway, thanks to Stupid Charlie's allergies.

Nellie pauses mid-staple and stares at the pile of freshly assembled copies. The cover is always in color now, printed on glossy cardstock. They've discussed having the booklets assembled by the local print shop, but Nellie likes that they still build each zine themselves. Something about the hesitation in Harper's question sends a shock of unease down her spine, but she ignores it. "Of course."

"Do you think maybe we could cut back to every other month?"

Nellie's unease grows from a shock to a sinkhole inside her, dark and unstable. "Why?"

"I don't know. It just takes up so much time. Stupid Charlie's after me to help out in his stupid office more on the weekends, and I'm thinking of trying out for track in the fall, and..." Harper hesitates, gnawing her lip.

"Okay," Nellie says, because she knows it's what Harper wants to hear, but she doesn't mean it. The sinkhole widens.

"Are you sure?"

"Yes." *No.*

"Because I just thought—"

"Harper, it's fine. We'll go to every other month." Nellie knew this was coming, although she'd hoped she was wrong. This isn't just about Stupid Charlie, or track, or free time. Harper talks a bit differently than she used to. She sits differently; she carries herself differently. She dresses differently, showing her legs and midriff and shoulders in ways that sometimes get her sent to the principal's office. She always seeks out Nellie after, and they sit and vent about the absurdity of dress codes and punishing girls because boys might get distracted. Nellie agrees that it's ridiculous, yes, of course boys should learn to keep their eyes to themselves if they can't handle seeing a girl in spaghetti straps, but she also misses the Harper who used to wear the same jeans and T-shirts Nellie does. She wants the Harper who demanded Disney movies and Flamin' Hot Cheetos and scary stories at their sleepovers, rather than makeovers and selfies and creeping the socials of the kids in their grade.

The changes had crept in gradually. More conversations about boys. More laments while staring in the mirror. More anxiety over the braces that had only recently come off or a haircut that was a little too short. More fishing for compliments. More shopping in stores that carried styles for Harper's shape, but not always for Nellie's, so now sometimes Harper goes shopping with their new friend Dia instead.

Harper, it's fine.

Nellie gathers the copies they've finished. She'll assemble the rest later, by herself.

"Good. Besides, Nellie, this'll give you more free time, too. Sitting in front of a screen as much as you do isn't good for you. Hey, maybe you should think about track, too. We could train together."

Nellie bursts into bright laughter until she realizes Harper is serious.

"No, really. You'd look so amazing if you toned up a little."

Somewhere in Nellie's torso, not far from the pit of her stomach, the sinkhole turns dense and swirling, a hungry black hole like in the deep corners of space. It sucks the breath from her lungs, pulling and tugging until she deflates. It fills with dark matter, invisible and unbearably heavy.

"Nah, I think I'm okay," she says.

"Don't you want to get a boyfriend, though? Then we could all go to the movies and stuff together."

Nellie puts the stapler back on her desk. "Who's *all*?"

"You know. You and a guy, and me and Ethan."

"Wait. Did he ask you out?"

"Not yet, but I know he's going to. He keeps flirting." Harper takes out her phone. "Let's take a break and look at his Insta."

A break? Harper hasn't even noticed Nellie quietly tucking away the elements of their zine. There's no break to be had when the work has ended.

Nellie wants to argue. She doesn't want to go on group dates. She doesn't want to go on group dates. She doesn't know if she even wants a boyfriend at all. She certainly doesn't want to run in the Florida heat instead of working on the zine.

But Harper has moved on. In so many ways. Now she squeals because the infamous Ethan recently posted a shirtless poolside selfie. Defeated, Nellie plays along, looking at the photo, holding back laughter when Harper accidentally hits the heart icon and panics. Nellie feels like she's observing an alien culture—she might be able to understand it on a logical level, might even sympathize with some of it, but she's not a part of it.

The things she thought were forever always seem to fade. Just like her old friend the shadow, which hasn't shown up in years. Nellie's fears are all her own now, made up in stories that she can control.

She wishes Harper would go home and let her get back to her writing.

Chapter Ten

W e could go into town for the afternoon," Tris says. We're still in the banyan's cradle seat, watching the tide come in. "Hang out there until Mr. Wonderful is gone."

I try to ignore the voice in my head that wonders if going into town with Tris would count as a date. Do I want it to? I think I do. "Yeah, let's go. I'll ask Dia to let me know when the coast is clear."

Tris hops down and grins, her boots landing solid and strong amid the roots. "Sounds good." I lower myself down more slowly and follow her to her truck, and we drive south.

We're approaching the gate when Dia responds to my text. Where are you? Can you come back? That's not like her. My stomach twists. "On second thought, maybe I should go back to the house."

"You sure?"

I nod. "I think Dia might need a little help."

"You got it. Just let me back up to a spot that's wide enough to turn around, and…" Her voice trails off, and she brakes but doesn't put the truck in reverse. Instead she stares south, squinting against the brightness of the day. "Do you see that?"

I follow her gaze toward what looks like a vague shimmer in the air near the gate. It's almost too faint to see, and at first I think it's an illusion caused by the heat and the sunlight, a mirage like the imaginary puddles that appear and vanish on the roads in the summer, but it's not like that. It's different, and it sends another unsettled tickle up my spine. "Yeah. It looks kind of hazy."

Tris nods. "Could be smoke. Shoot. I hope nothing's on fire nearby." She lets the truck creep closer, but neither of us see any flames. "Could be something on the mainland, I guess," she says finally. "The breeze off the water will clear it up soon." She glances at me. "You sure about staying here?"

I look at my phone. "I should really check on Dia."

"You're a good friend," Tris says, reversing on the narrow road.

Back at the house, we find everyone in the living room. Harper and Gavin lounge on one side of the sectional couch, her practically in his lap. Christopher sits on an ottoman with a colorful board game spinner, looking at Dia as he flicks the plastic pointer into a lazy whirl. Dia has her embroidery out, eyes fixed on the fabric as she pointedly ignores Christopher's gaze. I wonder if he's been pestering her, if that's why she wanted me to come back.

Harper's brows jerk upward when she sees Tris. "Hey! Trisha, right? I thought that was your truck. Did you need to fix something else? Trisha's dad owns the island," she adds for Gavin and Christopher before introducing them.

"There's always something that needs fixing," Tris says, glancing at Gavin, her expression cool and unreadable.

"Her name's Tris," I add.

"Of course. Sorry." Harper gives us an easy smile. I recognize that smile. It's a little bleary, a little wobbly. It's the same smile she had when she sneaked a bottle of Charlie's fancy bourbon into prom last year. There are beer cans and a blue-and-orange flask on the table. A flask in our school colors. That could only belong to Gavin.

I look from the table back to Harper. "Seriously?"

"Gavin brought a couple of beers," Harper says. "Sit down. Have one."

"I'll sit," Tris says, going to the couch and tilting her head for me to follow. The spot she chooses puts her squarely between me and Gavin, a move I'm sure is deliberate. "No beer for me, though."

"Suit yourself." Harper shrugs.

"Don't drink too much," I say to Gavin when he reaches for his beer. "It's a long drive back to Winter Park."

"That won't be for a couple of hours," he says, swigging. "I'll be fine."

Christopher spins the spinner again. "So who wants to play?"

I look from the spinner to the wide, flat Twister box next to Christopher's ottoman. "Where'd you get that?"

Christopher points to the cabinet under the TV.

"I don't think I'm up for Twister," I say. Not in a dress, in front of Tris. *Especially* not if Gavin is playing.

It's like Gavin reads my mind. Taking the spinner from Christopher, he says, "C'mon, Nell. It'll be fun."

Beside me, Tris straightens her spine. "I can't believe y'all are hanging out inside on such a nice day. You know there's fishing stuff in the garage, right? Want me to show you?"

I give her a quick glance that I hope conveys my gratitude. She returns it with a barely noticeable wink.

We get the supplies, and Tris leads the way toward the narrow dock. "Guys, no alcohol out on the bay," she says when she notices Gavin and Christopher carrying beer cans. "House rules. It's in the rental agreement. You'll need to leave those on dry land, okay?"

The boys look at each other, shrug, and chug what's left. They leave the cans on the back steps.

Tris leans close. "It's not in the agreement," she whispers. I can hear her smile, and the graze of her breath against my ear sends a delightful shiver through my shoulders even as I keep an eye out for any sign of my uke in the marshy shallows.

Soon we're all set up with rods and lures. I tilt my chin down toward the floating platform, where Gavin is casting his lure far across the bay, and grin at Tris. "You're a genius," I say quietly.

"Keep your friends close," she murmurs back, "and your enemies on an entirely different dock. Do you know how to fish?"

"Sort of. My dad used to take me sometimes when I was little." It always made me feel guilty, that unsettling moment when I'd haul a fish onto the dock and watch it flop and struggle. Still, I'd much rather be out here laughing with Tris than inside playing Twister.

My attempt at casting is atrocious; Tris sidles up just a little closer than necessary to help. Soon the muscles in my arms start to remember—the reach back, the long flick forward, the gentle resistance of the reel.

Harper gets the first bite, and Tris reminds her to yank the rod to set the hook. The fish she hauls up is reddish orange, about sixteen inches long.

"Nice snapper!" Tris holds up the fish by its gills so everyone can see. It gasps, drowning in air. "We doing catch and release?"

I'm about to say yes, but Gavin answers first, yelling up from the lower dock. "Keep it! I'll fillet whatever we catch." He reels in his line and jogs up to the platform to hug Harper. "Great catch, babe." He turns to Christopher. "Go grab a cooler with some ice. And a bucket, if you can find one."

"There's a bucket in the garage," Tris calls after him.

"So we're going to kill it?" Harper asks, eyeing the fish as it writhes and struggles, desperate to free itself and find its way back to the bay.

"That's generally how it works." Gavin takes the snapper from Tris without looking at her and pulls a knife from the tackle box. Then he nonchalantly rams the blade into the fish's head, making the move look as effortless as slicing pats of butter for bread. "Nice and quick. Right into the brain." The fish's eye goes wide and unfocused as it thrashes violently, fins fanning out. A dribble of blood splashes onto the platform.

Nice and quick. My lungs lock; my stomach lurches. "Jesus." I swallow against rising bile.

"What?" Gavin gives me an easy, smug smile. "You eat seafood, don't you, Nell?"

I nod, aware of the hypocrisy he's highlighting. "I don't generally look my meals in the eye first, though."

Harper grimaces. "Gav, can you at least put that thing out of its misery already?"

"It's dead," he says, despite the fact that the animal is spasming mightily in his grip.

"It's still moving!" I say, my voice going shrill.

"Those are just muscle contractions," he says as Christopher returns with the cooler and bucket. "Don't worry."

"Dude." Christopher puts down the cooler and chuckles. "That thing is *not* dead."

"It's as *good* as dead," Gavin insists as the animal continues to thrash. "Anyway, who cares? It's just a fish."

"It's suffering!" I snap.

"Yeah?" Gavin laughs and steps toward me, waving the fish near my face. "Here, you want it? Going to nurse it back to health?" Several drops of blood hit the platform near my sandals. I step back reflexively and feel a hand grab my forearm as Tris keeps me from falling into the bay.

"God, Gavin, cut it out," Dia says, her tone repulsed.

"God, Dia," Gavin says, mimicking her voice as Christopher doubles over with laughter. "Chill."

"Gavin—" Harper begins.

Gavin turns toward her, still dangling the dying fish. "What?" he says sharply. "You want to cuddle the dead fishy, too?"

She steps back, pressing a hand to her mouth.

"Jesus," Tris mutters, striding up to Gavin and snatching the fish and the knife. "You missed the brain, genius," she says, inserting the blade and finishing the job. Finally the fish goes still and limp. "If you're going to do something like that, do it right."

The efficiency of her kill is a sharp reminder that I don't know her well at all. How does she know how to do that?

Gavin glances from Tris to the knife, hesitating, as if seeing her do what he hadn't throws him momentarily off-balance. "Like it even matters," he says finally as Tris hands everything back. "It's a fish. We live in Florida. Thousands of people here go fishing every day."

I want to tell him that none of that justifies the torture he just put that animal through, but I lose the thought to revulsion as Gavin juts the knife into the fish's gaping gills, slicing an artery. "Got to bleed it out," he says, setting it tail-up in the bucket to drain. "Then we'll put it on ice for now. Later I'll fillet everything we catch, and maybe Dia can cook us up a feast."

"Why me?" Dia asks, frowning.

"You know," Gavin says. "Cuban style."

"Spicy," Christopher adds, grinning at her.

She rolls her eyes and glances toward Harper, waiting for a little help, but Harper keeps her eyes averted and stares down at the draining fish as Gavin heads back to the floating dock and crouches to rinse the blood from his hands.

I want to speak up, to tell both Gavin and Christopher to cut it out, but I'm still trying to stop shaking. *Nice and quick.* The line loops over and over in my head, always in Gavin's voice. Trying to move casually, I inch away from the others, reeling in my line and hooking the lure on one of the rod's guides. Then I sit on the edge of the platform and let the breeze cool my skin until the vertigo fades and I can breathe again.

After wiping her hands clean, Tris sits beside me. "Not a big fan of fish?" she asks softly.

"Not a big fan of..." I gesture toward Gavin. "Of that."

"I get it," she says. "That part of fishing isn't for everyone. It's not for me, either. When my dad and I go fishing, we usually stick with catch and release. But sometimes a fish gets too badly injured, and it wouldn't be humane to set it free. When that happens, I don't want them to suffer."

"It was just so brutal."

"Sometimes you have to be a little brutal." She gives me a tiny smile and tilts her head toward the floating dock. "Especially with clowns like him around."

"Yeah." I breathe slowly, willing the churning in my stomach to ease. "I don't want to catch any fish if that's what will happen to them."

"I got you." She uses a pair of tackle box snippers to discreetly trim the hook from my lure. "Now you can join in without dooming any fish. You'll just look unlucky."

I laugh a little. "Heh. Thanks."

"Know what's weird?" She turns and looks south. "I don't smell smoke."

"Should we be able to?"

"We saw that haze, remember? Usually you smell smoke before you see it. It's just weird."

"Maybe the wind's blowing in the wrong direction."

"Probably." Her shoulder presses gently against mine.

"I hope Gavin leaves soon."

"I'll nag him about it in a little while," she promises. "No extra overnight guests really *is* in the rental agreement, and I will totally get Dad to kick him and his friend out if it comes to that."

"You're the best. Seriously." I no longer want Harry to find out about Gavin and tattle and get our vacation cut short. I don't want to leave Straight Shot. Not when it comes with its very own Tris.

She grins. "You can pay me back with more stories."

Our eyes meet, and I know how I'd like to pay her back, and it's not with stories.

For a time, we all go quiet, and I start to wonder if perhaps my friends are as uncomfortable with Gavin's kill as I am. It feels like the mood on the platform has shifted; the bay almost looks a little darker than before. Then Harper squeals as she hooks another fish, and Tris jumps up to help, and the shift is gone. I pick up my unlucky rod and cast. For the next hour or so, the snappers keep biting. Everyone but me reels in a few, dragging them up for Gavin to dispatch—which he does more carefully now, perhaps to avoid getting shown up by Tris again. I try to ignore the squelching sounds as he stabs and bleeds.

Christopher pulls in an especially large fish. I call out, "Nice one," feigning some enthusiasm to match the others' excitement as they gather around to admire the catch, Gavin with knife already in hand. They're distracted, so I'm the first to see Harry storming toward us down the narrow dock, his expression a bared-teeth snarl of brotherly rage.

Chapter Eleven

W hat the hell, Harper?"

"Jesus, Harry, calm down." Harper shoves her fishing rod into Tris's hands and squares her shoulders, prepping for Round Two in the Spring Break Battle of the Siblings: Brawl by the Bay.

Harry pushes a hand through his hair. "Everyone back to shore!" he yells, nostrils flaring. "Now!"

I've never seen Harry so angry. Dia stares up from the floating dock, eyes wide, looking like she doesn't know whether to pee her pants or fling herself into his arms. Even Harper hesitates; her mouth opens as a screaming fit builds, but then she ducks her head and stomps down the long dock. We all follow, meekly filing into the house and gathering in an uncertain flock near the front door. Harry stops long enough to grab the empty beer cans from the back porch and grunt, "Really?"

Inside, he points at Gavin and Christopher. "You two. Leave."

Gavin's jaw tightens. He inhales. He's not as tall as Harry, but he swims and runs track, which builds more strength than Harry's history books. The muscles in Gavin's arms tense, and I worry that punches are about to be thrown, but then he exhales in a sharp, aggravated huff and drops his eyes. He snatches the blue-and-orange flask from the coffee table and pockets it, and he and Christopher take their beer cooler and head out the front door.

Harry turns to Harper. "Got anything to say before I call Mom and Charlie?"

"He was just visiting!" Harper's stare hardens, her eyes dark under scrunched brows.

"You knew the rules." Now that Harry has cleared out the intruders, his tone creeps closer to normal. "No boys. No drinking."

"I didn't know he was going to bring the beer!"

"Uh-huh. And I'm sure you didn't have any, right?"

Harper goes quiet.

Beside me, I sense Tris shifting her weight from one foot to the other. Her fingers graze my forearm. I wish I had the courage to reach down and catch her hand in mine. I want to apologize for causing her to be here for this mess.

"I trusted you," Harry says. "Mom and Charlie did, too. You couldn't live up to that trust for even a couple of hours."

"I don't fucking care about Charlie's trust," Harper mutters.

Harry huffs out an exasperated sigh and heads to the porch to make the call. Before he can close the door or dial, he says, "Oh, *now* what?"

We follow him outside and see Gavin's BMW returning to the house. "Maybe the gate isn't working," Harper says quietly. "I can go down with them and—"

Harry shakes his head and jogs down the front steps as Gavin gets out of the BMW. "What part of 'leave' don't you understand?"

Gavin stands still. "We tried. There's something in front of the gate." He looks a little pale. I squint, looking harder, thinking the sunlight must be playing tricks.

"What?" Harry asks.

"I don't know," Gavin says. His words carry a hesitant tremble. Gavin isn't usually the sort to tremble. "It's just...there."

"It's some kind of cloud," Christopher adds, getting out of the passenger seat. "It's blocking the way."

This time, I do grab Tris's hand. Her fingers twine through mine, squeezing. "That shimmer," she murmurs, her words matching my thoughts.

"I just drove through the gate fifteen minutes ago," Harry says.

"It was kind of hazy down there earlier," I say.

Harry frowns, rubbing his fingers along his jaw. "That was just a heat mirage," he says, but his voice carries a new undercurrent of uncertainty. He saw it, too. He saw it and he dismissed it as something normal, something born of rational circumstances. But it isn't normal, is it? I think back to the bus, the phantom ice-cream truck, and my lost uke. Nothing about this place is normal.

Finally Harry sighs. "Let's go see." We get into his SUV and follow Gavin's BMW back down the dirt road.

Whatever waits for us, it's no mirage. What was once a light shimmer in the air has congealed by the gate. The haze has turned soupy and rust colored, hanging like a thick bank of fog between us and our only path off the island. It's not quite solid, but it's close—the gate beyond is a nebulous form ghosting behind the brown murk. It looks *wrong*, uncannily so.

"What is that?" Dia looks at Tris. "Are there factories around here? Or a power plant? Maybe there was some kind of meltdown."

Tris frowns. "There's a chemical plant inland."

"What kind of chemicals?" Harry asks.

"No clue. The place almost got shut down over a spill when I was a kid. But if this stuff is from there . . . The plant is at least ten miles inland. And wouldn't you expect the wind off the ocean to carry it away from the shore, not toward it?"

"I don't know what to expect at the moment," Harry says grimly, pulling out his phone as our miniature convoy continues creeping toward the island's only exit point. "There haven't been any emergency alerts, at least not that I've gotten."

"I'll see if I can find anything," Tris says, but the search app on her phone stalls without loading properly. "Coverage out here usually isn't this bad," she mutters.

Harry stares at the haze. "I'd really like to get us out of here, but we have no way of knowing if that stuff's safe to breathe."

"Doesn't look too safe to me," Dia says softly.

I nod, too unsettled to voice my agreement out loud. The chemical plant is a rational source to blame, but if the haze is from some kind of meltdown or spill, it would have to be catastrophic to spread this far. I almost say so, but something about opening my mouth right now feels unwise. I'm reminded of how I felt when I was little, keeping my jaw clamped shut as the shadow reached toward me. Somehow this feels too much like that.

My shadow. I didn't do my ritual last night. I have no reason to believe the haze is somehow related to that, but the coincidence tucks itself into my mind and stays there like a whispered recording on an endless loop. *But what if? What if?*

We're still about a hundred feet away from the gate when the BMW stops ahead of us and Gavin rolls down his window. "What's he doing now?" Harry mutters. He gets out of the SUV, and we follow.

The air here is heavy and still, with a bitter, metallic tang. We're so near the ocean—the Atlantic is a short jog to the left—but there's no salted breeze here to carry the haze away. I take a few steps toward the cloud, going beyond the BMW, and the air weighs on me, pressing on my shoulders like I'm hefting an invisible sandbag. My lungs burn with each inhalation, my throat contracting until I cough, still trying my hardest to keep my jaw shut. With a hand over my mouth, I retreat, walking backward because turning my back on the cloud seems like a very bad idea. Tris's hand finds mine again, and she pulls me the last few feet to the SUV and holds tight.

"We'll have to drive through it," Harry says, his voice hushed as if he's afraid the haze will overhear.

Gavin shakes his head. "I'm not driving through that."

"How else are we supposed to get off the island?" Harry asks, bending slightly to address Gavin through the window. "We need to get out of here."

"That shit stinks, man. And we don't know how much of it there is!"

"Can it get inside the cars?" Dia asks.

Harry straightens and presses a hand to his forehead. "Look, whatever it is…It's a chemical, a gas. I just did a whole presentation on the chemical weapons they used in the First World War. There were things the soldiers did to protect themselves. We can do the same."

92

"What? Are you going to dig up some gas masks or something?" Gavin scoffs.

"Not actual gas masks, obviously, but…" Harry frowns. "Before they had those, they used cloth masks. They'd soak them in water, or a baking soda solution. Some of them even used urine."

"Jesus, Harry," Harper says shrilly.

"I'm not suggesting we do that, exactly," he says quickly. "But if we tear up a couple of shirts, that'll be enough fabric for everyone to have a few layers." He looks at Tris. "Is there any baking soda in the house?"

"There might be some in the pantry," she says, although her tone is doubtful. "People leave staples like that behind sometimes."

"Okay, so maybe we can make a solution and soak the masks. We just need to wear them long enough to drive through that stuff. That way, if it can get inside the cars…"

"There might be a couple of leftover painter's masks in the garage, too," Tris says, falling in line with his train of thought.

"Great!" Harry says, now on a roll. "We should protect our eyes, too. Some kinds of gas can blind you. Sunglasses won't do much. Are there any goggles for the pool? Swim masks? And we should cover up in case that stuff is caustic. Mustard gas used to cause horrible blisters; this might be like that. Jeans and long sleeves—"

"Are you fucking kidding me?" Gavin snaps. He opens his door with enough force to shove Harry back a step and gets out of the BMW. "Wet masks and long sleeves? That's what you've got?"

Harry glares at him. "I don't hear you coming up with anything better."

"Gav," Christopher says from the passenger seat, his voice reedy. "Just drive through it. Come on."

"That might be our best option," Harry says. "Get through it as fast as possible and hope for fresh air on the other side. It's what Canadian troops did during poison gas attacks—charge in and get through. The French troops would retreat instead, but that didn't—"

"Shut up about wars," Gavin yells. "This isn't a war!"

"We don't know what this is," Tris says.

"Fine. We'll drive. Right now." Gavin points at Harry. "You first, though. You open the gate, and we'll follow."

"The road's not wide enough for us to drive around you," Harry says. "Just go. Just…" He glances at Tris, an apology in his eyes. "Just drive through the gate. It'll give."

"I'm not wrecking my car on that—"

"Gavin, please." Harper's voice wobbles. "I'm scared."

"It'll be fine, babe." He drapes an arm around her and walks her a few steps away from the group. "I always take care of you, right?"

"Can I ride with you?" she asks.

"You know it's a two-seater."

"But maybe Christopher could—"

"Harper," Harry barks. "Come on back. You're coming with us."

"Go on." Gavin gives her a soft push. "We'll be right behind you."

Looking wounded, she comes back and puts her arms around her brother, their earlier argument forgotten. "I'm scared," she says again. I think of the time she and I secretly streamed a slasher movie when we were eight and she had to run to her brother for protection after the killer chased a screaming woman through a night-draped forest.

Harry exhales sharply in Gavin's direction. "Just drive through the goddamn gate, man."

The air grows hotter, heavier. Gavin starts to argue again, insisting that the SUV go first, but Christopher interrupts him. "Just *go*, Gav. Come on." Christopher stares through the windshield at the haze, his face pale. "We have to get out of here. Just go."

Gavin narrows his eyes, but he nods and gets back into his car. "Okay, okay. Stay close," he says to Harry before rolling up his window.

We pile back into the SUV, and Harry pulls up close to the BMW's bumper. Beside me, Dia is shaking. I link my arm through hers; my other hand is still safe in Tris's strong grip.

"What if this *is* a war?" Dia says quietly. "You know, an attack. Some kind of chemical weapon."

"Then we'll get through it and come out on the other side," Tris says. "Whatever this is, there's a rational explanation for it."

I still haven't opened my mouth. I can't shake the ghost of that long-ago terror, the fear that made me clench my jaw shut against the shadow. The haze is a mystery, but this feeling is too familiar, and I'm beginning to suspect our situation has nothing to do with a toxic spill or a chemical weapon. There's nothing rational about this moment.

I can't explain that, though, not in any sane way, so I stay quiet and hope I'm wrong.

Harry turns on his brights. Ahead of us, Gavin does the same.

We can see the gate more clearly now, although it's still like staring through etched glass.

"What the hell is that?" Harper whispers.

The gate is covered in...something. It looks like greasy black tar, shiny and wet. It's on the ground, too, and on the plants and trees nearby, and on the low, flat bridge. It drips off the Straight Shot sign in thick, moldering glops like mucus coughed up and spat from a smoker's lungs.

"Come on," Harry mutters when the BMW stops just before the bridge, its front bumper nearly vanishing into the haze. "Just fucking ram the gate already."

The BMW's engine revs with a jarring metallic squeal as if Gavin is standing on the gas pedal, but the car stays put. After a few seconds, the sound dies off and the taillights go dark.

"Why aren't they going?" Dia says, her voice shrilling into a squeak.

"Harper, call him." Harry taps the horn. "Tell him to keep going."

Harper already has her phone to her ear. "The connection's all staticky. I can barely hear him, but I think he said the car is dead."

"Damn it!" Harry smacks the steering wheel.

The SUV's engine shudders.

"It's the haze," Tris says.

"But we're not even in it!" Dia yelps.

"Doesn't matter," Tris says. "We're close enough. That stuff is doing something to the cars. It might be interfering with the phone signal down here, too."

"That can't be possible—" Harry starts, but he's interrupted by another shudder, this one more violent. "That's it. We need to get back to the house." He puts the SUV in reverse but keeps his foot on the brake.

Harper flails her hands toward the BMW. "We can't just leave them!"

"Tell them to get back here. *Now.*"

Harper relays the message, and the doors of the BMW fling open. Gavin and Christopher leap out, the collars of their shirts pulled over their noses and mouths. They sprint toward the SUV. Gavin stumbles, his head whipping around to glance behind him. The movement causes his shirt collar to fall, exposing his face. He appears to gasp, open-mouthed, and he doubles over, coughing violently, retching like something's stuck in his throat.

"Gavin!" Christopher screams from next to the SUV. He freezes, caught between retreating and going back to help his friend.

Gagging, Gavin glances up. He looks hunted, with the saucer-like gaze of a prey animal, but then he straightens and forces his feet to move.

"Hurry!" Harry says as Gavin and Christopher scramble into the SUV, bringing that metallic smell with them. They slam the doors and Harry floors the accelerator, hurtling us backward while the engine shakes and sputters. With no time to fasten seat belts, Christopher and Gavin lurch out of their seats. Gavin's chest crushes against the seat back in front of him, setting off another vicious coughing fit. I close my eyes and press my face against Tris's shoulder, hoping Harry won't fling us off the road and toward the ocean. A scream rises in my throat, forcing my jaw to unclench.

The SUV makes it halfway back to the house and dies.

"Run!" Harry yells, and we run.

Then

Three Years Ago

And then it happens, just as Nellie knew it would. The every-other-month compromise isn't enough. "I just don't have time for the zine anymore," Harper says one afternoon, a few months into freshman year. Her expression softens with something that's dangerously close to pity. "I've got track practice three times a week, and spring flag line tryouts are coming up. If I make the squad, my schedule will be even tighter."

Nellie swallows hard against the twist in her throat.

"You should try out, by the way," Harper says.

"For flag line?"

"Yeah. Dia's trying out. We could all be on the squad together. It would be fun!"

Nellie thinks of how the students in flag line are required to wear their uniforms to school on pep rally days. Tight bodices and tiny skirts flouncing down the hall. She shakes her head.

Harper presses her lips together. "You need to start being more involved. It's important for college. All you do is sit at home and write."

"I publish the zine." Nellie takes full credit. It's not like Harper has been much help for months.

"You staple papers together while you binge Netflix shows."

Nellie blinks away the burning in her eyes. The black hole in the pit of her stomach churns to life, feeding on Harper's dismissal of the project she and Nellie once obsessed over.

Harper shoves her bangs off her forehead. "That was harsh. I'm sorry. But I worry about you! I just want you to have fun!"

I always had fun working on the zine with you, Nellie thinks.

"You need to meet more people. Dia and I can't be your only friends."

Why not? Nellie thinks.

Harper's eyes brighten. "You know what you should try? Chorus. Whitney says it's really fun."

Nellie bristles at the mention of yet another of Harper's new friends.

"You don't even have to be a great singer. They take just about anyone."

Nellie is a good singer, but Harper doesn't know that, and it hurts that she automatically assumes otherwise. It feels like Harper is trying to push her into a new activity to be rid of her, and that hurts even more.

Yet Nellie finds herself nodding. "I'll think about it. I might try out." Maybe, just maybe, Harper's plan will backfire. Maybe, once Nellie is busy with something new, Harper will realize she misses her.

"Nellie, yes! It'll be so much fun. You'll see."

Nellie thinks of the issue of *Here in the Shadows* on her laptop, the one that's waiting for illustrations that will never come. Maybe it's time to keep her fears to herself once more. A new story blooms and twists in her mind, about a pair of mortician sisters too busy arguing over nonsense to notice the milky-eyed cadavers around them coming to life, with reaching arms and clamping, hungry jaws. She'll write it, but it will belong only to her.

Chapter Twelve

We run inside and slam the door. The metallic stink follows us.

Harper is the first to catch her breath. "What the hell was that?" she demands, rubbing Gavin's back while he doubles over, wheezing like his lungs are thick and putrid with pneumonia. She shoves a water bottle into his hands, encouraging him to drink.

"I don't know, but I'm calling 911." Harry gets out his phone and curses. "How can there be no signal? I had one a few minutes ago."

"I'll call." Dia looks at her phone. "Or not. No signal here, either."

"Anyone?" Harry asks.

We all check, except for Gavin, who's still retching. None of us have a signal.

"There's a landline." Tris goes to the kitchen and puts the handset to her ear. "No dial tone."

I try my phone's browser. "Wi-Fi is dead, too."

"That means the cable's out," Tris says.

"What the hell?" Christopher snaps, his voice taut with panic. "Why would everything cut out at once?" He puts his hands to his head, and that's when I see the source of the smell. His forearm is smeared with slick black tar, the same stuff we saw dripping off the gate. I point, and he follows my gaze and yelps.

Contaminated. The word buzzes in my mind, and I wonder if the others are thinking the same thing.

Gavin straightens up long enough to give Christopher a blood-shot glare. "What the hell, man?" he snaps, his voice as rough as gravel. "Go wash that shit off!"

Christopher runs to the kitchen to rinse his arm in the sink. "It's not coming off!" he shrieks, his eyes wide and bright with panicked tears. He grabs a handful of paper towels and scrubs harder, saturating the stuff with dishwashing detergent.

"Maybe we need some kind of solvent," Tris says. "I think Dad has some turpentine in the garage."

I grab her hand. "Don't go out there."

She points toward the window, where the afternoon sun filters through the gauzy curtains. "I'll be fine. Look how clear it is out there. Whatever that stuff is, it's way down at the south end of the island."

"That could change," I say. "I don't want you to go."

"I'll go." Gavin's expression hardens as he gestures toward a thick smear of tarry gunk on his calf. His breaths are shallow and cautious, but his cough is under control. "Whatever this shit is, it's on me, too."

"You and Christopher were closer to the haze than the rest of us," Harry says. "Did you see anything we didn't? Where it might be coming from?"

Gavin goes still. "I didn't see anything in all that muck, but..."

"What?" Harper prompts gently.

"For a second it was like..." Gavin hesitates, his tone quieting like he's back in the memory. "It was like something was pulling me. Trying to grab me. Reeling me in like a fish on a hook. I almost..." He swallows, then shakes his head. "I just stumbled. I stumbled and got a lungful of that hazy shit. Where'd you say the turpentine is?"

Tris describes where to look and Gavin heads outside. When he comes back with a plastic jug, we have rags ready.

"See anything out there?" Harry asks as we crowd into the kitchen.

"Not from here." Gavin splashes turpentine onto a rag and scrubs his calf. With a lot of rubbing, the gunk reluctantly breaks up, leaving a greasy stain on his skin. He saturates another rag for Christopher, who goes back to scrubbing like he's trying to remove his skin along with the tar.

Harper sits at the table, clenching her hands into fists, then stretching her fingers back out, over and over. "The phones are dead," she says. "And the cars are dead, too. So how do we get out of here?"

"Should we just...walk through the gate?" Dia grimaces like the suggestion carries a foul taste.

"You don't want to do that," Gavin says quickly. "My lungs still feel like they're on fire, and my vision's a little blurry. It's noxious down there."

"When we don't get back on Friday, our families will know something's up," Harper says. "They'll call the cops."

"Friday?" Christopher's head jerks up, his glare sharp and wild. "Are you kidding? It's *Monday*."

"Okay, so they report us missing," Dia says. "How do the police get through that stuff to reach us?"

"We don't even know what's going on over on the other side of the gate," Harry says.

"Wait." Tris pauses. "You think the haze is on the mainland, too?"

"I don't know," Harry says. "We don't know anything about any of this."

"What about if we go out to the dock?" I ask. "The other shore of the bay isn't far. It's close enough to see people on their docks on that side. Maybe we can signal someone."

"What if we get stuck out there?" Harry asks. "What if the haze rolls in and traps us?"

"No, I like Nell's idea," Tris says. "We don't even know if the haze *can* roll in this far. Maybe it'll stay to the south."

"We could have lookouts," Dia says. "If that stuff gets closer, we'd have some warning."

Harry's forehead creases with doubt, but he's outvoted. None of us want to leave the house, but we don't want to sit around and wait, either. Dia volunteers to keep watch from the road, and Harper stays in the yard. The rest of us head down the narrow dock to the covered platform. If the haze gets close, Dia will signal Harper, and Harper will signal us, and we'll all run like hell for the house.

Chapter Thirteen

While Dia and Harper keep watch, the rest of us cluster on the platform, close together and vulnerable, like fish in a tiny bowl.

Nothing about the bay looks out of place, and the fact that everything here seems so ordinary is itself disconcerting. There's no murky cloud hanging over the houses across the bay, no signs of carcinogenic slicks of dripping gunk. The normalcy of it makes me uneasy—how can things be sane out here after what we just experienced a few miles south?

The bay itself is midnight blue and slightly choppy from the breeze. It takes me a second to realize why that feels so odd. Down by the haze, everything was so still. How can it be windy here? I turn my face to the breeze and breathe deeply, letting the brine in the air draw the last hint of metallic bitterness from my lungs and carry it away. Far overhead, I hear the squawk of a gull. I look up in time to see it soar past the sun.

Harry shields his eyes from the light and stares across the water. "Looks okay over there," he says. "Looks quiet."

"Quiet." My eyes flit from dock to dock as I survey the opposite shore, analyzing why the placid view is so troubling. "Where is everyone?"

Every time I've been out to the platform, I've seen at least one other person—someone fishing off a dock or kayaking along the bay, or grilling in a yard or swimming or . . . or *something*. I listen for music from distant speakers. Children screaming and splashing in a pool.

"Maybe they're all just inside," Gavin says.

I shake my head. "On a day this gorgeous? During spring break? No. I've seen people on every single one of those docks, and in every yard. Those houses are all occupied. We should be able to see someone."

Gavin cups his hands around his mouth, bullhorn style, and hollers across the water. "HEY!" When no one responds, he tries again. "HELP! CAN ANYBODY HEAR ME? WE NEED HELP!" The other side of the bay stays eerily quiet.

Harry works his jaw. "Maybe there really is more of that haze on the mainland. Just because we can't see any from here doesn't mean it's not there. Maybe it's big news. Maybe everyone's staying safe until it . . ."

"Until it what?" Christopher rubs at the stain on his arm. The skin around it is red and raw from his violent scrubbing. He scratches nervously, drawing spots of blood that smear under his nails, darkening them. His nostrils flare. "I want this shit off me. I don't know how it got on me in the first place."

"It'll fade soon," I say, trying to keep my rising doubt out of my tone. I glance back toward Straight Shot and see Harper in the yard, facing away, watching for a signal from Dia.

"If we can't get out through the gate," Gavin says, "we'll cross the bay. Does this place have a boat?"

Tris shakes her head. I remember her mentioning her father's plan to stash a kayak in the garage. If only.

Gavin frowns. "Not even an inflatable one? Something for the beach? Rafts? *Anything?*"

"Sorry. No."

He points toward the floating dock. "What about that thing?"

Tris considers. "I'd need to grab my tools to detach the ramp, but maybe..."

Christopher stares across the water. "It's not that far," he says softly.

Gavin follows his gaze. "You saying we should swim for it?"

"It's, what? Maybe two hundred yards to that dock?" Christopher points to the closest platform on the other shore. "We could make it. No problem." He looks at Gavin, his eyes wide and determined. "We can swim for it and send help."

"Dude, I don't know."

"Why not? It's like a couple of laps. It's nothing."

I lean over, bracing my hands on my knees and staring down into the bay. "Was the water this dark before?" Or maybe dread has me imagining shadows where there are none. That's all I need in my life—more shadows. The thought makes me set my jaw against the bark of slightly deranged laughter that tries to bubble up.

"What?" Gavin looks down as well. "It looks exactly the same."

"Nell's right to be cautious," Harry says. "We don't know

what's going on. If there was some kind of spill, it could have gotten into the bay as well. It could be toxic. The stuff they used to use for mustard gas was released into the water sometimes—"

"Will you shut up about that already?" Gavin snarls. "Stop pretending you know what we should do."

Christopher shakes his head, the movement jerky with panic. "The water's fine and we're fast swimmers. We can make it."

"I just…" Gavin shoves a hand through his hair, mussing it as his usually slick demeanor cracks a little more. "If we had a boat or something, then sure, you know? It would be better if we had a boat." He looks back down at the floating dock, then at Tris. "Let's get your tools. We'll detach that thing and paddle across the bay." He sets off toward shore and gestures for us to follow.

We fall in line—Tris behind Gavin, then Harry, then me. Christopher hesitates for a moment, but finally he joins us as we walk up the narrow dock. Soon we're back on land, and Gavin and Tris head around the side of the house toward her truck while Harry fills Harper and Dia in on the plan. "We should see if we can find anything that can be used as a paddle," he says, and we scatter to search.

I head toward the branches Tris and I piled up yesterday and choose a few that might work if the others can't find anything better. As I'm dragging them back toward the shore, I spot a single figure walking down the dock toward the platform. I recognize Christopher by his turquoise baseball cap. He strides quickly, resolutely, determined and alone.

My throat closes as I realize what he's going to do. "Christopher!" I try to yell, but my voice seizes, going thin and high.

Down the yard, Harry notices and follows my stare. "Hey!" he hollers when he spots Christopher. "Hey, wait for us!"

Gavin and Tris reappear from around the side of the house. When Gavin sees what's going on, he drops the toolbox he's carrying, letting Tris's tools spill over the grass as he sprints toward shore. "Chris!" he yells when he hits the dock, shoving his way past Harry. "Wait! Don't do anything stupid!" He runs down the narrow pathway with Harry close behind. I quickly help Tris scoop her tools back into the box, and we follow.

"I'm getting the fuck out of here," Christopher is saying when I reach the platform. His voice trembles, and he rakes at the stain on his arm again, tearing at the skin. "I'm not waiting around any longer." He kicks off his shoes and tosses his cap and shirt on top of them.

"Let's think this through, okay?" Harry says breathlessly, positioning himself between Christopher and the edge of the platform. "Gavin is right. You don't want to go in there. Come on, we have a plan. We'll use the floating dock as a raft."

"I don't need a raft."

"Don't do it, man," Gavin says. He grabs Christopher's bicep, keeping his grip far from the bloody stain.

Christopher shakes himself free. "I'll come back," he says, swinging his arms like he's warming up before a race. "I'll come back with help."

"No." Still between Christopher and the platform's edge, Harry puts up his hands and braces his lanky form. "We don't know what's in the water. Look, we have tools, we'll just—"

"Out of my way!" Christopher charges, trying to dodge Harry.

Gavin grabs for his arm again and misses, his hands clenching air. Harry tries to catch Christopher, but Christopher shoves him away and dives. Thrown off-balance, Harry windmills his arms and falls backward off the platform.

Two splashes.

"Harry!" I barrel down the ramp to the floating dock.

Harry swims to the ladder and climbs, gripping the handrails. He's halfway up when his eyes snap wide and he's yanked back into the bay. He screams and clutches the ladder tighter, his fingers going white as he struggles to keep from going under. I grab him under his arms and pull until I'm sure one of us is about to break in two, and then he's free. He half flies, half stumbles onto the dock, falling on top of me. Needing to be farther away from the dark water, we scramble to our feet and run back up the ramp, collapsing on the platform.

"What was it?" I gasp. "What had you?"

"I don't know!" He grips his left ankle. "It didn't want to let go!"

Tris and Gavin look from us to the water, back and forth, back and forth.

I go to the edge of the platform. "Where's Christopher?"

Gavin points at the figure cutting through the bay.

Christopher is the best swimmer at Winter Park West, better even than Gavin. He's moving fast, fueled by panicked adrenaline, his long arms dragging him cleanly through the water, like a surgeon's scalpel through flesh. He's already not that far from the dock on the opposite shore.

Maybe he'll make it. For just a second, I let myself believe this, hope for this. Maybe. Just . . . maybe.

It happens fast. One second he's perhaps fifty feet from the dock. The next he's gone. He goes under, the bay swallowing him and closing over his head, erasing him from view.

"Christopher!" Gavin yells.

We watch. We wait.

Seconds go by, then a whole minute. We're all still staring toward the dock across the bay, so the splash nearby startles us.

The scream scares us even more.

Christopher is back on our side of the bay, clinging to the ladder of the floating platform with one hand. It's hard to tell amid his desperate flailing and splashing, but it almost looks like his other hand is just... gone, like his arm ends in a jagged mass of raw meat below his elbow.

I don't think that's the only part of him missing, either.

He screams for help, the word ending in a horrific burble as something yanks him back under. His hand stays clamped to the ladder, and that last show of desperate determination seems to anger whatever has him. It yanks the floating dock sideways hard enough to detach the ramp; we all scream as the main platform shudders from the force of the pull. Christopher's hand lets go and disappears, and the choppy water begins to calm.

I keep staring down at the now-inaccessible floating dock. If we had any hope of using it as a raft, the loss of the ramp took away that possibility. It bobs on the surface of the bay, drifting slowly downstream, still teasingly close but too far to reach without getting in the water. I know Christopher can't still be alive, not after that, but I can't seem to stop waiting for him to surface. In my peripheral vision I'm aware of Tris staggering a few feet away to cling to a piling. She glances down like some movement in the water nearby catches her attention. Her gasp knocks me out of my shock, unfreezing me, and I start to follow her gaze.

"No!" She shoves me back from the edge. "Don't look." Her stare is desperate, almost feral. "You don't want to see that."

Harry looks down, lets out a strangled cry, and vomits into the bay.

Alarmed by the screams, Harper and Dia race out to the platform. "What happened—" Dia begins, but then she glances over the edge, and now she's the one screaming. Harry straightens and grabs her from behind, pulling her to the center of the platform so she can't keep staring.

Gavin backs up without looking. "House," he whispers, and we tear down the narrow dock. By the time we reach the shore, Harry is throwing up again and Tris is sobbing. She drops to her knees, her hands over her face.

"We should get inside," I tell her, my voice as gentle as I can manage. She nods and lets me help her to her feet.

Harper wraps an arm around her brother, who has turned a terrible shade of gray, and leads him behind us. Inside, he moans softly and sits on the floor, one hand clasped over his mouth. "What kind of…" He pauses, working his throat like he's trying to hold off another round of vomiting. "What kind of chemical spill could do something like that?"

"It can't be a spill," Harper says quietly.

"But what else could it…" Harry's voice trails off, and he presses the heels of his hands to his eyes like he can somehow push the memory of what he saw in the water out of his head. My stomach twists as I watch him slowly realize what I already know— that whatever's going on has no easy, rational explanation. There was no meltdown nearby. We're not under attack.

Whatever's trapped us here—and whatever took Christopher—is far, far darker than anything like that. I know this already, but then, I have experience with dark things.

Dia leans against the wall nearby, her eyes wide and unfocused. "The blood," she whispers. "There was so much of it. So much blood." Her tone goes shrill and she punctuates her words with a harsh exhale that sounds almost like a quick bark of laughter; then she shudders and lets herself slide slowly to the floor. When I crouch next to her and quietly ask if she's okay, she gives her head a slight shake and swallows like she's fighting the rise of bile.

Gavin stays outside on the porch with his back to us, staring out toward the bay.

I lead Tris to the kitchen. She sits at the breakfast bar, takes a few sips of the water I offer, and buries her face in her crossed arms.

"What was it?" I can't help asking. "In the water. Was it Christopher?"

"Parts of him," she says, her voice muffled.

I sit beside her and rub her back and wish I knew what else to do.

After a few minutes, she raises her head and looks at me with bleary eyes. "Remember what I said about liking nightmares?"

"Yeah."

She lets out a shuddering breath. "Changed my mind."

Then

THREE YEARS AGO

Nellie frets about the spring semester auditions for Winter Park West's chorus—she has no real experience singing for anyone other than her shadow—but the director calls her a natural. Then she frets that he might assign old standards as performance pieces, and she's not sure how she'd feel about singing one old standard again in particular, one that she hasn't so much as hummed to herself in years, ever since she stopped singing and started writing. But the director is ABBA-obsessed and doesn't seem to realize that music existed before the 1970s. Nellie is safe with songs like "Dancing Queen" and "Waterloo."

Chorus practice is twice a week before school. While other members gather in small groups outside the chorus room, chatting and carrying on while they wait for the director to arrive with the keys, Nellie sits in the hall with a notebook on her lap, scribbling stories. Harper would cringe and tell her to talk to people—but that's Harper's thing, not Nellie's. She prefers to maintain a gentle sort of exile, especially this early in the morning.

Not that being at school this early is all that bad. Nellie likes the quiet at this hour, when an overnight hush still settles low and still in most of the halls, especially in the music wing. She can think. She can work. She can write, at least until the day the boy with ash-brown hair and green eyes shows up and sits beside her.

She ignores him. He's not in any of her classes, and she can't remember seeing him in the hallways.

"Hey," he says. His breath carries a hint of mint.

"Hey." She gives him a sideways glance and returns her attention to her notebook. He's nice-enough looking, she supposes. Cute, even. But she doesn't appreciate him invading her personal space. Why must he be so close?

"What are you writing?"

"Nothing."

He touches the side of the notebook, flipping the paper edges just enough to reveal page after page covered in her neat handwriting. "Doesn't look like nothing."

She closes the notebook and sets it aside, where he can't reach.

"I've seen you in the cafeteria," he says. "You sit at that corner table, right? The one by the mustang mural."

"Yes." She, Dia, and Harper share the small table near the mural of the school's mascot. Harper keeps nudging them to move to a larger table and sit with her track friends, but the cafeteria is overcrowded and there isn't room at the track table for three more people. Nellie often catches Harper glancing longingly across the room, and she wonders how long it will be before Harper moves to the track table by herself.

"This is really awkward," the green-eyed boy says, "but do you think I could sit with you guys today?"

Nellie looks at him, waiting for a punch line.

"I just moved here a couple of weeks ago," he goes on. "I can never seem to grab a seat. I'm tired of eating standing up."

No. Find your own table. "I mean, I guess? Sure."

He smiles. That smile gleams. "Thanks. All these changes have been kind of hard." He takes a breath like he's going to keep talking, like he's going to chatter on about the move and his struggle to make friends. People do that to her all the time. It's a thing she's noticed about being quiet—she is seen as a good listener by default.

She doesn't want to listen to this boy's problems.

Before that can happen, though, the director walks up and unlocks the chorus room door.

"So I'll see you at lunch," the boy says later, when they all file into the hallway after practice.

"See you then," she says, thinking about the story she didn't have time to work on this morning.

"Hey," he says. "You're Nellie, right?"

"Nell," she corrects. She's been thinking of changing what she goes by. She might save Nellie for her friends, and this boy isn't even close to earning that status.

"Nice to meet you, Nell. I'm Gavin. Gavin Richardson." He smiles again—there's something a little too slick about that smile, a little too sharp—and walks off, leaving Nell with an odd, unexplainable little pinch of dread in her stomach when she thinks about lunch.

116

Chapter Fourteen

A little while later, Harry stumbles into the kitchen and grabs the turpentine jug.

"You got it on you?" I ask.

Trembling, he points to his left ankle, the one that something in the bay had latched on to. The skin there is covered in tarry gunk. When he twists open the jug, his hands shake so badly that he drops the cap. The muscles in his jaw tighten as he soaks a rag with the acrid-smelling fluid, accidentally splashing extra onto the counter.

"Does it hurt?" I ask.

He shakes his head, his breathing loud and ragged as he scrubs at the gunk until it breaks up and wipes away. Unlike with Gavin and Christopher, on Harry it doesn't leave a stain.

Christopher rubbing and clawing at the stain on his arm. The memory tries to churn up fresh panic; I crush it down, settling back into shocked numbness. I've lost track of the time; the sun is low over the bay now, streaming copper orange through the gauzy curtains. Soon it will be dark. Soon it will be time for my ritual—the one I can't do without my uke.

What if? The thought dredges itself up and starts to loop again. *What if?*

We gather in the living room. Harper curls against Gavin, her face hidden against his neck. Dia mechanically shoves the Twister box back in the cabinet and pulls a floor cushion closer to Harry's chair. Tris and I take one end of the sectional, her hand clutching mine.

No one speaks. It's hard enough simply to breathe.

I glance at each of them in turn. Tris closes her eyes, her throat moving as she swallows. Gavin works his jaw, pulling it so tense I think it might snap near the joint, while Harper weeps quietly against him. Dia barely seems to blink; her hair brushes over her shoulders as she slowly rocks back and forth on the cushion, her arms wrapped tight over her stomach. I suspect she's in shock; I've tried to speak to her a few times, but she won't answer.

"We should probably eat," Harry says finally. "It's getting late. Right?" But he stays put and doesn't head toward the kitchen. His face is still gray, and his voice wavers like he's holding back, like he'd rather be screaming.

"The fish," Gavin mutters. When we look at him in confusion, he clarifies. "They're still out on the dock, on ice. I could…" His voice trails off, and he swallows hard. "Never mind. I can't. I can't."

"It's okay," Harper says close to his ear. She raises her head and rubs his shoulder, trying to soothe him.

Gavin shifts away from her. "Are you fucking kidding me, Harper? It's not. It's not okay."

118

Her red eyes brim with fresh tears. "I just meant—"

"My best friend just died in front of me!"

"I know." Harper's voice wavers. "Gavin—"

"He's out there!" Gavin hollers, standing and pointing toward the window that overlooks the bay. "In the water! In *pieces*!"

The louder his voice gets, the more my chest constricts. Rage, dark and feral, jockeys for position, shoving at my fear and my shock. "Don't yell at her!" I scream. Beside me, Tris's eyes snap open. Her grip on my hand tightens.

Gavin whirls toward me. "Stay out of it!" He steps toward me. "If you—"

"HEY!" The bark comes from Harry. I've never heard him be so loud; it's like whatever he was holding back finally escaped all at once, and I swear it shakes the house. He lets out a harsh breath. "Gavin. I'm sorry about your friend. We all are, okay? We're all… We're all traumatized right now, and fighting won't help. We have to stay calm and figure out what we're doing."

Gavin's nostrils flare. "We have to get out of here. That's what we have to do."

"I don't think we're going anywhere tonight," I say. Tris's hand squeezes mine again.

Harry nods. "It's getting dark. For now, let's focus on staying safe. We're stuck, but we're okay for the moment."

"Are you fucking kidding me?" Gavin says. "We're *okay*? Christopher isn't okay. My best friend isn't okay! How do we know that shit isn't going to cover the entire island?"

Harry rubs his face. "We don't."

"We should board up the windows and doors," Gavin says. "Keep it out."

119

I shake my head. "If that stuff does come up this far, I don't want it to corner us inside. I want to be able to run."

"Run where?" Harper asks.

"I don't know," I say quietly. "Somewhere. Away."

"Look," Harry says. "We're all supposed to be checking in with our parents this week, right? When they don't hear from us, they'll know something's wrong. They'll send help. We just need to stay safe until then. We can still make masks like I was talking about before, just in case."

"Masks," Gavin scoffs under his breath. "Bullshit."

"They might help if that stuff comes nearer," Harry says grimly.

"Yeah? You think? I got a lungful, remember? It was like breathing fire. You think some cloth is going to stop that?"

"They might help," Harry says again.

"I'm not just going to sit around and find out," Gavin says. "What if we try to signal someone?" He looks at Tris. "Does your dad keep flares or fireworks or anything around here?"

"So dumbass tourists can burn the house down? No."

"Then we'll build a fire out back. A big one."

"Did you hear what I just said about dumbasses burning the house down?"

"Who are you going to signal?" I snap at Gavin, pointing out back. "There was no one out there before, remember? The bay was deserted."

"Jesus Christ," Gavin mutters, glaring at me. "You just won't let up, will you?" He cocks his head toward Harper, gesturing for her to follow him into the kitchen. "Come on. I need to get away from this bullshit for a while." She throws me a quick glance, then trots off after him.

120

Harry sighs wearily. "The bay *looked* deserted, but that doesn't mean no one's there. The world hasn't just gone away. We've still got electricity and water, so some things must be okay on the mainland. Gavin's right—a signal might be a good idea."

"You're going to let him set the yard on fire?" I raise my brows at Harry.

"There are other ways to signal," Harry says.

"What about a sign?" Dia asks flatly. I'm almost shocked to realize she's still in the room; this is the first time she's spoken since her whispers about blood. We wait for her to say more, but she goes silent again, slowly picking at a line of fringe on the floor cushion.

"A sign could be good," Tris says after a moment. "Something big. Something that could be seen from a drone or a low-flying airplane. There are lots of amateur pilots with little planes in the area."

I think of every desert-island cartoon I've ever seen. The characters always spell out HELP on the beach in shells or driftwood or debris, trying to catch the attention of passing ships or planes. We could do that—but when it comes to signaling planes, wouldn't our message be more visible higher up? "The roof," I say. "If we can write *help* on the roof in big enough letters—"

"There's paint in the garage." Tris's tone goes short and eager. "Lots of it left over from the renovations. Dad and I left it here for touch-ups."

"That'll work!" Harry says.

Harry, Tris, and I brainstorm more plans to carry out tomorrow while Dia sits silently nearby. We'll make enormous HELP signs from bedsheets and hang them from trees, the platform, the house, anywhere they might be visible to a boat passing by in the bay or the ocean. We'll take down wall mirrors and keep them handy in case we need to reflect the sunlight as a signal. The more ideas we come up with, the more momentum we build, the more it feels like we might actually find our way back to safety. There's something strangling and desperate in our harried, frenetic planning. I doubt any of us truly believe bedsheet signs and closed windows will work, but it's all something to cling to, and we need that.

"There's other stuff in the garage we might be able to use, too," Tris says. "We can take inventory tomorrow as long as it's still safe to go outside."

Her comment blunts our progress, dragging it to a halt. Every plan we're making assumes we won't wake up to an island devoured by haze and blanketed in tar.

"Of course," Harry says as Dia starts to rock again. "We'll do all that tomorrow. As long as it's clear."

Chapter Fifteen

Night falls. Harper reappears from the kitchen and goes from room to room switching on lights, turning the world outside the windows even darker. Blinding ourselves to what could be going on outside feels unwise. I ask her to stop.

"What about the exterior lights?" she asks, but I picture moths drawn to flames, and I don't love the idea of making the house an obvious beacon.

"The security light down the road will stay lit all night," Tris says. "It runs on stored solar. That should be enough to let us see if anything's going on outside."

"Should we keep watch all night?" I suggest. "We could do it in shifts."

Harry nods and offers to take the first watch, and I volunteer to go second. Others fall in line behind me, all except Dia, who remains quiet and still. Even without her, though, we manage to work out a schedule that keeps us covered through dawn.

And then there's nothing left to do but try to get some rest.

When Gavin tries to follow Harper upstairs, Harry clears his throat. "You take the master," he tells Harper. "Gavin can have your old room. I'll crash on the couch after my watch."

Harper narrows her eyes at her brother. "Really? We're doing this now?"

"Yeah. We're doing this now."

Harper grunts and goes up to get her things.

"What about Tris?" Harry asks.

"She can stay with me," I blurt without thinking, and I blush. "I mean, she can have my room. Without me in it. I'll stay with Dia. Or out here. Or—"

Tris puts a hand on my forearm. "I'll get some blankets and sleep on the floor in your room. Okay?"

I swallow. "Okay. Help me get Dia settled first?"

"Of course. Let's grab some things, and then we'll take her upstairs." The linen closet is just off the kitchen, near the downstairs half bath. Tris and I gather blankets and pillows, and I lead Dia toward the stairs.

Before we go up, I glance at the sign that hangs over the kitchen entryway and turn to Tris. "What's what mean? What's it from?"

She looks up. "Island of no storms? It's a hurricane thing, I think. It's been here since before Dad bought the place. He's superstitious enough to insist we keep it." She leaves a few blankets on the couch for Harry and heads up the stairs, still talking. "It's kind of strange, actually."

I follow. "What is?"

"Florida gets more than its share of hurricanes, you know?"

Having grown up in the state, I'm well aware. "Several a year, minimum."

"Exactly. But it's been decades since St. Felicitas was hit directly. Longer, maybe. We get a lot of sideswipes and near misses, but that's it. It's like there's a barrier."

Tris helps me lead Dia to her room. We get her to lie down, and I take off her sandals and pull the sheets up to her shoulders. "Dia?" I say uncertainly.

She stays silent.

I sit beside her. "We're going to figure this out, okay?" I say, desperate to reassure her, to draw her out of her lingering shock. "Get some rest. In the morning, we'll . . ." I don't know what else to tell her. I have no idea what the morning might bring.

She doesn't respond, but at least she closes her eyes like she'll try to sleep.

In my room, we turn on one small, dim lamp, and I unload the armful of blankets on my bed and help Tris spread them on the floor. "You said it's like St. Felicitas has a barrier. I realize Straight Shot is a barrier island, but . . ."

"I don't mean literally," she says. "Not really. Or . . ." She pauses in the middle of fluffing a pillow. "Or maybe I do. I don't know. If a storm did come at us, all this place could do is take a tiny fraction of the brunt. Lessen the storm surge a little, maybe. And yet . . ."

"What?"

She shrugs. "We don't know who originally hung that sign, but Dad took it seriously. He says as long as it stays here—as long as the house is here—we won't ever get a direct hit. This is the island of no storms."

"I like that," I say.

She gives me a short, humorless laugh. "Like I said, he's kind of superstitious."

"It's a nice thought, though. Comforting."

"It is, but it doesn't mean we don't still prepare for the big one every hurricane season. Just in case. Every year the meteorologists predict that we'll get a direct hit. If they keep it up long enough, sooner or later they'll be right." She puts down the pillow. "This state is exhausting."

"Tell me about it," I say as I dig through my luggage for an extra nightshirt to lend. "Do you want to borrow this? It'll be over-sized, but…"

She smiles. "It's a sleep shirt, so isn't it supposed to be? Thanks."

I change into a T-shirt and sleep pants in the bathroom. When I get back to the bedroom, she's wearing the nightshirt and adjusting the blankets into a nest on the floor.

"Do you want…" I gesture toward the bed, trying to find a way to make it clear that we can share without the suggestion sounding, well, suggestive. "I mean, the floor's hard, and there's room—"

Another smile. "I'm good down here."

I set my phone alarm to sound in two hours and turn off the one small lamp we've been using. "Have you ever been through a hurricane?" I ask as I get into bed.

"I've always lived around here," she says, "so no, not directly. It's bad enough when they come close and veer off. What about you?"

"Not a direct one. You know how they charge north up the state sometimes? Winter Park is inland enough to tire most of them out. We've gotten plenty of rain and wind, but nothing like what you can get on the coast."

"The footage I've seen is brutal," Tris says. "A Category Four or Five would flatten this place." I can't see her, but I think I hear a shudder in her voice.

I close my eyes and think of my ukulele, and of the empty case that's still downstairs on top of the fridge. Not that I'd play it now and sing, not in front of Tris, *no way*, but the memory is jarring. Was it really only this morning that Gavin startled me out on the platform? It feels like it's been weeks.

For the second night in a row, I can't perform my ritual—and now I've lost a central part of it. I wonder how long it will be before the shadow dreams start again. I don't want to sleep, and I can't imagine that I even could after all that happened today, but I close my eyes and then my phone's alarm beeps and two hours have passed. I silence the alarm and get up, shuffling through the darkness, guiding myself with the beam from the Maglite so I don't have to turn on a light.

"Can I come with you?" Tris asks.

I jump a little. "Sorry, I didn't mean to wake you up."

In the Maglite's peripheral glow I can see her sitting on the blanket pile, her knees drawn to her chest. "You didn't," she says. "I've been awake."

"Of course you can come. If you want to."

"I want to." She stands.

We head downstairs, keeping the flashlight trained on the floor. Harry's sitting in the dark kitchen, his chair positioned by the large south-facing window. He raises a hand in greeting and gets up.

"Seen anything?" I ask.

"No. It's really dark out there, but the security light helps as long as you keep everything switched off in here." He yawns. "I don't know if I can manage any sleep, but I'm going to try. Give a yell if anything happens."

Tris pulls up an extra chair, and we settle by the window. I turn off the Maglite and stand it next to me.

"Since we're both here, should we keep watch in different directions?" I ask.

"I think we should stick together." Tris reaches across the space between us and catches my hand.

I'm glad it's dark in here. It hides the blush that must be glowing right through my sunburn.

Chapter Sixteen

It's after midnight. My watch will last until one o'clock, and then it will be Tris's turn.

I'll stay with her the way she's stayed with me.

"What do you think's going on?" she asks softly, her attention focused on the darkness outside. About seventy yards down the dirt road, the security light casts a dim orange glow. The air around it is clear; if the haze is moving, it's not moving fast. The moon tonight is new, and everything beyond the security light's meager reach turns to ink.

"I don't know."

Tris makes a tiny sighing sound that's almost a laugh.

"What?"

"It's just . . . well, you're a horror writer." Her tone lightens with what I'm almost sure is a grin. "If anyone should be able to figure out what's going on and how all this ends . . ."

I glance at her, the hint of a smile playing at the corners of my mouth. "When it comes to horror, the end is always the hardest part to write."

We fall quiet. I usually dread silence when I'm spending time with someone I might—*might*—have a little crush on, but this isn't awkward or uncomfortable. We sit and keep watch, and we just...*are*. Together. I wonder if that would be the case if Tris and I had met under more normal circumstances.

A few minutes later, something appears in the pool of orange light. It looks like a shadow, dark and sneaking, and I immediately go tense. But it's not my old friend, I realize after a moment. It's too small, and too solid.

Tris points at it and says, "Possum."

"There's wildlife on the island?"

"Not a lot, but yeah. A couple of raccoons and possums, at least. And birds, of course."

I watch as the animal creeps through the dim glow toward the beach. "Are you sure that's a possum?" Its tail looks too furry, although not raccoon-thick, and it's thin and sleek where a possum would be round and hunched.

"I thought so, but..."

"It's the wrong shape. Cat, maybe?"

"There shouldn't be any cats here," she says. "But I guess one could've jumped the gate."

My spine ices over at the thought. "Through the haze?"

"Maybe it was here before, and now it's stuck like us."

The cat steps out of the glow and blends back into the ink.

Three o'clock. Tris's shift is over. I hear footfalls on the stairs and stop breathing for a minute when I recognize the weight of Gavin's stride. Tris notices and squeezes my hand before letting it go.

"My turn," Gavin says when he reaches the kitchen. I grab the Maglite and head toward the stairs without a word. Tris follows.

"So what did he do?" she asks once we're back in the bedroom.

"He came between me and my best friend." I hope the short version will be enough.

"You and Harper?"

"Yeah."

She makes a face. "I hate guys who do that. Still, though—maybe I'm overstepping, but isn't that as much on Harper as it is on him?"

I nod and crawl back into bed. "It's easier to be mad at him, though."

"I hear that."

"Besides, he's just not a great person. It's a long story." A story I never intend to tell.

• • •

I'm not sure how long I've been asleep when a stifled yelp startles me awake. I bolt up and turn on the dim little lamp. Tris is sitting up in her nest again, clutching a pillow to her chest like a shield. Her entire torso heaves as she gulps air.

"Are you okay?" I ask.

She nods, but she's not okay. She's crying.

"Nightmare?"

Another nod, sharp and panicked. "I'll be fine in a sec. Go back to sleep." She almost chokes on the words.

"Do you want to come up here?" Asking is terrifying, but maybe she needs another body nearby. Maybe it will help.

"I don't want to move." She stares at the corner of the bed, her eyes avoiding mine. "Maybe . . . you could come down here?"

I get out of bed, turn off the lamp, and fold myself into her nest. It's more comfortable than it looks.

She swipes at her face before she lies back down beside me. "I'm sorry."

"You don't have anything to be sorry for."

"I'm just freaking out, and . . ."

"I think freaking out is pretty justified."

"Is it okay if I just . . ." She moves closer, tucking her head near my shoulder and putting an arm around me.

"Yeah. It's okay." I wrap an arm around her, too. "Want to talk about it? The dream?"

I feel her shake her head. "It was Christopher," she says, her voice muffled.

I don't ask for more details. Instead, I use my free hand to tuck the blanket higher over her shoulders.

We sleep.

Then

THREE YEARS AGO

Nell hopes the new boy won't show up to sit with them at lunch. When she sees him approach, she swallows that hope and introduces him to Harper and Dia.

"See, Nellie?" Harper says. "I knew meeting new people would be good for you!" She looks from Nell to Gavin, her gaze momentarily sharpening in a way Nell has never seen before.

Gavin tells them about the move from South Carolina. About the classes he's taking and the movies he likes. About wanting to join the swim team in the fall. "I just missed out on spring tryouts this year," he says. "At least we moved in time for me to join chorus." He glances Nell's way.

"So you're a singer?" Harper runs a hand over her dark hair, an unnecessary attempt at smoothing what's already strikingly sleek.

"Sort of, but I'm not serious about it. I'm not as good as Nell." He glances at Nell again, a very faint flush coloring his cheeks.

Nell bites into her sandwich to avoid thanking him. The

compliment makes her uncomfortable and jittery in a way she can't explain.

Harper keeps talking, pulling Gavin's attention back to her. When he says something slightly amusing, she laughs and reaches out, giving his forearm a quick, casual brush with her fingertips. Gavin seems receptive enough to her flirtations. He reacts to Harper's signals, laughs at her quips, smiles on cue.

But he also keeps glancing over at Nell, and the way his green eyes dart in her direction makes her go taut, guarded. Tension builds in her shoulders. Something sharp and dangerous, like an invisible surge of electricity from a downed wire, licks at the edges of her brain.

In the middle of an overcrowded cafeteria, she feels strangely alone and exposed.

The next day Gavin sits with them again. He joins them the day after that, too, over and over until he's one of them, a squatter settling in and making himself at home.

"Do you think he's dating anyone?" Harper asks one afternoon while she, Dia, and Nell lounge in Harper's big new bedroom in the big new house Stupid Charlie bought for his ready-made new family.

"Has he even lived here long enough to meet anyone?" Nell asks.

"He met us," Dia points out. "Harper, when's Harry getting home?"

Nell dreads the day Gavin finds a girlfriend, assuming that girlfriend isn't Harper.

And if it is? Nell dreads that possibility even more.

Chapter Seventeen

I wake up because Tris is stirring. When I open my eyes, her face is near mine, eyelids closed and heavy, lips slack. I look at her, and for just a moment I feel almost peaceful, especially with the way sunlight is pouring in through the thin curtains. It's clear and bright outside. The haze didn't drift north to trap us overnight.

Maybe it's not there at all anymore. Maybe it was some strange weather phenomenon, a meteorological oddity caused by humidity or heat or changes in air pressure.

I don't believe that for a second, but it's a comforting thought to wake up to, at least until I remember what happened to Christopher. I take a deep breath and push that memory away.

Tris's eyes flutter open. She smiles just enough to engage her dimple. "It's morning? Wait, did I actually *sleep*?"

"For hours," I confirm, checking the time on my phone. "I did, too." I get out a change of clothes. "I wish I had something you could borrow. Maybe Harper does."

"I'm good. Besides, I'm sure we'll get help today. My dad freaks out when he can't get ahold of me. He'll track me down." She gathers her clothes from yesterday and slips out toward the bathroom.

"Meet you downstairs," I call before closing the bedroom door to change.

We slept later than the rest of the house. Everyone else is in the kitchen; Harry's at the coffee maker, filling a mug, while Gavin sits at the table with Harper on his lap. His expression is blank, but then he smiles a little when she nuzzles his jaw. Even Dia, perched on a stool at the breakfast bar with her hands wrapped around another mug, looks a little better today, although her eyes are puffy and rimmed with dark circles.

"I just made more coffee," Harry says, "if you two want some."

"Yes please," I say, grabbing a mug. The kitchen is full of light, the drapes pulled back to let us revel in a dazzlingly clear morning. The sunlight ignites a hope that seemed impossible in the night's shadows, softening the memory of yesterday just enough. The scent of freshly brewed coffee curls around me like a blanket. In the distance, the Atlantic's waves pulse against the shore, sunlight glinting off the water's surface, so bright it's almost blinding. Except for the presence of Gavin, this morning almost feels like the vacation this week was supposed to be.

When my mind tries once more to bring up the fact that someone is missing from the scene, I shove the thought away again. Not now. I need to ignore that memory for just a little while longer. I replace it with another memory, that of the mantra my childhood therapist taught me. *I am safe.*

"Is anyone hungry?" I ask. "We have plenty of bread. I could make toast." I don't know if *hungry* is the right word for it—I don't really feel like I have the capability for hunger anymore, not after yesterday—but we didn't eat dinner last night, and we're going to have to refuel at some point. I get several nods in response, so I fire up the toaster oven and get out the butter.

Tris comes downstairs, and I hand her coffee and toast, and we settle next to Dia at the breakfast bar.

No one mentions what happened yesterday.

No one checks their phone for a signal or tries the house's Wi-Fi.

No one says anything about Christopher.

It almost feels like we can keep on pretending forever.

But Harry finally broaches the subject. He waits until the toast is gone and we're lingering over sips of lukewarm coffee. "Well...," he starts, hesitating until I almost jump up and put a hand over his mouth, forcing him to swallow the thought before he can voice it. I stay put, and he continues. "We should probably see if it's still there, shouldn't we?"

It's like the air is pulled from the room. The kitchen is still just as bright, but we're back in reality's shadow.

"We probably should." I regret the words as soon as I say them, but he's right. There's no use continuing to pretend.

Harper climbs off Gavin's lap and stalks across the room to scrub breakfast dishes at the sink.

Dia gives Harry a solemn, hesitant nod. "Who should go?" After last night, I'm glad to hear her voice again.

"We could draw straws," he says.

"Let's all go," I say. It seems like the only reasonable choice. Safety in numbers.

We travel in a herd, leaving the front door unlocked in case we need to get back inside quickly. The only working vehicle we have left is Tris's pickup, but it's not like we're in a hurry to head south. We can walk.

After a bit of a hike, we pass Harry's SUV, and then we can see the haze. It's still there at the south end of the island, blocking our escape from Straight Shot.

"Do we keep going?" Tris asks.

"A little bit," I say. "Let's make sure everything looks the same."

It doesn't. The rusty murk has expanded, swallowing Gavin's BMW. If I squint hard enough, I can see a vague shape where he abandoned the car yesterday. The shape is black-brown and sticky, running thick with tar.

When we're this close, I can smell that hot bitterness again. It smells like danger. It smells like death.

"Back to the house," Harry says softly, and again, we move as a herd.

The peace of the morning is gone.

When we reach the house, Tris points at the roof. "We should get that *help* message up."

I nod, eager to focus on something productive. Harper volunteers herself and Gavin to gather bedsheets for additional signs, and Dia quietly volunteers to work on Harry's cloth mask idea. When she asks if anyone has any spare hair ties she can use as ear elastics, I direct her to my toiletry bag, which has an entire pack of them inside. "Thanks, Mom," she says with a tiny smile that gives me hope that she'll be okay.

"Want to come with us to the garage first?" Tris asks. "I'm almost sure there's a painter's mask or two in there."

Dia nods, and she and Harry follow Tris and me to the garage. There's only one mask, but at least it's something. Dia grips it tightly, staying nearby as Tris hands us cans of touch-up paint from a shelf of tools and supplies. Tris pockets a large paintbrush and grabs the extension ladder, setting it against the house like she did to inspect the roof two days ago.

Two days. It feels like weeks have passed since then. Months.

She gives the ladder a few good shakes to check its placement, then hefts a paint can. "I'll need more than one. Can someone follow me up with another?"

Harry holds up one of the cans he's carrying. "I'll do it."

"No," I say, looking at Tris. "I can do it."

"You sure?" she asks. "It's pretty high."

"I can do it," I say again.

She nods and begins to climb, each footfall sturdy, each step solid. I don't know how she manages to be so confident as she goes up and up, higher and higher, hoisting herself onto the roof. For a moment, I can't see her at all from my spot on the ground.

Then she peeks over the edge and gestures for me to come up.

"Are you sure?" Harry asks. "I can go."

"No. I'll do it." I get ready to follow Tris with one of the paint cans, wishing I could hold its handle between my teeth so I could keep a better grip on the ladder.

"Wait," Dia says. She pulls the belt from her shorts and loops it through the can's handle. She then wraps it cross-body around my torso and buckles it so that the can hangs near my waist. "That'll be safer. Is it okay with your burn?"

The belt digs into the sunburn on my shoulder. It's irritating but bearable, and seeing Dia behaving like her old self does a lot to ease the sting. "Yeah. Thank you."

As Dia heads inside to get going on the rest of the masks, I start to climb, up and up like Tris. The distance I need to cover feels so much greater than a two-story house has any right or reason to be. I'm climbing into the stratosphere.

Tris won't let me on the roof, thank goodness. "Just let me grab this," she says, unbuckling the belt and taking the can. "Good. Bring up another."

I nod, but I don't step down right away. My hands are glued to the ladder. My feet won't move.

"You're shaking," she says, holding on to the top of the ladder.

I nod.

"Breathe," she whispers, resting a hand against my cheek. "You can do this. Go down, take a few breaths, and come back up when you can."

I'm so taken by the touch of her hand against my skin that I'm stepping onto the ground before I fully realize I'm climbing down the ladder. Harry is right there, ready to buckle another can of paint to me so that I can head back up.

When I climb high enough to peer over the gutter again, I see Tris standing on the roof. She holds the paintbrush in her left hand, smearing bold streaks of white against the dark gray shingles in the shape of a giant *H*. I watch her work, marveling again at how sure-footed she is on the slanted roof. When she runs out of white, she tosses the empty can down to the dirt road and opens another, which is the same light blue as my bedroom. When that one, too, is empty, she clomps back over to me for the next.

"You're not shaking anymore," she says when she bends to unbuckle the belt from around my torso again. The brush of her hands against my body makes me shiver—but no, I'm not shaking, not like before. She grins at me before she gets back to work, and I head down.

She walks the roof with such confidence, navigating its slope like she's on level ground. I know she knows what she's doing. I know she has experience. Still, one misstep could send her tumbling, and a fall from the roof of a two-story house wouldn't be pretty, especially when we can't call an ambulance or get her to a hospital. I track her progress and stand nearby. If she slips, I'll do my best to break her fall.

Finally, she finishes and climbs down. "What do you think?" she asks, holding out her phone. She took photos of her work—one enormous HELP is on the angle of the roof that looks out toward the ocean, and another is on the opposite side, facing the bay.

"Perfect," Harry says. "If any planes or drones come close enough, there's no way they'll miss that."

"How long have you known how to climb around on roofs like that?" I ask Tris as I help her carry the rest of the cans to the driveway, where we'll make the bedsheet signs.

"I've been helping Dad with roof repairs since I was fourteen," she says. "I wanted to try it even earlier, but he wouldn't let me."

"You're so sure-footed up there."

She shrugs. "When you're up that far, you don't want to doubt yourself. If you tiptoe around too much, you'll fall. Balance requires confidence."

"That's inspiring," I say.

"It sounds like something off one of those old motivational posters," she says, laughing. "It should be printed under a picture of a generic desert sunset."

"Or a kitten hanging on to a branch." I grin.

This makes her snort. "Hang in there, baby."

I almost giggle, but my amusement fades when I glance back toward the front porch. "Harper and Gavin should be out here with the sheets by now."

"Sheets." Harry curses under his breath and heads inside.

"Do you think they're...," Dia says.

That's not something I want to picture. "I wouldn't be surprised."

Harry marches them back outside pretty quickly, so I doubt he caught them in anything too involved. Still, Harper's hair is mussed and Gavin looks a little too pleased with himself.

We spread the sheets on the driveway and lawn and open cans of darker paint, spelling out more enormous HELPs, making six signs in all.

"Where should we put them?" Harper asks while we wait for the letters to dry.

"One can hang from the banyan on the north end of the island," I say, glancing at Tris.

She nods. "Let's put two out there. One visible from the ocean, one from the bay."

"One on the front of the house, maybe," Dia says. "And one on the pines."

"We should lay one out on the beach," Harry suggests. "We'll anchor it so it can't blow away. It'll be visible from the air."

I have another idea, but I almost can't bring myself to speak it out loud. "We should hang one from the platform. If anyone's across the bay, they'll be able to see it."

No one responds. No one wants to go back out there. Not after yesterday. Not after Christopher.

"I'll hang that one," Tris says finally. "I can grab my toolbox. I left it out there yesterday, when..." She goes silent.

"I'll help," I say quickly.

"Thanks," she says quietly, and we head toward the backyard.

"Are you sure you want to go?" I ask. "It's just hammering. I can do it." I didn't see what was left of Christopher yesterday. I don't have that image burned into my brain.

"We'll both go," she says. "It's okay."

We head out back, carrying the sheet down the long dock. Tris's strides are just as solid and sure as when she was on the roof, and I think of what she said about balance and confidence. I think of that, instead of what would happen if either of us lost our footing on the narrow walkway and splashed into the bay and its hidden underbelly of grasping, tearing tar.

On the platform, we hang the sheet from between two wide pilings, nailing it in place so that it casts a soft shadow over us. The breeze dances behind it, puffing it like a sail. Tris adds a few more nails, anchoring it securely while I stare across the bay, watching the opposite shore for signs of life.

"See anyone?" she asks.

I shake my head. The empty docks and yards feel almost haunted.

She sets her jaw and glances up. "We should put something on the roof of this thing, too," she says, "but I don't think I have it in me to climb up there."

"No. Definitely not." I reach for her, wrapping my fingers around her bicep before I even realize what I'm doing. "This is good enough. You're not going up there."

She puts down the hammer and looks at me, and the tension in her face softens a bit. "Are you saying you'd try to stop me?" she asks, her tone a little teasing.

"I sure would." I move a little closer.

She faces me and squares her shoulders. When she stands this straight, she's got a good three inches on me, maybe more. "And just how would you do that?"

"I'd find a way." I falter, knowing what I want to say but lacking the boldness to say it.

"That's not very convincing, Nell." She cups a hand over the angle of my elbow.

Balance requires confidence. If you tiptoe around too much, you'll fall. But what if I've already fallen, at least a little? "I'd kiss you," I say softly before I can lose my nerve and bite the words back.

"That would probably work," she murmurs, dipping her face closer to mine.

"Yeah?"

"Yeah. Want to try it and see?" She raises her voice just a little, exaggerating her words as she flashes me her dimple. "Gee, Nell, I think I'll go up on the roof after all and—"

I brush my lips against hers, and she returns the gesture, deepening the kiss. I sink against her, wrapping my arms around her waist. I used to dread that this moment, this first kiss with someone new, would find me too self-conscious to lose myself in it. Then I feared it would dredge up something that needs to stay buried, and I'd tense up and ruin it.

But neither of those are true. Instead, the kiss makes everything around us disappear, just for a moment. The gently flapping bedsheet, the bay, the haze, the memory of the day before, all gone. All lost to the gentle press of Tris's lips against mine.

"Still going up there?" I ask once the kiss ends.

"Nah." She smiles. "Suddenly I feel very attached to keeping my feet on the ground."

"Speaking of that, we should probably get back to the shore."

She picks up her hammer and leads the way back down the dock. We're passing over the marshy shallows when a glint of light from below catches my eye. I glance down and feel my throat tighten when I spot the source—sunlight reflecting softly off polished wood. It can't be. It's impossible. Like so many things on this island, it shouldn't be here, yet it is.

There, tangled in a nest of seagrass, is my uke.

Tris is several yards ahead of me. She doesn't notice me gasp and stop short. I can't let on. She'd never let me get close enough and low enough to the bay to grab my uke. But I need it. If I wait too long, if I don't come back for it soon, it might vanish again. Whatever's in the bay might take it back.

My chance presents itself after we go inside and Tris ducks into the bathroom. As soon as the door clicks shut behind her, I slip back out and jog through the yard toward the bay. "Please be there, please be there," I mutter, trying to remember exactly where along the dock I saw the uke.

It's there. It's still there.

The tide is at its peak, so there's only a few feet of clearance between this part of the dock and the bay. I lie down and start to reach...and freeze. I can't do this. It's incredibly foolish, beyond dangerous. I didn't see most of what the bay did to Christopher, but I saw my friends' reactions, and that was more than enough. I rise to my knees. I'll find a stick or something, and maybe I can fish it out.

A single syllable spoken in a hushed, throttled gasp comes from the shadow under the dock. "Con..."

I yelp and jerk back, scraping my hands and knees against rough wood as I steady myself, trying to stop the violent shaking in my limbs. I know that voice. It's jarringly familiar, and just like the uke, it's impossible.

I peek over the edge of the dock and ask, haltingly, "Is some-one there?" *Please don't answer*, I add silently.

"Con…st…" The word is drawn out, strained, like the speaker can't get enough air into his lungs. Something lurks behind the near-est piling, bobbing in the murky shallows and snagging on barnacles and seagrass. At first I think it's my childhood shadow, especially as it turns what's left of its head up toward me, and my fingers clench the unfinished edge of the dock until splinters shove into my skin.

But the thing staring up at me isn't my shadow.

"Christopher?" I ask, my voice drawing into a terrified squeak.

But it isn't Christopher, although it wears his face. The hazel eyes that used to follow Dia down the halls of our school have gone milky, and they roll and bulge in rotting sockets that drip with sticky tar. His peeling skin is a sickly, bloodless gray. His right arm is gone up to the shoulder, and it looks like there's not much of him left below his chest, either.

I hold my breath, watching him bob on the waves, and I'm reminded in the most horrific of ways of the time Harper and I lost a beachball to the ocean when we were young, the way it drifted and danced out of reach, and all we could do was watch it shrink as it headed toward the horizon, just bouncing and bobbing like what's left of Christopher, and when I remember to breathe, I catch the fetid smell of him, like meat that's gone off, oh God, the smell—

I retch and gag, although nothing comes up.

"Con…stan…," he moans again, the word fading into a wet death rattle, and I know it's not him at all, it's not Christopher, it's something else using him like a puppet. Each time it makes him speak, tar oozes and burbles from his mouth, and his jaw slacks sideways like it's no longer properly attached.

"I don't know what you're trying to say." My head reels with vertigo, and for a second I'm sure I'm going to fall in beside him.

"It has...begun," the thing that used to be Christopher chokes out.

"What?" I whisper, terrified by the way the thing's milky eyes roll toward me, but unable to look away. "What's begun? Tell me what's happening on this island!"

"What's...done...is done."

I force more air into my locked lungs. "TELL ME!"

"Con...stan...," he says again, and my eyes dart, panicked, from him to the uke. What is he trying to say? Con-stan...Constant? But constant *what*?

My stomach twists as I remember that I haven't been constant at all, not when it comes to my ritual.

Is this all my fault? Is that what the Christopher-thing is telling me? Is all of this happening because I let my shadow down?

"It can't be," I whisper, but guilt is already surging through me, flooding my veins with adrenaline and ice. *My fault.* But if the island is returning my uke to me, then maybe it's giving me a chance to make things right.

There *has* to be a chance.

I lie on the dock once more and stretch my arm toward the floating uke. My fingers nearly brush its polished surface, but I can't quite reach. Grunting, I inch forward, ignoring the resulting splinters, and try again.

"Con..." The Christopher-thing lets go of the piling to reach for me with his remaining arm. I freeze and watch his hand get closer, closer, and in some detached and disassociated corner of my mind, I notice a class ring with a blue stone still on his rotting finger.

In a desperate panic, I plunge my arm down once more,

stretching so violently that I almost think my shoulder will dislocate. My fist closes around the uke's fretboard, and I launch myself upward. Christopher's fingers graze my wrist; they're slimy, like wriggling slugs, and I almost retch again. Then, with a keening, crackling wail, he's sucked back into the shadows under the surface of the bay.

I fall back onto the narrow dock, anchoring myself before I can roll off the far side, and I clutch the uke to my chest. For a long minute, I don't move. I'm too afraid even to think. I stare up at the sky—so blue, so unrelentingly, soothingly *normal*—until my pulse slows and I can trust myself to sit up. I keep expecting a gray hand to shoot up and grab a piling, and my imagination feeds me too-vivid images of that milky-eyed face reappearing as Christopher pulls himself onto the dock, his jaw hanging askew as he drags his ruined torso toward me. He'll be back any second. I'm sure of it. I don't want to peek over the edge, but I do anyway, I have to. My eyes search the shadows, but there's no sign of the Christopher-thing anymore. When I see that he's gone, I let out a shuddering breath.

I inspect my uke, giving the strings a quick, experimental strum. It's out of tune, but it seems otherwise fine. There's no way there wouldn't be some water damage to the wood—the instrument spent a full day in the bay—but once I wipe the outside dry on my shirt, I can't tell it ever took a swim.

My fault. But I have another chance.

Tucking the uke under my arm, I stand and head back to shore, shocked that no one seems to have come looking for me. I feel like I was out there with the Christopher-thing for hours, but the sun hasn't moved in the sky, and apparently I haven't been missed.

Do I tell them what happened? Everyone's already so freaked

out. If this is my fault, there might be a way for me to fix it without them ever realizing. But the memory of the Christopher-thing claws at my mind with its slimy gray fingers, and I know I'll need to tell someone. Tris. I'll find Tris, and I'll explain, and I'll see what she thinks. She didn't know Christopher; maybe the story won't upset her as much as it might upset the others.

As I pass through the backyard, Gavin rounds the side of the house. He stops short when he spots me, his eyes flicking from my face to the uke and back, and he stands there watching until I go in. There's something blank and unsettling about his gaze.

Inside, I hurry through the empty kitchen and grab the ukulele case from on top of the fridge. I nestle my uke back in place in the padded interior, still wondering what its return might mean.

As I'm snapping the case closed, I hear someone on the steps. A moment later, Tris appears in the doorway. "Where were you?" she asks. "I thought maybe you went upstairs."

"Out back," I say. "Can we talk? Something just happened that…"

"What?" Tris's eyes go shadowy, her voice suddenly edged with dread. "What happened? Did someone else get hurt?"

"Nothing like that," I say quickly. I can almost see the fear and trauma rile up in her expression, and I know that I can't tell her about any of it. I'll have to keep the memory of Christopher's puppet corpse to myself. "Never mind."

"Are you sure?" she asks, still on the border of panic.

"Yeah. It wasn't important." I return the uke case to the top of the fridge; I'll come back for it later.

"Okay," she says quietly, like she's reassuring herself. "Okay."

I squeeze her hand and try not to think about gray fingers and bulging, milky eyes.

Chapter Eighteen

Once the distress signs are hung, we gather in the kitchen, where Dia quietly hands out masks made from layers of T-shirt fabric. Tris, remembering Harry's remarks from yesterday about soaking the masks in a baking soda solution, checks the pantry. She finds a box and puts it on the counter. "Just in case," she says, as if any of us really believe that cotton and baking soda will protect us from the haze.

I make sure not to face the windows that look out over the bay. I don't want to think about what—who—I saw under the dock earlier. Plus, it's cruel to see the opposite shore so close. The mainland is *right there*. It's right there.

It'll be okay, I tell myself. I just need to wait until nightfall. When it's dark, I'll grab my uke and figure out how to fix all of this.

"Think anyone is looking for us?" Dia says.

Harry frowns, rubbing a finger over the crease that forms

between his eyebrows. "I was supposed to check in with Mom and Charlie hours ago. They have to know something's up."

I look at Tris. "What about your dad?"

"Depends on whether he's tried to get in touch," she says. "I have an apartment near campus, so he doesn't know I didn't make it home last night. We're supposed to check a property down near Palm Coast later today. When I don't show up for that, he'll know something's up, but there's no reason for him to look here first." Her earlier optimism has fizzled.

"Even if he did...," I say.

"I don't want him trying to make it through that haze," she says softly.

"I don't want Mom or Charlie doing that either." Harry's voice goes grim.

Harper shrugs. "I mean, it wouldn't be *that* much of a tragedy if Charlie—"

"This isn't the time," Harry mutters.

"Fine." Harper points at Gavin. "What about your dad?"

Gavin's jaw tightens. "I doubt he noticed I wasn't home last night. He's dealing with a couple of really important cases. When his work gets like that, he doesn't pay much attention to anything else. It could be another day before—"

"That's enough for now," Dia says, her tone brittle. She stands, the movement sharp and sudden, like she's physically unable to stay still. Her fingers clench and loosen rhythmically.

"Does anyone want some lunch?" I ask quickly, mostly as a distraction.

Harry presses his mouth into a thin line. "I've been thinking about that. We don't know when...Or if..."

Harper gestures impatiently. "Say it. You're going to say it, so just say it."

"Maybe we should start rationing food."

"Jesus Christ." Harper buries her head in her arms.

Dia lets out a harsh breath and turns away from us, pressing her palms against the counter.

But he's right. "If that stuff doesn't go away," I say, "we might be stuck here for a while. We should plan for that."

"*Hunker Down*," Tris mutters.

I glance at her. "What?"

"Hunker Down," she repeats. "It's this awful hurricane preparedness program we had to do every year in school when I was little. Y'all didn't do it?"

We all shake our heads.

"Guess it was a coastal thing," she says. "Anyway, it was about how to be ready if a hurricane hits, and how to deal with the aftermath. There was a whole unit on food and water—how to conserve it, what lasts the longest, that kind of thing."

"That's exactly what we need," Harry says. "How much do you remember?"

She gives him a slight, wry smile. "Well, considering we did it every single year..."

"You're in charge, then." He gives her an awkward little salute. "Put us to work."

She does. "Perishables first. Harry, check the fridge and see what's fresh. Vegetables? Meat? That's lunch and dinner for today and tomorrow, assuming the electricity holds out."

"Where does the electricity here come from?" I ask. "Do you think we'll lose it?"

"Depends on what's happening on the mainland," Tris says. "Power comes through an underwater cable. With whatever's going on in the bay, I don't trust that to hold out. There's a generator in the garage, but it's small. It can't handle much."

She has Dia and me sort through the rest of the groceries, separating the foods that can last from the ones that will spoil or mold sooner. "Inventory everything," she tells Harper, handing her the pad and pen from near the landline. "We should know exactly what we have."

Then she points at Gavin. "You fill up the bathtubs. We get water from the mainland, too. If that goes, we need as much stockpiled as possible—for drinking, washing, flushing toilets. Anytime someone takes a shower, fill the tub again when you're done. I'll get the empty water bottles from the recycling bin, clean them out and refill them."

"This isn't just stuff you learned in school, is it?" I ask while she rinses empty bottles at the sink. It's too real. Too intense. She's been through this before. "I thought you'd never gone through a hurricane."

"Never got a direct hit," she corrects, glancing over her shoulder at me. "We've had plenty of close calls, though. Matthew caused all kinds of flooding. Irma knocked out our power for two days. Are you seriously telling me you don't do hurricane prep where you live?"

"I mean, we buy some extra jugs of water," Dia says. "A pack of batteries. A few cans of food that no one wants to eat. Mom stocks up on wine. We hope school might get canceled for a day. That's about it."

"I guess it's different when you're not on the coast," Tris says.

"Speaking of batteries, we keep emergency flashlights in all the nightstands. I'll round them up later. We should know where they are, just in case."

"I'll get them," Dia says, heading upstairs.

"Do you really think we'll need all this?" I ask once Tris and I are alone in the kitchen.

She shrugs and caps a bottle. "I don't know. Maybe it's all just a distraction, but right now I'll take every distraction I can find, just like when there's a storm coming."

I frown a little, not quite following.

"It's probably hard for y'all to understand," she says, "since you didn't grow up on the coast. When there's a hurricane coming right at you, you have all this nonsense to think about—how many gallons of water to buy per person, how many batteries to stockpile, when to put the shutters up and bring everything inside. There's so much stuff, and it's good to do, it's important. It keeps you safe. But it also distracts you from thinking too much about the storm itself, about this behemoth off the coast that might blow in like fucking Poseidon in a bad mood and, like, flatten your house and flood your city and tear your entire life apart." She pauses, taking a breath to still the rising quiver in her tone. "Maybe that's why the local news hypes it up so much and gets everyone so freaked out. Even that panic is better than thinking about the ... the enormity of the truth."

She's right. I've never had to take prep this seriously. Listening to her talk about it, though—hearing that tremble in her normally steady voice, watching the tension snake through her shoulders and up her neck, tightening her jaw—I think I understand at least a little of the dread she's gone through year after year, season after hurricane season. It's easier to focus on the practical, the immediate. It's almost soothing in comparison, and so I divert us back that way. "You mentioned hurricane shutters. Should we put those up, do you think?"

She shakes her head. "We have some in the garage, but it's not like they're airtight. Like you said yesterday, if that haze gets inside the house, I don't want to be trapped behind shutters. If I can run, I want to run."

Then

They don't sit at their little corner table in the cafeteria anymore. After Gavin makes the swim team as a sophomore, he tells Harper that the four of them should join some of the school's other athletes at one of the long center tables. Dia agrees since the group also includes plenty of flag line members, although joining the athletes means putting up with the attention of Gavin's besotted friend Christopher.

Nell argues for staying in the corner. She likes their seating arrangement as it is. She says they shouldn't give up prime real estate in a scarce market.

She is outvoted.

One evening the following spring, Harper invites Nell and Dia over to study for tomorrow's biology test and—more importantly—to discuss their plans for prom. None of them expect to have dates, so they've decided to go as a group, the three of them dressing up and dancing and having fun.

Nell arrives first. Harper's mother answers the door and sends her upstairs to Harper's enormous bedroom.

Harper's door is closed, which is odd because Harper always leaves it open when she's expecting Nell or Dia. Still, Nell doesn't even think about knocking. Harper is her best friend, after all. Even if they're not as close as they once were, they don't keep secrets from each other, and so Nell opens the door.

She stops short when she sees Gavin sitting next to Harper on the bed, too close, too close, his hand around her waist, his mouth against hers.

Harper's eyes snap open at the sound of the door opening. She leaps up, cheeks flushed, her alarmed expression morphing into relief when she focuses on Nell. "Oh my God!" She presses a hand over her mouth, stifling a nervous laugh. "Nell, you scared me! I thought you were my mom."

From the bed, Gavin chuckles.

With an effervescent grin, Harper sprints across the room and grabs Nell's hands, pulling her back into the hall. She lowers her voice, but her tone still fizzes with delight. "He asked! He actually asked!"

"Prom?" Of course it's prom. Nell feels their girls-only prom-night plans crumbling and sifting through her fingers like fine sand, or like ash carried away on the wind.

"Yes!"

"Does your mom know he's here?" Nell asks.

"Of course not. You know she'd never let us be up here alone. He climbed the *trellis*, Nell! It felt like something out of *Romeo and Juliet*."

"You remember how that one ends, right?"

157

The thrill in Harper's expression sours, just a little. "Can't you be happy for me? You know how long I've been into him."

Nell steels herself against her distaste. "I am. Of course. It's just ... We had plans for prom."

"I know. I'm sorry." Harper bites her lip. "Do you hate me?"

Nell deflates. "Of course not."

Downstairs, the front door opens and closes. Voices carry up the stairs, and Harper's eyes go wide. "Shit. Harry's home. He can't know about this. He'll tell Mom and Stupid Charlie."

A glimmer of temporary relief. "Maybe Gavin should climb back down, then."

"Gavin can do that," Gavin says, appearing in the doorway. He holds the sides of the frame and leans into the hall, smiling at Harper. "But he needs another kiss first."

"Get back inside!" Harper hisses, pushing him as Harry starts up the stairs. She pulls Nell in as well, and shuts the door behind them. Then she kisses Gavin, molding her body to his, rooting her fingers in his hair.

Nell sighs and stares at Harper's bookcases until the kiss ends.

"See you tomorrow," Gavin says to Harper as he climbs out her window. Then his gaze glides over to Nell. "Bye, Nellie."

Nell opens her mouth to remind him not to call her that, but there's something unpleasant about the way he holds her gaze, even though he's smiling. She stays silent until he's gone.

"Does he do that a lot?" she asks as Harper shuts the window.

"Only this once," Harper says. "We've been FaceTiming constantly, but I didn't think—"

"You never told me you were FaceTiming with Gavin," Nell says as the black hole in the pit of her stomach opens and pulls.

"We don't always tell each other *everything*, Nell," Harper says, laughing a little. "Don't tell about the trellis thing, okay? Don't be the mom friend this time."

"I won't."

"Good. And look! Look what he brought me." Still giddy, Harper takes a long-stemmed rose from her desk. "He carried it up in his teeth!"

"He should be careful." Nell tries her best to keep her tone free of the derision rising in her throat. "Those things have thorns."

"Not this one," Harper says. "They've been removed. He said he'd never give me something that might hurt me." She falls back onto the bed, giggling and holding the rose to her chest. "Are you sure you're okay with the prom thing?"

Nell sighs again. "Of course. I get it. I'm sure Dia will, too." She takes out her bio book and opens it to the chapter they'll be tested on tomorrow, about parasitic predators. She thinks of wasps that lay eggs inside caterpillars, leaving the caterpillars to nurture the larvae that hatch and grow and devour their hosts from the inside out.

Chapter Nineteen

I'm impatient for night to fall, although I can see its approach weighing on the others. It's easier for them to believe rescue is possible during the day. Then the sun tilts down toward the bay and the sky begins to dim, and as the sunset's fire extinguishes, their hope burns itself out, too.

"Should we check the haze again?" I ask. I don't want to, of course I don't, none of us do. But guessing is somehow worse than knowing, so we pack into Tris's truck—Tris, me, and Dia in the cab, everyone else in the bed—and head south together at twilight. We park before we reach Harry's SUV and walk the rest of the way.

The haze is still creeping north. It sits sleek and fat over the road, its tarry expanse halfway to the SUV. At this rate, if I can't reverse all of this, it will reach the house by the weekend.

Then what? We still have the north tip of the island. We can flee as far as Tris's hulking banyan. After that, there's just the inlet that connects the bay to the ocean...and whatever lurks below. Today we prepped while counting on rescue, but what if that rescue never comes? What if I can't placate my shadow and convince it to let us go? I plan on grabbing my uke tonight, once the house settles and I'm alone on watch. I'll sneak off somewhere private and alone, and I'll sing and strum and beg my shadow for forgiveness.

It will work. It has to work.

We're silent as we return to the house. When we go back inside, Gavin doesn't follow. He stands at the edge of the dirt road, staring at the woodpile on the side of the house. "Do you keep a saw here?" he asks Tris.

"I have one in my truck," she says. "And there's an axe in the garage. Why?"

"We should keep a signal fire going out back," Gavin says. "I can build one, but that woodpile probably won't be enough by itself. I might have to chop down a tree or two."

"Please do not go chopping down my trees," Tris says, sounding exhausted.

"We decided against a fire," I say.

"You all decided," he snaps. "Not me. I'm doing it."

"Who do you think is going to see it?" I demand. "We haven't seen anyone across the bay in over a day."

"That doesn't prove anything."

"Okay, so use the firepit."

"No. It's too far from shore, and it's too small. I'm going to set something up closer to the bay."

"What do you know about tending a fire?" I don't know where the urge to argue is coming from, but I can't bite it back. "This could be dangerous. Someone could get hurt."

"If anyone gets hurt, it'll be their own damn fault."

"That's a hell of a thing to say."

He steps closer. "Why do you give a shit if I do this, Nell?"

"I don't." I don't, I don't, I *don't*, and yet I do. I do because we had decided against it. Because it seems reckless and somehow violent. Because he's *insisting*, and that insistence crawls up my spine like the legs of a spider. He won't take no for an answer. Thunder rumbles in the distance, sounding strangely sympathetic.

Another step toward me. "Then shut up and stop bitching at me."

Every muscle in my body tenses as a panic I don't understand zaps through me. I stare him down, but inside I'm screaming.

Tris notices. "Okay!" she says, stepping between us. "That's enough. Gavin, if you want to build a signal fire, go ahead. Keep it away from the house and do not burn up my yard. Be careful."

Gavin glares past her, right at me. "See? Was that so complicated?"

"You just don't like being told no," I say, voice shaking. More thunder ghosts in from the horizon.

Before he can answer, Tris takes my hand and pulls me inside. The others follow, except for Gavin, who heads around the side of the house.

"What the hell was that, Nell?" Harper whirls on me. "Like things aren't already tense enough?"

Again, Tris places herself in the middle to keep the peace. "Let's all chill out for a little bit, okay? Nell, come help me grab a few more things for the supply pile."

Shaking, I follow her through the kitchen to the linen closet.

"Is there anything you want to talk about?" she asks once we're out of earshot of the others.

I shake my head.

"Are you sure?"

I nod.

"Are you okay?"

I stay still.

"All right." She exhales. "If you change your mind, I'll listen. The invitation's there." She kneels, ferreting out a box of pillar candles from the back of the closet. "I knew these were here somewhere! We were going to start arranging them in the fireplace for warm-weather renters." She stands and hands me the box. "They'll be good to have if..."

If the lights go out. If we lose power. If something's that wrong on the mainland, or if the tar and the darkness in the bay damage the underwater line. She doesn't say it. She doesn't need to.

She steps closer, although the box of candles keeps some distance between us, and she tucks a stray curl behind my ear. "We're going to be okay," she says. "We're going to be fine. You think so, right?"

I nod. Does it count as a lie if I don't actually speak?

And then our prep work is done. We've hunkered down, except for Gavin. There's nothing left to distract us. Harry bakes chicken with extra spices and fresh herbs from the porch planter for dinner, but nothing has much of a taste. Harper ignores me and takes a plate outside to Gavin.

After we try to eat, Harry stares out the window at Harper and Gavin. Gavin has gathered stones that once lined flower beds in the front yard and placed them in a circle near the shore, with a pile of wood at its center, and handfuls of pine needles as kindling. He sends Harper back inside for a lighter.

"How long is he going to stay out there?" Harry asks.

Harper shrugs. "All night, probably."

"I don't want you outside all night."

Harper huffs out a breath and heads back out without answering.

Harry looks ready to follow, but then he shakes his head, defeated, exhausted. "Looks like we'll have to revise the schedule for tonight, if we're down by two."

Spotting my chance, I say, "I'll take first watch. You all get a few hours of sleep."

"I'll go after Nell," Tris says. "We can keep watch together again," she says to me, gently thwarting my plan. I can't grab the uke and disappear while she's right there—I refuse to let my shadow that close to Tris, and besides, she'll have questions I won't be able to answer. Still, I can't find an argument that makes sense. I'll have to come back down for the uke later.

"Fine with me," Harry says. "I'll go third. Dia?"

She nods and heads toward the stairs. "I'll be down to take fourth." It's more than I've heard her say all evening.

Harry stares out into the darkness for a little while longer, watching as the fire in the backyard grows. "At least it doesn't look like that jackass will burn down the whole island," he says finally.

"Good," Tris says, "but just in case..." She produces a small fire extinguisher from under the kitchen sink and places it near the back door.

Harry gives her a small, blank smile, then turns away and spreads his blankets on the couch for the night.

Tris and I settle in the kitchen, taking our watches together again. The slivered-moon night is quiet and still; the thunderstorm

I heard earlier never came through, and there's not much of a breeze coming in off the water. We face the front yard and the dirt road, far from Gavin's fire, but it's bright enough to cause a subtle shifting of the shadows around the house.

At least I *hope* the fire explains the shifting shadows.

We don't react when Harper comes in from the backyard and stalks wordlessly to her room. Gavin stays outside with his precious fire.

A little while later the stairs creak. I glance around to see Dia come back downstairs. She is silent, aside from her footfall on that one creaky step; she drifts toward the couch like a ghost and sits near Harry. When I peek again a few minutes later, she's curled up against him, his arm around her. If I listen very carefully, I can hear muffled sobbing. If I stare, I can see her trembling.

I try not to listen. I try not to stare.

"Look," Tris murmurs an hour later. She points toward the security light down the road. The creature is back, slinking through the orange glow, and this time I'm surer that it's a small cat.

"It shouldn't be out there with the haze," I say. "What if it goes too close?"

"I'm pretty sure a cat would know better," Tris says.

"There's plenty of leftover chicken."

She turns, raising a brow. "Are you seriously suggesting we go out there to feed a cat?"

"Not now," I say. "Not in the dark. But maybe if we put out some food tomorrow…" I shrug. "It's stuck here just like we are. Maybe it's hungry."

She touches her shoulder to mine. "First the fish. Now a cat. You're a real softy, aren't you?"

"I guess."

"I like softies."

I don't have to look at her to know her dimple is showing. I can hear it in her tone.

My watch ends. Hers begins. My eyelids grow heavy.

"Go upstairs," she whispers when I nearly nod off. "It's okay."

"No, I'm staying."

She smiles at me and nudges her chair closer to mine, so that I can rest my head against her shoulder and doze.

"Look," she whispers.

I sit up, confused, wondering how much time has passed. "What?"

She angles her head toward the window that overlooks the porch. A small black cat sits on the sill, tail twitching as it stares in at us.

"Think we can get it to come inside?" I stand slowly and creep toward the window. The cat cocks its head and watches my approach, its eyes flashing in the dark. When I reach out to open the window, the cat slips away, skimming back into the shadows and disappearing. "Damn it."

"It'll be back," Tris says, her tone amused again. "There's no getting rid of cats once they realize there's a softy around."

Harry wakes up to take our place, and Tris and I go upstairs. As soon as she's asleep, I'll sneak back down. I turn away while she undresses. When I look back, she's in her blanket nest. She hesitates, then holds up the covers to invite me in. "Do you want to join me again?"

Of course I want to join her. Just until she falls asleep.

She fits herself against me, our faces close together. I can barely make out her features in the darkness, but I can tell that her eyes are locked on mine. "Just so you know," she says, "I'm not trying anything. I'm just kind of scared to close my eyes. Having you close makes that go away a little."

"I'm glad." I smile.

"Although...if I did try something..."

I catch her hand in the dark, and I find the words that I need. "I would tell you that we've only known each other for a couple of days, and that's a little fast for me."

"Understood."

"But I'd also tell you that I really liked kissing you on the dock today, and maybe you should try that again soon."

Her lips find mine. The kiss is gentle, with no hint of a demand for more. After, I lie still with my forehead touching hers. I listen to her breathing, waiting for it to go slow and deep with sleep so that I can slip away. I should go, it's time, but our nest is warm and soothing and I feel myself being lulled—

She startles awake, her body suddenly tense against mine.

"There's something in the corner," she whispers.

Chapter Twenty

I'm facing Tris while she looks past me. Behind me. I don't want to roll over. I don't want to follow her gaze.

I don't want to look in the corner.

But I have to. She's shaking and I have to know why.

I sit up, blocking her view. The room is so dark that I'm not sure how she managed to notice, but the corner beyond the bed is just a little murkier than it should be. The darkness is somehow thicker there, and my stomach sinks as I recognize the unique shade of that shadow. It's not a dream. It's not a hallucination. It's not something my troubled mind concocted as a frightened child, and it's darker and larger and more solid than ever.

Hello, darkness, my old friend.

Frost spreads over my spine. I can't let Tris know what I see. I have to handle this myself, and I have to do it *now*.

"It's nothing," I murmur, hating that I'm lying to her, hoping she'll believe me.

"What? No, something's there."

"There's nothing. Hold on. I'll prove it." As I stand, I give the corner an almost imperceptible nod. *Leave her alone. I'm the one you want.* I hope it understands. Two steps and I'm close enough to the nightstand to turn on the lamp. When I do, the shadow disappears along with the rest of the darkness.

Tris gulps air, each breath ragged. "I could have sworn."

"It's nothing," I repeat gently. I need her to believe the lie that I never believed when my father told it to me.

Her eyes are wide and watering, but she nods at me. "Nothing."

"Go back to sleep," I say. "I'll be back in a minute."

"Don't go," she says.

"I just need to pee." I stack up the lies between us.

She nods. "Leave the lamp on."

"Of course." I give her what I hope is a reassuring smile as I leave the room. I wish I could stop and grab my Maglite from under the pillow, but I don't know how to explain to Tris that I need it, not when she thinks I'm just taking a bathroom break. In the hall, instead of turning left toward the bathroom, I go right, toward the stairs.

The night has turned impossibly dark. The house is drenched in shadows deepened by the weak glow of the barely there moon through the windows.

One of those shadows, just a little darker than the rest, is watching me.

It folds itself along the staircase as I descend.

It lurks in the living room, peering out from under the coffee table on which we've stacked and organized supplies.

It slithers behind the couch where Dia sleeps. It pokes at her embroidery bag, peeking in and shying away.

When I go toward the kitchen, the shadow is somehow already there. It waits for me, staring from the pantry, neck bent, head hanging at a ghastly angle. It creeps close to Harry's chair while he keeps watch, his attention fixed on the night outside the window.

Only me, I think, trying to telegraph the words in its direction.

Harry turns at the sound of my footsteps. "Everything okay?" The shadow slips beneath his chair, thread-thin tendrils twining around his legs, and I want to scream, I want to cry out and demand to know why he can't feel them tightening, he has to feel them. I want to make him look down, just look, can't he see it, too?

But he doesn't look.

"Everything's fine. I just forgot something down here." I grab my uke from on top of the refrigerator. As soon as my fingers touch the case, the shadow wriggles away from Harry's chair. It unfurls itself in a far corner and watches me.

"Anything going on out there?" I make myself ask. My voice sounds normal, although my heartbeat feels loud enough to drown out the words. "Tris and I saw a cat in the window earlier."

"A cat? I haven't seen it. All quiet on the eastern front."

"Quiet is good." I turn to go.

"Nell? Can I talk to you for a minute?"

I repress a cringe. I don't have time for talking, not now. "I should get back upstairs."

"Just for a minute. Please?" He gestures to a chair, his expression— what I can see of it, at least—uncertain in the darkness.

I glance at the shadow. It stays very still, well out of his line of sight. I almost feel like it's giving me permission to linger, so I sit.

Harry stares out the window. "I wasn't sure if you saw anything from before. Dia and me, I mean."

I almost deny noticing, but then I nod. "Was she crying?"

"She's a lot more freaked out than she's been letting on."

"I think we're all pretty freaked out."

"No. I know. Of course." He runs a flustered hand through his hair. "I just didn't want you to get the wrong idea. Nothing's going on. I'm not, you know, creeping on your friend or anything."

The thought of sweet, awkward Harry creeping on anyone almost makes me chuckle. "I didn't think you were."

"She and I were getting closer even before everything started happening. I really like her."

Oh no. He has to pick *now* for this heart-to-heart? I glance over my shoulder, making sure the shadow is staying put.

"And I know it's awkward," Harry goes on, "and I know this is the worst time for it—"

"And you just got out of a relationship," I add.

"That too." The faint moonlight reveals a slight, humorless smile etching its way across his face. "But I really like her. If we get out of this—"

"*When* we get out of this."

He scrunches his shoulders. "Of course. When we get out of this...I know Harper will be weird about it, which is why I wanted to mention it to you first."

"Are you saying that you want to ask Dia out?"

"Yeah."

I think of how he held her on the couch while she cried. I think of the other day, when she told me about the conversations they'd been having, and how her expression lit up, the hope there bubbling and almost overflowing. I think of the little boy who used to tattle on Harper and me—not to be cruel, at least not most of the

171

time, but to keep his annoying younger sister and her pain-in-the-ass best friend safe.

"I really do like her," he says again, his voice dropping to a whisper. "I have for a while, I think."

I touch his shoulder. This really is classic Harry. We're trapped on an island by a deadly force none of us know how to battle, and he's sitting here stewing about his feelings for a friend. "You're probably the only guy I know who I'd actually trust with her," I say finally.

He exhales. "Yeah? You'd be okay with it?"

"It's not really my business either way, but yes. Of course."

"Harper will flip out."

"She'll get over it. Besides, it's not any of her business, either."

"Thank you, Nell."

I smile at him. "And you know Harper and I will kill you if you ever hurt Dia, right?"

"I assumed as much," he says.

"I mean it. Slowly and painfully." I poke him on the bicep and stand.

He gestures toward the uke case. "Are you planning on serenading someone up there?"

I gulp and glance toward the shadow. "Something like that."

When I go back upstairs, it follows.

Chapter Twenty-One

I'm not sure where to lead the damned thing.

I can't take it back to my bedroom, not with Tris in there. I need a dark room, but the bathroom is *too* dark—it has no window, and a shadow needs at least a hint of light.

I stop in front of Dia's room. She's still asleep downstairs, and the sliver of moonlight peeking through her window would be perfect, but do I dare pull this thing into my friend's bedroom and risk it staying there? Even as I shiver at the thought, I know it won't. The shadow belongs to me, not Dia.

I slip into the room and open the thin curtains wider, inviting as much moonlight as possible inside. The shadow is somehow already here, writhing in the corner, waiting for me.

"It's been a little while since I saw you," I whisper, opening the ukulele case. "Two months? Maybe three?"

A breath rasps from the corner, as rough as the scrape of a cat's tongue.

"You've gotten…bigger."

The shadow stretches, filling the corner, then an entire wall. Its limbs creep along the ceiling, as thin as thread. I almost think it's showing off. Reminding me that I'm supposed to fear it, perhaps.

If that's its intention, it's working. "I'm sorry. I know I haven't played for a few nights. I meant to."

Another breath.

"Are you…part of all this? Part of what's happening on the island?" It's a question I dread asking, but I have to know. "Is this somehow my fault?"

It doesn't answer, but those thread-thin limbs writhe overhead.

I check that the uke is in tune, strumming as quietly as I can. "I suppose I owe you a few songs." My voice catches, and I swallow against the tightness in my throat. "If I make it up to you—if I promise never to skip our ritual again—will you let us go? Will you let my friends be safe?"

It tilts its head.

"Please. I can't let them get hurt or…or worse, just because of something I did. You killed someone. *Killed* them. Why? Because I didn't sing you a song for a couple of nights?" My vision blurs with tears, and I'm thankful I don't have to read music while I play. "I swear I'll keep singing for you, okay? I'll sing for you for the rest of my life. Just please make this stop."

The shadow's breath rattles like a last dying gasp.

"Just tell me what you want with me. For once just *talk*." My tone goes reedy. "*Constant.* That's what it sounded like Christopher was trying to say. Was that really you talking? I know I skipped my ritual the other night, but I thought I'd already given you what

174

you wanted, years ago. I thought that I'd done this enough, been *constant* enough, and you'd stay away for good. I thought that for a long time, until..."

It stretches a thread-thin finger toward the uke and chokes out an impatient wheeze that I think may be a warning. "Okay. Enough talking." I strum the strings and murmur-sing its favorite song while it settles back into the corner and sighs.

Years ago I talked myself into believing what my father and my therapist told me, that the shadow's visits were harmless dreams. But I'm awake, I know I am, and the shadow is here. It's real. I can see it in the corner, its spindly limbs drifting back and forth in time to the music. I can hear the rasp of its breath. It's real and it's here and I've made it angry, all because I got lazy with my ritual. The more I ponder it, the more I know that this week is my fault. A chill zips through my limbs and I struggle to hit the right chords without trembling, but I manage to finish the song, and then I play others. I play until the pads of my fingers burn, until the shadow dissolves into the darkness. I hear a last soft sigh as it disappears, and I can hardly dare to hope that I've been forgiven. Will the haze retreat now? Could this actually work? As I put the uke back in its case, I consider slipping outside and walking down to check.

"Nell?"

The sound of my name being whispered makes me jump. Tris is in the doorway, her hand on the knob, holding the door open just enough for her to peek in.

"How long have you been there?" I ask. My heartbeat rabbits, and my tone is shorter and snappier than I mean for it to be.

"That thing … that was what I saw before, wasn't it?"

I sigh and nod.

Her eyes go wide in the near-dark. "What the hell was it?"

I can't make up another story, another lie. I'm going to have to tell her at least some of what I've been hiding from her.

What I've been hiding from everyone.

Then

ONE YEAR AGO

I wish I could go." Next to the school bus, Harper pouts.

"To a chorus competition in Tallahassee?" Gavin laughs and puts an easy arm around her shoulders. "I've been there, babe. You're not missing much."

"Not because of the destination." She ducks out from under him and gives his ribs a playful poke. "Because of the company."

Nell shakes her head. "It's just a competition. It's not like it's going to be fun."

Gavin scoffs. "Are you kidding? Every minute we're not performing—"

"Mr. Anderson will have us practicing," Nell finishes for him.

"Not *every* minute," he says, his grin growing wolfish.

"Ugh, Nell," Harper says. "Keep an eye on this idiot for me, okay? Don't let him get into trouble."

"When have I ever been in trouble?" Gavin asks. He puts his hand to his chest and pretends to be shocked at the thought.

It's true, though. Trouble chases Gavin Richardson, but it never catches up. The time he got caught sneaking beer into a pep rally, or the time the school deputy found those two joints in his locker, or the time he parked in the teachers' lot and his new BMW nearly got towed—his father always charged in and blustered legalities at the principal, and Gavin remained Teflon-clean. "Whatever trouble he gets into," Nell says, "he'll get away with it."

"Damn right I will," he says, chuckling. This time that easy arm goes around Nell, making her shoulders tense.

"Time to get on the road!" Mr. Anderson makes exaggerated herding motions toward the bus. "All aboard, people!"

Nell wriggles out of Gavin's grasp and hugs Harper. "Thanks for the ride."

"Of course. Good luck! I'll miss you."

"We'll only be gone for one night." Nell pulls back and sees that Harper is looking over her shoulder at Gavin. Those words were meant for him, and Nell is the block between them. She backs away, hoping the move seems casual as a flush colors her cheeks. As Gavin swoops Harper into his arms, Nell gets on the bus and heads to the back row. The seats ahead of her fill quickly. Through the window, she sees Gavin still kissing Harper outside.

When he finally boards, the only seat left is next to Nell. She sighs as he ambles down the aisle, grinning at her.

The trip from Winter Park to Tallahassee is supposed to take four hours, but now it will feel much longer.

Chapter Twenty-Two

Tris and I go back to my room, and we sit in her nest while I tell her about the sleep paralysis I used to experience, and my ritual with the ukulele, and the shadow that I wish was just a dream.

"No wonder you write horror," she says quietly when I'm done.

I pause, swallowing as I search for the words to say what's in my head. Finally I say, "I'm sorry."

"Sorry?"

Guilt sags heavy on my shoulders. "I wouldn't have let you share my room if I thought the shadow would show up. I should have been more careful. I should have kept up with my ritual, made sure to play my uke no matter what—"

"Nell." She touches my arm. "It's not your fault."

"But I didn't do what it wanted. I disappointed it; I made it angry." I clench my jaw. "I made it come back. What if this entire week is because of me?"

She frowns. "You think the shadow is connected to the haze?"

"No. Yes." I squeeze my eyes shut. "I don't know."

"None of this is your fault."

"You don't know that."

"But I believe it. And I believe *you*. I believe everything you just told me."

I open my eyes. "No one's ever believed me before. My dad, my therapist..."

"Did anyone else ever see that thing? I sure as hell did."

I shake my head. It had always been mine alone.

"After that, how could I not believe you?" She smiles a little, but that smile fades as quickly as it appeared. "It's...not going to come back, is it?"

"It shouldn't. Not tonight. And as long as I go back to singing to it before bed, that should keep it satisfied." *I hope.* "But I understand if you want to sleep somewhere else. Or if you want me to. You can have the room and I'll—"

She links her arm around mine. "Are you kidding? You're the only one who knows how to deal with that thing. If it shows up again, I want you nearby."

I laugh a little. "I'll protect you from the shadow monster."

She leans closer, her forehead touching mine. "Promise?"

"Yeah."

"Does that mean I get to hear you sing, too?"

I sigh and pull back. "There's no avoiding that, I guess. Not tonight, though. Tomorrow." I've sung more than enough for one night.

"Tomorrow," she echoes. "So if your shadow's happy now, does that mean the haze will go away? We'll be able to get the hell out of here?"

"I don't know." I don't want to get my hopes up, but they're already fluttering. "I was thinking about walking down to check, but..." I glance out the window at the darkness. As hopeful as I might be, I'm also hesitant. It's my inbox dilemma all over again, although in hindsight, email seems like such a foolish thing to have worried about. Now, though, if I don't check for the haze just yet, it both is and isn't there, and I want to cling to the possibility of *isn't* for a little longer. I think I'll keep Schrödingering the situation, at least until the sun comes up. "Harry will notice if I leave. He'll want to know what's up. I don't want him and the others to get excited if it turns out..."

"I hear you." She lies down, resting her head on my lap, and she gives me a small grin. That grin is hopeful. It fills me with dread; I don't want to see it dashed if my shadow decides not to let us go after all. "We'll check in the morning," she says.

I give her a half-smile and stroke my hand over her hair. She's taking my explanation extraordinarily well. But I suppose she's right—after the last few days, what's left to believe in but horror stories?

"That must have been so scary for you as a kid," she says, closing her eyes. "Seeing that thing every night."

"It was terrifying. I thought it would hurt me or my dad."

"How did you figure out how to deal with it?"

I lean against the wall and tell her about being too afraid to call for my father. "I couldn't scream, but one night I managed to sing a little. I did it mainly to snap myself out of the paralysis, to make myself feel safe, but then I realized the shadow liked it." I yawn. "It liked one song in particular, so I sang that one every night."

When Tris doesn't respond, I glance down and realize she's asleep. I make myself as comfortable as I can against the wall, and I close my eyes, leaving the little lamp burning. Just for tonight.

If only I could sleep.

I do manage to nod off a few times, but it never lasts. My system still vibrates with the chemical remnants of the panic that flooded my veins as I lured the shadow away from Tris. I won't be getting much rest tonight. I sit for as long as I can stand it, and then I cradle Tris's head in my hands, gently nudging her off my lap and onto a pillow.

This time I grab the Maglite before I head back downstairs.

Harry is asleep on the couch while Dia keeps watch in the kitchen. I pause near a rear window and see Gavin still sitting on the grass near his fire, elbows resting on his knees. He stares out across the bay, and if he were anyone else, I would empathize with his lonely task and the frightened tension visible in his form. I would head outside and offer my company. For anyone else.

Not for him.

I head to the kitchen. From the doorway, I see Dia yawn, and I softly say her name so my approach won't spook her. "I can't sleep," I say. "Want me to take over until dawn?"

"Are you sure?"

I nod. "Get a little more rest."

"Thanks, Nell." She pauses in the doorway, glancing from Harry's couch back to me. I want to tell her it's all right, that I know, that I approve, not that she'd need my approval either way.

But I don't. If she wants to keep it to herself for now, I won't prevent that. She gives me a small, exhausted smile and heads upstairs.

I sit down and place the Maglite on the floor by my side.

I keep watch, but there's nothing to see. I try to guess how much longer it will be before the horizon starts to lighten. I could sneak down now, just for a peek, but I'm not sure how my sanity will take it if the haze is still there. The fingers of my left hand move against my palm, miming ukulele chords.

Then I go still as goose bumps rise on my arms.

I'm being watched. I can feel it.

I glance to my left, toward the window that opens onto the front porch.

The small black cat sits on the sill again, staring in at me.

I creep toward the window, slowly, slowly. When I go to open it, the cat jumps down. This time, though, it stays on the porch, tail twitching as it looks back over its shoulder at me. It takes a few more steps, nearly merging with the night. But it doesn't go far.

I shine the Maglite out the window. The cat's eyes flash in its beam. "Come here," I say, holding out my hand. "You don't want to be out there with that hazy stuff."

The cat doesn't come closer, but it doesn't run off. It sits and watches and waits.

Maybe I can coax it in with the leftover chicken. I place a few small pieces on the windowsill and step back. The cat takes its time, but finally it jumps back up and crouches to eat.

I try to pet it, but static snaps through my fingers as they make contact with the cat's sleek fur, and I swear I see a spark. Images flash, too—things I don't understand, things that aren't there.

A man splayed out on a beach, wearing clothes that don't make sense. Plants sprouting near piles of sun-bleached bones. A woman's hand stroking sleek black fur. A threaded needle glinting in firelight. A human face covered in dark, dripping tar, with muck flooding its screaming mouth. An empty kayak drifting down a choppy bay.

I snatch my hand back as the cat yowls and takes off, claws skittering against wood as it tears across the porch and disappears. My heart slams in my chest and my breaths come short and shallow. The visions are already fading, like strange shards of memories from half-forgotten dreams. I shut the window and stumble back to my chair, and I sit very still, trying to stop shaking, hoping I won't start seeing things again.

I stay there until dawn breaks and Harry stirs and staggers in to make coffee. "Nell? Where's Dia?"

"She was tired. I relieved her."

"Ah." He turns on the coffee maker. "See anything?"

I pause. Then, because I don't know how to explain what I saw, I shake my head. "No. Nothing."

Chapter Twenty-Three

WEDNESDAY, APRIL 22

I'm almost too antsy to stay in one place any longer, but I can't face checking on the haze alone, so I sip coffee in the kitchen with Harry and Dia while I wait for Tris to come downstairs. When she appears, I see the same gleam of wild hope in her eyes that I feel in my heart. She cocks her head toward me in a question, and I answer with a small nod. "Tris and I are going to take her truck down to check the haze," I say, keeping my tone light but also final. I don't want the others to invite themselves along. Not this time.

We drive south, Tris going a little slower than necessary, like she wants to stretch out her hope just a little while longer, too. My anticipation turns to nausea as I watch the road ahead, waiting for the haze to come into view...or to be gone.

Please, please be gone.

By the time we spot Harry's SUV, I'm light-headed. I've never been so completely and entirely sure of two conflicting possibilities at the same time before, and the contradiction throbs in my temples. We draw closer, and I nearly convince myself that my singing worked, that we'll all be okay.

Then the haze comes into view. It lurks not far south of the SUV, which means it's nearly halfway up the island. The next landmark it will hit is the security light, then the pines to the south of the house. Then the house itself, and the banyan at the island's northern tip, and then...us.

"Damn it," Tris whispers, braking.

Mechanically, I get out of the truck and into the still, soupy morning air, ignoring Tris when she calls out to ask where I'm going. I have to feel the haze, smell it. Show myself that it's really still there.

I have to prove to myself how thoroughly and utterly I've failed.

I only make it a couple of steps before that acrid odor hits me and I go numb and drop to my knees. It's like my bones are gone, and my muscles. I'm only air, and then I deflate. I have nothing left.

"Hey!" Tris is right there, kneeling on the dirt road, her arms around me. "Hey."

"I thought it would work," I murmur, staring into the haze. "I'm so sorry. I really thought..."

"We don't know this is because of your shadow," she says.

"What else could it be?" I turn and press my face against her shoulder. "You saw that thing. It's a monster. I didn't give it what it wanted, and now it won't let any of us go."

"Maybe it'll just take more time," Tris says, her voice hinged with doubt. "If you keep up with the singing—"

I look south. "Time? How much time do you think we have left?"

"I don't know," she says quietly. "Come on." She stands, gently tugging me up beside her. "Let's go back." My disappointment is bitter on my tongue, but Tris is right—maybe it'll just take a little more time to appease the shadow.

I have to keep trying.

When we get back to the house, Harper has joined Harry and Dia in the kitchen. The three of them watch us with wide eyes, waiting for an update.

"It's closer," Tris says, and three sets of shoulders sag.

"How close?" Harry asks after a moment. "Has it reached the SUV yet?"

"No, but it probably will by tonight."

Dia gives a slow nod and drifts to the living room. She picks up her embroidery project and starts to stitch, as if focusing on fabric and thread is enough to let her escape, at least for a little while. When her tense grip dislodges the wooden hoop, she tosses it aside and stitches on the loose fabric instead.

Tris squeezes my hand and pours herself some coffee.

As the sun climbs higher in the sky, I glance out back and see Gavin still standing by his fire.

"He knows he doesn't need to keep that thing going all day, right?" Harry asks, joining me to glower out the window. "If he's so hell-bent on having a fire, he should conserve the wood for after dark."

"He needs to feel like he's doing something," Harper says from the kitchen table, her fingers wrapped around a mug. "Plus, like he said, if he runs out of wood, he can chop down a tree or something."

At the breakfast bar, Tris pinches the bridge of her nose and sighs.

"Yeah, and he'll probably make it fall right on the roof," I mutter, bristling as my disappointment sharpens at the corners, edging into frustration.

Harper puts down her mug a little too hard, sloshing coffee onto the table. "Why do you always have to be such a bitch about my boyfriend?"

The insult feels as jagged as a shard of glass, especially coming from my best friend, and I almost recoil at the sudden, stabbing pain of it. Trying not to let the injury show, I say, "I just think the fire is a ridiculous idea. He's going to burn something down or get someone hurt."

"No he's not. He goes camping all the time; he knows his way around building fires." Her gaze hardens. "What's your problem, Nell?"

"I don't have a problem."

"Obviously that's not true. You've never liked Gavin. What did he ever do to you?"

My throat constricts around answers I won't—can't—offer.

"Seriously, just give him a break," she goes on. "I don't care why you don't like him, but his best friend just died, and he's trying to figure out a way to save us. *Give him a break.*"

"People like Gavin get plenty of breaks," I say quietly.

Harper's jaw tightens as she works up a retort, but then she bites it back. "I'm going out to watch the fire for a while. So Gavin can rest." She whips past us and out the back door.

Harry snorts and gives the backyard one last glare before turning away.

"I think we're all a little moody today," Tris says quietly, one side of her mouth quirking upward slightly. "Can't imagine why."

"Yeah." I try to sip my coffee, but its bitter heat no longer appeals, and the mug trembles in my hands.

"You weren't wrong, though," Tris says. "About guys like Gavin."

I can't keep dwelling on the topic. "So what's next on the checklist? I need something else to think about. What other prep should we be doing?"

"I wish I knew." She stares into her mug. "I know you're no fan of Gavin, but I understand what Harper said about him needing to feel like he's doing something."

I get it, too, especially when I think of my uke upstairs in its case.

Tris starts listing some of the other things she learned from the Hunker Down program. Most of what's left are things like sourcing sandbags for flooding and plywood for boarding up windows and doors—tasks we'd have to leave the island to do, and that wouldn't do any good against the haze—but we brainstorm anyway because at least it keeps our minds busy, at least until we're interrupted by the sound of yelling from outside.

"Oh, what now?" Harry snaps, charging out the back door as Dia gets up from the couch to look. Through the window I see Gavin and Harper arguing near the signal fire. She gestures fiercely toward the house. He shakes his head and yells in her face. I can't hear what they're saying, but the rage in his expression, the coldness of it despite the heat of the sun and the fire, locks my lungs. When he grabs her wrist, some instinct zaps to life in my brain, as sharp and clanging as an ambulance siren. There's danger here.

I run outside, crossing the yard only a few steps behind Harry. "*Harper!*" I scream, and my voice startles Gavin into letting her go. I try to dart in front of her, to block her from the worst of his flaring temper, but she pushes me away, sending me sprawling onto the grass. She's not interested in being protected.

Harry puts himself between the two of them, glaring at Gavin even as Harper shoves at her brother, trying to move him out of the way.

"Stay out of it!" Gavin yells at Harry, hands clenched.

"Keep your hands off my sister!" Harry yells back.

Gavin's eyes blaze with fresh anger. "Are you telling me what to do?" he demands incredulously, as if being ordered around isn't something he's used to.

Harry hesitates, just for a second, and I can see him weighing the possibility of this becoming a physical fight. Then he squares his shoulders. "Yeah, I am!"

"Fuck this," Gavin mutters, trying to get around Harry to get to Harper. "Come here," he says to her, like he's ordering a dog to heel.

Harry pushes Gavin backward.

Gavin swings his fist.

Harry ducks and grabs for the collar of Gavin's shirt.

Gavin yanks away, the ferocity of the move knocking both of them off-balance.

Harper screams and grabs Gavin's arm, steadying him.

Harry stumbles toward the fire and falls.

Chapter Twenty-Four

Harry manages to fling himself clear of the fire, but the move sends him sprawling against the jagged stones around its perimeter. One slices long and deep into the flesh of his right calf, drawing an alarming spurt of blood. His face is pale, his teeth bared in a pained grimace.

Harper falls to her knees next to him. She presses her palms to her temples, her fingers tangling and yanking at her hair. Gavin stands over them both, eyes wide, nostrils flaring with panic. The three of them almost look frozen, posed like models for a Renaissance painting.

This is no time for freezing.

I know very little about how to treat anything worse than a sunburn, but someone needs to take charge. "Put pressure on his leg," I bark, and Gavin and Harper jerk back to life. Harper screams at Gavin for his shirt; when he yanks it off, she snatches it from his hands, balling it up and pressing it to Harry's shin.

The laceration is dirty, caked with smears of soil and ash from Harry's fall. "It needs to be irrigated," Tris calls, reaching us. She has the fire extinguisher with her, and she gets to work putting out Gavin's fire.

I nod. "Let's get him inside." Harper, Gavin, and I manage to carry Harry across the yard and up the back steps. He groans, his eyes wide and rolling, his face going even more ashen as his blood soaks Gavin's shirt. "Harry," I gasp. "Focus. Stay with us."

Dia waits in the doorway. Her face has gone gray, but her ghostlike drifting is gone, replaced by intense focus.

"We need to clean the wound," I say, but she's already on it. She orders us to the kitchen, where she drags a pair of chairs next to the sink for Harry. We sit him down in one and prop his injured leg on the other, and Dia uses the sprayer from the sink to irrigate the gash, sending a flood of blood-tinged water sluicing across the tile floor.

Eyes glassy, Harry hisses through clenched teeth as Dia focuses the flow deep into the laceration. "I'm sorry," she says, not relenting as he writhes against waves of fresh pain. "I'm so sorry. We have to make sure it's clean. I'm so sorry." She looks up as Tris hurries in, still holding the extinguisher. "First aid kit?"

"Under the sink," Tris says. "I'm not sure there's much in it, though."

"I have some stuff." I run upstairs and grab my enormous toiletry bag. Gauze, tape, antibacterial ointment—I've got it all, and after this, maybe I won't have to put up with any more teasing about being the mom friend, prepared for anything.

When I return, Dia is inspecting the laceration. "It looks clean," she says, her tone doubtful. She doesn't know what she's doing, really. None of us do. She presses a fresh cloth against it, trying to slow the bleeding.

"It's not stopping," Harper says, her tone weak and afraid. "He's losing a lot of blood."

"He needs stitches," Tris says. "This is dial-911 territory."

But we can't do that, so I look at Dia, the best stitcher we have. "Can you?"

Her face pales again, but she nods. "I think so."

"Keep applying pressure," I say. "I'll get what you need." Dia's project bag is on the couch, but her embroidery needles are on the blunt side, certainly not meant for skin. I go upstairs again and find my travel sewing kit. I also stop by the laundry closet for the jug of bleach—the only way I can think of to sterilize the thread.

Dia puts her hand out for the needle. "Embroidery," she whispers through clenched teeth, squeezing her eyes shut for a moment. "It's like embroidery." She focuses, breathes, and begins to work, easing the edges of the gash together with each careful stitch. Harry whimpers, his eyes squeezed tightly shut.

I look at Gavin, who hangs back near the entrance to the kitchen. "Where's your flask?" I demand.

"What?" He blinks at me.

"You had a flask the other day. I saw it. Harry needs whatever's in there."

"I— It's in my car," he stammers. "It's gone."

I glower at him and turn back to Harry as Dia finishes closing the wound. I hand her gauze and medical tape, and she wraps his leg. He's still pale and shaking, but at least the bleeding has stopped. We help him stagger to the couch, where he collapses while Dia arranges pillows for his shin. "You'll be okay," she says, and I think she's trying to reassure herself as much as him.

I squeeze her shoulder and look at Harry. "How's the pain?"

"Not great," he says through gritted teeth.

"I have ibuprofen." It's a blood thinner, just like whatever might have been in Gavin's flask, but we've mostly stopped the bleeding and I keep thinking about how bad things might get if Harry goes deeper into shock from the pain and we can't bring him back. I get the pills and some water, and we help him sit up enough to swallow.

"We'll watch for signs of infection," Tris says, and we all nod, but we don't point out the obvious—that there's not much we can do about an infection if we spot one. Tris ducks outside and returns with a handful of herbs from her planter. "I'm making him a tea," she says, muddling leaves in a large mug and putting water on to boil. "Rosemary and oregano for inflammation and pain relief. And chamomile to help him stay calm." When the kettle whistles, she fills the mug, letting the leaves steep. "It'll be ready in a few minutes."

"How do you know all that?" I ask. "Is it like when the pine trees tell you which branches to prune?"

Her jaw is tight, but one corner of her mouth quirks upward, just a little. "No. My grandma taught me."

Dia stalks into the kitchen and starts rage-cleaning the mess. When Harper and Gavin follow, she whirls on them. "What the *fuck* happened out there?" she snaps. "What did you do to him?"

"Don't you pin this on me," Gavin says. "He got in my face—"

"Because you were getting in Harper's face," I say. "What the hell was that about?"

"It was nothing," Harper says quickly, her face pale. "It was just a fight. It was stupid."

I shake my head at Harper. "Yeah. Okay. And then you saved *his* ass"—I jab a finger in Gavin's direction—"and let your brother fall."

"Bullshit," Gavin mutters.

Harper stares at me. Her chin wobbles, but her gaze is white-hot fury. I'm sure she's going to argue—I can practically see the words bubble up in her throat—but then she leaves the kitchen and shuts herself in the master bedroom, slamming the door behind her.

Gavin huffs like he's disgusted with all of us. "Whatever," he says, heading toward the back door. "I'm getting back to work."

Tris blocks him. "No way. No more fires in the yard. Too dangerous."

Gavin's eyes flash. "Fuck that. I'm not just going to sit around and wait for whatever's going on out there to come get me."

"And for once, your daddy can't come rescue you," I say, the words tumbling out before I can catch them.

He takes a step toward me, then sneers and heads back outside. "Fine, no fires in the yard," he yells over his shoulder. "I've got a better idea anyway."

"Oh God." Tris rubs her eyes. "Now what?"

"Maybe he'll try to swim for it after all," I mutter, joining Dia in her cleaning. I wring out the cloth she used earlier to slow the bleeding, and for the first time I notice what it is. A half-finished quote—*the rest*—is embroidered on it in her neat, patient stitches.

She sees me looking. "It's supposed to say, 'the rest is history,'" she says quietly. "It's for him. Or it was supposed to be. I was hold-ing it. I couldn't think of anything…It was there."

"He'll be all right," I say. "We all will."

She takes the ruined embroidery from me and looks at Tris. "You said you were making him some kind of tea? Is it ready?"

Tris is spooning out the leaves. "Yeah. It won't do much, I don't think, but it's something." She hands Dia the mug, and the three of us go back to the living room.

Harry's eyes are closed. When Dia says his name, he doesn't respond. He's so still, and at first I'm not sure if I can see him breathing. "Oh God." Nausea surges through my stomach.

Tris presses fingers to his neck, checking for a pulse. Her shoulders sag in relief when she finds one.

"Maybe he passed out from shock," I say, as the sick feeling settles just a little. "Or could he have hit his head when he fell?"

Dia puts the mug on the coffee table and combs shaking fingers through Harry's hair, searching for blood or knots or any sign of a head wound. "It doesn't seem like it." She glances back at the mug, eyes shining a little too brightly with tears she tries to blink away. "I'll make sure he drinks that when he comes to," she says, her voice thin and tense. "And I'll finish cleaning up the kitchen."

I get the message. She needs to be alone. "Banyan?" I ask Tris. She nods, and we head out together.

• • •

"So that was...something," Tris says once we've settled on our branch. She sounds overwhelmed, almost hollow, like she's trying to stay detached from what just happened.

I understand the feeling. I'm still trying to catch my breath from that horrible second when I thought Harry was dead.

"Do you think he'll be okay?" I ask.

Tris is quiet for a moment. "It's weird that he passed out like that, but I think so. I hope so. I don't know if we cleaned the gash out well enough. It was a mess. I wish we could have rinsed it with something stronger than water. If we'd had vodka or something..."

I nod, thinking again about the lost flask.

She stares out across the inlet and smiles a little. "Figures. Y'all are the only sober spring breakers in history."

"That's Harry's doing."

"Somehow I'm not surprised." She glances at me. "He's lucky you had all that first aid stuff. I've been meaning to check the kit between guests, but it kept slipping my mind."

"I like to be prepared." I explain how I've earned the reputation of mom friend.

"So you're the mom and Harry's the dad?"

I chuckle. "Pretty much, yeah, but what that insinuates is never going to happen."

"I would hope not," she says.

My face grows warm. I keep my eyes on the inlet.

"You know what?" she says. "This isn't the time. I'm not thinking straight. I'll stop."

"I really wish you wouldn't," I say quickly, because I so badly need the distraction.

She pauses. "I just meant that it would hurt my chances if you and he got together."

"Your chances with Harry?" I tease, deflecting.

"I think Dia might not appreciate that," she says. "But no, not with Harry. You know he's not my type."

I don't answer. The words aren't there. Instead, I nudge my hand closer to hers. Carefully. Hesitantly. A move as terrifying as it is small.

Her hand finds mine, our fingers twining together. My pulse rabbits in surprise, then calms because her touch feels so right.

"Once we get out of here," she says, "I'm asking you out. On a date. Fair warning."

"Fair warning back," I say, a little shocked by how easy it is to speak to her like this. "I'm saying yes."

"You'd better."

I close my eyes as the breeze picks up, tickling my hair around my shoulders. "You really want to go out with me? Even though you know my shadowy little secret?"

"That thing is not invited on our date."

I laugh.

We go quiet and still for a while, listening to the lull of the waves. A gull lands near the edge of the inlet, poking around the sand before the breeze startles it into taking wing again. There's still life beyond Straight Shot, then. There are other things out there beyond just us. "Should we go back?" I ask eventually.

"Nah," Tris says. "Not just yet."

I tilt my face up toward hers so she can kiss me. She does.

In the distance, we hear the sharp thwack of metal against wood.

"What was that?" I ask.

"I think your friend's jackass boyfriend is messing with my trees." Tris jumps down. "Come on. Let's go see."

Then

I wish they'd gotten us a charter bus." Gavin wriggles against the brown vinyl seat, getting comfortable as the bus pulls away from Winter Park West.

Nell presses herself a little closer to the window, trying to be subtle about it. "Why? This is fine."

"Sitting on a school bus for four hours sucks. If we were going to a swim meet, the school would've gotten us a nicer bus."

"That's sports. This is chorus. Sports teams always have it nicer."

Gavin scoffs. "If we do more of these competitions, I'll get my dad to donate a charter rental."

"I'm sure you will." Nell sighs and stares out the window, hoping for quiet.

Gavin doesn't catch the hint. Or perhaps he ignores it. "Can you believe Anderson's making us sing 'The Winner Takes It All' as part of our competition performance? What is it with that guy and ABBA?"

"I guess he's just really a fan."

"I guess. Hey, how's your English paper going? You're doing it on Romantic poets, right?"

Nell frowns at the thought of four hours of this kind of numbing small talk. "Haven't started it."

"I think I'm going to focus on the birth of horror. Frankenstein and Mary Shelley and all that." He looks at her as if he's eager for her approval.

She nods, hoping the lack of response will clue him in.

It seems to. He goes silent for a few precious minutes. Then he says, "Hey, Nell? I know we've never really gotten along."

This surprises her. She turns toward him, her brow furrowed. She doesn't know what to say, so she waits for him to continue.

"I just..." He tightens his jaw. "Did I do something wrong?"

You wheedled your way into my circle of friends. You caught my best friend's attention. You asked her out and now all she talks about is you. All she wants to do is spend time with you. You changed things.

It wouldn't be a fair response. She realizes that. Things with Harper were changing long before Gavin moved to Winter Park, but it hurts too much to be angry with Harper. Being angry with Gavin is easier to tolerate. Besides, there's still something off about him. Nell has felt it ever since that morning before chorus practice. She can't define it or describe it, but there's something about him that she doesn't like.

But she can't find the words to say so. Besides, she was raised to be polite, and the pull toward that is still strong. So what if Gavin makes her skin crawl in some confusing way? She remembers being little and having her father try to reason with her about the shadow. *You're being irrational, honey. Don't you see?* How is her baseless dislike of Gavin any less irrational?

Nell handled the shadow on her own. She made peace with it. She can handle Gavin, too, she decides.

"No. You never did anything. I'm sorry I made you feel that way."

I'm sorry.

The apology echoes in her head, feeling wrong, feeling undeserved. She ignores that echo and smiles at Gavin.

He smiles back.

Chapter Twenty-Five

We find Gavin smashing the blade of Tris's axe into the trunk of one of her pine trees.

"What the hell?" Tris yells.

"She told you the trees were off-limits!" I stride toward Gavin, ready to snatch the axe away. When he turns toward me, though, determined rage wilding his eyes, I stop short. His stare is sharp and detached, a challenge that pings an echo hidden deep in my brain.

Tris sees it, too. She grabs my arm and pulls me back. "It's not worth it." To Gavin, she says, "Why do you need the tree?"

"Fuel," he mutters, still watching us like he's braced for attack.

"What, like firewood?" Tris says. "I already told you—no more fires in the yard."

"It won't be in the yard." Without taking his eyes off us, he points behind him, toward the dock. I follow the gesture and see that he's carried armloads of firewood out to the raised platform.

"What's wrong with you?" I say as Tris's hand tightens around my arm. "You can't burn down the fucking dock!"

"It'll be more visible from the mainland," he says. "Someone will see. Someone will get me the fuck off this island."

"You won't have much luck with that wood," Tris says. "It needs to dry out."

"Wet wood makes more smoke," Gavin says, and then he repeats, "Someone will see."

"You can't just—" I start, but Tris pulls my arm again. When I turn to look at her, she raises her brows and nods her head toward the porch. She leads and I follow. Gavin goes back to taking down the tree.

"Let him do it," she says once we're out of earshot.

"Let him burn down the dock?"

"It'll keep him busy out there. If he actually gets a fire going and it gets far enough down the dock, we'll hose down the shore so it can't spread."

"I'm surprised you're okay with this."

"Docks can be rebuilt," she says. "I don't want him near us. Near you. The way he looked at you just now…" She goes quiet, setting her jaw in a way that looks painful.

I nod and we go inside. On the couch, Harry's eyes are still closed. He hasn't moved. The tea appears untouched.

The kitchen is clean. Dia is filling the sink to soak the embroidery fabric. "I know the stains won't come out," she says when she sees us. "But I have to try."

"How's Harry?" I ask. "He hasn't woken up?"

She glances toward the living room. Beyond the couch, the

door to Harper's room is still closed. "No. He's been out cold this whole time."

"And you? Are you okay?"

She looks at me, then goes back to rinsing the fabric.

•   •   •

At dusk, Tris and I volunteer to check the haze again. This time I'm not sick with hope and anticipation; I already know exactly what we'll find, and I'm not wrong. The stuff has begun to devour Harry's SUV. We don't get too close, but I can see a sheen of tar forming on the vehicle's windshield. The sour smell of it carries sharp and bitter through the unsettlingly still air, seeping into the truck's open windows.

"Why isn't there any wind here?" Tris says, her hand wrapping around my elbow. Near the house, the breeze still rolls in from the ocean, all salt and mineral. Here, less than a mile away, nothing moves. Saw palmettos and patches of beach grass sit as still as photographs, waiting to be shrouded in haze and swamped by tar.

I don't have an answer for her, but the stillness wraps me in dread. "Let's go back," I whisper.

Gavin is still outside when we return. He chops relentlessly in the fading light. Not long after Tris and I go inside, we hear the creak and crash of the pine coming down. Tris winces and mutters something about it not falling onto the roof, at least. Then the chopping starts again as he breaks down the tree into more portable pieces. He works until it's too dark to see.

"Making progress," he announces when he comes inside.

Tris, Dia, and I are in the kitchen. The sound of Gavin's voice brings Harper out from the bedroom. Gavin's shirt is plastered to his torso with sweat, and his eyes are sunken from heat and dehydration. "I'll take down one more tree tomorrow. That should be enough." He grabs a glass of water and chugs it.

"One more tree for what?" Harper asks, and Gavin explains his plan. "You really think anyone will see it?" she asks when he's done.

He raises his chin. "Yeah. I do. It'll be huge. Someone has to see. The other side of the bay isn't that far."

That's what Christopher thought, too. I'm not cruel enough to say it out loud.

"What if you hurt yourself out there?" Harper asks. "It's bad enough that Harry got hurt. If you—"

He catches her hands in his. "I'm getting off this island. I'm getting us both the hell off, babe." He glances at Tris. "I'm going to need all the lighter fluid in the house. And the gas from your truck, I think. It's not like we can drive anywhere anyway."

"Jesus." Tris puts a hand over her eyes.

"Gavin." Harper's voice grows more panicked. "You can't keep going out to the platform. It's not safe."

Gavin points at Tris and me. "They hung a sign out there and they're fine."

I almost want to tell him what I saw under the dock, but I don't.

"But Christopher—" Harper says.

Gavin's eyes darken. "Don't bring up Christopher."

"I'm sorry." Harper's voice wobbles. "But this isn't a good idea. It's dangerous. Just don't, okay? Please don't."

Gavin's expression blanks. It's like watching him put on a

mask. No. It's like watching his mask come *off*. "Don't tell me what to do, Harper."

"I'm not." She winces, and I realize it's because of how tightly he's squeezing her fingers, the force of his grip raising the tendons on the backs of his hands. I want to speak up, but that tiny, unexplainable echo of fear pings in my brain again, freezing me in place.

"People don't tell me what to do," Gavin says quietly.

Harper's voice drops. "I know. I wasn't. I'm just scared."

He lets go of her hands, but the unsettling blankness in his expression remains. "Damn it," he mutters. "I'm going to take a shower while we still have water." He stalks upstairs.

Trembling, Harper rubs her hands together like she's trying to return feeling to her fingers. I assume she's still angry with me, but our friendship used to be stronger than anger. Maybe it still is. When I put an arm around her shoulders, she doesn't pull away. "You okay?" I ask.

"He's not himself." She shuts her eyes. "The way he's acting… What if the fire gets away from him? What if he ends up in the bay? Like Christopher…" She presses her face against my shirt.

Dia wraps her arms around both of us. "He's tired," she says. "He's scared. We all are."

We stand there, the three of us pressed together like a single pillar while Harper weeps. Tris hovers nearby but doesn't join us. I would welcome her, but I understand.

"None of us are ourselves right now," I say, my face against Harper's hair. The scent of her shampoo knocks an old memory loose, of a time I slept over at her house and used her fancy shampoo the next morning. "Hey, what if we girls hang out for a while

206

tonight and try to relax? Slumber party in the master bedroom. What do you think? Like the old days?"

Harper pulls back and meets my eyes, and the rage from earlier is gone. "Are you kidding?"

"Not at all."

She smiles a little. There's doubt and disbelief in that smile, because what's more ridiculous than a nostalgic slumber party at a time like this? But there's also hope. "Like the old days," she repeats. "Sometimes I really miss when we were kids and we'd raid Harry's movie collection and stay up all night."

"Remember how mad he'd get when we'd screw up the order of his Blu-ray shelves?"

She sniffles and laughs a little.

A sleepover. It's an absurd notion, but it's all we have.

"I'll get you the blankets from upstairs," Tris says.

"You're invited, too, you know," I tell her.

She looks at Harper, then back at me. "Are you sure?"

Harper speaks before I can. "Of course we are."

Chapter Twenty-Six

It's a ludicrous idea, a slumber party in our situation.

It's also heaven.

We raid our food supply, grabbing Cheetos and Pringles and Oreos and cans of Coke that we'd meant to save and ration. What's the point in having weeks' worth of food when the haze is getting closer? Tris and I cart the blankets downstairs, and I grab a Sephora bag I've been hiding all week.

I also grab my uke case. After all, I have a promise to keep tonight.

Harper, Dia, Tris, and I settle on the floor of the master bedroom, nested in comforting piles of blankets and pillows, snacks piled within easy reach. "Should we keep watch tonight?" Harper asks in between Oreos.

I shrug. "I don't think we need to do that anymore. We know how fast that stuff is moving." It's odd, talking about the haze with such nonchalance, but it's also almost soothing. We can disregard the situation, at least for a few hours. For a little while we can be okay.

Apparently I'm not the only one who feels that way. "Agreed," Dia says, and Tris nods.

I look at Harper. "Remember the first time you slept over at my place? Or the first time you attempted to?"

She sighs, the corners of her mouth twitching upward in wry amusement. "I'm never going to live that down, am I? I was six! I'd never stayed away from my mom for a whole night before."

I turn to Tris. "She made it to ten o'clock. Then she wouldn't stop crying until my dad and I drove her home."

Tris laughs. "I can top that. The first time I slept over at my best friend's house, I got so nervous that I threw up on her bedroom carpet."

We tell more stories. Giggle over more memories. Dia talks about her first day at middle school after she moved to Winter Park. "Harper, you and I were friends right away, remember? We were wearing the same shoes—"

"Pink Chucks," Harper says. "I miss those things."

"But you were half of a set," Dia says. "You and Nell were already besties, and Nell, I'm sorry, but you were intimidating as hell."

Tris's mouth hangs open. "Nell? Intimidating?"

I've heard this before. "I wasn't scary. I was just quiet."

"Sometimes it's hard to tell the difference between quiet and angry," Dia says. "I felt like I was intruding on your friendship."

"You *can* be just a little bit possessive," Harper tells me.

I roll my eyes.

"But then I pulled that old Stephen King paperback out of my backpack," Dia goes on, "and boom, you wouldn't shut up."

"Friends ever since." I laugh.

"We bonded over horror. And you gave me a copy of that zine you used to make," Dia says. "It was so good. I miss it."

I glance at Harper. Her face pinks a little. "I miss it sometimes, too," she says, and I'm surprised.

"Do you ever draw anymore?" I ask her. "You were incredibly talented."

She grimaces. "Only the doodles I do out of boredom when Stupid Charlie makes me work. Other than that, it's been ages."

"I hope you get back to it."

"I do, too." She gives me a small smile. "I even brought a sketchbook with me this week, just in case."

We go a little quiet after that, mourning the week we were supposed to have—idle days languid with the peace of reading or sketching or embroidering or doing absolutely nothing. But we can still have a taste of that tonight, no matter what comes next. I force a smile and pull the Sephora bag from where I'd stashed it. "What kind of sleepover would this be without face masks?"

My friends' expressions brighten. "You really do think of everything," Harper says as I pass her the bag.

"That's what a good mom does, right?" I tease.

The masks distract us. We laugh at one another, our faces covered in pearlescent green goop or sheet masks as ghastly pale as the costumed villain from a slasher movie. We take selfies that we can't share without Wi-Fi or cell service. I notice as Dia opens and then quickly closes Snapchat. It's so easy to forget.

I encourage Harper to find her sketchbook. Dia has her embroidery bag with her, along with enough supplies to start a new project. Tris gives me a small, contented smile and nibbles on Pringles.

I get out my uke.

Dia's mouth falls open. "You've never played for us before."

"Yeah, well, don't expect too much." I fiddle with the pegs, fixing a flatness in the C string. "I like to play it at night. It's kind of a ritual." I glance at Tris. I know she'll understand why I need to do this. I also know she won't tell my secret.

She nods.

I don't start with the shadow's favorite. I choose lighthearted tunes, sweet modern love songs, lazy ballads that make me think of the breeze rolling in from the ocean. For the next hour, I sing for my friends while Harper draws and Dia embroiders and Tris listens with her eyes softly closed.

I end with the song I hope will keep us all safe tonight. I lose myself in the familiar chords, strumming dreamily, letting my body gently sway with the rhythm. Wherever my shadow is lurking, I know it will hear me. I hope it will accept my offering and consider letting us go. I finish the song, lingering on the final chords, and then I put the uke away.

When I glance up, my friends are all looking at me.

"That song," Harper says quietly. "My mom's old favorite."

"You taught it to me on the day we first met. In kindergarten."

She nods. "I remember that day. I didn't know you still remembered the song."

"I could never forget it." Eager to tilt the group's focus elsewhere, I point at her sketchbook. "What are you drawing?"

Her face flushes. "I don't know if I should show you. It's kind of dark. Like the stuff I used to draw for the zine."

"I'd really like to see," I say.

Her lips form a thin line. "It's from a dream I had last night.

I don't remember anything about the dream except for this... thing."

I know what I'm going to see before she turns the sketchbook. When she does, holding it up with her new drawing on display, a felt-tip version of my friend the shadow stares at me from a darkened corner. Its thread-thin arms, rendered in narrow scratches of black ink, stretch out as if it might pull me onto the page with it. The inquisitive tilt of its head is dead-on; Harper rendered it perfectly.

She's seen my shadow.

I hear Tris gasp.

"See, I shouldn't have shown you." Harper quickly turns the page. "It's too dark."

"No, it's just...really good," I stammer, struggling to keep a tremor out of my voice as the mood in the room shifts, growing heavy.

"Really creepy," Dia murmurs, her embroidery needle going still in frozen hands. "Is that a common dream? Seeing a shadow like that?"

"From what I understand, they're usually connected to sleep paralysis," I say. "Like a hallucination. A lot of people have similar experiences." It's the closest I can come to telling them the truth.

Dia slowly turns her embroidery hoop. Her new design is vague and loose, like she's sketching in thread. My shadow stares out from the fabric, creeping down a bare-bones illustration of the living room staircase. "I dreamed about it last night, too." She frowns a little, like the memory doesn't quite add up.

"It's probably a stress thing," I say quickly, very aware that Tris is staring at me.

Harper frowns. "Yeah, but both of us having the same dream on the same night?"

"Anxiety can do strange stuff." My words sound hollow. It feels like there's suddenly less air in the room. Our moods shift in tandem, snatching away our shared ability to pretend tonight really is just a slumber party.

Dia's gaze turns distant, almost disoriented. "I should check on Harry," she says, getting up.

Harper stands, too. "I'm going to make sure Gavin's okay."

The sound of his name makes my throat constrict. I look up at her. "After how he acted before?"

She sighs, sounding exhausted. "Can we not do this again, Nell?"

"He was hurting you," I say. I don't want her to leave this space, this temporary refuge the four of us created, especially not for Gavin's sake.

She stares down at her hands, like she's reliving the pinching tightness of his grip. Then she holds them up. "I'm fine. See?" She wiggles her fingers to prove her point.

"He didn't have to act like that, though," I say. "You were just worried about him."

She hesitates for a moment, but then she heads toward the door, and I feel something between us falter. "I know he's being weird," she says on her way, "but that's not him. Not really. It's this island. I just want to know that he's all right. Then I'll come back and draw us something happier, okay?"

"What the hell?" Tris hisses as soon as they're gone. "They're seeing that shadow thing, too?"

"I had no idea." I keep my voice low and scoot closer. "They've never mentioned anything about it before."

"Are you going to tell them?"

"I don't know. Not yet. Do you think it makes a difference? That it means something?"

"It's too weird not to."

"Let me think about it for a little while," I say. "I'll figure out what to tell them tomorrow. It shouldn't come around tonight, not after I sang for it."

"Are you sure?"

I nod, although I'm not sure about anything anymore.

Harper returns a few minutes later. "Dia will be back soon," she says. "She's grabbing some books for Harry, so he'll have something to do if—*when*—he wakes up."

"How's Gavin?" Tris asks.

Harper shrugs. "I got to his door, and I was about to knock … and then I just didn't. He has to be exhausted, so I didn't want to wake him up. He'll be fine tomorrow." She says this like she's trying to convince herself, and she sits and picks up her sketchbook again as Dia comes back in.

The sketch Harper does this time is a cartoony drawing of the four of us. She and I are in the middle; she's dressed in her warm-up sweats from track, and I'm holding a copy of *Here in the Shadows*. Tris is to my other side, holding a hammer. Dia is next to Harper, embroidery hoop in her hands. We're all smiling. It's a perfect caricature of four carefree friends.

It couldn't be further from the truth.

Finally we settle down and try to sleep. I doubt I'll get much rest despite the soothing presence of my friends, but I drift for a while. When I open my eyes again, the room is dark and silent and there's a vague shape in the window. I freeze, adrenaline tingling lightning-fast through my limbs, until I recognize the small black cat sitting on the outside sill.

The cat. I'm drawn to it even as I recoil at the memory of soft fur and crackling sparks. I want to approach it. I want to shoo it away. I want to open the window. I want to close the curtains.

Before I can do anything, before I can shake off my shocked inertia, the cat sits up on its haunches and places its front paws against the window, yellow eyes flashing as it stares in at me. Four additional forms appear behind it, human-shaped but barely visible, as vague as dreams.

The voice I hear doesn't come from outside. It echoes in my head like an unearthed memory.

It has begun; what's done is done.

You are not the first, poor darlings. Nor will you be the last.

There is no justice without sacrifice.

No matter how costly, no matter how dear, we all pay our debts in the end.

The figures fade into the night, but the cat stays a moment longer, cocking its head curiously. It turns away, then glances back, and I find myself standing, moving, creeping out of the bedroom, past Harry's too-still form on the living room couch, right out the front door.

The porch is gone, and although the night looked calm and quiet from inside, now I'm standing on a storm-battered beach. Gusts of wind pummel me, threatening to shove me sprawling onto the shoreline, bending the tall crowns of palm trees to their will. Rain pelts my skin, each drop keen and so needle-sharp that I'm amazed I'm not bleeding. The wind picks up bursts of sand in miniature cyclones, slamming against me until my eyes are gritty and I have to blink against pain to clear my vision. In front of me, the ocean roars like a whitecapped demon.

A shattering creak from behind me announces the fall of a nearby tree, the grinding scream giving me just enough warning to jump out of the way before the trunk crashes onto the sand. I fall to my knees as the wind carries a large sign through the air, lifting it like it's a sheet of scrap paper and not a slab of wood. I recognize the sign; we passed it when we arrived on the island. Five days ago I cracked a joke about it, and now it's spiraling over my head, a lethal projectile spinning like a propeller through the storm.

The wind finally sets it free, sending it hurtling to the ground, where it splinters into pieces. I crawl toward it through the rain, and I realize it's not the Straight Shot sign at all. I grab the broken sections, piecing them back together like a puzzle.

THE ISLAND OF NO STORMS. It's the sign from above the kitchen doorway, the one Tris's superstitious father insists on keeping.

I hear a sucking inhale, like a gaping maw gasping for breath, and I look out to see that the ocean is vanishing. No, not vanishing, not entirely. Pulling back. It retreats, exposing hundreds of yards of wet sand, leaving countless fish flopping helplessly. I follow, my feet sinking into the oversaturated ground as I pass dying creatures and clumps of seaweed. I chase the ocean as it pulls away. It goes and goes until I can no longer see it.

It retreats... and then an endless wall of water comes roaring back.

Then

A few miles outside of Gainesville, the bus leaves I-75 and parks at a rest stop. "Let's be back on the road in twenty minutes, people," Mr. Anderson says. "Don't make me have to track you down."

When Nell leaves the women's restroom, Gavin is nearby eating a strawberry ice-cream bar. "They have an ice-cream vending machine here," he says. "I don't think I've ever seen one at a rest stop before. It plays music and everything. It's so cheesy. Look." He feeds another dollar into the machine and chuckles as it jingles to life, playing a few out-of-tune notes before spitting out another strawberry bar. The music sounds like something from an old ice-cream truck.

Gavin holds out the second bar. "For you."

Nell wants to turn it down. *Be nice. He's your best friend's boyfriend. Find a way to make this work.* She smiles a little and accepts the ice cream, ignoring the brush of Gavin's fingers against hers as she takes the wooden stick.

They sit at a picnic table, out of earshot of the other students. Nell nibbles the ice cream while mentally clawing for something, anything to say. She hates moments like this, when her mind blanks and she feels empty, devoid of any thought worth expressing. She stares at the bus and pretends her heart isn't beating just a little too fast, that some deep and primitive corner of her brain isn't forcing hypervigilance. The ice cream is too sweet on her tongue, and the chunks of strawberry have an off-puttingly mushy texture, but she keeps eating anyway.

"Can I tell you something?" Gavin asks.

She nearly jumps. "Sure."

"You might think it's weird."

"Go ahead," she says, keeping her tone measured.

"You have to promise not to tell Harper."

She squints at him.

"Just promise. You know I'd never want to hurt her."

She hesitates, then nods. "I promise."

"Okay, so don't get me wrong. I'm really into Harper. She's great. But when I met you guys...I was into you first."

She almost chokes on a bite of ice cream. "Yeah. Right." Her vigilance spikes. People like Gavin rarely pay attention to people like her. Instead, they're drawn to Harper like magnets to metal. Like attracts like, and Gavin's admission is jarring because it doesn't follow that disappointing but reassuring pattern.

"I'm serious." His face is sheepish and open, and she almost thinks she can see a slight blush rising in his cheeks. "I had this wild crush on you."

"I have a really hard time believing that."

"It's true! Why would I make this whole embarrassing confession if it weren't true?"

"I don't know. Why are you telling me this?" A dull ache throbs behind her eyes, and she's sure it's not from the ice cream.

"I wanted to be honest about it. I thought maybe that would help us be friends. Like you'd trust me more." He rubs the back of his neck. "I almost asked you out. Almost. But I was so afraid you'd say no."

She opens her mouth to respond, but her words dry up.

"I debated it with myself for weeks. Months. But you were always so hard to read. You're really mysterious, Nell."

"Most people just say I'm shy."

"It's more than that. There's this...this depth to you that I couldn't understand. I still don't, really. But I liked it. And it kind of killed me for a while that you obviously weren't into me."

"I wasn't, Gavin. Not in that way. I'm sorry."

"No, I get it. And I mean, I'm over it. I've got Harper, and she's amazing. Like I said, I wouldn't do anything to hurt her, so don't think I'm coming on to you."

"Okay. Good. Because that would be a problem." She forces her shoulders to loosen.

"Obviously. Yeah. I just thought you should know. I'd like it if we could be friends."

"Me too," she says. The words feel like strange shapes against her tongue.

"You're the reason I've stuck with chorus all this time." He reaches across the table, and for a terrible moment she thinks he's reaching for her hand, but instead he takes the wrapper and stick from her now-gone ice cream. "Here, I'll get those for you," he says, tossing them in the trash along with his.

"Thanks. We should get back to the bus. It looks like Mr. Anderson's about to do a head count."

He nods. "Okay. And, Nell?"

"Yeah?"

"Remember, don't tell Harper."

"I won't." It feels like her last bite of ice cream is still stuck in her throat. She swallows against it, willing it down.

Chapter Twenty-Seven

The tide roars back in, snagging me in its grip, sending me somersaulting and sucking me under. I can't find which way is up, can't tell sand from sky. The world has gone churning and murky and dim. I try to kick, to claw, to propel myself back above the surface, but there *is* no surface anymore, there's just dark, and the salt burns my eyes and the water pours into my mouth, flooding my lungs when I fight for breath—

A voice, hushed but urgent, yanks me back. "Nell! Nell, wake up! It's just a dream!" Hands grip my shoulders, shaking me.

I wake up gasping. The air is back and I want all of it, every last molecule. It takes a moment for me to orient myself, to recognize that I'm not lost in a surging sea. I'm on the floor of the master bedroom, tangled in heaps of blankets and pillows, and Tris is leaning over me, still gripping my shoulders tightly enough to pinch. "Are you okay?" she asks.

I press my hands to my chest as if they can calm my urgent heartbeat.

"You were gasping in your sleep."

"I dreamed that I was drowning." I want to tell her more, to pour out everything I remember, but someone stirs in the nearby bed and I shut my mouth and press a finger to my lips as Harper sits up and stretches. Dia must be showering; I hear water running in the bathroom. Beyond that, a dull, steady *thunk thunk thunk* drums from somewhere outside. Gavin is back at work, cutting more wood for his fire.

Stiff from the floor and still a little disoriented, I stand up. As soon as I do, Harper is there, hugging me. "That was a perfect idea for last night," she says. "Thank you, Nell."

"I think we all needed it," I say.

"No weird dreams, either," Harper says. "No creepy shadows. How about you?"

I shake my head and ignore the quick, sharp look Tris tosses me.

Dia leaves the bathroom, towel-drying her hair. "None here, either." She sits on the edge of the bed. "I checked on Harry again a little while ago. We need to unwrap his leg today and make sure it's not looking infected."

"We'll do that first thing," I say. "Is he awake yet?"

Dia frowns, her forehead creasing with worry, and I know the answer to my question before she can speak it. "No. Do you think that's a sign of some kind of infection? Sepsis, maybe?"

"I doubt that would set in so quickly," Tris says. "Is he feverish?"

Dia shakes her head.

"That's a good sign," Tris says, before a brutal crash from outside makes her cringe as Gavin claims another of her trees. She shakes off obvious discomfort and stands. "Actually, let's take a look at his leg right now."

We go to the living room. If I didn't know about his injury and all that happened after, I would assume he was napping. His eyes are gently closed, his breathing slow and deep. I touch his forehead, double-checking for a fever, but his temperature seems normal.

Dia's washed, half-finished embroidery lies draped over his chest. She sees me notice it. "I don't know why I left it there. It felt right."

"Maybe it'll bring him a little luck," I suggest.

Dia shrugs and gently unwraps his calf. "This can't be right," she murmurs, staring down at the wound.

I hesitantly crane my neck to see, expecting inflammation, infection. Instead, the gash seems...better, at least a little. It's still jagged and angry, but it doesn't look like something that happened yesterday. There's no redness. No swelling.

"How?" Harper asks.

"Maybe the gash wasn't as deep as it seemed," Tris says, but her tone is heavy with doubt. It *was* that deep. We all saw it. We cleaned it out and helped Dia close it. A day ago it was deep and angry and gushing; now it's well on its way to healing, and although I don't know how that's possible, I'm not in the mood to question it. Right now I'll gladly cling to every bit of good news I can find, and this is definitely good news.

While Dia rebandages Harry's leg and Harper heads outside to find Gavin, Tris tilts her head toward the kitchen, indicating that I should follow.

"That's not possible," she whispers when we're out of earshot. Eyes wide, she points back toward the living room. Toward Harry. "You saw his leg yesterday. He was practically bleeding out!"

I don't know what to tell her. I'm as confused as she is. "Maybe it really wasn't as bad as it seemed. It's not like we're medical experts. Maybe it's more of a surface wound, and once Dia closed it up—"

"That was no surface wound," Tris says. "I could almost see bone."

"At least we probably don't have to worry about infection. This is a good thing."

"It's good," she agrees, still deeply bothered. "It's just not possible."

"How much of what we've seen over the past few days is possible?"

"You have a point." She sighs. Then her gaze grows keen, her eyes locking with mine. "What were you dreaming about when I woke you up? Was it the shadow?"

I shake my head. "There were some figures I couldn't make out, but they weren't like my shadow." I tell her about the cat at the window and the dark shapes beyond.

" 'No justice without sacrifice'? What does that mean? What sacrifice?"

"I wish I knew." I start to tremble as I reach the part of the dream where I went outside. "It was... I think it was a hurricane, Tris. I was on the beach during a hurricane, and then the ocean disappeared."

She pauses. "You mean like the tide went out?"

"Yeah. No. It wasn't just low tide. The ocean was *gone*. Then it came back really, really fast, and it was much higher than high tide. There was so much of it. It swamped me, and I couldn't find the surface. I couldn't..." The strangled, gasping feeling returns, wrapping iron around my chest. I wish I could shove the memory away. I wish I could vomit it up.

"Hey." She puts her arms around me, pulling me close. Her hands move over my back, soothing me. "Breathe. You're okay. Just breathe."

"I was drowning."

"You're not drowning now," she murmurs against my neck. "I've got you. I won't let you drown."

I feel the honesty in her words, and I cling to that. To her.

When I finally calm down a little, she says, "What you're describing sounds like storm surge."

I pull away enough to give her a questioning look.

She gives me a small, humorless smile. "You inland kids and your lack of proper hurricane education. Okay, during a hurricane, the wind can blow the ocean up onto land. If a really strong storm hits from just the right direction, though, sometimes the wind sort of sucks the water away first. Then it all comes back at once."

"That's exactly what happened in my dream."

"That's how a lot of flooding happens during a hurricane. The surge we got around here from Matthew a few years ago was a mess, and that storm only skimmed us. The wind shoves the water inland, and the ocean just...swamps everything. It takes out cars. Houses."

"And it drowns people."

She nods grimly. "There are always at least a few people who don't evacuate when they should. Sometimes they even think it's funny to walk out where the ocean used to be. Then the water comes back."

225

"It comes back and takes what it wants," I murmur, letting Tris pull me close again. Over her shoulder, I can see through the front window. Gavin crouches next to her truck with a length of hose and a bucket.

The sight of him must make me tense up, because she moves back and follows my gaze. "He's siphoning my gas," she says after a moment. "That fool's going to blow himself up."

"God, I hope so." The words slip out; I can't bite them back.

We watch Gavin head toward the backyard with whatever gas he managed to extract sloshing in the bucket. As he makes his way toward the dock, Harper peeks inside. "He's almost ready to light it up," she says uncertainly.

Tris shakes her head. "Come on," she says to me. "There's another fire extinguisher in the garage. Let's grab it and the back-yard hose and go watch the show." Dia joins us as we head outside.

The pile Gavin has built on the raised platform is impressive. All the rest of the firewood is there, along with logs and branches from the trees he chopped, and massive mounds of pine needles and other kindling. He splashes gasoline over everything, then jogs back down the dock toward us.

"How are you going to light it?" Tris asks when he gets near. "You've got a nice big cloud of flammable vapor out there, thanks to the gas. You can't just stand there and light a match."

"I know." He narrows his eyes slightly and picks up a branch. A bundle of pine needles and paper has been twined to one end, creating a makeshift torch. "I'm going to throw this at it and run like hell."

"Shouldn't you wait until it gets dark?" Dia asks.

Gavin shakes his head. "I'm not doing this for the fire. I'm doing it for the smoke. It'll be more visible during the day." He takes a lighter from his pocket.

"Wait." Harper steps toward him. "This is too dangerous."

"I know what I'm doing, babe."

"But—"

He takes a step back, his gaze hardening. "I keep trying to save us, and all any of you can do is tell me not to. It's like you don't even want to get off this island."

Harper's shoulders droop. "Of course we want to get out of here."

"Yeah?" Gavin gives her a cold, measured look and holds out the torch. "Prove it."

"What?"

"You're a faster runner than I am. Light the fire and run back down the dock."

Harper's throat works like she's swallowing a sob, but she steps toward him and raises her hand.

The suggestion of sacrifice rushes back from my dream, making me panic. Dia and I lunge forward at the same time, each of us catching one of Harper's arms to hold her in place and keep her on land. She doesn't fight us.

"That's not happening," I say to Gavin. "This is your plan. You do it."

"Fine." He gives us one last glare, lights the torch, and heads down the dock. He inches as close to the platform as he dares, stretches his arm back, and flings the torch.

Chapter Twenty-Eight

The pile of wood fireballs, devouring the roof of the platform and sending a mushroom cloud of flame and thick black smoke several stories into the air. The force of the explosion sends Gavin sprawling, and for a moment I think he might trip right off the dock and into the bay. No, I don't just think it, I *hope* for it, and as he regains his footing, I imagine rushing out and pushing him into the water myself. He would flail in the shallows, unsure of whether he should battle forty yards of mud back to us or try to swim for the opposite shore like Christopher. Then he'd be sucked under, another meal for the darkness lurking beneath the gentle waves of the bay. If the island wants a sacrifice, perhaps that would be enough.

But of course I don't charge down the dock toward him. Of course I stay safely on shore.

He's halfway back when he pauses, planting his feet like something startled him and staring down over the lapping waves.

"Did you see that?" Tris says.

"What?" I ask, but before she can clarify, it happens again. The dock...moves. It lurches several inches to one side, and although the movement is relatively minor, it's enough to make Gavin drop to his knees. The narrow dock, after all, has no handrail. Nothing to cling to.

"There's no way," Tris murmurs, her hand covering her mouth. "The dock is solid. It can't—"

"Gavin!" Harper screams as the dock trembles again. Something underwater is tugging at one of the pilings ahead of Gavin. Something *massive*. The dock lurches, creaking and shuddering as a section begins to lean, angling more and more toward the water. Gavin needs to run, to clear that part of the dock before it gives way, but he crawls backward instead, only stopping when the heat of the fire reminds him that there's no escape in that direction.

I've never seen him so afraid, so alarmed, and somewhere beneath my genuine fear and panic and horror, a little part of me likes what it's seeing. I'm about to watch Gavin Richardson die, and even if I could save him, I don't think I would.

The piling gives way, splashing backward into the bay as whatever's in the water moves on to the next support. Its pulls grow rhythmic, each wrenching heave twisting the dock more violently toward the water. The wood begins to splinter, cracking harsh and sharp as gunfire.

"GAVIN!" Harper shrieks. "RUN!"

Her voice snaps him out of it. He leaps to his feet, swaying dangerously as the dock tilts more, more, more. Just as he begins to sprint, another piling falls and the section of walkway ahead of him gives out, planks of wood jerking loose and flipping into the water.

This time Gavin doesn't freeze. He doesn't hesitate.

He jumps.

This is it. This is when I watch him die.

But he clears the gap, stumbling but maintaining his footing, and he keeps going. Seconds later he reaches the shore, tumbling onto the sandy path as another section of dock rips apart. "Holy shit," he gasps, his face going shroud white. "Holy shit." He looks stricken—eyes ghoulishly wide, brows low and shadowed, mouth gaping like a fish drowning on land.

Crying, Harper runs to him, throwing her arms around his shoulders. "I told you it was too dangerous," she chokes out between sobs. "The island won't let us leave."

Gavin turns back and stares at what remains of the narrow dock. Whatever tore it apart has gone dormant again, like it knows it missed its chance. Still gulping air like a hooked fish, Gavin shakes himself free of Harper's grasp and rakes his hands through his hair. Then he spins and strides toward the house.

Harper sinks to her knees, still sobbing. Dia, Tris, and I sit next to her, surrounding her. We're a pillar again, sturdy and strong together.

"He could have died," she says once her sobs lessen.

"He was trying to do a good thing," Tris says. "He was trying to save us."

He was trying to save himself. I don't say it out loud, but I saw his face before he lit the fire. I saw the unhinged determination in his eyes. Gavin's first priority was Gavin.

Harper shakes her head. "It was reckless. He wouldn't listen. He got Harry hurt. And that stupid fire…" She stares out toward the burning platform. "That mess was our last hope."

"It could still work," Dia says, her voice thin with doubt. "Someone has to see all that smoke."

"No one's coming," Harper murmurs. "No one's out there. I don't know what the hell happened, but no one's left. It's just us." She starts crying again.

"No," I say softly. "We're going to figure something out."

"Nell's right," Tris says. "We're not giving up. Not yet."

"I don't want to go back to the house," Harper says.

I stand. "Let's stay outside for a while. We can go up to Tris's banyan for a bit."

"Banyan?" Harper asks.

Tris gets up and takes my hand. "You'll love it," she tells Harper. "Come on."

Harper stands. Dia holds her hand out. Harper takes it, and I catch Harper's other hand so that we're all connected like paper dolls. We trek across the side yard, past the remnants of Gavin's fallen trees, and we stand on the dirt road, facing the beach. The sun warms our faces, and the salted breeze carries in from the ocean, briny and comforting as it fills our lungs and dances back through our hair.

"Should we go down and check the haze first?" I ask.

"We don't need to go anywhere to check it," Dia murmurs. We follow her gaze south.

The haze is visible from here. It's still quite far down the road, but we can see it from where we stand. By tomorrow morning it will reach the security light. Then it's just a matter of time until it engulfs the house.

I swallow the lump rising in my throat.

"Um, Nell?" Tris says softly. I glance at her. She's staring over her right shoulder at something on the ground. I turn to look. Dia and Harper do the same.

Our shadows range over the dirt road behind us, hands tethered, a second row of paper dolls. All four shadows are tall and narrow, stretched taut by the morning light, but mine is different. It pulls much farther than it should, impossibly long, with thread-thin arms and a curiously tilted head.

My own head swims. My vision shimmers. I blink, and my shadow is my own again.

"We all saw that, right?" Harper says haltingly.

"Yeah," Dia whispers. "That was the thing I saw on the stairs the other night. I'm sure of it."

"It was the thing I drew," Harper says. "The shadow I dreamed about." Her gaze flickers my way, and the new fear in her eyes almost breaks me.

"Nell," Tris says, "you have to tell them. Something's going on, and they need to know."

"I can't." I stare out toward the ocean, unable to look at any of them. The fear I saw in Harper's face haunts me.

"Please tell us, Nell," Dia says, but her voice is heavy with dread, like she's not sure she truly wants to know.

My best friends are afraid of me.

I can't do this. Can't bear this.

Blinking back tears, I shake my head.

"You have to," Tris says gently. "Because somehow…that thing is you."

Chapter Twenty-Nine

Before I can respond, Dia swallows back a strangled gasp. "I should go check on Harry," she mutters, turning away and jogging toward the front steps.

"Yeah," Harper says. "I need...I don't know what I need." She pulls her hand from mine and walks toward the beach.

I look at Tris. "They're afraid of me."

"They're afraid of the shadow," she says.

"That thing isn't me. It isn't."

"It's part of you, though."

"How can that be true?" My voice catches like a nettle in my throat.

"I don't know. We all saw it, though. That thing isn't just a shadow. It's *your* shadow."

I shake my head. I might call it my friend sometimes, but it's not me. It can't be. Why would I have put myself through so much childhood panic knowing on some subconscious level that I was manifesting it? The idea is ghastly. If it were true, it would make *me* ghastly. And if the shadow is me, does that mean everything that's happening on the island is somehow me as well? Did I kill Christopher? Have I trapped us all here to die? I wait for Tris to stare at me in horror, to back away, to distance herself from the monster she must think me to be.

Instead, she steps forward and hugs me. "It's okay. We're going to figure this out."

For a moment, I let myself lean into her, my cheek resting on her shoulder. Then I pull away. "I'm sorry. I need to be alone. Just for a little while. I have to think."

She nods and lets me go, and I head inside. Harry is right where we left him, of course; Dia sits nearby with his St. Felicitas history book closed on her lap. She looks at me when I come in; I glance at her without a word, grab my uke from the master bedroom, and go upstairs, shutting myself in my room.

The shadow isn't part of me. It can't be, and I'm going to prove it right now. After all, if it *is* my own manifestation on some subconscious level, I should be able to summon it. Control it. I can't do that.

Can I?

I shut the gauzy curtains. They still let in too much light, so I drag the comforter from the bed and drape it over the curtain rod, making the room darker. It's not perfect—light still seeps in around the edges of the blanket like a growing water stain from a slow leak—but it should be enough. After all, shadows can't exist without at least a little light.

I sit on the bed, legs crossed, my uke loose and light in my hands. I sing through my shadow's favorite song. When it ends, I keep strumming, but instead of singing along, I talk. "Come on. Come out. I know it's the wrong time of day for you to visit, but if we're connected—if you're part of me—you have to listen to me."

Nothing. I stare into the darkest corner of the room, where the thing would most likely appear, but the shadows there remain still and calm and not alive at all. I listen for that wheezing, hitching breath, but all I can hear is my own voice and my fingers brushing over the uke's strings.

"What are you? What do you want with me?"

Still nothing. My fingers find the chords of the shadow's favorite song. I play them over and over, hoping to tempt the thing out.

"Everything that's going on here, whatever's keeping us trapped on the island...Are you behind that or not?"

I strum harder. Louder. Faster. The normally winsome tune turns staccato and impatient.

"You have to talk to me. I don't know if you even *can* talk, but there has to be a way for us to communicate. Tell me what you want!"

I strum too hard. The uke's E string breaks, snapping against my hand like a striking snake. I put the sore spot to my mouth, sucking away the sting as I glare at the corner.

The one time I want my darkness to be here with me, the one time I dare to demand its presence, of course it stays away.

Then

One Year Ago

It's like Gavin has removed a mask Nell never realized he wore. After his confession, he loosens up, relaxes, and Nell finds herself relaxing as well, as though the weight of his truth had rested on her shoulders rather than his. Now she knows what she's been picking up on all this time. The relief of knowing that he's over his crush is a comfort. It's in the past and the slate is clean.

They spend the rest of the bus ride laughing at memes and videos on Gavin's tablet, their heads close together as they focus on the screen. He shows her a GIF of a litter of puppies trying to navigate a flight of stairs, and she can't stop giggling because the clip is hilarious and the puppies are adorable and she can finally breathe, actually *breathe* around Gavin.

There's another feeling, too, one that jitters around the edges of her mind. One that she tries to ignore because it feels prideful and disloyal. Sometimes it's a little difficult to be friends with someone like Harper, with her gleaming smile and her lithe runner's body and her easy extroversion. Now Nell knows that Gavin—attractive, popular Gavin, who gets everything he wants, and who can weaken the knees of nearly any girl in school with just a glance and a smile—liked her. And he liked her *first*.

It's a relief that he no longer does, but there's a certain satisfaction in knowing he did.

She'll keep her word. She won't tell Harper. She would never want to chip away at her best friend's granite-solid ego. Besides, it's shameful to feel this kind of pride, she tells herself, embracing the resulting guilt. She doesn't want to compete with Harper. That's no way to be a friend.

But that pleased little corner of her brain is content to hold the secret close.

After a stop for a fast-food dinner, the students settle in at the hotel, four to a room. Mr. Anderson announces that they're welcome to use the hotel's facilities until nine, at which point they're to stay in their rooms for the night.

Gavin pulls Nell aside. "The guys and I have something planned for later. You and your roommates come to our room after ten."

"We probably shouldn't. What if Mr. Anderson catches us?"

"Don't let him." When Gavin grins at her, his teeth seem sharper than they should.

"I don't know. Maybe."

"I'll be sad if you don't come, Nell."

She swallows. Harper would do this. Harper would dare. "Okay. I'll try."

Chapter Thirty

THURSDAY, APRIL 23

I give up on my shadow and head downstairs, the rumble of distant thunder echoing my footfalls on the steps. I slip silently through the living room and into the kitchen, where Tris, Harper, and Dia sit at the table. It's almost like they're waiting for me.

"There she is," Harper says while Dia waves me over. They *are* waiting for me.

"Tell them about the shadow," Tris says to me. "Tell them everything."

I freeze. It's like the sleep paralysis is back, only I'm wide awake. Three expectant faces watch while I go statue-still, utterly trapped.

"Nell?" Dia prompts gently.

"Please," Harper adds. "Whatever it is, you know you can tell us."

I force my jaw to unclench. "No. No, I can't. I really, really can't."

"Why?" Dia asks. Her brow furrows with concern. Maybe it's that concern that breaks me, or maybe it's the exhaustion and fear I see in her weary expression. Something in me snaps like an over-stretched rubber band; I go from frozen to limp, all at once, and I start to stumble. Tris leaps up and catches me before I can collapse onto the tile, and she leads me to a chair while Dia gets me some water. I bury my face in my arms and start to cry. My sobs are quick and rough, violent enough to build an ache in my chest. I feel someone's hand on my shoulder, and another rubbing my back.

It takes me a few minutes to catch a breath. Once I manage, I raise my head, my eyes swollen and scratchy. "If I tell you what's going on," I say, feeling hollow, "you'll know this is all my fault."

"It's not," Tris says softly. "You're trying so hard, Nell. I know you are."

"I don't understand," Harper says. "What's your fault?"

"All of it." I raise a hand and gesture weakly toward a window. "The haze. Us being trapped here. Christopher. I did this. I didn't mean to, but that doesn't change the fact that it's all happening."

"Tell them about when you were younger," Tris nudges. "It's okay. They're your friends."

I don't want to, but I know she's right. It's time, now that they've seen the shadow as well. There must be a reason for that, and so I sit with them and tell the story of the little girl who learned to soothe a shadow with a song. I tell them almost everything. There's just one secret left by the time I'm done, one last hazy memory that I won't share. After all, I can't very well explain a memory I barely remember myself. I leave that one where it is, locked in darkness where it belongs.

It's late afternoon by the time my story is told. Outside the window, the sun blazes off the bay. "I knew my shadow was back," I say finally. "I should've known not to come on this trip with you, but I came anyway, and I brought that thing with me. Then I got lazy about the one way I knew to keep it at bay. I caused this. It's my fault."

"No," Dia says simply.

"No?" I echo.

Dia shakes her head. "Whatever's going on, I refuse to believe it's your fault."

"Right?" Tris says, taking my hand but addressing Dia. "I've been telling her the same thing. We don't even know if the shadow is really causing all of this."

"What else could it be?" I say, my voice shaking. "I'm...I'm haunted. And now the island is haunted, too."

Harper puts her hand on my forearm. "Even if it *is* all related, it's not your fault. You didn't mean for this to happen."

Dia stands and walks around the table so she can wrap her arms around my shoulders. "I'm so sorry you've been carrying this around," she says. "Not just this week, either. All of it, since you were little. That had to be so terrifying."

"It was," I whisper. "It is."

For a long moment we sit, silent and connected. I start to feel calmer; my breathing returns to something resembling a normal rhythm.

"So you can control the shadow with music?" Harper asks finally. "Or you used to be able to?"

I shake my head. "I wouldn't call it control. I communicated with it, sort of. I used the song to make friends with it, but it never just did what I said, and it sure doesn't now. The song doesn't seem to work anymore." My recent attempt to summon it proves that.

"Still, though." Harper's brow furrows with thought. "Maybe there's something there. What about other songs?"

"She sang so many songs last night," Dia says, "and the haze is still there today."

"I'm still not sure I buy that the shadow's the one causing everything," Tris says. "What's going on feels bigger somehow, don't you think? The shadow might be part of it, but..."

Harper nods. "We need to work out what's really going on here. Somehow, it's all connected; we have to figure out how everything fits together."

An idea hits me, and I turn to Dia. "Where's Harry's history book? I saw you with it earlier." It's not much, but without internet access, it's the only connection we have to St. Felicitas's past. "Wasn't there something in it about an island?"

"I left it on the coffee table. Hold on." She slips into the living room and gets it for me, and I page through it, looking for the legend Harry shared the other night, when we were gathered around the firepit. He read us the summary, but there's more to the story. I find the chapter marked with a torn scrap of lined, cream-colored paper. It looks like part of a list of names, written in unfamiliar script—I can't read most of it due to the angle of the tear, but I can make out *Dennis Taylor* and *Rachel Taylor*.

Dia looks at it and frowns. "Okay, weird. I found something like this on the floor in my room."

"Seriously?" Harper says. "I found one in my room, too."

"Harry must've found this one," Dia says.

"Who are Dennis and Rachel?" Tris asks.

"No clue," I say as Harper shrugs.

"Okay, but these papers had to have come in with y'all," Tris says. "Dad always has rentals deep cleaned between guests. The crew would've thrown out any random scraps of paper."

"I don't think so," I say. "I've never heard of these people."

"Weird," Dia says again, frowning. "Maybe the crew just didn't see them."

"Maybe," Tris says doubtfully. She points to the open book. "Is that the legend you were talking about?"

I nod and start to read. According to the book, the women who fled the mainland in the seventeenth century really were witches. Banished by the local priest and pursued by witch hunters, they escaped to a small island, which they then secured with a protective charm that made the island unfindable, or at least inaccessible. After that, the legend loses track of them. Some versions claim the women spent the rest of their days on the island, shielded by the charm; when they died, their magic remained in place, letting the island be found only when it wanted to be. Other versions claim that their pursuers discovered them and dragged them back to the mainland to be executed, and others suggest the hunters made it to the island only to vanish. A hurricane hit the area in the 1800s, devastating St. Felicitas but supposedly leaving the mythical island untouched. After that, the legend sprouted the idea of the Island of No Storms.

I glance up at Tris. "Like your dad's sign."

She shakes her head. "It's a coincidence. Or someone heard the legend at some point and liked the ring of it."

"And put up a sign? On this exact island?"

"This isn't the island from that legend, assuming that island ever really existed. Dad bought Straight Shot from a woman, who'd bought it from someone else, who'd bought it from a couple who built this house back in the 1980s. I've seen the original plans. One of them had to have hung the sign." She shakes her head. "There are probably dozens of islands in Florida with that nickname."

"I've never heard the phrase before we got here," I say, going back to Harry's book. What I find on the next page makes me gasp.

The woodcut illustration is black and white, simple in a way that makes every detail feel deliberate and integral to the whole. Four women pose in front of an enormous pillar of a tree, its canopy a draping shield against the darkness surrounding them. The women's dresses are frayed and patched, the bodices well-worn, the skirts stained at the hem, but the women stand proud, staring defiantly from the page. One holds a thin brush, another a bit of cloth. The third has a large feather and a book; the fourth, instead of holding an object, rests a hand on the trunk of the tree. At their feet, a sleek black cat twines its way through masses of gnarled roots. Underneath the illustration is a small caption in verse. It reminds me of a nursery rhyme, something a child might chant:

> One to illustrate a truth
> And one to tell a tale
> One to nurture, one to bind
> So none who seek shall ever find
> Beyond this conjured veil

The women—the witches—seem too familiar. It's like some small part of me knows them, even though I don't recognize their

243

faces. The feeling reminds me of the stories I used to write, and how Harper would draw my characters, tugging them from my brain and my words and making them all the more real somehow. I touch the illustration like I can somehow reach through it. Like I can somehow reach *them*. "We need to know their story," I say, picking up the torn scrap of paper so that I can mark the illustration and close the book.

Tris understands what I'm trying to grasp at. "You're our storyteller," she says. "Do you think you can—"

Before she can finish, Gavin appears in the kitchen doorway. He stares silently at us, his green eyes cold and strangely dark. My hands curve into fists.

Harper jumps up. "Are you okay? I tried to check on you before, but your door was locked."

"I was sleeping." He goes to the sink and fills a glass with water. "Trying to save half a dozen people can wear you out. Speaking of that..." He pauses, sips. "I haven't heard a single thank-you."

Tris raises a brow.

"I risked my life building that fire," he says. "I almost got myself killed trying to save your asses."

I stand. "You were trying to save yourself."

He steps toward me.

I take a reflexive step back.

Harper comes between us, glaring up at him. "Hold on. Are you kidding? I told you it was dangerous. I begged you not to do it. You wouldn't give it up. Even after Harry got hurt, you just kept—"

"At least I've been trying," he says. "What have you done? Any of you? Put up a few signs? Sort food? What have you done to get us the hell out of here?"

I stare into his eyes, into the darkness there. "Too bad you couldn't do what you usually do when you're in trouble and have your daddy take care of it."

He shoves Harper out of the way and steps toward me again. Something clenches in my throat, reminding me of how it felt to choke and drown in my dream. My head feels like it's floating, like I've lost my anchor.

"Hey." Tris is on her feet. She plants her hands on his chest and pushes. "Enough with the toxic macho bullshit, dude. We all want to get out of here. Acting like an asshole won't make that happen any faster."

I need to escape. I spin on my heel and head for the front door. Angry voices rise behind me, and Tris calls my name, but I don't turn back. Outside, I head for the banyan because that's as far away as I can get from Gavin.

When I go to climb onto the cradle seat, I realize I'm holding something. I open my clenched left hand and find the scrap of paper from Harry's book, now crumpled from my grip. I don't remember taking it, but Gavin's appearance in the doorway had startled and distracted me. As I stare at it, I realize I've seen that shade of cream-colored paper before. Not sure just what the memory means, I pocket the scrap for later.

It's hard to hoist myself up onto the cradle branch without a boost from Tris, but I manage. Then I sit with the setting sun to my left and the darkening ocean to my right. I stay very still and try to breathe, to find my missing anchor, but the floating feeling stays with me. It's like I'm drifting in and out with the tide. I hold tightly to the tree and imagine rooting myself in place.

After a little while, Tris approaches hesitantly. "You were right about that guy," she says. "What a jerk."

"You have no idea." My hands tighten even more, digging into the tree's bark, clenching like I might fall. I'm not so sure I won't.

"You okay?"

"I don't know."

"Want company?"

I shake my head. "I need time. I need..." But I don't know what I need. Something's calling me, pulling at me like I'm flotsam caught in a riptide, but I don't know what it is.

"Don't stay out here too long. It'll be dark soon."

"I won't," I say, although returning to the house is the last thing I want to do. I reach into my pocket. "Do me a favor?"

"Of course."

I hand her the scrap of paper. "Get the other pieces from Harper and Dia. See if they fit together."

"Why?"

"I'm not sure yet."

"Consider it done. Nell?" She touches my arm. "Be careful out here, all right?"

I nod again. After she leaves, I drop to the ground and huddle amid the enormous tangle of roots. I stare up at the tree, at its canopy silhouetted against the darkening sky, and I imagine that canopy stretching huge and wide over other people, other eras, tucking the island's secrets away in the crooks of its mammoth branches. "What am I supposed to know?" I murmur, brushing my hands over the roots while I puzzle and fret. My fingers close

246

around a small white stone that isn't a stone at all, but a broken sliver of bone. There are other fragments as well, some bleached pale by salt and sun, others newer and fresher and still stained dark from more recent deaths. Do birds gather here to eat, pelicans and herons and ospreys scattering the remains of their dinners? I never noticed the fragments before, but now they seem obvious. The glint of gold looping around one catches my attention. I reach down and pick up a class ring set with a blue stone.

I remember seeing that ring very recently, on the finger of the Christopher-thing under the dock. He's not under there anymore, though, is he? The ring proves it. He's been taken by the island, absorbed by it, and his ring and a few slivers of bone are all that's left. Shivering, I drop the ring back among the roots. It belongs here now.

Slivers of bone. Fragments. Tiny hints that used to fit together.

I remember my thought from earlier—that if this really is the island from Harry's book, we need to know its story, and that of its witches. I have the puzzle pieces, or some of them at least. What if I can fit them together, just like I used to do with the stories I wrote to scare myself? But I need more pieces, more details. I need a hint.

I'm not surprised when the small black cat saunters up, picking its way gracefully through the root system. There's no spark when I touch its fur this time, no disturbing electric buzz. There's just one line, one phrase that flows through my mind like water, so germane and natural that I'm not sure if it comes from the cat at all, or from me. I say it out loud, letting it slip over my tongue.

"They called us witches, so witches we became."

The cat blinks at me, looking pleased. Then it slips away

247

toward the beach and disappears over a dune. It shouldn't be here on Straight Shot, but it is.

The banyan shouldn't be here either, a misplaced behemoth anchoring such a tiny island, thriving in sand and salt, but it is.

Gavin shouldn't be on the island, but he is.

And I shouldn't feel like I have to fight for every breath. I shouldn't feel like I'm drowning. I shouldn't have a storm building in my chest. But I do.

So witches we became.

To my left, the sun sinks in the clear sky, close to meeting the bay. I half expect the tar to surge up from the water and devour it, just tug it down into the depths like it did with Christopher. The sun will hiss and steam as it goes out, leaving us all in endless shadow.

Shadow.

I hold my hand out, watching to the right as the shadow of my arm stretches across the roots. It grows impossibly long, reaching halfway to the ocean, becoming as thin as thread.

At its far end, it meets a separate sort of darkness. It yields at a crooked joint that might almost be a shoulder below a bent neck and a curiously tilted head.

"There you are." My friend. It's not me. I'm not it. Or maybe I am. We've always been connected, ever since I was a child, and it's time to stop resisting that bond.

It's time to embrace it instead. It's time to *become.*

I stare at the shadow. "Come on, then."

It approaches slowly, unevenly, jerking forward on legs like charcoal-blackened spiderwebs. It's almost solid now, so different from the indistinct blur that crept into my childhood bedroom at night. It's grown into so much more. I pull my hand back, reeling it in like a fish on a line.

It inhales. That creaking, churning gasp. My earliest nightmare. I resisted the shadow for so long; I pushed the fear away and replaced it with the frights of my own fiction. That let me cope, at least for a while, until reality grew worse than anything I could write.

Become.

My throat constricts again. The shadow steals the air, taking it all, gobbling it while I drown on dry land, my mouth gaping wide.

I don't know what this means, but I have to do it.

When the shadow grasps forward with its free arm, I let that thread-thin, slithering appendage reach for my face, my mouth. I remember how I would clamp my lips shut against it as a child while thunder growled in the distance.

This time I let it in.

It begins to disappear down my throat.

As it blocks my airflow, I try to cry out. It nearly cuts off my voice, but some part of my scream escapes, echoing overhead in strange harmony with a jarring thunderclap despite the cloudless twilight sky.

We are one and the world goes dark.

Then

At almost half past ten, Nell peeks into the hallway. There's no sign of Mr. Anderson; he did final room checks fifteen minutes ago and told them to get plenty of sleep before tomorrow morning's big performance.

The boys' rooms are one floor up. Nell and her roommates creep down the hall toward the elevator, but Nell imagines the doors sliding open to reveal Mr. Anderson on patrol. She veers toward the stairs instead, because who would ever use a dingy stairwell when there's a shiny mirrored elevator right beside it, and the others follow, slipping up the stairs and toward Gavin's room like silent ghosts.

When they knock, Gavin opens the door, a red Solo cup in his hand. His eyes brighten when he sees Nell, and he ushers all four of them inside. The room is packed with chorus kids dancing to music playing through someone's Bluetooth speakers. Liquor bottles sit on display on the small hotel desk, along with multiple cans of beer on ice. How Gavin got his hands on everything, Nell can't guess, but that's the indefinable magic of being Gavin Richardson. If he wants something, it appears. If he desires it, it's his.

He serves the other newcomers drinks, then turns to Nell. "What'll you have?" he asks, flashing that too-sharp smile again.

Her mouth goes dry. "Nothing. Thanks."

"Aw, are you sure? I make a killer rum and Coke."

She shakes her head.

"Come on. Just one. You'll have a lot more fun."

She tries to ignore the pressure. "I don't really like to drink."

He sighs. "Fine. How about just a Coke, then?"

"I guess. Okay."

He grabs a ready cup of ice, pops open a can, and pours her a soda.

She goes to take it, then hesitates. "Promise there's nothing in this but Coke?"

"You watched me pour it, didn't you?"

She accepts it. Sips. No bitter bite of alcohol at the back of her throat. The fact that he was telling the truth loosens her shoulders a little.

He glances at the party going on around them. "I was hoping we'd have a minute tonight to talk."

She gives him a quizzical half-smile. "We talked for most of the afternoon."

"This is about something important." He wraps his fingers around her elbow, his grip gentle but firm, and he leads her back toward the door, the only area not full of dancing bodies.

"What?"

He looks at her. Shuts his eyes. Brays a strange, barking laugh that puts her back on edge. "I'm a little drunk," he says, still chuckling.

"I can tell." She takes a nervous gulp of Coke.

"Okay, so it's just... What I told you before wasn't entirely true."

She tenses even more. His confession earlier was a lie, a joke, and now he'll deliver some cruel punch line at her expense.

"When I said I used to have a crush on you…" He pauses, his face going red from bashfulness or alcohol or both. "I still do."

"What?" she says again.

He leans toward her. "Harper would never have to know." His hand strokes her arm.

"I don't know what you're suggesting, but—"

"I think you do." He steps closer, backing her against the door. "We could go somewhere for a while." His voice drops to a murmur, and he brings his lips close to her ear, his teeth grazing the lobe. "Everybody's here. The other guys' rooms are empty. Or we could go back to your room."

She huffs out a breath and darts away, fleeing the imposition of his proximity. "Are you kidding me? You're going out with my best friend."

"That's why I said she wouldn't have to know." He traps her close again, his breath warm against her face. She smells mint, but no alcohol.

He's faking, she thinks.

He's sober.

"Gavin, no. Just *no*."

His stare goes oddly blank. "Are you going to tell her?"

She finishes her Coke and shoves the cup into his hand. "I don't know."

"It'll just hurt her. You don't want to hurt her."

"I know. I just…" She presses a hand to her forehead, trying to think. The room is too loud, too warm. "Let's pretend this conversation never happened, okay? Let's pretend this entire trip never happened." She turns and shoves through the crowd until she finds her roommates—they're not her close friends, but they're a group, and she very much wants the safety of a group. For a while she tries to join their conversation, but they're tipsy and it's harder and harder to follow their words. Finally she tells them she's going back downstairs. Then she pushes past Gavin, who is still stationed by the door, and she leaves.

The hallway is too warm, too. She doesn't remember it being so warm earlier. Did the hotel's air-conditioning break down? It's the kind of drowsy warmth that presses in and invites sleep. She hopes she can remember her room number.

She hopes she can remember her *floor*.

Wait, it's one floor down, that's right, just one floor. And she shouldn't take the elevator because…she can't remember why, but she assumes she has a reason. The stairs, that's right. One set of stairs, a landing, and one more set, and she'll nearly be back to her room.

She pushes the stairwell door open, and she counts the stairs as she descends. They seem so much steeper than they should be. One, two, three, four, five, and she's falling. She lands hard on her knee, catching herself with her hands before her face can meet the grimy painted concrete. She tries to stand, but her vision blurs and her head swims and it's warm, so warm, and maybe she'll just stay here for a minute and rest. She settles into a corner, tilts her head against the wall, and closes her eyes.

Somewhere above her, a door opens. Heavy footsteps descend the stairs.

"There you are." A voice. Familiar. Masculine. Arms around her. The smell of mint. "I'll help you." A laugh that feels nearby and distant at the same time. "Come on, Nellie. Nice and quick."

Then nothing.

Chapter Thirty-One

THURSDAY, APRIL 23

I wake to night and the tickle of rain on my face. The drops filter through the banyan's crown and pelt the exposed inlet. Lightning flashes overhead, silhouetting the treetop in stark blackness against the white-hot electrical flare, and a simultaneous thunderclap signals that the storm is directly overhead.

Rainwater runs into my eyes; I blink and rub them to flush it out and clear my vision. Then I remember, and I run my left hand down my right arm, all the way to the fingertips. They end just where they should, with no thread-thin shadow anchored to them. Experimentally, I touch my throat. I remember gasping, strangling, screaming, but now I can breathe just fine.

"Nell? Where are you?" Tris's voice, nearby. I sit up and look around the banyan's massive trunk, and I can kind of see her standing near the edge of its root system. Another blaze of lightning ignites the sky, startling her.

I stand, finding my footing among the roots. It's difficult to see where to step. "I'm over here!"

"Please come back!" she calls. "I know you don't want to be near him, but it's not safe out here in the storm."

She's right, I know it, and I'm already picking my way to her, doing my best not to trip. By the time we reach the house, we're both drenched.

Dia runs up and wraps a large towel around my shoulders. She hands more to Tris. "This storm came out of nowhere!"

I think of the shadow, of the feel of it in my throat, of the way my scream grew to thunder. It feels like that happened hours ago. Days. I'm completely drenched, and the towel does little against the resulting chill. "How long has it been raining?"

"Just a couple of minutes," Tris says. "There wasn't a cloud in the sky when I left you by the tree."

"No clouds in the sky," I murmur, teeth chattering. "Just one in the road."

"Maybe the rain will wash that stuff away," Dia says, but it's clear she doesn't believe in the possibility, not really.

"We can hope," Tris says, trying to rub warmth into my shoulders. "Nell, you're shivering. You should jump in the shower and warm up."

I nod, but I stay where I am. My thoughts feel foreign and far away.

"Come on." She takes my hand and leads me up the stairs. My feet move slowly, mechanically. It's as if I'm wearing shoes of concrete and being controlled like a marionette. She finds my sleep pants and a dry T-shirt, and she hands them to me and walks me to the bathroom. "Do you need help?"

I shake off a little of the fog. "I can manage. Thanks."

"Warm up. And hey, when you're done, remind me to show you the scraps. I think we found most of them." She gives me a little smile and shuts the door, leaving me alone inside.

I run the water, letting it heat up until the mirror steams and the room grows misty. After peeling off my wet clothes, I step under the showerhead and tremble as the hot water pinks my skin. It's almost too warm. A heady, drowsy warmth.

Warm. My eyes snap open. My shoulders tense. Then the surge of adrenaline abates as suddenly as it began, and I shove down the echo of a memory, willing the water to rinse it away.

Tris is right. The heat helps. It penetrates my skin and makes its way to my core, and I feel my mind defrost. I can think clearly again. I don't know what to make of my experience under the banyan, but I faced my shadow and survived. I took a step—

they called us witches

—and now I need to puzzle out what that step meant. I take in a generous gulp of steamed air and breathe out the last of the fog.

Then something tickles in my throat. I cough, but that only makes the sensation worse. I open my mouth to the shower's spray, trying to drown the itch, but the water does nothing. I gag, doubling over in the tub, waiting to vomit. No food comes up, but I feel something on the back of my tongue and I retch again, trying to bring it up. I jam my fingers into my mouth and catch it, and I pull. A long, thin thread like something out of Dia's embroidery tote emerges from my throat.

No, not like embroidery thread. It's too slick and strong for that, like fishing line but slightly thicker. A ukulele string. It keeps coming and coming, and I keep coughing and gagging until it's all up, two feet or more, and then I stare at it as it hangs wet and limp from my hand. I want to fling it away and let it sluice down the drain, but instead I find myself winding it without knowing why. I loop it around my hand until it's small and neat and bundled, and I put it on the edge of the tub while I finish my shower. After I dress, I tuck the string into the pocket of my sleep pants.

I'm detangling my wet hair when the lights go out.

Chapter Thirty-Two

I stumble through the darkness, feeling my way to my bedroom, where the Maglite waits faithfully under my pillow. Its weight in my hand is reassuring, and I follow its stark beam downstairs, where Dia and Tris are scattering pillar candles around the living room. The house feels still and quiet, almost hauntingly so, and it takes me a moment to realize why—the subtle, constant hum of the air conditioner has stopped. The ceiling fan overhead drowsily spins to a halt, leaving the air in the room unmoving and the candle flames tall and undisturbed.

"What are the chances we lost power because of the storm?" Dia asks. "And not because of..." She doesn't finish. She doesn't have to. We all know.

Tris exhales. "Maybe we just blew a fuse. The circuit breaker's out in the garage. I'll go check."

"It's not the storm," I say softly. "And it's not a fuse." This was inevitable. Another link to the mainland—to reality and safety—is gone.

Dia's eyes glimmer with tears in the flickering light. "We can still hope."

"Of course we can," I say quickly, but I know better.

"I'll go ahead and check the circuit breaker," Tris says. "Just in case. And I'll see if I can get the generator going. It can't do much, but it'll give us enough juice for a few lights."

"I'll come with you," I say, pulling on my wet sneakers.

We head outside. The rain has stopped, leaving the air humid and heavy. Opening the garage door is difficult without electricity, but we yank it upward together and manage to get it halfway. I pull a stack of storage tubs over to block it from closing with us inside while Tris heads for the breaker panel.

Flipping the switches does nothing, so she drags a sizable generator out from below a set of metal shelves. "We have to move this thing away from the house before we start it up," she says.

"Let me help. It's heavy."

"I've got it. You grab those and follow me." She points to a couple of orange gas containers, then hefts the generator outside, disappearing into the dark.

I pick up the containers, one in each hand. They lift too easily, and my stomach twists as I think back to Gavin and his fuel-soaked fireball. "Tris?" I put them back and jog after her.

The sky has cleared. In the slivered moonlight I find Tris standing in the wet grass near the road, the generator forgotten at her feet as she stares south. I follow her gaze.

Down the road, the orange security light is still functioning, running on stored solar energy. It's dimmer than I remember. Indistinct. I squint through the darkness until I realize why. The haze has reached it, hanging heavy and low, slowly devouring the pole and suffocating what's left of the light's reassuring glow. There's no breeze rolling off the ocean anymore, nothing to wear away at the dense cloud.

"It's so close," Tris murmurs.

I hear a growing buzz cut short by a sharp electric snap. The light sparks searing-bright for half a second and goes out.

"Like the cars," I say. "It killed the light just like it killed the cars."

Tris looks at me and swallows. "Let's get this thing going and get back inside. Where's the gas?"

I hold up my hands. "The containers were empty."

Her jaw tightens. "Are you kidding me?"

"Gavin must have found them."

"No. I don't think it was him." She shakes her head. "Dad was supposed to make sure the containers were full. I kept reminding him, but I bet he still forgot to check. Damn it! I'm going to give him such a hard time once we..." Her voice trails off and she goes still.

"Tris."

She turns to me in the darkness. "I'm never going to see him again. He might never even know what happened to me. Where I went. Why I disappeared." Her voice breaks.

"We don't know that. We'll find a way to—"

"No." She swipes the back of her hand over her eyes. "I'm done. No more hoping. And no more guessing." Her gaze meets mine, and I'm surprised by the sharpness in it. "What else do you know,

Nell? What are you keeping from us? There's something, isn't there? It's important and it's part of all this and you just won't…" She lets out a strangled, frustrated huff and stalks off. I catch her hand and try to pull her back, but she wrenches away and keeps going.

"Tris!"

I'm terrified she's going to give up, just head south and march right into the haze and accept whatever awful fate it has planned for her, for us. But she goes north instead, and once I see that, I know exactly where she's heading.

I also know exactly what I need to do.

I run back inside, grabbing the Maglite from where I left it near the door. Dia sits on the sectional near Harry. "Where's Harper?" I ask her, shining the flashlight's beam toward the master bedroom's closed door. "In there?"

Dia nods. "I think so."

I knock. No answer.

"She might be asleep," Dia says. "She's been in there for a while."

"I need to talk to her," I say. "You too." I open the door and shine the flashlight around the room. It's empty. "Harper?" I check the bathroom. The closets. Under the bed. Nothing.

Somewhere upstairs, a floorboard creaks. It's a slight sound, so quiet that the hush of the air conditioner might have masked it if we still had power. I look up, and I know exactly where Harper is.

"What's going on?" Dia asks when I run back through the living room. I ignore her question and tear up the stairs, taking them two at a time. Dia follows, still questioning me as I slam open the door of Harper's original bedroom.

The room is dark, its shadows cut only by the flashlights on a pair of cell phones on the nightstand. Harper and Gavin sit on the bed. She's giggling as she sips from a blue-and-orange flask; he has one arm locked around her while his other hand nudges the bottom of the flask upward, encouraging her to drink more deeply. My entrance surprises her; she gasps and sputters as a mouthful of who-knows-what goes down the wrong pipe. The flask splashes to the floor, its contents gurgling out.

"Come on." Shoving Gavin's arm off her shoulders, I yank Harper to her feet and hand her off to Dia. "Get her out of here," I tell Dia. "I'll catch up in a minute."

Gavin stands and steps toward me, his gaze hard and clear in the Maglite's beam. Harper is drunk, but he's sober. "What the hell was that?" he demands, and he's close enough for me to smell the mint on his breath. Something surges in me, dark and feral. Before I can stop myself, I snarl and swing the flashlight by its head, bringing the heavy handle down on his skull. He crumples.

"I am so fucking done with your bullshit," I mutter, heading back downstairs. Dia follows me outside, dragging a confused, protesting Harper. I don't want to leave Harry unconscious and vulnerable in the house with Gavin, but based on how Gavin went down, I hope he'll be out cold for a while.

Thunder echoes in the distance as we head north toward the banyan, with me leading the way.

Then

Nell wakes before her roommates. She's groggy and grumpy and there's a dull, deep pounding behind her temples, which seems unfair. Shouldn't headaches be reserved for the members of chorus who spent half the night drinking in Gavin's room?

At least the bathroom is free. She gathers her clothes, trying to shake off a slow, drowsy vertigo, and limps across the room, her knee protesting every step. Did she bang it on something? She can't quite remember.

She uses the toilet while the shower water warms. When she wipes, the toilet paper is tinged with blood. She squints, counting back. It isn't time for this yet. Her period shouldn't start for another week. At least she always travels prepared with a few pads, even if she doesn't expect to need them.

She showers mechanically, waiting for the haze to lift from her mind. A thought floats just out of reach, scratching at the inner corners of her memory, teasing without revealing itself.

She's toweling off when a twinge of soreness from her knee clears her thoughts a little, just enough to let her realize she doesn't remember getting back to her room last night, just like she doesn't remember why her knee hurts. She was at Gavin's impromptu party; she can recall their conversation, his come-on, the way he acted drunk when he was sober, the scent of mint on his breath.

Then nothing.

No, something. One more thing. Footsteps on stairs. The stairwell. She fell in the stairwell, right? She fell and then...

When she leaves the bathroom, her roommates are awake. She asks them about last night.

One laughs, then winces at the apparent effect of that laugh on her head. "How much did you drink, Nell? You were wasted. You could barely talk."

"All I had was a Coke."

"Girl, it's fine. We were all wasted. Gavin made sure you got back down here okay."

Nell goes quiet. That doesn't sound right. She watched Gavin pour her Coke. She never left it alone.

When they board the bus to head to the competition venue, Gavin sits up front with a couple of his friends. Nell ends up next to a girl she doesn't know well. They ride in silence.

Backstage, she catches Gavin by the arm. "I need to talk to you."

He frowns. "Sure. About what?"

She pulls him aside, behind a set piece, out of sight. "What happened last night?"

"I pulled off an epic party and Anderson never caught on." He grins, proud, smug.

"You know what I'm talking about."

"What? You don't remember?"

Her vision shimmers. She blinks tears away. "Not all of it."

"You did kind of have a lot to drink." He chuckles softly.

"I did not!" Confusion swirls her thoughts until she's not sure which memories are real and which ones are her mind making up horror stories again.

His brows tilt in bemusement. "Everyone saw, Nell. You were at the party with a drink. You got drunk, so I helped you downstairs."

"What else did you do?" she asks through clenched teeth.

He rubs the back of his neck. "Nothing you didn't want me to."

A frozen stillness settles over her. "What?"

"Well..." He pauses, giving her a crooked half-grin.

"What did you do?" she demands again, speaking slowly, clipping each word between her teeth.

He steps forward, cornering her against the set piece, and he leans close. "I want you to think very hard about a few things before you go making assumptions or accusations. Okay, *Nellie*?"

His use of the nickname crawls along her skin like a spider. "Accusations about what, Gavin?" She tries to duck away, but he puts up an arm to block her.

"Everyone saw us get ice cream at the rest stop. Everyone saw you flirting with me on the bus."

"I wasn't—"

"They saw us together at the party. They saw you drinking. They saw you leave, and they saw me go after you to make sure you were all right."

The frost dissipates and she begins to tremble. "But I wasn't drinking!"

He gives his head a slow shake. "Whatever you think happened last night…"

"Did you—"

"Before you keep going—before you start telling anyone else about this—you need to think about who will believe you. And who will believe me." He ducks his head until his lips are near her ear, and he places a hand on her shoulder, and she can't move, she can't make herself push him away. His hand is a little too close to her neck, his thumb pressing against her throat just enough to send alarm surging through her veins. He doesn't choke her, doesn't prevent her from inhaling…but he could.

"If everyone saw us, they'll talk," she says, her voice faltering.

"Doesn't matter," he murmurs. "It only matters what Harper thinks. If she hears anything, you'll deny it. Right?"

"I'm not going to lie to my best friend."

"Yeah? What will she think if you start accusing me of things?"

"She'll listen to me. She'll stay the hell away from you."

His grip tightens, and now it's a little hard for her to breathe. Something sharp and acidic creeps into his tone. "She's not allowed to do that. She can't."

"What do you mean she's not allowed?"

"I won't let that happen," he mutters, speaking quickly. "Besides, where's your proof? If you tell, Harper will never talk to you again. If you tell, no one will believe you. You'll ruin your life, and nothing will happen to me. Think about that, Nellie. You know it's true."

She remembers his father the lawyer. She pictures the array of alcohol at the party. She imagines Harper's expression twisting into betrayed anger. Disbelief. Hatred.

She shuts her eyes. Shudders. "I won't say anything."

"Good." He presses in with his thumb one last time before he leaves her behind the set piece and goes back to the group.

Coughing, she stares into the shadows where he used to be as something dark and frightened and full of rage rises in her. It strains and writhes, fighting to unfurl like an ink-black flag. She shoves it down, encapsulating it in a snug cocoon of denial deep in the pit of her stomach. This is a story, she decides. Nothing more. She stuffs it away, and she stuffs her other stories away with it. No more darkness. No more fear. She locks it all in place and loses the key, and when a shadow that's just a little darker than the rest slinks past, slipping by in her peripheral vision, she pretends not to see it. She pretends not to notice how much more it has become.

Onstage, she mouths the words without singing, terrified that the tremble in her voice will betray her.

They come in last in the competition. Mr. Anderson isn't happy. The ride back to Winter Park is quiet, the bus maneuvering down the highway through a ripping thunderstorm.

At home, she throws her copies of *Here in the Shadows* in a box and shoves it onto a high shelf in her closet. She archives the stories saved on her computer; they're findable, but she won't see them unless she looks for them.

Tonight, for the first time in years, she will play her uke and sing. The shadow will be back, and it will be hungry. She can deal with that; she knows how. It's a known fear, and that's better than whatever's lurking at the edges of her memory—the echo of footsteps, the feeling of pressure at her throat, and a ghosting of cold, bitter mint.

Nell prefers the shadow to any of that.

Chapter Thirty-Three

I take Dia and Harper to the banyan.

When we reach it, I aim the Maglite at the ground so that we can pick our way through the roots. Tris isn't on her cradle branch; she huddles where I sat earlier, her knees drawn to her chest. She glances up when we appear. The crown of the tree is still wet and dripping from the storm.

"Why'd we come out here?" Harper demands, the words slurring into one another as she clumsily wipes a drop from her forehead.

Ignoring the dampness, I sit her down among the roots and peer at her face, trying to see her clearly without blinding her with the flashlight. "What was in the flask?"

"Whiskey, I think."

"How much did you drink?"

She squints. "Jesus Christ, Nell, I only had a couple of swallows. It wasn't much."

"And you don't think it's a little weird that you got this drunk from that?"

"I'm not fucking drunk." She sneers at me.

"Yeah, you are." Dia sits beside her. "You could barely walk by yourself."

"It was just a swallow or two," Harper insists.

"That might have been more than enough if there wasn't just alcohol in that flask." I jam the Maglite between the roots so that it stands upright, projecting its beam at the treetop. The residual glow is enough for us to see by, but it paints our faces with shifting shadows.

Dia frowns. "You think it was drugged or something?"

"That's exactly what I think."

Harper shakes off a little of her stupor. She stares at me, eyes narrow. "You're talking about Gavin."

I swallow. "Wouldn't be the first time he's done something like that."

Off in the distance, thunder shakes low against the dark horizon.

Harper squares her shoulders, drawing herself up. "What the hell are you saying, Nell?"

Tris stands and walks over. I feel her settle close behind me, her hand on my shoulder. Her touch steadies me. I take a breath. "I'm saying that Gavin put something in my drink once."

"Don't," Harper snaps. "Don't you fucking dare."

But it's coming out. It has to. Voice shaking, I go on. "It was last year, on that chorus trip. I wasn't even drinking. He poured me a Coke, and I think he put something in the cup first."

"Seriously? You're just going to sit there and accuse him?" She looks at Dia. "And you're okay with that?"

"I'm listening to what my friend—*our* friend—has to say," Dia responds, seeming to choose her words carefully. "I don't have any reason not to believe her."

I go on. "I think he had it all planned."

Harper gulps in a deep breath and closes her eyes. "Stop."

"I blacked out. I don't know exactly what happened after that."

"Nell." Harper's voice grows low, a warning tone.

"I think Gavin raped me."

I've never even let myself think the word, let alone speak it. The taste of it is bitter and metallic on my tongue, its shape against my lips alien and wrong. I'm shivering almost violently now, despite the humid warmth of the night.

Lightning strobes in the distance.

"I think he raped me," I say again, "and I think maybe he was planning on doing the same thing to you tonight. Whatever was in that flask, Harper, he wanted you to drink it."

Dia scoots closer to me. "Oh my God, Nell." She wraps an arm around my shoulders. "You never said anything, oh my God. Why didn't you tell us?"

"She didn't tell us because she's lying," Harper says through clenched teeth. She slowly rocks back and forth. It's like she's trying to burrow deeper into the roots and disappear. "Why would he even...I'm his girlfriend! Why would he want to do that to me? It doesn't make sense. And why would he want to do that to *you*?"

I don't know how to take that last question. I don't know if she means for it to sting like it does.

She shakes her head. "I heard the gossip after that trip. I heard what people were saying, and I ignored it because you were my best friend and I knew you wouldn't do something like that to me, you wouldn't sleep with my boyfriend, and now—"

My face is wet. At first I think the rain has started again, or that the rivulets are more drops from the banyan's highest branches, but salt hits my mouth and I recognize the tears for what they are. "I didn't *sleep* with him. I didn't consent to anything. Whatever happened, it wasn't my choice. I didn't want it."

"No," she whispers. "He wouldn't do that." She stands and moves a few yards east, her feet tripping over roots. She faces away from us, staring toward the Atlantic, her arms wrapped tightly around her torso.

Dia is weeping. She curls around me, warm and protective, and she presses her face to my shoulder. "Oh God, Nell, you've had to spend so much time around him, pretending everything was okay. You've been carrying around so much, all by yourself."

"I didn't think I had a choice. If I'd spoken up, he could have claimed it was consensual. So many people saw us together. He made sure of that. I didn't know how to…" I pause to pull in a shuddering breath that my lungs try to reject. "So I hid the truth away. I slammed it down and hoped I'd never have to think about it again. I needed to forget what I can't remember."

Tris closes in, too, taking my other side, holding me, her fierce grip enveloping me. We are a pedestal, the three of us, a column, connected and strong.

But not as strong as we could be. Not as strong as we need to be.

"He wouldn't," Harper says again, speaking to the sea. "I mean, he's been kind of weird lately, but…"

"Weird how?" I ask, trying to steady the tremble in my voice.

She turns back toward us, shoving her hair out of her face. There's anguish in the set of her jaw, and I think my revelation is beginning to settle and root, no matter how hard she fights to push it away. "I don't know. He's been...intense. I thought it was just because school's almost over and so much is ending. He's been clingy. But he wouldn't..." She sits back down nearby, her head in her hands. "I'm kind of dizzy. I seriously didn't drink that much."

"If you're right," Dia asks me, "how do we help her? What do we do?"

"We stay with her and make sure she's okay. There's nothing else we *can* do." I pull free and go to Harper, settling hesitantly beside her. Her earlier anger still stings like a snakebite, and I don't trust her not to strike again, not when she's feeling this defensive, this vulnerable. But when I put an arm around her, she leans into me.

"I've been thinking about breaking up with him," she says against my shirt, her tears seeping through the thin fabric. "I didn't say anything to you or Dia. I didn't know how, not after all the times I bragged about what a perfect boyfriend he was. But I figured we'd break up once we went to college."

"Even though you're both going to school in Connecticut?" Dia asks, joining us. Tris follows her, and we are four again, a stronger column.

"I withdrew my UConn application a few months ago." Harper sniffles. "He doesn't know. I knew he'd throw a tantrum if I told him, but I think I'm going to stay closer to home and go to UCF, at least for a year or two." She lets out a shuddering sigh. "I wanted to be far away from Stupid Charlie, but I don't know.

Maybe Harry and I can get an apartment near campus or something. I have to get out of Charlie's house, and for a long time I told myself that going to UConn with Gavin was the answer. I thought he was my escape, my security. He made me believe that, and even when I realized it wasn't true, I didn't want to admit it. It's just... it's been a lot."

"I had no idea you were trying to figure out so much," I say. "I wish I had known."

"How could you? It's not like I said anything." Her shoulders tense. "Gavin's going to go nuclear when he finds out, but I feel like things need to be over. We haven't even had sex lately. It's been a couple of months. I haven't wanted to, and he hasn't forced it or anything, but he's been impatient. He really pushed for me to invite him out here, especially when I mentioned that Harry wouldn't always be around. And then tonight, with that flask..." She starts to sob. We encircle her, holding her while she cries.

Something begins to rise in me, something dark and frightened and full of rage. It strains and writhes, fighting to unfurl like an ink-black flag, and it's so much more than it used to be.

I'm not going to shove it down anymore. Soon I need to set it free.

In the distance, thunder growls again.

When Harper stops crying, she's a little more sober. If things were normal, I'd insist we take her to the emergency room and call the cops. I'd demand that someone seize Gavin's flask and analyze the residue of whatever was inside it. No wonder he lied to me about that thing. It wasn't lost along with his car; he just had other plans for it.

We can't do any of that for Harper, so we surround her and

watch her and do our best to make sure she's okay. While we do that, I tell my story, the one bit of horror I never, ever wanted to share.

I tell them everything. I explain what I remember from the chorus trip. And I describe my encounter with the shadow earlier that evening, the way we joined together, the way I screamed the thunder.

Lightning beats against the horizon as if to prod me along.

"I've been placating the shadow for so long, trying to keep it happy so it wouldn't hurt me," I say. "But what if it never wanted to hurt me at all? What if it's just...part of me? What if it's all this anger and grief and fear—real fear, not the stuff in my stories— I've never dealt with? Everything I've hidden? What if I can harness that somehow?" I pause. "Maybe I already started to do that tonight."

"You think the shadow had something to do with that thunderstorm?" Tris asks.

"It came out of nowhere. You said it yourself—there weren't even any clouds, and suddenly it was pouring rain. I connected with the shadow, I invited it to join me, and *boom*, thunderstorm. The shadow made it happen." I pause. "No, *I* made it happen. I didn't realize it at the time, but I called that storm. I created it. It was part of me, just like the shadow."

"What does that mean?" Dia asks.

I can't believe what I'm about to say, but the words tumble down before I can doubt them into oblivion. "I think it's time for me to *really* let the darkness in. And then...I have to learn how to set it free."

Chapter Thirty-four

Set it free," Tris repeats, her voice quiet and tense with hesitation. "Set it free how?"

"The storm this afternoon wasn't enough," I say. "It couldn't touch the haze. But what about something bigger? Something strong enough to blow that stuff away, or dilute it, or... Whatever works. Whatever lets us reach the gate and get the hell out of here."

"And you think you can use the shadow to do that?"

I tighten my jaw. "I have no idea. If that storm showed up because of me, maybe I can do it again. I just need to figure out how."

Harper chews her lower lip. "What about Gavin? What do we do with him in the meantime?"

"We make sure he's not in the position to hurt anyone else," Tris says grimly.

I stare at her. "Are you saying we should..."

She squints. "No, of course not. But we need to lock him up or something."

"Once we get off the island," Dia says, "we'll tell the police everything and they can come back here and arrest him."

"Sure, and then his daddy will bail him out like usual." I'm resigned to that part of the story. "Where do we put him? I don't want him in the house. What about the garage?" I ask Tris. "Is there a way to lock the door?"

"There's a security lock, a slide bolt, but he could open it from the inside if he figures it out." She presses her lips together, thinking. "I might be able to disable the interior mechanism so that it only works from the outside. And we can nail the side door shut. That should hold him, at least for a while."

I nod. "Let's try that. I want him locked up as soon as possible." I hope he's still unconscious; the thought of him coming to makes me shudder.

We head to the garage, where Tris smashes the interior portion of the door's locking mechanism with a hammer from her truck until it hangs limp and useless by a single screw. To test it, she has us lock her in. From outside, we hear her fussing with what's left of the mechanism, trying to worry the slide bolt free. It stays in place. After a minute, she bangs on the door and we let her out. "It'll hold," she says, so we go to work on the side entrance, driving nails into the frame until the door won't budge.

"Do you think he can hear the hammering?" Dia says.

Dread rises in my throat, cold and thick. "I hope not."

Tris frowns. "How are we going to get him out here?"

"If he's awake," Harper says, "I'll lure him out." Her voice is weak, nauseated.

276

My fingers tighten around the barrel of the Maglite. I don't want Harper to have anything more to do with Gavin. If he's awake, I'll knock him out again.

But we're lucky. He's still crumpled in the bedroom, a trickle of blood drying on his forehead. The Maglite's weight seems to increase, pulling me down as I remember how hard I hit him. For the first time, I make myself acknowledge that I might have done more than just knock him out. I can't stand Gavin. I hate him. But can I live with myself if I . . .

Tris checks for a pulse. "Alive. Come on, let's make this quick."

I keep the Maglite ready as we half carry, half drag him down the stairs and through the living room. We make plenty of noise, but Harry doesn't stir, and I can't let myself think about that, not yet, not right now when there's so much else to do. We heft Gavin outside and lay him on the garage floor, leaving him in darkness as we shut the door. Tris slides the exterior bolt into place.

I exhale as my body starts to shake. "I thought I might have killed him."

"I could totally kill him right now," Harper says dully.

I look at her. "No, I'm being serious."

"So am I."

Chapter Thirty-Five

T ime. I need a little time to think. I can figure this out; I just
need *time*.

I send the others inside and head back to the banyan. It's after
midnight by now, and the crescent moon fights to filter through
the treetop, staying tangled in the uppermost branches. After
climbing onto Tris's cradle branch, shifting so I have a view of
the dark Atlantic, I shut off the Maglite and wait for my eyes to
adjust. It's so dark out here that my friend the shadow could sit
right beside me and I might not even know.

My friend. I never thought I'd truly consider the shadow a
friend, an ally. I don't know if its presence is part of what called the
storm earlier, or if I did that on my own. What if it was trying to
teach me? I wish I could just talk to it, ask it questions. But shadows aren't known for holding up their ends of lively conversations.

The horizon is quiet now, but there was thunder and lightning in the distance when I confronted Harper and told my least

favorite story. Did I cause that? Or was it a coincidence, a whisper of typical coastal spring weather?

There's only one way to find out.

I scoot along the branch until I'm close enough to lean against the banyan's enormous trunk. Bracing myself, rooting myself, I stare out over the ink-stained ocean and call back how I felt when I spoke to Harper. I remember the sting of her denials. I think of my devastation and fear, and the dark rage hidden beneath. The thunder answered those emotions in kind.

I inch back further, to the snap of fright I felt on the platform over the bay when Gavin showed up on Straight Shot. I keep going, to the memory of his voice a year ago. *You'll ruin your life, and nothing will happen to me.* I let the recollections rise until they feel ready to burst from my chest. This is the worst sort of meditation, slicing through the scars of old wounds to reach the infection still festering beneath. I pull at the pain until it nauseates me; I bathe in it until my thoughts swirl with vertigo.

Nothing. No streaks of lightning in the sky, no distant rumbles of thunder. I drench myself in dredged-up pain, but the island around me stays dry.

Holding tight to the trunk, I close my eyes, digging deep for more. "Where are you?" I mutter to my first nightmare, my oldest friend. "Why won't you help me?"

Next to me on the cradle branch, something breathes. A gasping strangle of an inhale.

My eyes fly open. "Have you been here the whole time?"

No answer, of course. Just another breath.

"Please. There's something I'm missing here, and I know you know what it is. Tell me what I have to do."

Silence.

"Show me, then. Show me what to do."

Something as thin and tickling as thread brushes my cheek. It's like the irritating tease of a stray strand of hair, or the scuttling dance of an insect on my face. I resist the urge to recoil, to slap it away. The tickle moves to my mouth, resting against my closed lips.

The shadow inhales again, nightmare-close this time. It has a mouth, this thing. I remember the way its face hangs open, a gaping cavern, wide and dislocated. Yet it never speaks. It breathes and gasps and chokes, but it doesn't talk.

It has no voice.

But I do.

"I need to use my voice," I say. "Is that what you're telling me?" I remember the uke string I coughed up, and that's when it hits me—whatever needs to happen to save us all, it has to come from me. From inside me. It's not about a ukulele. It's not about a song. It's what I carry with me. "It *was* you who returned my uke, wasn't it? Even then, you were trying to get me to understand. You weren't the one trapping us. You were showing me how to save us." It's not about the uke. It never was. But when I play, I also sing. I use my voice.

That's the key.

Once more, I let the shadow in. When it slips inside my mouth, I fight the reflex to cringe and pull back. It doesn't block my airway this time; it crouches low in my throat and encourages me, and finally I think I understand.

I climb down and pick my way through the roots toward the Atlantic. My feet find grass, then the soft give of sand. I don't stop until I'm a few feet from the tidemark. Wind still rolls off the ocean this far north; the haze hasn't stolen it yet. The moon slivers overhead, letting its light reflect in shards off the waves, dim stars shivering against ink.

I inhale deeply, letting the salt air brine my lungs.

Then I scream.

I give voice to my shadow, to every hint of darkness I've spent my life shoving down and tucking away and allowing to fester. I cry out, releasing the memories I've been sitting with for too long—all the pain caused by Gavin, Harper, even my own mother. Instead of digging deeper, I drag it all upward and out, setting each wound free like scraps of paper dancing away on the breeze. I fling them into the ocean like offerings.

No matter how far I throw them, I know they'll never leave me, not completely. I'll carry their ghosts for the rest of my life, whether the haze engulfs me tonight or I escape and live to be a hundred. But speaking them, screaming them, lessens their weight on my shoulders.

The shadow is pleased with my progress. I feel a strange shiver where it huddles in my throat, and I almost think that it's laughing.

Lightning arcs into the ocean, impossibly close.

I scream again and the sound turns to thunder as clouds that didn't exist seconds ago move to blot out the moon. Rain pelts my skin, battering my face and arms. I welcome each tiny, splashing sting.

I keep yelling, releasing, whipping the storm into a frenzy. It needs to be bigger, so much bigger than the last one. It needs to be powerful enough to wash away the haze and tar and clear us an escape path. It needs to be as enormous as the rage I feel toward Gavin, so I curse his name, throwing it into the thunder. I howl out the story of that night again and again. I cry out until I'm exhausted, and then I lie on the beach and let the thunderstorm soak me. It pummels the sand and beats the ocean into a whitecapped, foaming beast. As wild and furious as the storm is, though, I can tell it's listening to me. It's here because I called it, and it will stay as long as I have the strength to hold it.

I keep it corralled for what feels like hours, for what I hope is long enough to wash away the haze, although I've lost track of time. Was I under the tree for a few minutes, or did I spend most of the night there? I don't know anymore, but I hold the storm until dawn licks the eastern horizon. Surely that's enough. I let the memories rest, no longer shoving them down and encapsulating them, but allowing them to settle where they wish. The rain dies away and the sky brightens.

When there's enough light to see by, I grab the Maglite and make my way to the dirt road, where I jog south. I need to see what I've done.

I need to see that it worked.

The northern clutch of pines comes into view first. Then the house, its wide porch peeking around the tree trunks. There's Tris's truck. There's the garage, Gavin's makeshift jail cell.

I'm not Harper; I'm no runner. My lungs burn like overfilled balloons about to burst, and the muscles in my legs threaten to cramp, but I keep going.

Harper waits for me on the porch. She raises an arm, waving for my attention, and she shakes her head, but I ignore her. She has to be wrong.

I keep going until the air around me stills. Bitter heat smolders inside my throat when I inhale. Ahead, the haze sits dark and heavy. It has devoured the security light; I can barely make out the tall slash of the pole through the rust-colored cloud. The haze nibbles at the thicket of pines to the left of the house near the garage, another appetizer before the main course. I can already see tar dripping from some of the branches.

It wasn't enough. Disappointment drops my heart into the pit of my stomach. I put everything into that storm, screaming until my throat seared and my voice threatened to turn to gravel, but the haze is still here. I couldn't tear it to shreds. I couldn't even beat it back a couple of feet.

"Come inside," Harper says behind me. She puts a hand on my shoulder, guiding me back toward the house before my knees can give out. I feel like collapsing.

"I thought it would work," I murmur, walking backward while I stare at the haze. "I was so sure."

"That was an incredible storm."

"But it wasn't enough."

"We'll figure out something else."

"I don't have anything else."

"At least there's a silver lining." Harper forces lightness into her tone.

"What do you mean?"

She points to the garage, and to the haze beyond. "That stuff will get Gavin before it gets us."

Chapter Thirty-Six

Harper leads me inside, where Dia and Tris wait in the kitchen. I can't tell them I failed. I can't even look at them; I stare past them, over their heads, while Harper quietly reports that the haze is still in place.

Tris comes to me. "You need to rest. You look like you're about to collapse."

She's not wrong; I'm wavering on my feet, blank and dizzy. I let her guide me through the living room again, toward the stairs, but they look so incredibly steep. I can't imagine lifting my feet high enough to climb them.

Behind us, Harper notices my hesitation. "She can have the master," she says, so Tris takes me there instead, closing the door behind us.

"Your clothes are soaked. Let me help you."

I shake my head. I can't undress. I can't do anything; I'm too tired. The Maglite falls from my hand and rolls under the bed.

She nods and brings towels from the bathroom, wrapping one around my trembling shoulders and spreading others on the bed. She helps me lie down, and I curl on my side and close my eyes, lost in a fog of relief and crushing inadequacy. When I feel her untying my wet sneakers, I don't react.

She covers me with a throw, and the mattress shifts as she sits down. "Want me to leave you alone?"

"Stay." The word comes out like sandpaper.

"Okay. I'll be right back. Then I'll stay." She leaves, and I float in nothingness until I hear the door open and shut again as she returns. "Drink some water before you pass out."

The last thing I want right now is more water, but I open my eyes and sit up enough to drink from the bottle she offers. It gentles some of the scratchy hoarseness in my throat. Once I've drunk enough to satisfy her, I collapse and drift again, my mind meandering to the idea of a storm bigger than anything I can conjure, and then to women fleeing persecution and harassment and finding their way here, to what they hoped was safety. What went wrong? What went *right*?

So witches we became.

What did they do here that, centuries later, led to everything that's happened this week? It all ties together, I'm sure it does—the legend, the haze, the visions, the tease of a nonexistent ice-cream truck, the rusted remains of a school bus, the damaged guest book that lost its memories. There's something here, some connection I'm not seeing. It's like when I'd write a story and the plot wouldn't quite gel, the frustration that came from not fitting the details into place in the right order, and then that moment of invincible brilliance when everything finally snapped together.

285

I need to reach that moment, but first I need rest. As sleep tries to steal me, I feel Tris lie down. She puts an arm around me and holds me close, ignoring the dampness of my clothing. I feel so much stronger this way, when we're connected.

When we're connected.

So witches we became.

I drift off with the story still just out of reach. But I'm close, I can feel it. "Tell me." I mouth the words silently, talking to my shadow, to the island, to whatever might be listening.

I dream of scraps of cream-colored paper.

When I wake up, Tris is still asleep behind me. Careful not to disturb her, I creep out of bed and into the living room. Dia is there, sitting near Harry's unconscious form. She stands when she sees me. "How are you doing?"

I try to say that I'm fine, but after all the screaming I did earlier, I can't manage much more than a croak. "Papers," I whisper. "Tris said you found them."

"Oh!" Dia's eyebrows shoot up. "Right. The scraps. Here. Look." She takes a taped-together sheet of lined, cream-colored paper from the table. "It's a whole list of names. I don't recognize any of them, though."

I don't, either, but I finally recognize the paper. I gesture for Dia to wait, and I go upstairs and take the guest book from its spot on my bedroom's bookshelf. By the time I get back downstairs, Harper is there, too. I take the taped sheet from Dia and puzzle it into the book. It lines up perfectly with the torn edge near the spine. This is the missing page.

Each line on the taped paper carries a single name, all written in the same bold, unfamiliar script—Don Pedro de San Marcos,

Felipe de Luna, Carlotta Fuentes, Maria de Colon, Constance Smith, Thomasin Baker, Mark John Spenser III, Bridgette O'Hara, Arnold Kavanaugh, Vanessa Gordon, Dennis Taylor, Rachel Taylor, name after name after name, with no other information, no dates or comments or the kinds of things typically written in guest books. Bewildered, I read the names over and over.

"They must be other guests who've rented this place," Dia says, frowning.

"Some of these don't sound like modern names, though," Harper says. "I mean, Don Pedro de San Marcos? Thomasin Baker?"

"And Constance," I murmur as I realize why that name feels more familiar than the others. What if the horror lurking under the dock—the thing that wore Christopher's face and used his voice—hadn't been saying *constant* at all, but *Constance*? Perhaps it thought I was Constance Smith, whoever she was, or it was comparing me to her. Connecting me to her. Informing me—her—*us*—that something on the island had begun and could not be undone.

"Sometimes people have old-fashioned names." Dia takes the book from me and flips through the blank pages. "This really just seems like a regular guest book—oh!" A piece of yellowed newsprint flutters out from between the pages. She catches it before it can fall. "Look how old this is." She points to the date at the top of the page; the article was published in 1947.

I take it from her and read the headline, holding the brittle paper with care. "Honeymooning Couple Goes Missing." My eyes widen as I scan the first paragraph, and I clear my throat, fighting the lingering rasp. "Their names."

She takes the article back. "Dennis and Rachel Taylor. Like on the list."

"Right," I say, and the three of us gather close so that we can all read the article. After recounting what was known about the disappearance of the Taylors—they were never seen again after hiring a boat from a local marina—it compares the situation to another unsolved missing-persons case from the same area two decades earlier. "Another couple," I say. "Mark John Spenser III and Bridgette O'Hara."

"They're on the list, too," Harper says.

"As of when this article was published, they hadn't been found." I press my lips into a thin line, thinking. "As far as we know, Dennis and Rachel were never found, either. What if everyone on this list went missing?"

"Do you think they made it to this island?" Harper asks.

I think back to the class ring on the sliver of finger bone tossed in the banyan's roots, and I feel something click in my mind, the same way story details used to click together when I'd write. These are names I'm meant to know. "I think maybe they did, but they never made it back off."

"Like us," Dia says quietly. She points to the blank lines at the bottom of the list. "There's just enough room left for all of us."

"Not if I can help it," I say as an idea that's irrational and wild and utterly mad begins to whirl. I stack the guest book on top of Harry's history book, and I clasp both to my chest. "Give me a little time to puzzle this out, okay? I'll fill you in soon."

Dia's brow is creased with confusion, but she nods. She trusts me.

I return to the master bedroom and sit at the small desk, and

I find the woodcut illustration of the witches in Harry's book. There's a detail in it that none of us noticed before. Maybe we weren't ready to see it yet, but it's plain as day now. As the gears in my brain start turning, I make a list in the guest book of the visions the cat showed me. The empty kayak. The screaming, tar-covered face. The sewing needle. All of it. It all fits together somehow.

Then I open the guest book to a blank page, and I start to write. I get a lot wrong, I'm sure—it's not like I can Google research questions—but maybe I can get just enough right. The tale that pours out is the roughest of rough drafts—I scribble fiercely, almost violently, slamming the story onto the guest book's pages. It doesn't have to be perfect; it just has to *become*. Like me.

Maybe, just maybe, like *us*.

For once, I don't write to frighten myself. I'm already more than scared enough. But there's a story here, a plot smashed into a thousand pieces. If I can puzzle them back together just right, maybe I'll find some answers, truths wrapped up in fiction.

I write like I'm in a trance or a dream. By the time I finish, my hand is cramping around the pencil and I'm exhausted again. I need the others around me, but my eyes won't stay open. I slip the guest book under my pillow and curl back up with Tris. I still need to anchor the story in the reality of what we've been through this week, but I'm close to the truth now.

I'm so, so close.

Chapter Thirty-Seven

I awake surrounded. Tris's arm is around me again. Harper is on my other side, dozing on her back, while Dia naps stretched across the foot of the bed like a cat.

My friends. The storm I screamed to life didn't set us free, and now the story that made perfect sense earlier feels too silly to share. I let them all down, yet here they are.

I can't sit up without waking them. One by one, they stir and rise until we're sitting in a circle on the bed.

"Did you figure it out?" Dia asks.

"I'm not sure," I say, feeling increasingly foolish that I ever thought I could somehow fiction us all free. My voice is still raspy from so much screaming, so I switch to a whisper. "Throat drops. I have some in my makeup bag."

"I'll get them." Harper jumps up and leaves. When she returns, she has the makeup bag in one hand and my uke case in the other.

"I thought you might want it nearby," she says, nodding toward the uke before she hands me the bag.

"You really do travel prepared," Tris says as I unwrap a drop.

The thick, honeyed sweetness soothes my throat, and I can speak a little more clearly, although my voice is still rough. "You never know if someone's going to get a cough or a sore throat or something."

"Classic Nell," Harper says without a trace of teasing. She gives me a gentle smile.

"Sometimes it's nice to have a mom type around," Dia says.

Harper swallows and wipes at her eyes. "I miss my mom." Dia hugs her.

My vision blurs with tears. "I'm sorry. I was sure the storm would work."

"You have nothing to be sorry for." Dia frowns. "That storm was incredible. I can't believe you did that."

"It wasn't enough," I say. "*I* wasn't enough."

Tris shakes her head. "Nope, we're not even going to acknowledge that train of thought. There's a way to use this. We just need to figure out how."

"If I had more time," I say, "if I could practice, really learn how to control it..."

"The haze is just too close," Harper finishes for me.

"There has to be some way to amplify what you can do," Dia says. "I mean, you summoned a storm."

"Two storms," Harper points out.

Dia nods. "Right. And the second was enormous compared to the first. You're going in the right direction."

"I put everything I had into the second one." I rest my head on my hand.

"How does it work?" Harper asks. "How'd you do it?"

I consider how to explain. "I pulled up all this anger I've been holding in, and I set it free. The more I dug up, the more I seemed to have. Anger at Gavin for what he took...for what I assume he took from me. Anger at the holes in my memory. There was so much of it, so much anger, and it just kept coming. Anger at my mom for leaving when I was little. Anger at my dad for not believing me about the shadow, and for never telling me the truth about why he and Mom divorced, and...He doesn't know this, but I got into his email once, a few years ago. I found these old messages between him and a couple of women he used to work with. I think Mom left because he cheated. He drove her away. He broke her heart." Another truth I'd never planned to say out loud. "It was just...everything. Every bit of anger I've been keeping inside."

"Anger at me?" Harper asks quietly.

My instinct is to lie. To appease. Instead, I slowly nod. "Yeah, I guess there was some of that, too."

"I don't blame you." Tears pool in her eyes. "I've been an awful friend for a long time."

I start to reassure her, to walk the admission back, but my voice cracks when I try to speak.

"Don't," she goes on. "You always say that everything's fine, and you carry the weight for everyone else. You don't need to do that for me. I know I haven't been a great friend."

"You've been pushing me so much," I say when my voice comes back to me.

Her chin trembles. "I know."

"You stopped wanting to do all the things we used to do. You kept changing." My eyes overfill and I let the tears spill. "And okay, people change, it's normal. But it was like you were leaving me behind."

"I didn't want to!" she says. "I wanted to pull you with me."

Something inside me unravels, something that was buried so deep that I couldn't reach it when I summoned the thunderstorm. Storms are rage and howling fury; this is grief, quiet and stagnant. "I felt like I wasn't good enough for you anymore unless I forced myself to change. I didn't want to do that."

"I just started wanting different things." She presses her mouth into a thin line. "It was terrifying. I felt like I was doing everything wrong."

I think of how easily it all came to her. New friends. Teams. Popularity. A relationship that seemed to make her swoon. "That's not how it looked to me. You were so confident."

She shakes her head. "I was faking it. It scared me that you didn't seem interested. If you'd wanted the same things…"

"You didn't need my permission for any of it."

"No, but I needed the validation. I thought if I could get you to come along with me, that would mean it was okay for me to change. That was why I kept pushing. I wanted to keep you with me, and I felt like you were drifting away."

There's a tissue in my hand. I don't notice who put it there, Tris or Dia, but I'm grateful as I wipe my eyes. "I thought you were the one drifting."

"I couldn't. I wouldn't." She sniffles. "Can we fix this?"

I hug her tightly, fiercely. "I think so. I hope so."

She cries against my hair.

"It'll take time," I say. "We'll both need to accept each other as we are now. We're not two little dorks publishing a zine anymore, but our friendship was always more than that. It can still be more."

"I just wish I had talked to you instead of making such a mess."

I pull back. "I wish I'd talked to you, too. Years ago. Let's promise not to keep these things buried anymore."

She gives me a wobbly smile. "So from now on, if I'm mad at you, I should just say so?"

"Yeah. And if you're annoying the hell out of me with endless track-meet talk or obsessing over some guy's Insta, I'm going to call you on it."

"And if you're being judgmental and grouchy, I'm calling *you* on *that*."

"It's a deal." I smile a little. "But you have to admit that sometimes my judgments are pretty accurate."

"I'm so sorry," she says, the hope in her expression deflating. "I'm sorry for what he did to you."

I shake my head. "You're not the one who needs to apologize, and there's no apology from him that would ever be enough— even if he felt any remorse, and I promise you he doesn't." My voice trembles, and I inhale slowly to calm it. "He broke something in me. I'm still putting myself back together. I'll never be quite the same again, but I think, with enough time and enough work, I can assemble some other version of myself that's just as good."

"Damn right," Tris murmurs, moving close so that she can rest her chin on my shoulder. Her hand finds mine and squeezes.

I sit up a little straighter as the first hint of something bright and buoyant sparks in my chest. "And I'm only going to have time to do that if we manage to get off this island. Should I go out and try again?"

"You need more rest," Tris argues.

"There's no time for that," I say. "The haze is too close." But even the thought of calling another storm, of dredging up all that fury and hauling it to the surface again, is so exhausting that I close my eyes.

"Maybe one of us should try," Dia says. "We've all seen your shadow. Maybe my voice would work, too. Or Harper's, or Tris's."

"What about the rage that goes with it?" I ask.

Dia's shoulders fall. "I don't think I have that. I'm sure we're all mad about something, but... not like that. I mean, I used to get so pissed off when Christopher would send me dick pics, but—"

"He *what*?" Harper's eyes go wide.

"God, yeah, all the time." Dia shrugs. "And he'd bug me for nudes."

"What an ass," I say.

Dia's cheeks flush. "It was more annoying than anything. Or I convinced myself of that, I guess. Mostly it was just gross. I didn't want to look at that, you know?"

Tris grimaces. "It's more than gross. It's harassment."

"I guess."

"Did you tell him to stop?" Tris asks.

"Of course! I think he liked how uncomfortable it made me. And I didn't know who could help me."

"I'm surprised your dad didn't hunt him down," I say.

"I think he actually would have, if he'd known," Dia says. "That's why I didn't say anything to my parents. And I thought that if I went to someone at school, like a guidance counselor, they wouldn't take it seriously. It'd just be, *oh, boys will be boys*, you know?"

We all nod. It's too familiar. Too disheartening.

Too infuriating.

"I think part of why I freaked out so bad when he…" Dia pauses. "You know, in the bay."

We all nod.

"I mean, it was horrifying," she goes on. "I wish I hadn't looked in the bay. I don't think I'll ever get that image out of my head. But I also felt kind of… satisfied, almost. It was like some dark little part of me thought he got what he deserved. That really scared me."

I think back to the Christopher-thing I saw lurking under the dock. The memory isn't as troubling as it used to be. "If it makes you feel any better," I tell Dia, "I feel a lot less sorry for him now that I know what he was doing."

She catches my hand and gives it a squeeze.

"My dad used to have this business partner, Pete," Tris says quietly. "I stopped going to properties with Dad for a while because Pete was always there, too, and he'd get weird."

I thought my anger was spent, but her comment reignites it. "What did he do?"

"Nothing," she says quickly. It's a reflex, an automatic denial that rings false and empty. "He'd wait until Dad was out of earshot, and then he'd try to get me to give him my number, which was weird because he was so much older than I was. Or he'd ask if I had a boyfriend yet—and when I told him that was never going to happen, that I only liked girls, he just seemed even more interested. And there was one time..." She shuts her eyes and shakes her head. "It was nothing."

Harper puts a hand on Tris's shoulder. "Sounds like it was a lot more than nothing."

Tris sighs shakily. "I was fourteen. Pete and Dad were inspecting this house that they wanted to buy and flip. Dad went outside to look at the foundation, so I was alone with Pete. He walked past me, and he sort of stumbled, and he grabbed me to steady himself, and his hands stayed on me a little too long. It creeped me out, you know?" Her jaw tightens. "I pulled away and backed up a few steps, into a bathroom, and I tried to close the door in his face. He blocked it with his foot and pushed his way in, and then he stood there in the doorway. He gave me the weirdest look. There was something in his eyes that... I don't know what it was, but every time I watch a nature show, the predators make me think of him, of the way he looked at me. I froze. It was probably only a couple of seconds, but it felt like longer. Then he stepped aside just enough to let me pass. I had to brush against him to get away." She shuts her eyes.

I wrap an arm around her.

"I stuck close to Dad until we left," she goes on, "and after that, I just started avoiding Pete. I couldn't tell Dad about it. He and Pete had so much money wrapped up in their properties, and I was terrified Pete would pull his funding and make Dad go bankrupt if I said something. So I told myself it was nothing."

"We all tell ourselves that, don't we?" Harper asks, her tone stretching thin.

"Oh, Harper." My heart sinks when I see the reluctance in her expression. "You too? Who was it?"

She hesitates. Parroting Tris, she says, "It's nothing."

"Sounds like it's a lot more than nothing," Tris says gently, turning Harper's earlier words back on her.

"Charlie," Harper says, her voice dropping to little more than a whisper.

"Charlie? Your *stepdad*?" My stomach clenches as rage I didn't think I had the strength to conjure rises and twists. "What did he do?"

"It's not any one thing," Harper says quickly. "He's just...I don't know how to describe it. He's just weird." She looks at Tris. "Like what you said about Pete."

"Weird," Tris mutters. Dia and I nod. We all know what *weird* means in this context. Lingering glances. Smiles that are more like leers. Vague creepiness. That predator-prey feeling.

"He's creeped me out since he and Mom got together," Harper goes on. She can't meet our eyes; she focuses on the tangle of bedsheets, running a finger along the edge of a blanket. "I told myself I was being stupid. Here's this successful guy who's changing our lives for the better, and he's good to Mom, and for once she doesn't have to worry about paying bills and making rent anymore, and I don't like him because, what? The way he looks at me sometimes makes me uncomfortable? I mean, so what, right?" She shrugs.

"No," I say. "Not right. Not at all. What has he done?"

"He's never touched me or anything," she says quickly. "It's little things. Like he never knocks on my bedroom door before he comes in. He says it's his house and he shouldn't have to knock. But sometimes he does that when he knows I'm getting dressed, and it's just..." She grimaces. "A couple of times I've noticed him peek in my room at night, too, and he won't let me have a lock on my door. He says we're family, and families don't lock each other out. And sometimes he makes these comments. Like he'll say I look hot in my new dress, and I don't know, it doesn't feel right."

"Definitely creepy," Tris says. "Definitely *weird*."

"And the way he makes me work for him," Harper goes on. "On Saturdays it's usually just him and me in the office. I hate being alone with him. I hate how close he leans in when he's looking over my shoulder at the computer. He puts his hands on the desk on either side of me. It makes me feel trapped. He gets too close to me in general. And sometimes he tells me to smile—"

Dia, Tris, and I all groan. We're too familiar with that command.

"Exactly!" Harper says. "He's never done anything worse, but, like…" She pauses, chewing her lip. "I've always felt like he *could*. He could and he wants me to know it. I'm always on guard around him. I feel like I have to be."

"Have you told your mom?" I ask.

She shakes her head. "I can't. Nothing's actually happened. If I say anything, it'll mess up their marriage. She'll go back to struggling. We all will, her and Harry and me. I can't do that to my family." She shuts her eyes. "I just need to stick it out until college. Then I can escape, even if I stay local."

"That's why you want to get a place with Harry instead of living at home," I say.

She swallows and nods.

"I wish I had known what was going on." I frown in sympathy. "You never told me."

"I was embarrassed. I felt like I had to keep it a secret for my family's sake. And part of me wondered if maybe I did something to make him act like that. Maybe I invited it."

"You didn't," I say. "Of course you didn't."

"I know, but I couldn't help wondering."

Tris points at her. "You blamed yourself." She swings her finger toward Dia. "You knew you'd just hear some *boys will be boys* garbage if you spoke up." She looks at me. "You thought you'd lose your best friend and no one would believe you." She shakes her head. "This world has been feeding us some serious bullshit."

"At least we're starting to see through it," Dia says. "We don't have to hide these things from each other. We've all had similar experiences. We get it."

"We can support each other," Tris says. "Protect each other. Help each other become stronger than any of this."

"Become," I murmur. Something clicks in my head, a realization as simple as it is huge. "That's it. That's *it*. Maybe I was on the right track after all."

The others look at me quizzically.

"The shadow showed me that what I needed to summon the storm was inside me. My voice. Everything I carry with me— the darkness, the fear. The rage. But don't you see? We all carry those things. We carry them like it's normal, like it's just...what we're meant to do."

"Like it's just expected of us," Harper says. "Nell, remember when I got my training bra and those boys in our class kept snapping the straps? And the teacher wouldn't do anything about it? Now that I think about it, I'm still pissed about that."

"Or when they'd make you cover up your tank tops because boys might be distracted," I say.

"Right?" Dia says, sitting up straighter and squaring her shoulders. "How come we're always the ones who have to cover up? Or compromise? Or put up with guys' nonsense?"

"I told Pete I was gay," Tris mutters. "I *told* him. You should've seen the way his face lit up when I said it. Like I was going to invite him to join in or something." Her lips curl with disgust. "Like the whole idea of it was just there for his enjoyment. I was *fourteen*."

"This!" I say. "This rage. This is what I'm talking about. This is what we carry. What if the shadow isn't me at all? Or rather, what if it isn't *just* me?"

"What is it, then?" Harper asks.

Tris's eyes widen. "It's *us*."

"All of us," Dia says. "I don't think there's a woman on earth who hasn't felt it at some point."

"We carry it for each other," Tris says. "We help each other."

Harper nods. "We're stronger when we're together."

"Look." I grab Harry's history book and show them the wood-cut of the witches. "I think they carried these things, too. I don't know how we didn't see it before, but..."

Their eyes grow wide and shocked as they see my shadow. *Our* shadow. It surrounds the illustration, stretching taller than the banyan, its thread-thin arms tangling in the tree's branches. It encircles the women, but I know now that it's not trapping them.

It's connecting them. Uniting them.

Tris runs her fingers over the illustration like it has to be some sort of trick. "How did we not..."

"I don't know, but I need to read y'all something." I pull the guest book from under my pillow and open it to my newest story, the most important story I've ever written. Undoing the original magic is too big of a job for me, but I'm not the only one here carrying rage-fueled secrets.

It's time for us to join together. It's time to *become*.

I begin to read.

THE ISLAND OF NO STORMS
By Nell Douglas

They were called witches, so witches they became.

There were four of them, sisters not in blood but in spirit, and each had a gift all her own. Those gifts brought renown.

Those gifts sealed their fates.

Maria was an artist of exquisite caliber. She drew, she painted, she carved and printed woodcuts, and even her quickest sketches conveyed almost unbearable beauty. Carlotta's embroidery turned plain dresses and coats into enviable and intricate fashions rumored to charm the wearer with tantalizing mystery. Under Thomasin's gentle care, plants flourished in the harshest conditions. And Constance was a storyteller, weaving words into tales, each more fantastic and fascinating than the last.

Their skills inspired envy throughout the village of St. Felicitas, and the well-to-do came from miles around seeking a taste of those talents. They commissioned Maria to create flattering portraits. They paid handsomely for Carlotta's bewitching

fashions. They begged Thomasin to bless and
nurture their crops, and they came to Constance to
hear her irresistible stories.

In the end, those stories were perhaps *too*
irresistible. Sometimes awestruck envy turns to
bitter jealousy and demanding entitlement, and that
is what happened when a pair of travelers, Felipe
de Luna and Don Pedro de San Marcos, passed
through the village on their way to the fort of St.
Augustine and became aware of the sisters. They
saw Thomasin's citrus trees, each branch heavy with
fruit. They admired a fantastical painting in the local
alehouse and learned about Maria. In the village
market, they passed Carlotta and marveled at the
intricate sprays of lavender blossoms embroidered
on her dress. And they came across Constance
weaving tales in the village square, surrounded by a
crowd of dazzled children.

They stopped to listen, and soon they were
dazzled themselves.

The mysterious sisters were blessed with exquisite
gifts, and that realization fascinated the travelers.
They would court these women, they vowed, with
each keeping his favorite sister for himself. But it
was not to be—over and over, their attempts came
to nothing. When the sisters would not submit,
fascination turned to resentment. Felipe and Don
Pedro would have their revenge, and all it took was
a whisper here and there. Such unholy talents, they

suggested, could not possibly come from God. They muttered rumors and nudged lies through the village until its residents turned against the sisters and drove them out of St. Felicitas. Under the cover of new-moon darkness, the four stole a little boat and escaped to an island off the coast.

But that was not enough for Felipe and Don Pedro. They followed, still bent on possession. The island was small, and the sisters couldn't hide forever.

"They called us witches," Constance said. "Let's prove them right." And so the sisters got to work.

Carlotta tore a scrap from her skirt, and using the needle and thread she always kept close, she embroidered the men's names, whispering a curse into every stitch before tossing the fabric into a bonfire, setting those curses free.

Thomasin went to the north end of the island, where a lone palm tree stood guard. There she planted a special seed and coaxed it to sprout. Its vines would embrace the palm and strangle it, a sacrifice made to anchor and protect.

Maria used a branch to draw in the damp sand near the shore, sketching the men lying dead on the beach, illustrating what she most wanted to see.

Constance wrote spell after spell, choosing each word with care and rage and hatred as dark as tar. She had no paper, so she kept the words safely in her head.

"Let them come," she said when the men reached the island. "Let them come and regret it. It has begun; what's done is done."

Together, the sisters woke the island. And the island, it turned out, was hungry. When the men approached, the island claimed them, tearing and wrenching and drowning them in tar until they lay still and dead in the sand, just as Maria had drawn, just as Carlotta had whispered into every stitch, just as Constance had written in her head.

Under Thomasin's guidance, the sisters dragged the men to the north end of the island, to where she had planted the seed pod. A tree grew there overnight, wrapping the bodies in massive roots and devouring them, leaving nothing but bone behind.

"No one else will find us," Constance said. "We are safe here." But there was no justice without sacrifice, and the island was hungry still—hungry and owed a deep debt. Soon it reached for the sisters themselves, all tar and choking haze, and when they weren't strong enough to control what they had conjured, they knew their bones would come to rest amid the roots of the enormous tree as well. It was not their intention, but it shaped their fate, and the fate of the island itself.

Resigned, the sisters vowed to leave behind a warning for anyone else who might find their way to the island's shore. What form the warning might take was a topic of debate until Maria, with a sly smile, drew a creature in the sand. "What better choice for witches to make?" she said, and the others agreed. Carlotta tore another scrap of fabric from her dress and embroidered dark fur, and wary eyes, and long, twitching whiskers. Thomasin coaxed life into the creature, the same way she'd always coaxed plants to grow, and Constance imbued it with their story. When the island claimed the sisters, they left behind an animal to hold their memory close, an animal quick and clever enough to do what they could not—survive on the island.

They left behind a small black cat.

Seasons passed, then years. The island returned to its slumber, and perhaps the cat slumbered as well, content in its solitude. Some hint of the sisters' protective spell remained, keeping the place safe from the storms that threatened the rest of the coast every summer; however, the sisters and their pursuers were all but forgotten, as was the island itself, more or less. Others still found their way there now and then, and still the island slept....

Until a certain sort of visitor, a certain sort of threat caused it to stir. "Let them come," the island whispered to itself—or perhaps it was the echo of Constance's voice carrying on the ocean breeze. "Let them come and regret it. It has begun; what's done is done." And then there were more debts to pay.

One was owed by Bridgette O'Hara, whose burlesque routine caught the eye of millionaire playboy Mark John Spenser III in the 1920s. Bridgette believed Mark's empty promises, even when he was handsy, even when he was violent. She suggested a picnic on that pretty island just offshore, the one with the big tree.

Neither Bridgette nor Mark were ever seen again.

In the 1940s, newlyweds Dennis and Rachel Taylor went missing during their honeymoon, after hiring a boat from the St. Felicitas marina. Rachel's closest friends quietly wondered what Dennis had done. He had that way about him, they whispered. It wouldn't be the first time he hurt Rachel.

In the 1970s, Arnold Kavanaugh and Vanessa Gordon visited St. Felicitas. Vanessa loved Arnold's free spirit—and if his temper flared when he drank too much, wasn't that just further proof of his passion? They crossed the bay in a kayak, rowing out to explore the little island with the big tree.

The kayak was found adrift the next day, but Arnold and Vanessa were gone.

Now and then, it happened. People disappeared. It wasn't unheard of, officials reasoned, to drown in the Atlantic, to vanish into the waves and drift into oblivion. The island dozed, allowing itself to be searched, keeping its secrets close. Eventually, it even allowed a house and a road and a bridge to be built. It let visitors wander its shore and play on its beaches. Those visitors stayed for a week or a season or a span of years, and then they left, unaware of the fate they escaped. The island wasn't hungry for them.

When the girls showed up on their spring break trip, the island welcomed them. It expected to sleep through their visit. They were perfectly safe....

Until one invited a boy named Gavin to join them. She gave him access to the island, and the island awoke once more.

It has begun; what's done is done.

It was time to find a way to break the dark and dangerous spell. It was time, once again, to become witches.

The End

Chapter Thirty-Eight

When I finish, Dia opens the history book to the woodcut illustration and reads the first line of the rhyme. *"One to illustrate a truth."* She points at Harper, then hands her the book.

"And one to tell a tale," Harper continues before passing it to me.

"One to nurture," I go on, giving it to Tris.

"One to bind." Tris hands the book back to Dia.

"So none who seek shall ever find, beyond this conjured veil," Dia finishes.

"You all see it, too," I say.

"They're like us," Harper says. "One draws. One embroiders. One grows plants."

"And one tells stories," Tris finishes, squeezing my arm.

"I don't know what really happened here," I say. "It's not like I can research, not without internet access or a library. But the island has shown us things here and there. I piled up those things, and the illustration from Harry's book, and I ran with them. I took control of them."

"Like the storyteller you've always been," Dia says.

"What if whatever's going on here is as strong as it is because the four of them worked together?" I ask. "I don't think they meant for any of this to happen. They just wanted to be safe. They didn't intend to build a trap."

"Sometimes a drawing doesn't look right, no matter how much time I put into it," Harper says.

"Sometimes my stitches won't come out as neatly as I'd like," Dia says.

"Sometimes a plant won't thrive," Tris adds, "even under perfect conditions."

I nod. "And sometimes a story won't end the way I want it to. Maybe that's what happened to these women. They tried, but things didn't go as they intended. They wanted protection from Felipe and Don Pedro, but that protection came at a price."

"But if they worked together to set all of this in motion...," Tris begins.

"Maybe we can work together to stop it," I finish as the others nod.

"We all have things to be angry about," Harper says, and I put an arm around her shoulders and squeeze. "We all have rage to set free." She looks at me. "Will it be enough?"

"I don't know, but it's worth a try." A shiver of hope straightens my spine.

"Do you really think we can connect like that?"

"Harper, you and I already have," I say quietly. "You taught me the song I always sang for the shadow. You didn't know I needed it, and I didn't know it would work, but we just…connected that day, without even meaning to. Imagine how strong we could all be together, doing this on purpose."

"We'll need to conjure one hell of a storm," Dia says.

"We need a hurricane," I say. "Even then, I don't know if it'll be enough to clear out that haze."

"A hurricane," Tris murmurs, frowning. "Wait. What if we don't need to clear the haze? What if we can get rid of the water instead? If we drain the bay, maybe we can walk off the island."

My chest tightens as I remember my dream, and what Tris said when I described the ocean roaring back to drown me. "Storm surge."

"Not so much the surge itself," Tris says. "We need what can happen right before. We'll summon a storm that's strong enough to suck out all the water temporarily. It'll empty the bay. If we're lucky, it'll take whatever's lurking out there with it, at least for a little while."

I nod slowly. "And then we run like hell before it all comes back."

Harper pauses. "And if things don't go the way we intend?"

I don't say anything. We all already know the answer to that. The island will take us, just like it took the witches. Our bones will rest amid the roots of the banyan tree, slowly bleaching in the dappled sunlight.

Chapter Thirty-Nine

Wait," Tris says. "If we have to get out of here fast, what do we do about Harry?"

Dia is already on her feet, heading to the living room with us following to gather around the sectional. I take the guest book and the history book with me; I can't stand the idea of letting them out of my sight.

"We can't carry him," Tris says.

"We can't leave him," Harper counters, her tone thin.

Dia touches his bandaged calf, then looks back at me. "The witches are us, right?"

"You've seen the illustration in Harry's book," I say. "Four of them. Four of us."

Harper turns to Dia. "What does that have to do with Harry, though?"

Dia takes her ruined embroidery project from Harry's chest. She managed to wash out most of the blood, but the wrinkled fabric still carries some light stains. "This was supposed to say, 'The rest is history,' but it's only half done. See?" *The rest* is stitched in her impossibly neat calligraphic script; the space below is empty. She looks from the fabric to Harry. "I was making this for him, and then I used it on his injury."

"Rest," I say softly.

"It's impossible," she says. "I know. But, Nell, if you're right and we have to be witches, what if this was some kind of accidental spell?"

"His leg has been healing impossibly quickly," I say. "That has to be because of your stitches."

"Okay, but what if he won't wake up because of what I embroidered for him? Because I told him to rest? I didn't mean to, but—"

"If that's what happened," Harper says, "can you undo it?"

"I don't know." Dia picks up the fabric, her fingers tightening around it, creating new wrinkles. "I have to find my project bag. I need my seam ripper."

"I think it's still in the master," Harper says. "I'll come with you so I can grab my sketchbook. If there's a chance we can make any of this work, we each have to do our part."

"Nell already did her part," Tris says. "She told us the story." She frowns. "What about me, though?"

"You know the island better than any of us," I say. "Your banyan anchors this place. Ask it for help." I'm not sure what that help might look like, but I remember her saying that the pines almost seemed to tell her which branches to prune, and I think of how lush her herbs and succulents grow. The banyan is at the heart of whatever magic is going on here, and if it's capable of listening to anyone, that person is Tris. She protected the tree when her father wanted to chop it down to make room for a gazebo. Perhaps it will return the favor.

Harper comes back with her sketchbook, opening it to a blank page. "If I'm the artist, what do I draw?"

"Whatever feels right," I say. "Use your intuition, just like they did." I touch the illustration of the witches again. "We don't have a lot of time. We'll meet at the banyan in an hour."

Dia wiggles the seam ripper under a stitch, worrying it until the thread breaks. Harper sketches furiously.

Tris heads outside. I follow her as far as the porch, and I sit on the front steps with the guest book balanced on my knees. She's right. I've already done my part; by writing the story, I've begun my spell. For the next hour, I read and reread it, over and over and over until I know it practically by heart. I murmur the words to myself with intention, giving them power, strength, a voice. *My* voice.

So witches we become, ready to finish what those who came before us began.

Close to an hour later, I hear the door open behind me. I turn and see Dia gesturing me inside. She holds up the fabric; the old project is gone, replaced with hasty stitches spelling out *wake up*.

"Did it work?" I ask, looking over her shoulder at Harry. He's still unconscious.

"I'm afraid to try," she says.

I touch her arm and nod, encouraging her on. I understand. I'm afraid, too. But we're running out of time for hesitation.

She goes to Harry and places the fabric back on his chest, over his heart. "Please wake up," she whispers, pressing her hand to the embroidery. "Please."

314

Harper closes her sketchbook, clasping it to her chest as she watches. She's holding her breath.

So am I.

After an unbearably long moment, Harry's eyelids flutter. Dia lets out a laugh that's more of a sob. When he tries to sit up, she gently grasps his shoulders, keeping him in place.

He blinks sleepily, still somewhat out of it. "What's going on? What happened?"

"Just stay here," Dia says. "We'll tell you everything when we get back."

"Get back from where?" he asks, rubbing his eyes, but we're already heading out the door, Harper with her sketchbook, me with the guest book and history book.

It's time.

Chapter Forty

We find Tris on her cradle branch, eyes closed, one hand pressed against the banyan's trunk. She opens her eyes and jumps down when she hears us coming.

"Ready?" I ask her.

"I think so," she says, her voice full of doubt. She touches the branch once more, like she's sending a final silent plea. "I don't know if I'm doing this right."

"None of us do." I open the history book to the illustration of the witches because I feel like they should be here with us for this. "Neither did they."

"Did y'all do your parts?" she asks.

"Dia woke Harry," I say.

Tris raises her brows. "Wow. Just like that? He was really out of it."

Dia pulls another bit of fabric from her pocket. "I did this, too." I recognize it as the embroidery she did of the shadow, but she's added our initials underneath in quick, long stitches. We're connected now, in thread and in whatever strange magic we're conjuring. The thought gives me a burst of fresh hope.

I look at Tris. "If we can make this storm surge thing happen, how long will we have to cross the bay?"

"The tide should stay out for a couple of hours, at least until the eye passes over us," she says. "We'll have time." She turns to Harper. "And our artist witch?"

Harper opens her sketchbook. "I didn't really know what to draw," she says, but her choice is perfect. Rendered in quick, sharp pencil strokes, the four of us stand amid the banyan's roots. Harper took inspiration from the history book, but the witches in her version are very much us. Tris has one hand on the trunk of the tree; her other hand holds a bundle of herbs. Dia pulls a threaded needle through a cut of fabric, embroidering the *p* in *wake up*. Harper holds her sketchbook and a pencil, and I have the guest book in one hand . . . and a ukulele in the other.

"My uke?" I ask.

"It felt right," Harper says. "What are songs if not stories set to music?" She gives me a small smile that sends a gentle flush over my cheeks. I never thought of my singing and playing that way. It was a ritual born from fear and meant to protect, to appease. Now, though, I look back at how I used music to cope, and how it connected my shadow to me. Harper is right. Music is part of this. Part of me. Part of *us*.

I point at the uke in her drawing. "Do you think I should go back and get it?"

"You brought your voice," Tris says. "I think that's what we need."

I nod. Together, we head down to the beach. I toss the guest book, story and all, into the ocean. Harper follows it with her sketchbook. Dia sets the fabric free to drift on the waves, and Tris adds a seed-heavy fig from her banyan. Offerings.

Tris points to the southeast. "A hurricane would come from that direction. It would strengthen over the warm water and curve northwest toward Florida." Her brow knits. "What if the water's too cool, though? Hurricane season doesn't start until June, and the big storms don't usually hit until late summer, when the ocean's at its warmest."

"We'll just have to hope it's warm enough," I say. "It's not like we can wait until August."

She nods and goes on. "When Hurricane Matthew skirted us, the track skimmed the coast. We'll need our storm to follow a similar path, but we'll have to bring it much closer. If we get the angle of approach just right, we should be able to get the winds going in the right direction to draw out the water."

Harper crouches and uses her finger to draw an outline of Florida in the damp sand. "Show us what the path should look like."

Tris kneels beside her and traces a track that curves up toward the Atlantic shore, making landfall near St. Felicitas.

"Wait." Dia frowns. "This isn't going to affect just us. If we manage to conjure a hurricane, we'll be putting a lot of people in danger."

For a moment, we're all quiet. I just want to get us off the island; I haven't let myself think about the consequences of our plan beyond our own escape. "As soon as we're safe," I say finally, "we'll push it back out to sea."

"Do you think we can?" Harper asks, straightening up.

"The storm I made this morning didn't stick around once I let it go. It dissipated."

Tris stands, brushing the sand from her knees. "That would disrupt the surge, too. Slow it down. We might be able to avoid flooding the coast."

"*Might*," Dia repeats. "I don't know if that's enough. What if we hurt people? What if we kill someone?"

"I don't want to kill anyone," Harper says softly, "but I also don't want to die." She looks south, toward the haze. "I don't want that stuff to get me. To get *us*. I don't know what other choice we have."

Dia shakes her head, a gesture that echoes my own doubt. "Of course we have a choice," she says.

Harper steps closer. "What? Let the haze devour us?"

"What makes us more important than all those people?" Dia waves her hand toward the bay and the mainland beyond. "You're all okay risking thousands of lives?"

"Of course not," I say. "But we're also not okay with just giving up. I'm not, at least."

"Neither am I." Tris comes to stand beside me.

Dia says, "Tris, your own father is out there."

Tris's expression pinches. "He'll be okay. He knows his way around hurricanes."

"If we don't do this," Harper says, "we might as well just walk into the haze right now and get it over with."

"Harsh," Tris mutters.

Dia's eyes shimmer as she fights against tears. "I can't, you guys. I'm sorry. I just...I can't." She turns and heads south.

"Dia!" I start to follow her, afraid she's taking Harper's suggestion to heart, but she veers toward the house instead of the road.

319

Tris catches my hand. "Give her a minute. She's not exactly wrong."

"I thought you agreed with us," Harper says.

"I do. It's just complicated." Tris sits on the sand, legs crossed, and stares out at the Atlantic. "You know, every time a hurricane comes anywhere near St. Felicitas, Dad and I watch the weather maps and keep track of the spaghetti plots, and we hope like hell that the storm goes somewhere else. That it doesn't hit us. That it turns just enough to keep us safe."

Harper sits beside her. "Why wouldn't you hope for that?"

Tris chews her bottom lip. "When you hope for a hurricane to turn away from you, you're hoping by default that it hits somewhere else. You're not outwardly wishing it on anyone, but you want it to stay far away from you. If that means it turns and makes landfall a hundred miles north or whatever, well, at least you're safe. You're thankful. You're *glad*. You feel awful for the people in its path, but at least that isn't you." She swipes the back of her hand over her eyes. "It's such a selfish thing to hope for, and yet I still hope for it every damn time. I get where Dia's coming from. She needs to process the fact that we have to be selfish. We *have* to. Once she accepts that, I think she'll come around."

"And if she doesn't?" I ask.

"Then we'll try it without her," Harper says.

I rub my forehead. "I don't think it'll be enough. We need to be as strong as possible when we try this."

Tris nods. "We need to be four."

I can't stand waiting. "I'll be back. I'm going to talk to Dia." I jog south, following the path she took toward the house. I pause on the porch and peek into the living room window. Inside, Dia perches close to Harry on the couch. He's fully conscious, sitting up on his own, his arms around her while she hides her face against his shoulder. When I open the door, he looks up. She doesn't.

"Did she tell you what we're trying to do?" I ask him.

"She told me enough," he says, although he still looks confused. "Do you really think it can work?"

"I think we have to try," I say. "We don't really have a lot of other options."

Dia pulls away enough to look Harry in the eye. For a long moment, she just stares, like she's weighing a decision.

"You won't hurt anyone," he says quietly.

"You don't know that," she says.

"You'll do your best. No one can ask for more than that." He uses the embroidered cloth that woke him to wipe the tears from her cheeks.

"I need proof," she says. "Proof that this plan is more than wishful thinking."

"You woke Harry up," I remind her.

"Maybe that was a coincidence." She touches Harry's bandaged leg. "Can I look at this?"

Bewildered, he nods.

She unwraps the bandage and gasps. When I step closer, I see why. The gash is almost entirely healed.

"See?" I say quietly.

"Not possible," she murmurs, looking at Harry. "How does it feel?"

"A lot better." He flexes his calf. "A little sore, and a little tight, but maybe that's just the stitches."

"I should take them out," she says.

"That can wait," I say gently. "Dia, we need you. It needs to be all four of us. Will you help us?"

She swallows and looks at Harry again. I see his forearm flex as he squeezes her hand. Finally, she stands. "Yes."

"Thank you," I say.

"Once we're safe," she says, "we'll send the storm back out to sea. Promise me we can do that."

I take a cue from Harry. "We'll do our best. It will be our storm. We'll be able to control it." A shadowy pit of dread opens in my stomach, and I hope I'm not lying to her. It's the closest to a promise that I can offer. We tell Harry to wait in the house, and we head back to the shore. Back to the others.

Tris gestures toward the storm path drawn in the sand. "So we're all in agreement? This is the plan?"

Dia, Harper, and I nod.

"Okay." Tris raises her brows at me. "Tell us what we need to do."

"We've already done our individual parts," I say. "We've set things in motion." *I think. I hope.* I don't know if I can adequately explain the next step, that feeling of pulling every dark vine of rage and wrath and sour anger to the surface and giving voice to them, flinging them all toward the horizon. "It will hurt. It will burn. It's like salt water in a wound, but I got through it, and so will all of you."

Facing the Atlantic, we join hands in the afternoon sunlight. Our shadows are squat paper dolls on the sand in front of us, but then mine begins to grow. It stretches until it's long enough to flirt with the tidemark.

My friend the darkness surges through me. Its thread-thin

arms are my own, and I feel Tris reflexively try to pull away. "It's okay," I murmur. "Let it in and set it free."

To my left, she inhales, taking in a deep, shuddering breath. Harper does the same to my right, and I hear Dia gasp as well. Their shadows lengthen to match mine, four impossible monsters stretching and writhing on the sand.

"Oh God," Harper whispers.

I tug at her hand, nudging our line toward the southeast. "Let it in and set it free," I say again. "Give it a voice."

And then I begin to scream.

My voice is still rough from earlier, but I give the shadow and the storm all that I can manage. I drag up the rage from where it settled, and I picture it casting out over the Atlantic, gliding and skipping to warmer waters. I imagine it drawing in clouds and starting to churn, to swirl, forming the vortex of a hurricane.

Harper joins in, then Dia, then Tris. With our hands still clasped, we scream and cry and holler, four witches, four hurricane girls building something massive. We make our offerings, setting them free on what's left of the ocean breeze.

I swear I feel my shadow laugh with triumph, and I know that our spell is working.

I keep going, shoving everything I have at the darkening horizon, pushing and flinging and heaving until my vision pales and my hearing fades. Everything around me goes still and white, a perfect void, and I fall.

When I open my eyes, I'm lying on the sand with my friends collapsed and unconscious beside me. I'm the first to wake up. I roll into a sitting position.

I've never felt so empty. I'm hollow, like the trunk of the banyan.

The others start to wake a minute later. One by one, they sit up. For a long moment, we look at one another in silence.

"Did it work?" Dia asks finally, her voice low and rough from screaming.

I point toward the horizon, where the sky is gray and angry. The storm won't rage in for hours, but I can *feel* it. It swirls in my blood just as it swirls through the Atlantic. It's part of me, just like the shadow, and it's coming.

"Now what?" Harper says, standing up.

"Now we wait for the water to retreat," Tris says, "and then we get ready to run."

"I hate to ask," Dia says, "but what about Gavin? If we can't avoid some surge, the island will flood. He could drown in the garage."

"Let him," Harper mutters, and a cold agreement pricks my heart.

"Let's just hope we can send the storm back out to sea," Tris says.

Harper nods. "Then we'll do what we said earlier and send the cops out here, and they can deal with him."

Dia looks troubled, but she doesn't protest.

But when we head south, we realize there's no decision to make. "Shit," Harper says as we approach the house. She points toward the garage. One corner of its door bends outward at a strange angle, allowing a glimpse of the darkness inside. It's not a very large gap, but it's wide enough for someone to squeeze through if they're determined.

Gavin is free. The realization churns the ocean in my veins until every heartbeat becomes the crash of a whitecap. I feel the hurricane scream its rage in thunder as it speeds toward us.

Chapter Forty-One

W e need to be careful," I say. "We don't know where he is."

Dia's face goes pale. "Harry!" She sprints toward the house with Harper close behind.

"We can take the bastard," Tris says as she and I follow.

Dia flings open the front door. Harry is still on the couch, inspecting the nearly healed gash on his leg. He looks up as we pile inside. "Is it done?" he asks. "Did it work?"

His questions have to wait. "Where's Gavin?" I ask, surveying the front hall and what I can see of the stairs and the kitchen.

Harry frowns. "I haven't seen him. What the hell's going on?"

"We'll explain when we can," Harper says, her expression alert and hypervigilant, a rabbit in an open field. "So he didn't get inside? You've been here since you woke up? You haven't left the couch?"

"I've been here." He pauses, then points at the half bath near the kitchen. "Except for when I was in there."

"How long were you gone?" Dia asks.

"A few minutes, I guess?" He puts his hands up in exasperation. "Why?"

"We should assume he's inside." I drop my voice and draw Tris, Harper, and Dia close. "Do we try to subdue him again? Or do we just get the hell out of here and wait by the banyan? From there, we'd be able to see him coming if he tries to follow us."

"Banyan," Tris says, and the others nod.

"We'll grab weapons and go," I say. "Be careful." The others head to the kitchen, but I think back to where I left my Maglite. Did I have it with me when I got back this morning? I imagine the heft of it in my hand and try to remember, but my recollection of the time right after the second storm is elusive, half-lost to the oblivion of my exhaustion. If I did bring it back to the house, it would be in the master bedroom. I vaguely remember the muted thunk of it dropping to the floor before I fell asleep.

The door to the master is almost closed. I shove it open and glance around the room. It seems empty, so I head toward the bed, where I most likely dropped the Maglite.

Something comes down hard on my head. Stars burst in my field of vision, and at first I think the muffled crack I hear is my skull, but I keep my footing and spin around, raising my hands to shield myself from a second blow.

Gavin stands there, breathing hard, with my uke case raised and ready to hit me again. When he tries, I catch it and yank it away. He snarls and hurls himself at me, knocking us both to the ground with him on top of me.

I freeze. It's like I've stepped outside of myself, like the world is placed on pause and I'm watching the moment on a movie screen.

This feels familiar; it shouldn't but it does, and the resulting surge of panic snaps me back to the present. I heave against him with my entire body, kicking and shoving, fighting, but he's too heavy. I can't buck him off.

Someone nearby screams, a sound that shouldn't even be possible after all we did to summon the storm. A body collides with Gavin with enough force to send him thudding sideways. He rolls off and I skitter back until I slam against the nightstand, pain blossoming bright and fierce through my elbow. I cry out and hunch forward against the throb, and from that angle I can see half an inch of the Maglite peeking out from under the bed.

I snatch it up and leap to my feet in time to see Gavin stagger sideways with Tris latched on to his back, her arm hooked around his throat. She bares her teeth as she squeezes, and his eyes go wide. But then he spots me watching, and he gives me a feral grin as he charges backward, smashing her into the wall. Her head collides with the whitewashed shiplap and she goes slack, slipping off of him. Her body puddles onto the floor, limp and still.

I stare him down. He steps forward.

"You hit me, Nell," he says, his eyes darting from my face to the Maglite and back. "That hurt. And then you locked me in the garage."

"You were supposed to stay in there."

"I didn't want to." He shrugs and takes another step toward me. "You haven't been too nice lately. Let's figure out how you're going to make it up to me."

"Is that what you want?" I edge toward the door, keeping the flashlight ready.

"It's only fair." Another step.

I remember how he's backed me into corners before. How he's trapped me.

Not this time. Something dark and delicious flows over me, drenching me in some strange new instinct. My shadow coils in my chest, encouraging, urging, and I know what I have to do.

"Then come and get me." I surge past him and out of the bedroom. He grabs my hand, but I yank it away and keep going. He takes the bait and charges after me.

Let him come and regret it.

I sprint toward the front door, dodging past the others on my way. I try to will them to step aside, to stay where they are and let me do this. Let him follow. I'm the one he wants, after all, and doesn't Gavin Richardson always get what he wants?

I tear down the porch stairs with his footsteps thundering after me. He's too close. I know where I need to lead him, but I'll never make it. He's an athlete, stronger and faster than me. I head north, pumping my legs until I'm nearly flying, but the rhythmic thumps of his sneakers on the dirt road grow nearer and I know above all else that I can't let him catch me.

I can't let him win.

To the west, the late-afternoon sun cuts through the cloud cover. I glance to my right, where my shadow runs beside me, matching me step for frenzied step.

The words come to me—the song, my old friend's favorite. "Here in the shadows you're mine," I gasp under my breath, and my shadow grows into something impossibly tall and spindly. I will it back, forcing it to arch behind me, and I hear a skid as Gavin stumbles. It's not much. He's up and running again in seconds. But it lets me pull ahead, just a little.

When he catches up, his fingers grazing the back of my shirt, I send the shadow back again. He trips, curses, jumps back to his feet, back to the chase.

We reach the banyan.

I hurtle toward its massive trunk, trusting my feet to land in just the right spots, hoping that Tris's part in our magic means that the tree is a friend. It almost seems like the roots and vines unwind in my path, dodging aside to let me through. Gavin follows with far less grace, stumbling and yelling.

I turn to face him. I raise the Maglite, ready to lash out, but I feel the banyan shudder behind me, and I realize my instincts were right.

He stops and stares at me, his eyes dark with rage. "Nowhere else to run, Nellie."

"Here in the shadows you're mine," I murmur again, and my shadow stretches longer, unfurling nearly to the beach and winding its tendrils through the banyan's massive root system, joining itself to the tree, *becoming*. In a chorus of groans and snaps, the roots pull free, lurching like striking snakes. They catch Gavin, wrapping around his ankles, twining up his legs, pulling him to his knees.

"What the hell?" he snarls, and although his voice is angry, his eyes are wide with shock and terror. He fights in vain to free himself as more roots rise to encircle his wrists, vining along his arms, around his shoulders. The more he screams and struggles, the tighter the roots become. I know because I can feel their movements twining through my veins, just like I can feel the storm. The shadow, the hurricane, the tree—I am all of them. My free hand forms a fist, tighter, tighter, until my nails cut into my palm, drawing blood, and the roots constrict in kind. *Strangler.*

Gavin's breaths come fast and short with panic. "What's going on?" he demands, the tendons in his neck standing out as he strains to break free. "What is this?"

His tone grows almost shrill, and I see fear and disbelief and resentment swirling together in his face as he learns that there are others on this island far more powerful than him.

That has to be a shocking realization for someone like Gavin.

"Have him face the ocean," I say, and the roots nudge him toward the east. "I want him to watch the storm come in." Dark clouds pile in from the Atlantic, and the wind grows harsher. Its rising howl reminds me of gasping breaths from a gaping mouth, and I cough as I reach into the pocket of the sleep pants I've been wearing all day. My fingers find the neatly wrapped length of ukulele string. I duck behind him and wrap it around his wrists, slipping it between the roots and tying it off. The roots don't need the help, but the string feels like it belongs. It's part of my magic, part of the spell.

Gavin hollers my name, trying to twist enough to see me. "Nell! Please!"

I pause. "*Please?* Really?"

"I'm sorry!" he barks. "I shouldn't have—Nell, let me go! *Please!*"

I consider coaxing another root to muffle his mouth, but I like the sound of him begging. I decide to let him scream for a while. It's only fair.

Chapter Forty-Two

I leave Gavin by the banyan and walk back to the house as the sky darkens. "We can wait for the storm here," I announce when I walk inside. "We don't have to head north."

Harper stands frozen in the front hall, clutching the handle of a large knife. Nearby, Dia huddles against Harry. The fact that Tris isn't with them snaps me out of whatever shadowy spell I've been under, and I run to the master bedroom.

She's sitting up, rubbing the back of her head and wincing. She launches to her feet when she sees me, and I fly into her arms.

"Are you okay?" She gets to the question first.

"I'm fine." I press my forehead to hers. "What about you? He slammed you so hard against the wall."

"My head's killing me. Other than that, I'm in one piece. When I saw him pinning you down like that..." She pulls back. "Where is he?"

"He's up by the banyan," I say. "He won't hurt us again."

"Wait, you didn't—"

I shake my head. "He's alive. He's tied up. Your tree helped."

Tris lets out a short, humorless chuckle. "I thought she might."

Harper joins us, and Dia and Harry hover in the doorway. "Are we leaving him out there?" Dia asks. "When the storm comes? When we run?"

We all look at one another. It was easier to talk about leaving him when he was locked in the garage. He had shelter. He might even have survived the surge in there, with shelves to climb if the tide forced its way inside. Now he's exposed and shackled.

"We can't," Harry says, but his voice is full of doubt.

"We'll decide what to do about him when it's time to go," I say, and no one argues.

We have hours to wait. I feel the storm coming, but it needs to stay over warm, open water to gain strength. I'll know when it's close. I'll know when it's time to run.

In the living room, we fill Harry in, and while I can see the skepticism in his expression, he can't argue in the face of the gray sky and the rising wind, especially not when he's standing on a nearly healed leg. And of course, our story has to include the sources of our rage.

"What the *fuck*?" Harry snaps when Harper explains about Charlie. "You have to tell Mom."

"I can't," Harper says. "I can't make Mom go back to struggling on her own."

"She won't be on her own. She has us. Besides, she'd rather struggle than make you stay in a situation like that." Harry's hands clench into fists. "If you don't tell her, I will. Or I'll...I don't know what I'll do."

"I'll find a way to tell her," Harper says quietly.

"When you evacuate before a hurricane," Tris says, gently changing the subject before Harper can grow more uncomfortable, "you're supposed to take important stuff with you. If there's anything y'all want, you should get it ready to go."

Harry leans over to pick up my uke case. "Nell, I'm sure you want to take this."

Remembering the muffled crack when Gavin hit me with the case, I open it gingerly. The body of my poor uke is partially split up the middle, with the headstock half snapped off and bent at an odd angle. It's still intact, sort of, but even if I can get it fixed, the sound will never be the same. When I pluck one of the remaining strings, I cringe at the new sourness in its tone. I close the case like a coffin. "I think it would rather stay here. I doubt I'll need it anymore."

"I need to go out to my truck," Tris says. I'm about to ask if she wants me to come with her, but she takes my hand and leads me, answering the question before I can voice it.

The world outside is strange. To our left, the rising wind makes the pines shiver and bend. To our right, closer to the haze, the trees stand still and wait to be devoured. The sky has turned a uniform charcoal, and the dropping barometric pressure plants a dull throb behind my eyes.

Tris crosses her arms and stares at her ancient, rust-dotted truck. She stays silent for a long time before she says, "I guess I couldn't exactly drive this thing across the bay, assuming it would even start."

"I think you'd get stuck in the mud pretty quickly," I say, a little confused.

"Yeah. Of course. I wasn't really thinking of trying." She wipes the back of her hand over her eyes.

"I take it you're attached?"

"It was my grandma's truck," she says. "She taught me as much about building and repairs as my dad has. He's the one who expanded the property business to what it is today, but Grandma started it. This truck is my favorite thing I have from her."

I put my arm around her. "It might make it. If we can turn the storm around in time—"

She shakes her head. "I'm not thinking that way. It's just a truck. Grandma would be the first one to remind me of that. And Dad's been after me to replace it anyway. It's a wreck. I'll just... miss it." She pulls away and opens the driver's-side door, and she unloops something from the rearview mirror. When she comes back to me, she holds her hand out so I can see. It's a rabbit's foot on a chain, old and battered by years of sun and heat. Most of its white fur is gone, exposing the mummified flesh and curved claws beneath, with delicate bone jutting up against desiccated skin in a way that reminds me of the banyan's roots.

"She always told me it was lucky," Tris says, chuckling a little. "I'd tell her it wasn't too lucky for the rabbit. But she never had an accident while this thing was in the truck. And she never got pulled over, which..." Her expression settles into something grim as she studies the charm. "That was pretty significant for her."

"Maybe she had a little magic, too," I say, thinking of how she taught Tris about herbs and teas.

"If anyone did, it was her." Tris closes her fingers around the rabbit's foot and slips it into her pocket. "I can't take her truck with me, but I can take this. Hey." She looks at me, brow furrowed. "What about your cat? Should we try to find it? Take it with us?"

I'm tempted, but I shake my head. "I doubt it wants to be

found. It already showed me what I needed to know. Its job might be done."

Back inside, we pause by the kitchen doorway and stare up at the sign that hangs over it. "Do you want to get it down?" I ask. "Save it for your dad? We can try to carry it."

She snorts at the absurdity of my offer and points out the window at the charcoal sky. "I don't think it applies anymore, do you?"

I laugh a little and shake my head as thunder growls near the horizon, carrying across the ocean. It's not like the thunder from last night and this morning. It's not just mine. It's bigger. The hurricane is giving birth to squalls that will travel ahead of it, rushing forward to herald its arrival.

We gather in the living room to wait. Without air-conditioning, the house has grown stuffy and uncomfortably warm. We open the doors and windows, inviting in the wind as long as it will blow. It's already dying near the house as the haze drifts closer, although I know it's still whipping up the north end of the island. I can feel the banyan's roots bracing against it.

Harper perches tense and stiff on the corner of the sectional, gripping a bottle of water. "It's getting darker out there," she says, staring out the front door. "It's too early to be this dark."

"It's just the storm coming," I say, but I know what she means. An uneasiness blankets the room, settling low and close around us. What if this doesn't work? What if the bay doesn't empty? Straight Shot won't survive a direct hit from a hurricane. Barrier islands sacrifice themselves to shield the mainland.

Better to die in a hurricane than in that awful haze, I reason. Better to drown in the surge while trying to escape than to sit still, waiting to be devoured.

And there's still the matter of Gavin's fate. When I sit quietly and concentrate, I can feel the echo of him struggling against the banyan's roots. He won't break his bonds, not by himself. If we spare him, I'm the one who will have to set him free. I wish I could hope that this week will have taught him a lesson, but I'm not optimistic. If I let him go, he might hurt someone else.

If I let him go, I'll always know he's out there.

While there's still enough light to see by, Dia sits next to Harry on the sectional and has him rest his leg across her lap, and she goes to work on the stitches with her embroidery scissors. The gash has healed so well that she has trouble pulling the bits of thread free; after each tug, he winces and she apologizes. When she's done, all that's left of his injury is a long scar that looks like it's been there for years.

"That's extraordinary," he murmurs, stretching his calf, testing it. "It barely even hurts anymore." He looks at Dia, and when he speaks again, his tone is reverent. "You're a witch, all right, and I mean that in the best way possible. Thank you."

Dia shakes her head. "Don't thank me. I just couldn't stand seeing you in pain. I didn't want you to hurt. I had no idea it would work like this."

"But it *did* work. You might have saved my life. That's amazing. *You're* amazing." Harry's voice goes quiet, hesitant. "Dia?"

She looks up at him. "Yes?"

"It's just... I've been waiting for a good time to... What I'm trying to say, I mean, is...," he stammers, blushing so fiercely that the color in his cheeks is visible in the dim gray light.

Dia's brows tilt. She bites her lip, waiting.

"It's just that I..."

"Jesus, Harry," Harper says, cutting her eyes at her brother. "Spit it out before you choke on it."

He throws her a quick glare before his gaze returns to Dia. "Can we talk in the other room for a minute?" he asks. "Away from my *favorite* sister?" When Dia nods, he leads her into the kitchen.

If he wanted privacy, he should have taken her upstairs. The house has settled into the sort of quiet that comes from an electrical outage. Without the white noise of fans and air-conditioning, we can hear every word.

"We don't know what's about to happen," Harry says, "but if we make it through this, would you like to go out with me sometime? We could get dinner, or just coffee if you'd like, or there's always, I don't know, mini golf or a movie or—"

"I'd love to," Dia cuts in before he can make an entire list.

Harry exhales. I can almost hear the tension in his shoulders loosen. I can't imagine being so nervous about asking someone out right now, with all we've been through and what we're still facing, but I also can't imagine Harry being any other way.

"That's so great," he says. "Okay. Thank you. And there's one more thing."

"What is it?" Dia asks.

"Normally I'd ask at the end of our first date," he says, "but given the, um, uncertainty of the situation, I don't think I want to wait."

On the sectional, Harper sighs and covers her eyes with her hand. "Oh my God."

Tris and I shush her at the same time and go back to listening.

"Dia, may I kiss you?" Harry asks.

Their conversation goes quiet in a way that makes Dia's consent clear.

Beside me, Tris giggles and whispers, "Okay, I am officially shipping this so hard."

"Don't encourage them," Harper says, but she's smiling, too. "My brother and one of my best friends. Dating. This is going to get weird." She holds up her water bottle. "Oh, well. Here's to honoring and adapting to changing friendship dynamics, I guess," she says, glancing at me before taking a swig.

Harry and Dia return, unaware they were overheard, and we settle back into waiting. Resting my head on Tris's shoulder, I close my eyes and listen to the storm—not the distant thunder drifting in from the first approaching squalls, but the heart of the hurricane itself, beating like whitecaps in my core. I envision reaching out to it, my arm a thread-thin shadow, and I beckon, encouraging it toward Straight Shot.

It's strong enough now, I can tell—strong enough to whip its wind around us and empty the bay when it arrives. Strong enough to drag the water and whatever lurks beneath it out far before sending it roaring back. I drift with the storm while night falls around the house, hidden beyond the thickening clouds. My eyes stay shut, but I'm aware of someone—Dia, I assume—moving around the room, lighting what's left of our candles.

The first squall moves through, a rush of wind and rain pummeling the island. It's oddly enthusiastic, an excited puppy in weather form. Another follows; they tumble through quickly and go on their way, clearing a path for their mother.

A little while later, my skin grows warm and I realize the breeze through the windows has gone still. I stand and go out to the porch, shining the flashlight to the south.

The haze has reached the house. It mutes the flashlight's beam, and it bitters my lungs. Dark tar drips from the edge of the porch. Meanwhile, another squall churns over Straight Shot's northern tip. I shut my eyes and feel. This is the last one. The next storm to arrive will be ours.

"Time to move," I say, going back inside. "We'll wait by the bay." We gather flashlights and anything we can't bear to leave behind. "Got your rabbit's foot?" I ask Tris.

She pats her pocket. "Got it."

"Any luck left in that thing?"

She gives me a half-smile. "God, I hope so."

We leave through the back door and walk north, looking for the best place to cross the bay when the time comes. The water is choppy in the darkness, frothing and churning, as angry as a kicked beehive. It hasn't gone anywhere, and for a moment I panic, sure that our plan has failed. Then I swing the flashlight's beam back toward what remains of the narrow dock, and I see a barnacled waterline on the closest piling, marking the bay's typical low-tide point. That line is at least a foot above where the highest storm-borne waves can reach.

It's happening. The water is pulling back. The others see it, too, all of us watching the pilings, squinting through the fading squall.

Now that the retreat has begun, it goes fast. It's like someone opened a drain in the murky bottom of the bay. Within minutes, we're staring out over dark, stinking mud. The smell is incredible—the sour, fetid odor of rotting fish and algae and sandy muck that has never known open air.

"Is it safe to walk out there?" Dia yells over the wind.

"Do we have a choice?" Harper inches down the shore and takes a few experimental steps into the goop. The mud sucks at her feet, turning each step into a struggle, but nothing surges up to grab her. Nothing drags her under. After a few more steps, she turns and gestures for us to follow.

"Nell?" Harry says. "Are we leaving Gavin behind?"

Of course we can't leave him to face the coming storm. But...

I pause.

Footsteps on the stairs.

The scent of mint.

The brown vinyl seat at the back of a school bus.

The sourness of an ice-cream-truck melody and the cloying taste of strawberry on my tongue.

Memories I'll never find. Things I'll never know. Rage he needs to answer for. Darkness descends over me, enveloping me like a shroud.

"You all go on," I say. "I'll catch up. I have to get Gavin."

Tris catches my hand, trying to hold me back. "Leave him," she says.

"Let me do this. I have to."

Tris's face tightens like she wants to argue, but then she nods and lets me go. "Be careful."

"Nell!" Harper yells from the empty bay, but I'm already running back toward the house. I need one thing before I head to the banyan. I have to sing to my shadow—my *real* shadow, the darkest part of me, the part I never wanted forced upon me—one last time. It's too dark to see my shadow, but I know it's there beside me, stretched and spindly and thin as thread.

Part of me.

All of me.

Now

He stopped struggling more than an hour ago.

He might have been able to tear himself free from the roots if it weren't for the string binding his wrists. He fought until it bit into his flesh, until his hands grew wet and sticky with oozing blood.

His legs ache terribly, every muscle cramping and screaming in protest at being made to kneel for so long. His back hurts no matter which way he leans. The squalls batter him with raindrops like pinpricks, leaving him shivering. The wind snaps a branch from the banyan and flings it spinning against his shoulder, the impact hard enough to bruise.

The latest squall dies down, but he can see what's coming behind it. The sky to the southeast is impossibly black. When the ocean begins to pull back from the coast, he thinks he's hallucinating in the chaotic darkness, but no, the Atlantic is retreating, *disappearing*, the waves sucking out to sea without returning.

A strumming sound, sour and sad, carries over the wind. It wisps its way to him, planting a bloom of cold panic in his chest. He tries to turn toward it, but the roots hold him still as the sound moves closer, louder, more curdled, accompanied by footsteps nearing the tree.

The strumming stops, and a flashlight blazes to life behind him. He cringes, remembering the crack of that flashlight's handle against his still-aching skull, and he braces for another blow, but it doesn't come. Instead, someone appears around his left side and wedges the flashlight into a tangle of roots, tracking it on him like a spotlight. He blinks against the sudden illumination. How can a little bit of light make the dark even darker? The shadows beyond the flashlight's beam lurk like eager predators among the roots.

The strumming begins again, bitter and wrong, and the girl steps into view. He's surprised the ukulele can make any sound at all in the shape it's in, with its headstock half-cracked and bent like a broken neck. One string is missing and the others are hopelessly out of tune, making each chord flat and unsettling.

The girl doesn't seem to notice. She begins to sing.

"Here amid the shadows, here amid the gloom."

The gentle sweetness of her voice, that tone so soft and true, has not changed. He remembers hearing it on the platform over the bay before she knew he was there. He had thought he'd gotten what he wanted from her last year, but that craving surged back to life when he heard her voice again. How dare she make him feel this way? How dare she be uninterested? How dare she deny him the right to possess her?

"Here amid the echoes of this lonely room." Against the uke's sour melody, that lovely voice sounds blasphemous. She circles him, her steps slow, soft. Still keeping time with the terrible song. "Together in our solitude, you'll come to recognize you're mine."

She comes closer, and now he can see her, the state of her. Her hair hangs loose in rain-soaked waves that are almost too heavy for the gusting wind to dance through. The indirect glow from the flashlight slashes shadows across her face. She regards him coolly with eyes that go hard and blank as she smiles. Something twines around her legs, its gaze glowing gold when lightning flashes. A cat—where'd she find a goddamned cat on this island?

"I know you've other things to do, another life to live."

Something rises behind her like a long shadow on a wall, but of course there's no wall on which for it to rest. It's a shadow cast on air, writhing, pulsing, breathing through an impossibly gaping mouth. He hears the nightmare rasp of its inhalation, and then it, too, begins to sing. Its voice is a pained, ruined echo of hers, and the two twist around each other in sour harmony.

"Your heart does not belong to you, it isn't yours to give."

His eyes grow wide. His pulse slams in his throat, a choking vibration. "Nell," he gasps. "Nell, please stop this."

She tilts her head, still strumming the broken instrument. The thing behind her trembles with something almost like laughter.

"Tomorrow you'll be far away, but first I'll claim my prize—you're mine."

Their voices mingle almost playfully, the girl's and the shadow's, teasing each other through the uke's spoiled chords.

"I'm sorry, okay?" His tone grows shrill. "I shouldn't have done it. Any of it!"

She steps closer, drawing the shadow along with her.

"You don't have to do this," he says.

"I like to dream it's otherwise, pretend the world is fine," she sings while the storm and the shadow loom behind her. He barely recognizes her, and perhaps there's no more of her left. But then her gaze warms, letting him glimpse a hint of the vulnerability to which he's always been drawn, that prey-animal glance that always made him want to chase, to catch, to devour.

"I know you'll soon be on your way, but here in the shadows you're mine."

He remembers how she'd gone from guarded to open that afternoon at the rest stop. He had won her over that day; he'd tossed out bait and reeled her in. He can do it again. He can stop this.

"Please," he says, struggling to get his voice under control, softening it, trying to sound sincere. "Please, Nell. What I did was unforgivable. I know that. I see it now. Let me go, okay? Let me go and we'll get off the island and I'll turn myself in."

"This night can't last forever, too soon we'll see the dawn."

He fights against the roots. "I swear I will! I'll turn myself in and I'll confess to everything. You'll never have to deal with me again. I'll go to jail. Let me prove how sorry I am. Please."

She takes another step. "Too soon the sun will rise again, too soon you will be gone."

"You can stop this. Nell, you *have* to stop this!"

"But as long as we are covered by dark and starry skies, you're mine."

"Nell! This isn't what you want."

Her stare hardens again, and he realizes his misstep. "What I want?" she murmurs, still strumming. "Since when do you care what I want, Gavin?" The thing behind her writhes, grows, unfurls.

344

"That's not what I meant! I just—"

"If I let you go," she says, "can you honestly tell me you'll never hurt anyone else the way you hurt me?" Behind her, the shadow flickers.

"I didn't hurt you," he says, his tone hardening again. "You just don't remember what happened."

"I remember enough," she murmurs.

White-hot anger licks like flame at the edges of his terror, clouding it with smoke. He bares his teeth. "You should have been grateful," he says. "You should have been flattered that I wanted you."

She steps directly in front of him and sings the final lyric. "Here in the shadows you're mine."

"Nell!" he screams. "You can't do this!" His voice cracks. "Look, I'll leave you alone. I promise. Okay? I'll never talk to you again. I'll be in jail and—"

"We both know that's not how the world works, Gavin. It should, but it doesn't."

He gulps. She's right. His father won't stand for him seeing the inside of a cell, no matter what confession he makes. "Then I'll go away! I'll move. You'll never see me again."

"But you'll still be out there."

"Does that matter? It won't affect you. You can go on with your life and—"

"And hope the hurricane hits someone else, just so it won't ever hit me?"

"What?" He can't follow the argument, so he veers to another. "How will you live with yourself if you kill me?"

She hesitates, murmurs, "I'm not going to kill you," and he

345

knows he's done it, he's won again, he doesn't like to leave it until the last second like this, but at least he's won, that shadow thing behind her is already shrinking, and he'll be—

But then, as the shadow disappears back into her, she smiles. "I'm just not going to save you."

"NELL!"

"Nice and quick," she whispers, as the roots that hold him turn to tar, thick and hot, searing his flesh as he's pulled down, out, up, in a thousand directions at once. With a tender smile and a last sour strum, she takes a few steps back, reaching the safety of the sand. Laughing and crying, she watches until there's nothing left of him but scraps of flesh and fabric, a knotted bit of ukulele string, and bones picked clean and stark. She tosses the broken ukulele into the ruins of the roots and squints through the pelting rain to the south; the haze is almost upon her, and the tar from the tree seeps closer, closer, pooling near her feet.

She has witnessed the island's justice. She sits, ready to make the sacrifice it will surely demand in return.

A small black cat pads up beside her. It butts its forehead against her side, urging her back to her feet. Beyond, four shapes rise from the melting roots. They don't speak, yet she knows exactly what they've come to tell her.

The spell has been changed. The island has set them free.

All of them.

The girl takes off running, giving what's left of the banyan a wide berth. With the cat at her heels, she races toward the empty inlet before the Atlantic can come crashing home.

Chapter Forty-Three

I pick my way through the stinking muck toward the far side of the bay, looking for my friends, my sisters, my witches. At first I can't find them, can't see them through the sheets of rain that pelt and prick my skin like splinters. Then I hear Harper hollering my name over the howling wind, and I follow the sound west until I'm with them once more.

Harper glances past me, waiting for Gavin to appear from the darkness.

"He's not coming," I tell her, and she accepts that without question. They all do.

The four of us join hands and stand on the gale-soaked mainland, facing the storm together. It's time to finish what we started. We scream, pushing back, releasing the hurricane, sending it back out to sea.

Only…it won't go. The rain grows heavier and the wind threatens to knock us off our feet. Our monster has outgrown us, and it's hungry. I feel its refusal pounding in my veins as it charges toward us, toward St. Felicitas, toward so many innocent people caught in the path of something we created. Panic seizes in my chest. People are going to die, and it will be our fault.

Someone catches my free hand, and I look up to see Harry beside me, facing the storm with his eyes narrowed and his jaw firmly set. He glances at me, nods grimly, and joins his voice with ours. Later, he'll explain about the girl who had made a habit of harassing him on campus and online for months. And the guy who kept hitting on him at an event in downtown Orlando and got aggressive when Harry refused to give him a phone number. "I always figured it was all nothing, you know?" he'll say, shrugging. "Or that's what I told myself, at least, that it wasn't a big deal. But it was. I'm still mad about it, I guess." If Harry had turned in exactly the right direction that night in the kitchen, I think he would have seen the shadow, too. He carries it, just as we do.

With him beside us, it's just enough. We're five now instead of four, and we set the storm free, guiding it back over open water, letting it calm and fade and die. We stay as long as we dare, and then we head away from the shore as the water returns home to the bay and the ocean begins to surge inland. The tide crests over the shore of the bay, but it doesn't make it much farther than that, and it recedes quickly.

We did it.

As the water pulls back and the storm lets up, we see that the bay is no longer a bay at all. There's no island on its far side—no majestic banyan, no house, no Straight Shot. It's just... gone, and all that's left in its place is ocean.

"Barrier islands sacrifice themselves for the mainland," Tris murmurs.

"What are we going to tell people?" Dia asks. "What do we say to our families?"

"I don't know," Harry says. "We'll figure it out."

"We just need a good story," Tris says, looking at me. "Nell?"

"I'm thinking," I say as the small black cat twines itself around my legs, its wet fur cold against my skin. Apparently I have a cat— or a familiar, or the remnants of a spell, or whatever it is—now. "I'll come up with something."

"We'll help." Tris brushes my wet hair out of my face, tucking it behind my ear. "You don't have to carry it alone. Not anymore."

I put an arm around her shoulders and press my forehead to hers. "I'm glad."

"Should we get going?" she suggests to the group. "It's a bit of a hike to town. Maybe someone in one of the houses nearby will let us use a phone."

"Let's walk for a while," Harry says. "It'll give us time to get our story straight."

As we head down the wet road, Tris takes my hand. "Hey," she says softly. "I'm sorry about your uke."

I laugh a little. "I am so, so not concerned about my uke right now."

"I know." She bumps my shoulder with hers. "You really loved that thing, though. It was important to you. I'll get you a new one if you want. I know it won't be the same, but..."

"I think I'd like that," I say after a moment, surprised by my own response.

"Then consider it done." She glances toward me. "And you'll sing for me again sometime?"

349

"Yeah. I will."

"Not…that song, though," she says with a slight chuckle. "No offense, but I don't think I'll ever be able to hear that song again without freaking out."

"Agreed." I already know I'll never sing "Here in the Shadows" again. I won't have to. My shadow is part of me now—part of all of us—and we'll carry it together.

No, not that song. Never again.

But there are other songs to sing.

From *The St. Felicitas Tribune*

ST. FELICITAS—Residents of St. Johns County and the surrounding areas braced for the effects of an unnamed storm Friday evening. Hurricane shelters opened. Interstate 95 grew clogged with panicked evacuees. Meteorologists predicted wind gusts of over 140 mph and the potential for as much as twenty feet of storm surge in some low-lying areas, a recipe for certain devastation in some of St. Felicitas's most beloved historical districts.

Then, in a seemingly impossible move, the storm turned back out to sea and vanished, dissipating as quickly as it formed.

Local experts remain stunned. "That's not how any of this works," said Channel Five's local chief meteorologist Heidi Peng, speaking from her station's emergency storm center. "Florida hasn't been affected by an off-season hurricane since Alma moved across the state back in 1970. The wind patterns around this weekend's storm, its speed, the rate at which it formed—there's no way it should have been able to make that kind of turn, but we're lucky that it did."

Peng's colleague, meteorologist Ken Shelling-Smith, shared a time-lapse video of the storm's track from the station's satellite radar. The video clearly shows the storm, technically a subtropical system with the strength of a Category 4 hurricane, approaching the region from the southeast before veering sharply back toward the east just before making landfall. "It's a phenomenon we're going to keep studying very closely," he promised. "This activity flies in the face of everything we know about hurricanes. We shouldn't be seeing storms of this magnitude at all at this time of year, let alone storms with tracks as unusual as this one."

"Never seen anything like it," St. Felicitas resident Hattie Parker said while inspecting the windows of the Crow's Nest Lounge, which she's run for more than two decades. "Maybe it was a climate change thing. Maybe it was an act of God. All I know is that I never want to get a surprise like that again. Didn't have time to board up or anything. We were lucky, but what about next time?" She shook her head. "And there's always a next time."

St. Johns County didn't completely escape the effects of the storm. Early squalls took down branches and damaged roofs and power lines, leaving several neighborhoods without electricity for nearly a day, and the hurricane's approach caused an alarming blowout tide as rough winds emptied local bays and caused the Atlantic to temporarily pull back. This rare phenomenon, also known as a water level set-down, typically indicates the possibility of a major storm surge. However, the storm's unusual path meant that, when the water returned, the area experienced tides only about a foot higher than normal. This still meant minor street-level flooding in some low-lying areas, but Heidi Peng pointed out that the situation could have been far worse.

"We were extremely lucky," Peng emphasized again. "If we'd gotten the full brunt of that storm surge, all of St. Felicitas would have been underwater. Countless lives might have been lost." As it is, only two possible fatalities have been connected to the storm so far. Two Winter Park high school students, Gavin Richardson and Christopher Leon, were reported missing earlier this week. Cell phone records show that they last connected to towers in a popular vacation neighborhood just south of St. Felicitas, and there's been no trace of them since. Officials continue to search, but it's feared that Richardson and Leon may have fallen victim to the storm.

HERE IN THE SHADOWS YOU'RE MINE

Here amid the shadows
Here amid the gloom
Here amid the echoes
Of this lonely room
Together in our solitude
You'll come to recognize
You're mine

I know you've other things to do
Another life to live
Your heart does not belong to you
It isn't yours to give
Tomorrow you'll be far away
But first I'll claim my prize
You're mine

I like to dream it's otherwise
Pretend the world is fine
I know you'll soon be on your way
But here in the shadows you're mine

This night can't last forever
Too soon we'll see the dawn
Too soon the sun will rise again
Too soon you will be gone

But as long as we are covered
By dark and starry skies
You're mine

Here in the shadows you're mine

Author's Note

This book began as a hurricane story inspired by my experience with Hurricane Irma. When I started drafting it, however, the news cycle was full of stories about a Stanford swimmer who received a minimal prison sentence for assault, and a Supreme Court justice nominee who really liked beer (not to mention a certain then-president who had infamously bragged about his grabby habits). The US had reached a tipping point, and more victims felt empowered to come forward; yet for every man who faced consequences, it seemed like half a dozen more escaped with nothing more than a temporary career ding (if that).

After all, *boys will be boys.*

Hearing that over and over while witnessing the backlash against those who were brave enough to name their abusers made me so, so angry. I know so many people who have been assaulted. *So many.* Few of their assaulters were prosecuted or punished. The more I thought about that, the stronger my anger became. It whipped itself into a froth. It spun and twisted into a hurricane of rage.

I had been thinking of the storm in this story as the villain, but that soon shifted. Hurricanes devastate, but they don't do it on purpose. They're forces of nature. The real villains are the Gavins of the world, who abuse and manipulate and take advantage, and who have the resources and privilege and connections to get away with it. The real monsters are human.

That rage became the heart of this story. We tend to call it "feminine rage" or "female rage," but it's important to remember that this anger and the violations that inspire it aren't exclusive to women. People of all genders can be victims of assault, and they deserve to be heard. Seen. Believed. Respected.

Believe women. Believe *people*.

Resources

RAINN (Rape, Abuse & Incest National Network), the United States' largest anti–sexual violence organization, offers a variety of resources at https://www.rainn.org. RAINN also maintains the Sexual Assault Hotline: (800) 656–4673.

ADAA (Anxiety & Depression Association of America) has extensive information on topics like anxiety, depression, and post-traumatic stress disorder at https://www.adaa.org.

Planned Parenthood offers information on sex, relationships, and related care for teens at https://www.plannedparenthood.org/learn/teens.

Thinking about therapy? *Psychology Today*'s therapist directory is one place to start (and it's how I found my therapist). The US directory can be found here: https://www.psychologytoday.com/us/therapists.

Acknowledgments

I would be remiss if I didn't start with my absolute hurricane of an agent (and I mean that in a good way!), Eric Smith of P.S. Literary. Eric, thank you for sticking with me and believing in my work. Thank you for taking on my witches even though you don't normally handle horror. Thank you for your excitement when good things happen. It means the world. I'm grateful to be part of #TeamRocks.

And another ENORMOUS thank-you to my Little, Brown Books for Young Readers team, especially Alex Hightower and Crystal Castro, who championed my witches and gleefully encouraged me to go darker and make this story stronger. You are delightful, both of you. Thank you to Kelley Frodel for so brilliantly catching my typos and hiccups, and to Jake Regier for your thoughtful and much appreciated input.

To Jenny Kimura and Marco Mazzoni—thank you for creating the dark, lush, *gorgeous* cover of my dreams!

To Jeri Baguchinsky, Dava Butler, and Laura Kittens—thank you for being the first readers of early drafts, for spotting the strengths amid the messes, and for always supporting and encouraging and believing. (And thank you, Mom, for buying me as many Stephen King novels as I wanted as a kid even though I was probably way too young for most of them!)

And while I'm at it, thanks to Stephen King for writing the kinds of nightmares that enchanted and inspired my dark little childhood heart and led me to write stories like this.

To my amazing beta readers, Shelley Wells, Chrissy Skinner, Rekka Jay, and Jillian Koenigsmark—thank you for your time and your constructive honesty. Your help on this project has been priceless. I couldn't have done it without y'all. (And even when you're honest, you're still so darn NICE about it!)

To Susan Edgington—thank you for always having faith in me and always wanting to read, whether I'm writing about princesses or witches. Thank you for being a friend.

To Rhonda Jones and Renee MacKenzie—thank you for listening if I needed to complain about characters or drafts or the inevitable frustrations on the business end of publishing. Y'all know how it is, lol.

To Jesse Baguchinsky and Sara Naval—thank you for including my books in your reading nook. It always makes me happy to see. Got room for one more?

To Patty Angileri—thank you for giving us a safe place to stay during Irma, and for letting us give Alex one fish.

To those who reached out and helped Mom and me with cleanup and fixes after the storm—y'all saved our sanity, which was hanging on by a frayed thread in 2017. Thank you. There's a lot of good still on Marco Island. (And thank you to Sami of

Sami's Pizza & Grill for doing so much for the community after *every* hurricane.)

To Cara Nixon—thank you for helping me pull through and process my Irma anxiety, and for encouraging me to write this book, and for sharing my excitement all along the way.

To Drover—see? I included a black cat, just like I promised. Thanks for being my fuzzy little void-muse.

And I guess I should say thank you to Hurricane Irma for the inspiration. Ugh, *fine*. I still hate you. Let's never meet again.

J. Baguchinsky

JILL BAGUCHINSKY

is an award-winning author who grew up on a barrier island just off the coast of Southwest Florida, where she read too much Stephen King and dodged more hurricanes than she could count. After one storm too many, she and her mini menagerie of rescue animals moved inland. Aside from the manatees she used to watch in her backyard canal, Jill doesn't miss much about island life. She invites you to visit her online at jillbaguchinsky.com.